A COMMON ROOM
ESSAYS 1954-1987

REYNOLDS PRICE

A
COMMON
ROOM

ESSAYS 1954-1987

NEW YORK

ATHENEUM

1987

ATHENEUM
Macmillan Publishing Company
866 Third Avenue, New York, N.Y. 10022
Collier Macmillan Canada, Inc.

Library of Congress Cataloging-in-Publication Data

Price, Reynolds, 1933–
A common room.

I. Title.
PS3566.R54C66   1987   814'.54   87-27064
ISBN 0-689-11948-8

Macmillan books are available at special discounts for bulk purchases for sales promotions, premiums, fund-raising, or educational use. For details, contact:

Special Sales Director
Macmillan Publishing Company
866 Third Avenue
New York, N.Y. 10022

Designed by Harry Ford

10   9   8   7   6   5   4   3   2   1

Printed in the United States of America

FOR TEACHERS

LUCY LEIGH LOVETT

JANE ALSTON

CRICHTON DAVIS

HOWARD POWELL

EUNICE MARTIN

PHYLLIS PEACOCK

CELESTE PENNY

PHILIP WILLIAMS

HAROLD PARKER

FLORENCE BRINKLEY

HELEN BEVINGTON

WILLIAM BLACKBURN

DAVID CECIL

NEVILL COGHILL

PREFACE

Every veteran of western education knows what the essay is—the place where you get to say what you mean. (If you're still in school you know in addition that what you mean had better be what the teacher means also—or the American Legion, if you're entering their essay contest.) Given the human propensity to sound-off and to listen to the sound-offs of others, the essay was until recently among the most prolific and admired literary forms—with numerous near-priestly specialists. Anyone born as recently as the 1940s learned a respectable part of what he knows about prose rhythm and strategy by reading and writing the "informal essay." I can still all but sing you whole paragraphs of Bacon on marriage, Swift's "Modest Proposal," Virginia Woolf's "Death of the Moth," H. L. Mencken's "Sahara of the Bozart." But despite a false spring in the sixties and seventies with the inflated claims of the New Journalists—many of whom were burnt-out or never-airborne novelists, and in the face of an insatiable reader-hunger for information, prophesy, and hateful ego-theatrics disguised as arts reviews—in America now the essay is generally practiced on invitation only by writers who would rather be doing something else.

Since the death of E. B. White (and with the exception of a few *New Yorker* regulars and a small stable of poltical columnists), there are almost no writers who confine themselves to the spotless white cube of the essay with its window on the sea, land, sky, or city. Though the public shows a decreasing appetite for serious fiction and poetry and though we're in the midst of one more amusing effort by critics to claim aesthetic parity with their colleagues in fiction, drama, and poetry, the curious fact is that most of the energy of contemporary writers is fed into novels, plays, and poems—even when those forms bring smaller financial rewards than essays. Maybe that's why so many writers are grateful when an editor phones to commission a review or an article.

Luckily, I've been steadily rewarded for my own prime work. Still— far into an essay career that began with high-school-newspaper editorials —I have accumulated a great stalagmite of paper in my office, the invitations and assignments of more than thirty years. They constitute my

solicited advice on subjects as disparate as country cooking in the 1930s
and the functions of the chorus in Greek tragedy.

I call them *advice* because they are frankly that. Mankind, uniquely
among the species, welcomes the chance to expatiate—to rear back beaming and deliver an individual's findings and knowledge. How to tenderize
a bear, write an epic, read a computer manual. As much as any border
collie or seduction lyric, the essay works to nudge its clients in what it
believes is a beneficial direction. So the tone of the informal essay from
Montaigne till now assumes a recalcitrant reader—one who needs turning
but is likely to put up a resistance that ranges from mild to adamant. The
ability to advise and persuade pleasurably, and more or less invisibly, is
the second most indispensable skill of a good essayist (the first is a precise
and readable prose). Contemporary readers will linger only briefly for red-
faced hectoring or the brand of oak-paneled Dutch-uncle mutter that was
popular even thirty years ago.

And I can honestly call the advice *solicited*. The occasion for all but
two pieces in this pruned collection was an assignment, by a teacher or
an editor. Only two came at me from the smoky ether out of which stories,
novels, poems, and plays so unexpectedly land.

Once assigned, to be sure, I was often permitted to choose the subject.
And that freedom has yielded me most of the considerable pleasure of
my many-hundred hours of essay writing. What invitation is more welcome than one which offers to pay you to say what you're currently
thinking? Still, the occasions and the audiences have almost invariably
been chosen for me. An editor had a particular curiosity—or a glaring
hole in a forthcoming issue—and the audience was to be the regular
readers of, say, *Esquire*. (A writer should seldom flatter himself that the
editor is urgently curious to know his opinions on a particular subject.)

Such facts should be kept in mind by the rare reader who studies
the structure and portents of such volumes. A serious American novel,
in the late twentieth-century, is likely to be altogether generated by internal
pressures—the novelist's own pressing ability to write long narrative, a
specific emotional curiosity or urgency. There are no magazines that
publish serial fiction; I can't remember hearing of a good modern novel
that was specifically commissioned. And there are very few journals that
solicit poems; most of them hunker under improvised shields to take the
withering avalanche that inevitably descends once they've hung out a we-
print-verse shingle. So no contemporary poets can claim influence from
editors. If there's a shape to the work of modern essayists then, that shape
was partly generated by a series of random invitations and prompt responses.

A few notes about the origins of some of these essays may help define the point. The oldest of the pieces is printed because it illustrates the ambiguous nature of the essay, solicited but personal. It was required from me by my teacher in a class on Representative British Writers when I was a college sophomore, but I took the compulsory occasion to state hotly-held convictions. I was a fervent age twenty, it was the spring of 1953, and the essay was first published in the student literary-magazine a year later when I'd become associate editor and saw my chance to ventilate a personal position-paper.

I set such early work in an exposed position here, not because I'm besotted with pride in my adolescent brilliance. On the contrary, its inclusion has required some wrestling with my annoyance at a young man's humorless arrogance. But it states, in—God knows—unabashed pure form, most of the principles that undergird the remaining essays and most of my imaginative work. An aesthetic marching-banner then, an unmistakably audible warcry—youth on the gray barricades of the lie-low-and-eat-what-they-feed-you 1950s.

Continuing with essays related to my student- or teaching-career, "Finding Work" was written in 1967 (on the cusp of the exhilarating and exhausting turmoil that we call the Sixties) at the request of the Duke undergraduate yearbook. "Dodging Apples," with its discussion of the origins of my first short story, originated as a lecture to freshman short-story students. "A Fairly Crucial Choice" was requested by the university's president for a series of pamphlets he was circulating to the student body. The remainder of notes on my own work were also solicited—the remarks on another story, "Waiting at Dachau," by an anthology in which American writers selected a favorite story of their own and explained why; the extended look at my second novel, *A Generous Man*, was for a volume in which novelists discussed one of their novels. "A Place to Stand" served as preface to *Mustian*—a collection of my fiction, to that point, concerned with a single family.

A further symptom of the controlling ambiguity of the form is revealed by the names of the writers whom I've examined at length—Milton, James, Hemingway, Faulkner, and Welty. They are all large figures whom I admire and who, with the exception of Faulkner, are important to my sense of procedure and dignity. Unless I announced the fact however, a casual reader would never suspect that other writers came earlier and counted most heavily for me. But in all the above cases, except Milton's, I was invited to expound for a particular occasion. I've never been asked to write about three of the four writers most decisive to my own sense of literary vocation—Flaubert, Tolstoy, and Hardy. Hence their regrettable absence.

The fourth of my early formative heroes is John Milton. And the essay on Milton's *Samson Agonistes* began early, as my graduate thesis at Oxford—a project conceived in anxiety, delayed by personal pleasure (the delights of early love and continental travel when I should have been chained to a clammy desk in the misty Bodleian Library), and completed two years later in a near-panic of duress literally one hour before deadline. It was expanded in my relaxed years of teaching Milton at Duke where, with steady reward, I continue to offer him annually to astoundingly eager students—no writer in any language seems to me deeper or more genial to the human predicament in most of its tragic varieties.

All the pieces about Jimmy Carter, his Georgia hometown, and his irrepressible family were commissioned by *Time* and *The Washington Post* during those years of the late 1970s when Southern writers, who had fast been going out of vogue, were suddenly attractive again as guides to our own huge mysterious, partly glamorous, partly repellent subcontinent. The disaffection had been an understandable response to the withering triumph in the 40s and 50s of a virtually preemptive Southern school of writers—Williams, Porter, Faulkner, Warren, McCullers, Capote, and Welty—an earned triumph that had nonetheless been annoyingly trumpeted by a national critical establishment that was staffed largely by Southern critics. Even more unfairly, those of us who began to publish in the early 60s were tarred with our region's filthy Civil Rights brush. The somber ceremonial flourish called "Pictures of Pride" was solicited by the *Post* for its Inaugural Day issue. In it I took the welcome occasion of Carter's ascent as permission to engage in one of the oldest and most complex species of American rhetoric—the courthouse steps or Confederate Memorial address, with vivid loopings and with every stop pulled: all very much from the heart and, in retrospect, certainly not shamed by Carter's unfortunately brief tenure.

"Pantherine, Leonine, Orchidaceous" is a look at the singing voices of women—in particular the voice of Leontyne Price, the most phenomenal of American sopranos. It was commissioned by *Dial*, whose editor knew of my enthusiasm for the splendor of Price's achievement. More than most invitations, this one gave me time to expand upon an even older and studious admiration for female voices that (since my early teens) has meant as much to my own writing as the examples of my literary predecessors. I've learned the greater part of what I know about prose and verse architecture not from other writers but from the performances of supreme singers (Caruso, Farrar, Ponselle, Melchior, Flagstad, Lehmann, Anderson, Bjoerling, Callas, Price)—and from their own first resource, the great works of persuasive vocal music.

"For Ernest Hemingway" provided a similar opportunity. Requested by Theodore Solotaroff for his *New American Review* series in which writers discussed an older writer to whom they were especially indebted, it permitted me not only to acknowledge a debt that had escaped the notice of almost all my influence-sniffing reviewers but also to explore the central bafflement, quest, finding, and failure of Hemingway's life-work.

All the book reviews were requested, usually on short notice, by papers and magazines. Once past a regrettable, and long-buried, first piece in which I did an unforgivable reviewers' tap-dance on the prone body of serious work, my principle has been that I only review a book I respect. In the present glut, a bad or mediocre book does little if any harm that requires active combat (what book since *Mein Kampf* has done considerable harm?); and there are adequate huddles of under-employed book-journalists yearning in alleys to do the dirty work for paltry sums.

Of the five memoirs—"Penny Show," "A Gourmet Childhood," "Christmas Food," "Real Christmas," and "Man and Boy"—the first four were elicited by journals in search of personal recollections; and the last was an address to the Friends of the Duke University Library, a group that includes many of the old friends and colleagues of a long and rewarding professional association.

And onward similarly through the table of contents—with the sole exceptions of "A Single Meaning" and the concluding "What I Believe." "A Single Meaning" was written to introduce *A Palpable God*, a collection of my own literal translations of stories from the Old and New Testaments of the Hebrew-Christian Bible, and was an entirely self-generated effort—the outcome of a long project dedicated to understanding the genius of the most successful narratives in world literature and thus to the purification of my own story-telling procedures in fiction, poetry, and drama. I have not attempted to launder out of it all references to the volume which it introduced, but I have provided an appendix with translations of the three Bible narratives closely studied in the essay.

The external and deadline-ridden origins of the essay explain its frequently ephemeral air. Anyone like me who has gone on writing essays for more than thirty years past his own college needs, and who sets out to winnow the results, must take care not to attempt narcissistic resuscitation on pieces that are now dead and better off left underground.

The contents of this volume represent then what seem to me the readable and useful essays that I've written in the past three and a half decades. Some of the earliest of the literary-personal essays are repeated from an out-of-print collection, *Things Themselves* (1972). Of the ways to arrange such a miscellany, a simple chronological order seems to rouse the fewest objections—certainly fewer than arrangements based on vague thematic resemblance or one which implies a false degree of planning. So the order is chronological, with some exceptions. I've herded a few short pieces, mostly reviews, out of order and up against longer essays which they may serve as footnotes or marginalia. In each case, I've indicated the date of first publication.

While readers should understand that the opinions expressed in old essays may no longer be those held by the writer who continues to sign himself with the same name, I mostly continue to agree with my younger selves. In any case, I have not revised or homogenized the essays beyond the odd clarification in syntax or the correction of a factual or typographical error. Punctuation has occasionally been revised for clarity but not for consistency. My own house style of punctuation has evolved through the years in an effort to provide a maximum of courteous guidance to the reader. Any attempt to tune it all to some present constant system would be misleading, so would a rooting out of repeated ideas and phrases.

Good or bad, the pieces appear as I first released them with original titles. One of the first forms of revision a writer learns to dread but accept is the inability of editors to resist a thrust at creativity, or at least saleability, when it comes to other men's titles. For instance, the essay here called "Uses for Freedoms" was solicited by *Esquire* and published with their title as "What Did Emma Bovary Do in Bed?"—an inviting inspiration but too promising and not mine. The essay called "A Vast Common Room" was commissioned and published by *The New York Times Book Review* as "Men Creating Women." I chose the topic, one that had long concerned me; but the *Times* substituted a title which proved an inaccurate and combative flag to fly over an essay whose main intention is to tend the deeper wounds of gender warfare. "Real Christmas" was commissioned by *Harper's Bazaar* and published as "A Child's Christmas in North Carolina," a pointless reminder of Dylan Thomas's very different kind of memoir. And if the present texts of the essays often differ from the ones first published, again it's because I've returned to my manuscripts and discovered that I wished to reverse the arbitrary changes of editors.

The decision not to assist, repair, or sophisticate my younger selves confronts me with matters of style and opinion at which I may now occasionally wince. But better a current wince than the permanent mistake of imposing an inappropriate later style and thought on headlong youthful work. My own principle is—print it as conceived; stand by it or discard it. But don't forge the altered sensibility of someone who now calls himself Reynolds Price onto the work of a younger and often substantially different writer. Trust patient Time to wound all heels.

In any case, the stalagmite in my office—from so many years and places and with such various causes—has yielded after all a book as personal as a novel or a sequence of poems. At the behest of others and with steady indirection, a man appears. If it's not the entire man (the one known only to intimate friends), it is at least the dressed and honest public-figure, saying a good part of what the entire man believes. Since the later pieces are more obviously personal than most of the earlier, I decided to conclude with a bare statement of conviction.

Several of my respected contemporaries have recently included, in similar collections, interviews in which they responded to questions about life and work. I considered such a conclusion. Like most writers I've participated in hundreds of miles of interviews; but eventually I decided against it—too externally controlled, too boring, and more self-loving than even I wish to be at the end of a long book of essays. I've chosen instead an outright credo—a line scored in the earth beneath this much at least of a career grounded in the beliefs described. Credos are dangerous coats to wear; they may alienate readers to whom the beliefs look absurd or excluding.

I trust that for the patient reader, my conclusion will prove to be neither. In one sense at least, it may come as a relief. Since I have flashed the self-regarding glare of the essay so often here, and from so many angles, I've chosen to end in a reckless thrust behind all mirrors toward the heart of a lifetime's motive-passion—an owning-up, a thanks, a bow to all walls and corners of our common room: the world I think I see around us, all we've got.

R.P. *1987*

CONTENTS

A COMMON ROOM
ESSAYS 1954-1987

VANITY FAIR

A PERSONAL REACTION

As CRITERIA for the judgment of any work of art, one might well revise and adapt to his own use something on the order of those principles which Coleridge set down in his *Biographia Literaria* as "a solid foundation, on which permanently to ground my opinions, in the component faculties of the human mind itself, and their comparative dignity and importance." Any work of art which I can call great must be found to exhibit certain characteristics:

1 It must be uncompromisingly faithful to truth and to the nature of things.
2 It must arouse pleasure for the aim of great art is to please.
3 It must exert an undiminishing attraction. Great art is not that which the sensitive man considers once. It is that to which he returns with deepening pleasure throughout his life.

It is by these principles that I must judge Thackeray's *Vanity Fair*, a novel which since its publication in 1848 has received the general accolade of discerning critics. One usually hears the novel called great and mentioned in the august company of such panoramic novels of society as *War and Peace, The Human Comedy,* and *The Remembrance of Things Past*. I cannot call *Vanity Fair* great. I cannot find from my experience with it that it satisfies any of the three personal criteria stated above. It is neither pompously nor dogmatically that I state my opinion; but *Vanity Fair* deeply offends my personal concept of the high purpose of art, and I must try to show why.

Is it possible to say that *Vanity Fair* is faithful to truth and to nature? In a distorted sense, yes. It records a series of observations, delivered without compassion, of a world of men and women who range from utter moral depravity to an almost equally despicable and maudlin sentimentality. There *are* such people, and thus one might say that Thackeray has drawn his portraits from a very real segment of life. But no where—thank God—is there a world composed entirely of such specimens. There is not in the whole of *Vanity Fair* one character for whom I can feel love or pity or admiration. There is not one breath of clean air or health in that whole vast wasteland.

The only pleasure which I could conceivably derive from the novel would be in admiration of its architecture and style. Thackeray is a magnificent technician, but technique is not enough to draw me back to *Vanity Fair*. Indeed, it is in something like horror that I reconsider the novel for the writing of this essay. If the choice is mine I do not think that I shall ever read it again. I shall try not to think of it.

I do not argue for any Pollyanna view of life or literature. I am aware of the existence of wrong, of tragedy. Yeats wrote, "We begin to live when we have conceived life as tragedy." I have attempted to justify *Vanity Fair* as a tragedy. In measuring it against Aristotle's definition of tragedy, something like this emerges: *Vanity Fair* is the imitation of a grave and complete action of a certain magnitude in language with all pleasing ornament. But here the parallel collapses. The characters and incidents of *Vanity Fair* can arouse no pity (it is certainly possible that fear might be evoked), and nothing resembling catharsis is achieved. One might be misled into calling Becky Sharp's fall a tragic one. It is an awesome spectacle like Satan's, but like Satan she finally becomes ludicrous in her plight. There is none of the grandeur of the Great Sinner Fallen about her—none of the baleful magnificence of a Medea, a Cleopatra. The fate of Dobbin is little better because, I am afraid, Dobbin is a put-upon fool. He proves toward the end that he at least has a moral sensibility; but he sets it aside in marrying Amelia, a gesture which, though penitential, is hardly noble.

The final question then is this: if *Vanity Fair* represents Thackeray's honest, passionately held view of human life is not the novel's existence justified? I must answer for myself—no. For I have not found life to be what Thackeray would have me see. There are classics of despair in world literature—*Job* and *The Wasteland*, to name two—but even these indicate a means to a significant life.

Thus I am forced to reject *Vanity Fair*. It is not true. It is not tragic. Concealed under its facade of social amenity is a human viciousness of the most awful kind. Chekhov observed in one of his letters,

> Let me remind you that writers who, we say, are for all time, or are simply good, and who intoxicate us, have one common and very important characteristic. They are going toward something and are summoning you toward it, too, and you feel, not with your mind, but with your whole being, that they have some object. . . . The best of them are realists and paint life as it is, but, through every line's being soaked in the consciousness of an object, you feel,

besides life as it is, the life which ought to be, and that captivates you.

Thackeray leads one *toward* nothing; he rather abandons his reader in the backwaters of a black pessimism to escape to truth and light as best he can. There is not the least glimpse of life as it ought to be; there is not even a picture of life as it is.

I pity Thackeray that he came to see life as he did. The tragedy of *Vanity Fair* is not that of its own loathsome people—mean little insects that they are—but that of its author. I can only feel that English literature would be a prouder thing did its annals not include a *Vanity Fair*.

1954

COUNTRY MOUSE, CITY MOUSE

AFTER A WRITER is called *regional* three times, he knows that the word is neither complimentary nor merely descriptive; that it ranges in flavor from condescension to distaste in the mouths of urban journalists (so often decamped regionals themselves). At their most generous such journalists equate the word with *rugged, naif, pastoral*; at their meanest with *quaint, homey, folksy*. Indeed in the past twenty years their snobbery has been so insistent that many a good writer may have half-believed the charge and dreamt of himself being ultimately gathered to the bosoms of Henry Timrod, William Gilmore Simms, Kate Chopin, Petroleum V. Nasby—because he was not born or reared in a city and has chosen to write of what he knows, his home and the people there.

But relief comes with the recollection that *regional* also includes (if it does not cover) Emily Bronte, Hardy, Lawrence, Hawthorne, Twain, Faulkner, Hemingway, half of Tolstoy, Turgenev, Chekhov, Flaubert, Verga; that the most nearly whole and comprehending recent American fiction has been regional or at least provincial—James Agee, Eudora Welty, William Styron, John Updike; that the classic American novels are regional or non-urban—*The Scarlet Letter, Moby-Dick, Huckleberry Finn*. There are of course bad sorts of regional fiction, but they are seldom bad in an especially regional way. All bad novels are alike—they do not tell sizable, understandable truth. So blanket condescension—the notion that life is realer, more significant in cities—is one more absurd form of the ancient Country Mouse, City Mouse game.

I propose to limit the word. *Regional* shall mean *rural*. It shall be inaccurate to describe as regional any novel set in a town of more than ten thousand inhabitants—or perhaps more accurately, a town from whose center open country cannot be reached by a fifteen-minute walk. If I may limit the word thus, I will claim that the best American fiction of the next twenty years is likely to be regional, *rural*.

The claim is rash. The novel as a common form postdates the rise of great cities in western Europe. Its mainstream rose in those cities and has flowed so deeply and freely through London, Dublin, Paris, Berlin that we are tempted to think of the novel as a metropolitan form, dependent for theme and manner upon the physical and spiritual reality of cities. Such a view naturally sees rural fiction as eccentric. But such a view forgets that the early picaresque novels spent more than half their time wandering in the countrysides of Spain, France, England and that with almost no exceptions the great urban novels of the nineteenth and early twentieth centuries make frequent and extended excursions into the country—not merely into Hyde Park or the Bois but into a world not made by man. Think only of *Great Expectations, Anna Karenina, The Remembrance of Things Past.* Why these excursions? Were they only "getting away," an earlier version of the weekend in Westchester, a later version of Marie Antoinette at Trianon?

No. First they were the results of an early and passionate relation between a writer and nature. Second, they were his technical means of expressing a conscious or unconscious perception: that the city of pavements, traffic, stone buildings, bridges does not provide a framework of imagery sufficiently rich or varied to support novels concerned with emotions other than hate, rage, and anxiety. Think of the artists who maimed their work (or some portion of it) by a strict reliance on the imagery of city life—Pope, Baudelaire, Rimbaud, James, Eliot. And where are their heirs?—interred in the hundreds of bad poems and novels full of neon light on wet asphalt, unshaven chins, scalding coffee at four a.m. And surely Kafka's *The Trial* is the only totally urban novel of distinction in our century? (How much more terrible it could have been if Kafka's vision had encompassed trees and fields, as it threatened to do in *The Castle* and at the end of *The Metamorphosis.*) So the city has played us false in one more way. It has not borne the scrutiny of poets and novelists; has not reverberated, only horrified, petrified.

Wordsworth knew that the city was lethal to art and was the first to say why in his preface to *Lyrical Ballads,* 1800: "Humble and rustic life was generally chosen [as subject] . . . because in that condition the passions of men are incorporated with the beautiful and permanent forms of nature." The vital word is *permanent.* It is only permanent or permanently recurring objects which provide a sufficient reserve of imagery, an adequate sounding board for any but the most claustrophobic novel.

What has been proved by a century of attempts to deal with the city in art if not that we cannot successfully inflict the pathetic fallacy upon manmade objects (buildings, bridges), only upon natural objects (think of Levin in the hay fields, Marcel at Combray, Pip in the Thames marshes)? A city is now more vulnerable, destructible than a man. But trees, fields, stones preceded us; will almost surely survive us. So they condemn our folly and our virtue, chasten our fret (scratch a farmer and find the tragic sense of life). Yet they still can console us—the things we have not made—because they will absorb all our emotions, not simply our destructive emotions; and if we wait they will return those emotions to us, clarified. Consolation is not always (perhaps not often) the reward of an honest return to nature; but illumination, some measure of understanding will be. That is not merely the experience of Wordsworth and Thoreau but of Aeschylus, Sophocles, King Lear.

Those are the bases of my claim that the richest, wisest, most nearly complete fiction of the next years will be regional. In so far as the claim is a prophecy, it teeters on the rim of absurdity. The future of no art can be predicted, even its most minor turnings, precisely because art exists and continues, not in obedience to trends or schools or *zeitgeists* but by a series of miraculous births—the births of geniuses. The death of every art form seems imminent at least once in every century; but while the very funeral arrangements go forward, some child is born who is Michelangelo, Picasso, Yeats. Of all great literary forms perhaps only the epic has died (and I cannot find it in my heart to pray for its fiery rebirth).

Thus the past permits us to hope that there will soon again be novelists of a breadth and depth to combine country and city and so give us the fullest novel again. The great whole rural-urban vision of Dickens, Tolstoy, Proust paused at the end of its most profound product, Forster's *A Passage to India*. Since 1924 we have had no novelist who has dealt with the *world*. Let anyone in a novel by Faulkner visit a city larger than Memphis; the blood drains from him instantly. And no one in Hemingway should ever have left Michigan or the Abruzzi or the trout streams of Spain. It is possible that the whole world is now too varied, too terrible; and of course that is said on every hand—but how I doubt it. The world of the fifteenth century was clearly too large for any man, but there came a Leonardo who tried to grasp it all and nearly succeeded.

We only await a birth, the birth of a single child (and now for the first time in our history, we are rearing what Europe has reared for centuries—an enormous generation of children who have intimate experience of both city and country). But novelists at least can only await it as the Jews awaited, await, the Messiah—in active patience, preparing the way by living their lives in the places they know, probing those lives and homes in the hope of comprehending and controlling them, ordering their vision however narrow into art which is true enough to be a world, as though one county of North Carolina, say (red dirt, green pines, black men, white men scratching out lives, occasionally standing into them) were as perfect a mirror of man's estate as all the boroughs of New York together, all the cities and wastes of Russia. Which of course it is.

1964

THE THING ITSELF

Any NOVELIST who reads notices of his work will soon wish (whatever his larger reactions) that it was within his power to retire certain ritually chanted words from future considerations of his work. I for example have published three volumes of fiction and have each time suspected, as returns rolled in, the existence of a syndicate dedicated to the lightning distribution throughout America of a small critical vocabulary pre-selected for each book and designed solely to fog public understanding of the book's intentions and achievements. Even the most gratifying notices of my first novel, A Long and Happy Life, echoed one another with the word *simple* (when I knew in every detail the novel's technical complexity, its emotional and thematic density, its attempt to deal with and order the larger part of my own observation and concern). My second volume was short stories, *The Names and Faces of Heroes*; and the national adjective was *autobiographical* (because I used my own name in a single story which was, at most, historical fiction). The third volume has recently appeared—a novel called A *Generous Man*—and the new word is an old but potent fog-bomb, *myth*.

Those were only minor blemishes in three encouraging receptions, but the word most frequently used by reviewers in dealing with all three books has become a serious grievance to me. The word is *influence* and its almost universal—and universally imprecise—use by even respectable critics is an unmistakable symptom of a tumor of misunderstandings of the narrative imagination, the purposes and strategies of an individual novelist.

First, what do they mean by *influence*? The context is always lamentational if not derogatory— "If only X could throw off the burdensome influence of Y"—and the object of their attack is always X's "style." What they mean is *imitation*. They assume one of two things—that the writer has made an intense study of another writer's methods, every tone and tic, which he then forges and calls his own or that the younger writer, mesmerized by his encounter with the older writer's voice, mimics that voice each time he speaks (as a child will unconsciously mimic his father's stance or tone). There are even extreme advocates who suggest that a

writer may be possessed by another, usually dead, writer to the extent that
what the possessed produces is automatic writing—analogous presumably
to the plight of those ancient but uneasy evangelists in seventeenth-century
painting whose hands are firmly gripped and steered by attendant angels.
In short, reviewers seldom mean more in proudly identifying an "influence" than that X *sounds* to them more or less like Y.

It does not occur to them that there are any number of explanations
for such similarities of sound—none of which need assume that X has
consciously or unconsciously mimicked Y. The broadest and truest explanation is that X and Y have attempted to deal, at different times, with
similar, occasionally identical forms of life. The apples of Cezanne resemble the apples of Chardin; and the apples of Norman Rockwell resemble those of both, not necessarily because any one of the three influenced
either of the others but because, given their common attempt to render
an imitation of the visible palpable thing *apple*, they have produced necessarily but superficially related pictures.

Let me consider some possible valid meanings for the word *influence*, some clear examples of one artist's being influenced by another.
There are cases of profound *formal* influence. It is clear that *Paradise
Lost*, maddeningly original as it is, would not have had its shape without
the existence of Homer and Virgil; and it is not conceivable that even
Shakespeare could have sprung full-grown from the womb of time, a five-
act tragic verse drama spontaneously formed in his own head, quite unassisted at his birth by Seneca or Kyd or Marlowe. One could name the
obvious formal ancestors of every great writer—his architectural masters.
Even such apparent sports as *Tristram Shandy* have visible roots into a
rich past; even *Finnegans Wake* has conscious precedents in the games
of children, the private art of schizophrenics, in the first of all poems—
dreams and nightmares. And more, we can often unearth in the work of
one writer undeniable fragments of the precise language of another, the
words in their order, the identical similes. Shakespeare's use of North's
Plutarch is the obvious example; Milton's lifelong raids upon his immense
memory of the Greeks, Ovid, Horace.

Such bald resort to another man's diction, however, is a phenomenon
of poets. I can think of no serious novelist who has made such resort.
Conscious resort to the structural principles and solutions of older masters,
yes; but not a repetition of phrase and image. Why? The reason is simple
enough. Poets are primarily concerned with language. It is both their
subject and object. But despite the labors of Flaubert and Henry James
and James Joyce, the novelist has not been primarily obsessed with language. His subject is the world—*a* world at least, that only-just-invisible
world which he alone perceives beneath the infinitely seen and rubbed

world of other men; and his object is not a demonstration of the ritual power of language but the clear transmission of that total vision, that broad expanse of experience which he alone knows. The difference is a matter of time—clock time.

Among poets, only the epic poet and occasionally the verse dramatist are concerned with sweeps of time. A poet's subject is the instant, a novelist's the years. Thus the poet's reliance on language, his means of achieving intensity. Keats exclaimed that "the excellence of every Art is its intensity." Intensity *is* the excellence of verse—an intensity achieved through arrangement of language, an arrangement that invites and receives imitation—but it would be more accurate to say that the excellence of the novel is its stamina, an excellence of long-term understanding exerted over the lives of inconsistent human beings who move without rest through modifying time, eroding space. Such a forbidding excellence has never invited imitation nor submitted to imitation.

Then are there genuine influences at work in any novel? Of course—thousands, though to be precise, the influences work upon the novelist not the novel. Are these influences visible to anyone but the creator of the novel (if him)? Are they discussible influences? No. Why? Because the only influences worth knowing, the influences whose knowledge might illuminate a man's work (its origins and aims) are unknowable, incommunicable.

To speak of myself. It is all but mandatory in discussions of my fiction to claim—and regret if not lament—the influence of William Faulkner. There is no such influence, formal or emotional. But I am not alone in receiving this reiterated charge. No Southern writer who has chosen to write about the South within the past twenty years has escaped the burden—so perhaps it is time to attempt to disperse a cloud of misunderstanding which has been thrown over my work and over the work of many other artists as different from me as we all are from Faulkner.

To begin, a formula and a true one—serious writers of fiction born in the American South, setting their work in the region which they possess and must comprehend, do not imitate the obsessive themes or the private language of a single distinguished elder, William Faulkner. They imitate the South, *their* South, as Faulkner imitated his South—his private relation to a public thing, a place larger than France, inhabited by millions of people united by an elaborate dialect formed in syntax and rhythm (like the people themselves) by the weight of land, climate, race, religion, history. And so the Souths of Eudora Welty, Robert Penn Warren, Flannery O'Connor, William Faulkner resemble one another because they all resemble an existing *thing*. The apples of Chardin, apples of Cezanne.

The service of Faulkner to subsequent Southern writers has not been that of a rich lode to be prospected by night for plots, characters, rhetoric but the service of father to son—to demonstrate a few of the things a man may do, to sketch in the air some of the shapes of possibility. I did not read a novel by Faulkner until I was a college freshman; and I began with *Sanctuary*, for a freshman's reasons. Baffled, I did not continue until my sophomore year when I read *As I Lay Dying* in order to write a paper on his use of the child narrator. Baffled again. In short, my introduction to Faulkner left me admiring but coldly, feeling no sense of dialogue between my own beginning work and his. It was only when I read *The Sound and the Fury* in the summer after my junior year that I recognized the grandeur of his genius, distant grandeur. To that time I had written only one story of any seriousness—the first draft of a story called "Michael Egerton"— and I still took no imaginative fire from Faulkner.

The next year however—my last undergraduate year—I read the work of another, very different Southern writer, Eudora Welty; work which did instantly ignite my imagination, illuminate my own experience because I recognized in Welty what I had not in Faulkner—many of the landmarks of my own world. What her work showed me was what is vital for any beginning novelist, the most valuable possible *literary* influence —that the world I had known for twenty-two years (the people, places, language) was a possible subject for serious fiction. That was all but it was genuine revelation. What her work had said to me was what all good work says to the listening fellow-artist, not "Go and do likewise" but "Go and do as well with what you know and need to know."

Once that great service has been acknowledged, the remaining important question is—what has made one's work, one's vision of that world? My answer is unsatisfactory but true. All of my life has made my world, has shaped my work—all the people I have loved or hated, all the places I had lived in, and many people I have never touched, places I have only passed. My work is made from my entire life not from other books, though books have been a part of my life.

I do not mean to deny the large value of reading in my life and artistic education; but I must point out that books entered my life quite late, as they enter most lives. By the age of six or seven, when books become available to most children, those events have occurred, those sights been seen which will or will not make a man a writer. Indeed, by the time a potential novelist begins to read, most of the encounters and relations about which he will write have passed, are history and lie in the mind pure as diamond, unyielding to one's long education, waiting only to assert their power, to challenge one's life and all one has learned to a battle which is the battle of understanding against mystery, in which victory can only be a work of art—an act of temporary understanding, temporary order or, if not so much, a celebration of mystery itself.

There are of course books which I am sure fed—and feed—my imagination. I do not recall having a favorite book as a child. I did not read the brothers Grimm or Andersen or *Tom Sawyer*. Aside from the comic books of the forties, Sidney Lanier's King Arthur and the entire run of Hardy Boy mysteries, I mostly read and reread Bible stories, not the Bible itself but a child's retelling which nonetheless spared me little; for some of my earliest obsessions were the stained relationships of Cain and Abel, Abraham and Isaac, Jezebel and Jehu, or the appearance of the risen Jesus in the breaking dawn by the Sea of Tiberias to the disciples fishing off-shore—"Children, have you any meat?" I must move ahead years in my memory (to the age of fifteen) to find similar food, similar wounds demanding care. It was then that I first read Tolstoy, *Anna Karenina*—well before I discovered that for me, given my life, it was write or choke in chaos, self-hate; and nothing since, even Shakespeare or Dante, has mattered so much.

As to formal influence, there have been times when I faced technical problems in my own work and turned to masters in search of help. When I arrived at the scene in *A Long and Happy Life* in which Rosacoke and Wesley must at last make urgent love, I studied comparable scenes in *Anna Karenina* and *Madame Bovary*; and though my own scene bears no visible relation to either, it was shaped in part by Tolstoy's elliptic power, Flaubert's timid failure. When I came to introduce a ghost into *A Generous Man*, I read Japanese Noh plays—the great credible portrayals of spirits returned. (Must I say though that I should never have come to such scenes at all had I not encountered both love and the lingering dead from the start of my life?)

And as to specific influences, moments of mimicry in my work, a far truer influence than Faulkner upon the sound of my prose would be Milton, the fact that I spent nearly three years of my early writing life also daily engaged in a study of *Samson Agonistes*, my mind stocked with lines of coiled power like "Them out of thine who slew'st them many a slain."

I could go on but my point, I hope, is made. The study of influences in a novelist's work is doomed to trivial results; worst of all, irrelevant obscuring results. A serious novelist's work is his effort to make from the chaos of all life, *his* life, strong though all-but-futile weapons; as beautiful, entire, true but finally helpless as the shield of Achilles itself. And the truest list of a novelist's influences, his helps in that effort would be a list of names, a list not of other artists however grand but of private names, household gods, like that list with which Marcus Aurelius begins his *Meditations*—

> From my grandfather Verus I learned good morals and the govern-ment of my temper. From the reputation and remembrance of my father, modesty and a manly character. From my mother, piety and beneficence and abstinence. . . .

My own list would begin: Elizabeth Price, Will Price, Will Price Junior, Ida Drake, Grant Terry; and so it would move through a few new places, a few new voices to the present, the names which demand the words I am writing now, the causes, final judges.

1966

FINDING WORK

$\mathbf{M}$OTTOES, LIKE HEROES, are out of fashion. Perhaps wars have come too closely on us lately; and we have not had time to forget the savage poverty of wartime mottoes, the brief and lethal imperatives— *Remember the Alamo!*; *Lafayette, we are coming!*; *Remember Pearl Harbor!* Oddly the Korean War and now the Vietnamese seem to lack battle cries. Perhaps their purposes and possibilities have been and are too complex and appalling to submit even to the simpletons who manufactured our earlier shouts. (That might be our hope, that now we at least know the *density* of war, were the hope itself not such a black end.)

But when I was a child in North Carolina in the Second World War, private mottoes still had almost magical power for me and my elders. Several of my grammar school teachers urged us to choose our mottoes then in time—as though a motto were as vital as one's health, one's name. (What did one do with one's motto, once found?—write it on one's walls? tattoo it on one's chest? One lived by it, was the answer of course.)

I looked for years, without satisfaction. Surrounded in the threatened air of that wartime America by a cloud of service corps and battalion mottoes dedicated to destruction—*Semper Fidelis, Semper Paratus, Keep 'Em Flying!*—I was relieved to discover that the motto of my family had been for a long time *Vive Ut Vivas*—Live That You May Live—but while I saw even then how vigorous it was, it seemed nothing personal: an old Welsh family's slogan, not mine. So I lacked a motto.

But when I reached college—Duke, September 1951—I almost at once encountered a sentence that steered a large part of my time for those years. Harold Parker said it to his freshman history class of which I was a member in my second semester (and he was quoting Waldo Beach of the Divinity School)—"Education is an ever-widening vision of greatness." It seemed long enough for a motto (though my dictionary conceded that a motto might be "a maxim adopted as a principle of behavior"), its verb should have been conditional, and it ended vaguely—what was the "greatness" of which I was to be seeking an ever-widening vision in these four years and had presumably been seeking for twelve years already? "Greatness" was, even in the fifties, a word tarnished nearly beyond cleaning. What was the meaning of any quality which common speech agreed to accord to, say, Napoleon, Hitler, Roosevelt, and Gandhi?

Beach and Parker were right however. Thanks to them and to a handful of other remarkable teachers, I came in that four years to know fewer and fewer things worthy of an educated man's pursuit and devotion.

That is to say, education had been for me—and I hoped would continue to be, hoped my life would be—an understanding of what in the world and beyond the world (people, things, abstractions) was worth one's life, worth the full exercise of the mind and strength of a single human being, complex as that mind and strength are: appallingly fragile. Another sentence which I discovered in my sophomore year was important for me also—both a confirmation, expansion and deepening of the other. It is Milton's famous definition of education from his essay *Of Education*:

> The end then of learning is to repair the ruins of our first parents by regaining to know God aright, and out of that knowledge to love Him, to imitate Him, to be like Him. . . .

It was in England, at Oxford—after my graduation from Duke in 1955—that I encountered still another sentence which seemed to have both steering and braking power. It was told to me by my teacher, Lord David Cecil; and it had been said by his grandfather Robert Cecil, Lord Salisbury, Victoria's Prime Minister. As I recall the story, Lord David's mother had said to the old man, "Father, don't you think it matters *very* much for the children to do thus and so?" And Lord Salisbury had replied, "My dear, nothing matters *very* much; and few things matter at all."

The remark seemed to me then—as it does now—both moving and shocking, consolatory and subversive. It is not at all a new observation. It appears at first sight to share the weariness of Marcus Aurelius; the easy disillusionment of *Ecclesiastes*, the *Rubaiyat*, and a million sophomores' diaries—*Vanity of vanities, all is vanity*. But that is not what Lord Salisbury said (though well he might, having presided for years over the largest empire in the history of the world), not "*All* is vanity" nor "Nothing matters" but "Nothing matters very much and few things matter at all." What few things?

My own formal education lasted nineteen years (my whole education will be, I hope, conterminous with my life), and the list I have made of the few-things-that-matter would be irrelevant and intolerably presumptuous here now. In any case, the list has altered; is altering yearly. And the fullest record of the effort to make it and keep it, such as it has been, is contained or implied in my stories and novels. Summary, as usual, would only be a lie.

One of the things however has become so central to the continuation of my own life, to my slim convictions about the needs of others, and to my few certainties about the ends of education that I must discuss it. It is something I learned in the process of the inadequate life and education I have had—ridden by the seven deadly sins, most heavily by sloth—but which I assert as universal. And it can be briefly stated, almost a motto, a hated motto—*Work Makes Free*. I could even extend it (truly, I think) to make my own definition of education. Education is the process by which a man discovers, as early as possible in his brief life, the nature and duties of his personal work.

There may be no reason why a man should work, provided he lives in a society which charitably supports its unemployed. The only abstract reason for working may in fact be that a God exists who created man and set man to work to glorify His creation. (The second chapter of Genesis says that God made Adam "and put him in the garden to till it and keep it.") If a man does not acknowledge such a God—and his own duties to God—then perhaps he is a fool to work. Let him sleep till noon seven days a week, leave the house only to cash his welfare checks, buy his beer, and return to watch television all afternoon, half the night, surrounded by his loud and growing family.

Yet to speak of myself—even if I did not acknowledge God, even if I were adequately supported by the state, I am sure that I would work. And my first simplest reason for working would be one universally expressed in proverbs—that "The Devil finds work for idle hands." But my next reason would be that one expressed in the motto which Adolf Hitler cruelly inscribed across the one-way gates into many of his death camps —*Arbeit Macht Frei*: Work Makes Free. Few if any men freed themselves from Dachau or Belsen or Auschwitz by the work required of them there. But the truth of the motto survives that hideous distortion. Work frees a man. Frees him from what though?

First, from want—physical want, hunger, cold, disease. But I have suggested a society which would supply these wants. Exactly so.

In such a society I would work to be free of others. Free from prolonged economic obligation to the state, which is self-diminishing (and a man's obligations to his state increase paradoxically and terrifyingly as that state becomes increasingly impersonal, unreachable). But at least as necessary, free through the exercise of my proud and growing skill from other human beings, free even from those people I love, especially them. This will require explanation. I do not mean that I would wish to be— or would ever become—free of the duties and debts of love toward my kin, partners, friends. What I mean is that only through my own early discovery of, cultivation of, absorption in some work—building houses, teaching schools, laying roads, writing novels—could I free myself from the crippling emotional dependence upon other human beings which infects and afflicts any man who has nothing in his life upon which he can rely, nothing more permanent than other people. A craft, a skill may—given good health—last a man all his life; very few friends, wives, sons, daughters will prove as enduring. Age, disease, death—and worst, disloyalty—exist and will in time win all that we love. The hardest shield for ourselves will be our work, if we have troubled to discover and master and commit ourselves to some rewarding work.

But our *selves* also exist and are as frail, vulnerable as any other person we may have loved. Yet it is ourselves which will remain true to us longest of all. All our weaknesses—our vanity, greed, dishonesty, cruelty, fickleness—will accompany us closely to our graves. What shield is there then against our own loyal flaws? What may free us from ourselves, our final enemy?—work, perhaps only work, the daily commitment to a task which will demand from us full and strenuous exercise of our strongest selves: our comprehending, foreseeing, order-creating minds, our miraculously complex physical competence.

So work frees a man. Yet I have only spoken negatively, denyingly of the things work frees us *from*. The difficult but necessary question remains—what things can a man's work free him *for*?

I will—can only—answer for myself, by attempting to explain briefly but truthfully my discovery of my own work, its nature and function in my life, perhaps in the life of the world. I was the son of parents who, like most Americans at the time of the Great Depression, suffered profound humiliations—economic and thus emotional—which were inevitably filtered through their screening love to me, their first child, born in the black winter of 1933. Yet though I was faced in my early years not with actual poverty but certainly with the threat of poverty (the Depression continuing into the Second War) and though my father (a small-town North Carolinian with only a small-town education) hoped that I would want to study medicine, I have no memory of ever wishing to be anything but an artist. At first, a painter; then a musician.

But when I had tried and proved to myself that my gifts for painting and music were insufficient; that whatever my ambitions, I could not implement them, then (in my last years of high school) I began to write—poems, stories, novels. Through all those years of school and college, I worked naturally, almost unthinkingly, never seriously wondering why I was painting or finally writing. Yet since college had given me freedom to choose, I had chosen for myself an education likely to feed my wish and ambition (the study of language, literature, history, art, religion, anthropology, psychology)—had chosen without seeing that the wish to become an artist was more than a wish, more than a bent, more than a choice made for me by elimination of all I could not do.

What I had not seen was that my wish was a need, forced on me apparently by two large forces—birth (gifts, talents) and environment—and it was only toward the end of my formal education (and largely through the gathered weight of comprehensions and failures which comprised that education) that I came to understand that what I had wanted was what I had needed, that my wish was work, that most of my education—my life—had been a process both of creating a need for my particular work and of preparing me for it. But why is the writing of fiction my work?

A complete answer would require total understanding of my needs and motives, an understanding which I do not have. Yet this much at least is true. I have worked for twelve years now in the solitude necessary to a writer, then subjected my work to the judgment of an unpredictible, often uncomprehending public so that I might, first, understand (or at least examine and set in order) the threatening mysteries of the world, of my fellow human beings and of myself; second, that I might communicate my understanding, however inadequate, to other human beings as baffled and endangered as I by all the controllable and uncontrollable mysteries of the universe, God, human nature.

My work then is what all honorable work is—the attempt to control chaos. It has freed me till now from physical want, from prolonged dependence on my fellows, and occasionally from myself. It has freed me for the attempt to understand, if not control, disorder in myself and in those I love. It has even freed me at time to participate in the richest, most dangerous mystery of all—the love of what otherwise I should have feared and fled, a few human beings.

1967

PYLON

THE POSTURE OF WORSHIP

$\mathbf{M}$OST GOOD NOVELS, however they triumph over life in their orderly structure and clarity of language, will obviously complicate and enrich themselves on second readings—returning, as they move, to a truer imitation of human life; growing more mysterious as they are contemplated, mirrors which cloud from behind or whose depths deepen. (*Anna Karenina*—which seems at first like a broad river uncovering, washing, revealing all life—can come, on successive readings, to seem more mysterious than Kafka or the murkiest Dostoevsky. What can they offer which is stranger, more menacing, than this sentence from Anna's last monologue?—" 'No, I will not let you torture me,' she thought, addressing her threat not to him nor to herself but to that which forced her to suffer, and she walked along the platform, past the station buildings.")*

Some of Faulkner's strongest works move in that direction, from apparent lucidity toward opacity—*As I Lay Dying*; *Light in August*; *The Hamlet*; *Go Down, Moses*. But as many or more of them reverse the movement in that they clarify, simplify (sometimes oversimplify) on second reading. They are initially thickets, forbidding puzzles, which mount a great show of threat or at least of indifference to solution—indeed, to mere reading—but which, if one makes a commitment of will, surrender their secrets with grateful and alarmingly loose-limbed ease (secrets which occasionally prove to have been no secrets at all).

Absalom, Absalom! is—its admirers insist—the most richly rewarding of Faulkner's bristling puzzles; and certainly *The Sound and the Fury* will not yield its staggering load to any straight-line reading (it demands to be read in all directions, at once). A *Fable* seems, on the testimony of its survivors, to be all puzzle; its final secret a puzzle—why was it done at all? But *Pylon*—though it is usually waved aside as Faulkner's second-worst novel (it is his eighth in order of composition) and though even its few defenders do not succeed in making its solution (*their* solutions,

* Leo Tolstoy, *Anna Karenina*, translated by Louise and Aylmer Maude (Oxford, 1933), II, p. 379.

symbol-logged) seem grandly worth the effort—does yield curious and (for Faulkner) unique answers to a second reading. While not so complex as it looks, it is a more interesting book than it promises to be, and finally a surprising one—touching, oddly lovable, more needful of us than we of it.

Any tenth-grader can see, at first glance, what its weaknesses are—the willful havoc with grammar and spelling, the homemade artiness (the resort to Eliot and Shakespeare in chapter titles, the tired stream of un-illuminating compounds and obstructive neologisms, which even in 1935 must have been old hat); the flirtation with objects and events which appear to be gathering emblematic functions but which finally are abandoned, unemblematic debris (the pylons themselves; the time of the novel—Mardi Gras, the entrance into Lent, time of mourning and repentance preceding rebirth; the airplanes as numinous receptacles of *eros* and *thanatos*); the coyness in refusing ever to reveal the name of the chief character and the resulting confusion in passages involving several men, all referred to as *he*; the failure to distinguish by rhythm or diction between the interior monologues of the few characters who think at all—or between their thoughts and those of the narrator-author; and the placing cheek-by-jowl of a passage perfect in its precision with a long spin-off into bad prose-poetry (*bad* because unusable—viscid, obstructive, proceeding from no visible needs of character, plot or mood).

Why? The quickest answer would be the one given so often by Faulkner's early critics (most of the above weaknesses are common to all his work except *The Sound and the Fury*)—that Faulkner was a genius almost entirely dependent upon inspiration, afflatus, and therefore peculiarly lacking in the milder resources of joinery, stamina and taste which would have eased his way between seizures. That may finally be the truest answer (at least until someone learns to reproduce the phenomenon of artistic inspiration and production, at will, under laboratory conditions). Meanwhile, anyone seriously interested in discovering why *Pylon* is the book it is might begin by trying to establish what Faulkner thought he was making when he began the novel and what he believed he had made at the end.

In March 1957, a member of the English Club at the University of Virginia asked Faulkner, "do you regard *Pylon* as a serious novel, and what were you driving at in that novel?" Faulkner said,

> To me [the pilots] were a fantastic and bizarre phenomenon on the face of a contemporary scene, of our culture at a particular time. I wrote that book because I'd got in trouble with *Absalom, Absalom!* and I had to get away from it for a while so I thought a good way to get away from it was to write another book, so I wrote *Pylon*. They

were ephemera and phenomena on the face of a contemporary scene. That is, there was really no place for them in the culture, in the economy, yet they wouldn't last very long, which they didn't. That time of those frantic little aeroplanes which dashed around the country and people wanted just enough money to live, to get to the next place to race again. Something frenetic and in a way almost immoral about it. That they were outside the range of God, not only of respectability, of love, but of God too. That they had escaped the compulsion of accepting a past and a future, that they were—they had no past. They were as ephemeral as the butterfly that's born this morning with no stomach and will be gone tomorrow. It seemed to me interesting enough to make a story about, but that was just to get away from a book that wasn't going too well, till I could get back at it. *

Notice that he does not directly answer the first half of the question—"do you regard *Pylon* as a serious novel?" He might be taken to imply both that he does and doesn't. He expands on his *idea* of the barnstorming pilots of the early 1930s; but he ends with the possible hint that the book was—and remains for him—a short dash away from the difficulties of *Absalom Absalom!* We could not in any case press close textual analysis upon a remark which was impromptu and courteous. What is clear enough is that the conscious motive-to-work in *Pylon* was people—the sight of certain people in action, at their work. It is clear from all Faulkner's remarks about his work assembled in *Faulkner in the University*, that his imagination was invariably triggered by pictures of people—knowledge of and curiosity about character, always arrived at through visual experience. He says of *The Sound and the Fury*, "It began with the picture of the little girl's muddy drawers, climbing that tree to look in the parlor window with her brothers that didn't have the courage to climb the tree waiting to see what she saw." And of "A Rose for Emily," "That came from a picture of the strand of hair on the pillow." In answer to a question about the theme of *Light in August*, "I was simply writing about people." And again, "the writer himself is too busy simply writing about people in conflict with themselves and one another and their background to wonder or even care whether he repeats himself or whether he uses symbols or not."

It is clear too, in his statement about *Pylon*, that the people whom Faulkner thought central to his impulse were the racing pilots and their retinue. He does not name them but he discusses only them. He does

* Frederick L. Gwynn and Joseph L. Blotner, eds., *Faulkner in the University* (Random House, 1965), p. 36.

not refer at all to the non-pilots—the nameless reporter and Hagood, the editor. Faulkner had apparently seen a good deal of such people, though how intimately he had known them we cannot yet say. He had himself learned to fly in 1918 in the Canadian air force; and while he did not fly in the war, his interest in aviation remained strong enough for him to fly with barnstormers while he lived in New Orleans in 1925 and to purchase his own plane in 1933 with the profits of the first film of *Sanctuary*. He flew this plane to New Orleans for the dedication of Shushan Airport in February 1934 (the month in *Pylon* is February—the novel was published in March 1935); and he seems to have continued flying until his brother Dean was killed in November 1935, while barnstorming in a plane Faulkner had given him. Barnstormers had been central to two of Faulkner's early short stories, "Honor" and "Death-Drag."

But *Pylon* is not about airmen—or about flying. On first reading, it appears to be. The title is *Pylon*, the posts round which air races are flown; the airmen seem at center-stage with their hard meager glamor—but that appearance is the cause of more than half our initial bafflement and irritation with the novel. Why do we spend almost no time actually in the air? Why are Shumann and Laverne and Holmes so vaguely seen, so physically impalpable? Why do they do so little (they are off-stage half the time), say so little? Why do they almost never think an audible thought? Why do we have no material for understanding them (that is, knowledge of their pasts) until the novel is thirty pages from the end?

Because we are not meant to "understand" them. The three of them are the literal center of the novel; but our geographical or spatial relation to them is the same as that of the nameless reporter—the relation of circumference to center. The subject of *Pylon* is that relationship—and a picture of it, at that (however murky), not an investigation.

For in a careful second reading of the novel—with eyes now trained for avoiding debris—one sees that, though the pilots may be the object for Faulkner's curiosity, even yearning, it is the reporter whom he inhabits and sends toward them in an effort to comprehend, an effort which becomes (for the reporter only?) a helpless offer of love and finally a balked isolated bitterness. The fact that the reporter does not begin the novel (Jiggs the mechanic has the first dozen pages, solo) and that he is at times intensely inhabited by Faulkner (to the point of identification—the reporter's vision coinciding with the narrator's) and then without apparent reason flung beyond not only our comprehension but our sight—these are red herrings which are too successful in a first reading. But the bones of the novel can be made to appear—and most of them relate to the reporter. This, I think, is the anatomy of *Pylon*—a young man, age twenty-eight (born on April Fool's Day, the son of a multi-husbanded mother) who will remain nameless to us (the name by which the other characters know him is apparently a pseudonym), is a newspaper reporter and has been assigned by his impatient but paternal editor to cover an airshow held to celebrate the opening of a city airport in a thinly-disguised New Orleans during Mardi Gras. We first see the reporter through the eyes of Jiggs (the hot-eyed musclebound mechanic for a team of airmen) as

> something which had apparently crept from a doctor's cupboard and, in the snatched garments of an etherised patient in a charity ward, escaped into the living world. . . . better than six feet tall . . . about ninetyfive pounds, in a suit of no age or color . . . which ballooned light and impedimentless about a skeleton frame as though suit and wearer both hung from a flapping clothesline; a creature with the leashed, eager loosejointed air of a halfgrown highbred setter puppy.

And these are the terms in which the reporter is seen again and again throughout the novel by everyone, including the narrator—a scarecrow, a skeleton, Lazarus, an escaped ghost; in fact, a disembodied, unphysical being as contrasted with the cocked and "vicious" (as Faulkner so frequently calls it) physicality of the airmen.

It is only some thirty pages into the novel, when the reporter has returned from the first day of the air show and is talking with Hagood his editor, that we see how his assignment to cover the show is becoming for him an assignment to cover three of the participants—Roger and Laverne Shumann and Jack Holmes. The growth of that involvement from curiosity to fascination to infatuation to abject devotion is complicated more by bad prose than by complexity in structure, and may be dissected. Hagood gives the first prod. He says that the reporter has a marked instinct for events but not for "the living breath of news. . . . just information" (*vision* perhaps as opposed to *comprehension*); and in a crucial passage, Hagood asks the reporter, "Can it be by some horrible mischance that without knowing it you listen and see in one language and then do what you call writing in another?"

The reporter will not accept the charge and rushes to say that he has given the editor only what he thought the paper required—bare news. Then he tells Hagood all that he has learned so far about the Shumann menage—that Roger is the pilot, Laverne an assistant mechanic, Jack the parachutist; that Laverne is technically married to Shumann but that she serves both men sexually and that none of them knows the paternity of the six-year-old child with them, though he has been named Jack Shumann through a roll of dice. Hagood urges the reporter "to write it." The reporter accepts enthusiastically. But at once Hagood says, "Go home . . . and write it. . . . And then set fire to the room"—present it, understand it, but burn it because, Hagood says, "I don't even care. Why should I find news in this woman's supposed bedhabits?"

The reporter is appalled, for two reasons. He has been lured now into revealing his own great ambition to be a writer (the classical ambition of young reporters), only to have it callously waved aside as useless; and he has suddenly seen the Shumann menage by Hagood's new scalding light, not as he'd seen them a moment before ("They ain't human") but, in their homelessness and poverty and outcast state, as forlorn and needful as himself, differing from himself perhaps only in their violent physical plenitude, their—as he thinks—rich sexuality, all of which has made them paradoxically defenseless in a world of the asexual, the condemning, the uncaring. He finds them derelict on the first night (the novel begins on a Thursday afternoon and continues through the following Monday morning), broke and unable to collect their share of the first day's prize money. He at first tries to help them find free lodging, then makes an impassioned call to his editor to explain the dilemma and to ask for help from the paper (what help is not clear). The editor, enraged, fires him; and the reporter takes them all, including Jiggs and the child, to his own room in the old quarter, moved by "the sheer solid weight of their patient and homeless passivity."

By now—a third of the way in—it is becoming apparent that the three are not interesting to the reporter (or to Faulkner, or us) as airmen—as a new phenomenon, new types demanding new modes of comprehension and judgment—but as what Faulkner might have called the present and temporary avatars of an archetype: the seductive rascal, the glamorous and lethal tramp. Alcibiades, Antony, knights-errant, goliards, Hell's Angels. Nor are the present instruments of their obsession—airplanes—essentially new. The great seducers have always possessed and displayed certain objects to which they were helplessly attached but which seemed, to the witnessing world, charged extensions of their superior vitality, bristling monstrances of their fearful and enviable sexuality—swords, shields, armor, champing steeds; lutes, tight hose, laced codpieces; biplanes, leather clothing, goggles, boots; motorcycles. What occurs too late to us, their victims, is that these objects are never the weapons or threats of the seducer but are his literal attempts at defense and escape (escape from what?—world? time? self? us? All, of course; always); thus our relation to him is constant and predictable and is partially described by Johannes de Silentio—

as God created man and woman, so too He fashioned the hero and the poet, or orator. The poet cannot do what the other does; he can only admire, love and rejoice in the hero. Yet he too is happy, and not less so, for the hero is as it were his better Nature, with which he is in love.*

The word *love* is accurate—for the poet, for Faulkner perhaps, certainly for the reporter. What Johannes does not say is that the love will end—is, anyhow, refused. And the end occurs when love produces in us, as it must, understanding—when adoration and contemplation tell us that the Hero differs from us in *degree*, not kind; that his body is rigid with fear, not fullness; that all his strength is cocked only for flight or revenge on us; that he is (to return to Faulkner's discussion of *Pylon*) "outside the range . . . not only of respectability, of love, but of God too." Why beyond the reach of God?

Because the Heroes are always incapable of love, gift or receipt. And indeed they never deny this to us. The airmen announce it to the reporter from the start—in their scorn, in Holmes' explicit jealousy, and, most strongly, on the morning of the second day when Laverne and the others rob the reporter of six dollars as he lies blind-drunk in the alley beside his house. Yet his knowledge of the theft only baits him deeper into fascination and commitment. Now he must make them confess the theft, must make *Laverne* confess (because by now his need is focused largely on her, though never entirely)—"it seems I am bound to offer her the chance to tell me that they stole . . . not the money. It's not the money. It's not that." What is it then?—their defiling his unsought generosity, his offered unneeded love.

And he does achieve a moment of triumph. He forces a moral act from them. After he has given them the key to his room to use as they like, Laverne briefly thanks him and confesses the theft; and a little later (after Shumann's first crash, at almost the exact center of the novel), he wrings from her another bleak word of thanks and apology and—at last —rudimentary affection.

"We're going on to your house," she said . . . . "You have changed your plan about leaving town, I imagine?"

"Yes," the reporter said. "I mean no. I'm going home with a guy on the paper to sleep. Dont you bother about me." He looked at her, his face gaunt, serene, peaceful. "Dont you worry. I'll be o.k."

* Quoted as the epigraph in *Heroes and Orators* (McDowell, Obolensky, 1958), a novel by Robert Phelps which would be of interest to any reader of *Pylon*. Johannes de Silentio was Kierkegaard's pseudonym for *Fear and Trembling*.

"Yes," she said. "About the money. That was the truth. You can ask Roger and Jack."

"It's all right," he said. "I would believe you even if I knew you had lied."

Now he is unleashed and his fantasy races hungrily ahead. He dares to tell Shumann (who has also betrayed the chance of warmth) of his desire for Laverne, a desire which he all but admits to be focused now upon the three of them, the old dream (dreamed most fully in the sonnets of Shakespeare) of the *ménage à trois*.

Sometimes I think about how it's you and him and how maybe sometimes she dont even know the difference, one from another, and I would think how maybe if it was me too she wouldn't even know I was there at all.

(We recall his obscure and drunken remark of the previous night—"Did you tell him I was married? Did you tell him I got two husbands now?") Now he extends the dream—still aloud to Shumann—to the possibility of replacing Shumann in the event of Shumann's death in the faulty plane the reporter has found for them.

His infatuation is complete. He believes at last in his chance for love—participation, completed gestures, nodded receipts. Hagood (who has reinstated him in his job) says, "Why dont you let these people alone?"—"I can't," the reporter says, "Yes. . . . I tried." Even Shumann sees him now as "patron (even if no guardian) saint of all waifs, all the homeless the desperate and the starved."

One last moment of hope is allowed him. After he has managed to find a new plane for Shumann to fly in the final race, co-signed the note of purchase, made a dangerous first flight with Shumann to establish the plane's weight-distribution problem, he then persuades Colonel Feinman to waive qualification on the plane and can bear the news as a gift to Laverne—

"Yes. It was all right. Like I told you."

"They did it," she said, staring at him yet speaking as though in amazed soliloquy. "Yes. You fixed it."

"Yes. I knew that's all it would be. I wasn't worried. And dont you . . ."

This further triumph frees him, minutes later as he holds the Shumann child just before Shumann's fatal crash, to return to his first description of the three—"That's it . . . they aint human. It aint adultery;

you can't anymore imagine two of them making love than you can two of them airplanes back in the corner of the hangar, coupled." The reporter has not known (and will never know) what we have possessed for some thirty pages now—Shumann's memory of Laverne's first attempt at a parachute jump, her ecstatic return from the wing to the cockpit to mount him in frenzy, then float to the ground, bare to all viewers—nor did the reporter witness, with us, the Shumanns' metallic preliminaries to copulation in the reporter's own bed.

But though his initial insight seems to him now confirmed in experience, his need remains firm and desperate. When Shumann crashes into the lake before their eyes and Laverne runs toward the seawall, the reporter follows (both are holding the child) "at his loose lightlyclattering gallop like a scarecrow in a gale, after the bright plain shape of love." Laverne instantly withdraws what little she has given—"she turned, still running and gave him a single pale cold terrible look, crying, 'God damn you to hell! Get away from me!' "

The next chapter (the next-to-last) is called "Love-song of J. A. Prufrock." The lines from Eliot which seem especially relevant (though not given by Faulkner) are these—

> Would it have been worth while,
> To have bitten off the matter with a smile,
> To have squeezed the universe into a ball
> To roll it toward some overwhelming question,
> To say: "I am Lazarus, come from the dead,
> Come back to tell you all, I shall tell you all"—
> If one, settling a pillow by her head,
>   Should say: "That is not what I meant at all.
>   That is not it, at all."

For while the reporter seems, however dazedly, to realize that his hope of involvement in these three lives (perhaps in *life*) has died with Shumann, he is still compelled to haunt Laverne, posted back again at the circumference where he can only watch her as she watches the grim attempts to snag Shumann's body from the lake. His compulsion, which he states several times, is to make Laverne understand—in fact, to step forward as Prufrock cannot dare to do and speak his love, to "tell you all." But she never looks or speaks to him again and he does not dare. He is able to say to Jiggs later that night, "I keep on trying to explain to somebody that she didn't understand. Only she understands exactly, dont she? He's out there in the lake and I can't think of anything plainer than that." But the plain acceptance of death is not an understanding of love; and what has Laverne not understood?—the mere fact of his infatuation, his abject loyalty? Or the chance that he may have more than half-unconsciously procured a faulty plane for Shumann in the hope of assuming Shumann's place? What, after all, would his love have consisted of? (No more, surely, than he had offered in his confession to Shumann—"I'd just be the name, my name, you see? the house and the beds and what we would need to eat. . . . I could anyway buy her the pants and the nightgowns and it would be my sheets on the bed and even my towels.") And what has the reporter understood of the motives and needs of Laverne, Roger, Jack? Nothing—for, again, he has imagined them different from himself only in degree, not in kind. His trust, his gamble, has been that their hectic lives were—like his own—in search of love, family, rest; solutions to a dilemma which he has assumed to be also his—loneliness, homelessness. But they were not in search of love.

Why? No answer—either from them or the reporter or from Faulkner. After nine o'clock that final night, the reporter never sees Laverne again. He accepts from Jack Holmes the money to forward Shumann's body to his parents in Ohio; he works with Jiggs to conceal a gift of money in a toy for the child; but his truest response has been a question said only to himself—"How could it be?"

The last fifty pages shed no light, for him or us. The reporter hears from Jiggs of Shumann's Ohio boyhood, Laverne's Iowa orphanhood (both, in effect, obituaries which in their pathos and credibility, their late position in the novel, and their failure to *explain* the lives that ensued, closely parallel the glimpses of Jay Gatsby's early years which Nick Carraway receives from the father at Gatsby's funeral). He sits through an all-night blackjack game and vigil for the body with other reporters and hears their coarse unhelpful version ("It's because they have got to do it. . . . They can't help themselves")—hears it passively, offering no contradiction or justification. Then, with dawn, he sees the search abandoned, a wreath dropped into the lake in lieu of salvage; and having no knowledge (which we have, in full) of Jack and Laverne's trip to Myron, Ohio to abandon the child with Roger's old parents (the child's predicament now paralleling the reporter's own childhood—and Laverne's), he returns to the paper and writes as his last visible act two short passages. The first, resurrected from the trash by a copyboy, is the reporter's attempt to make "literature" (not *meaning* but *decoration*) from Shumann's death—

Thus two friends told him farewell. Two friends, yet two competitors too, whom he had met in fair contest and conquered in the lonely sky from which he fell, dropping a simple wreath to mark his Last Pylon.

The second attempt is for Hagood's desk—

> At midnight last night the search for the body of Roger Shumann
> . . . was finally abandoned by a three-place biplane of about eighty
> horsepower which managed to fly out over the water and return
> without falling to pieces and dropping a wreath of flowers into the
> water approximately three quarters of a mile away from where Shu-
> mann's body is generally supposed to be since they were precision
> pilots and so did not miss the entire lake.

Is this a final admission by the reporter that Hagood was right?—
that the reporter listens and sees in one language and writes in another?
Or that he has not seen at all, but misseen, misapprehended, merely
hoped? Or perhaps this ending (the whole book, in fact) makes those same
self-condemning admissions for Faulkner himself?—that the years and
energy which he had spent among pilots and planes (seduced there by
something) had yielded only turgid bafflement, ashes-in-the-mouth? None
of those questions can now be answered—the reporter is off for a thorough
drunk; and we do not yet know (perhaps we never will) what actual
relationships, if any, from Faulkner's own life lie beneath the story.

Yet this sphinx has its secret and keeps it closely, a secret whose
answer even it does not know—not "Why are these airmen reckless
and godless?" but "Why do the Orators (even this reporter) adore the
Heroes (even these three, so tawdry and small)? What is the source of
their need to love, on their knees thus, smiling?" And the fact of the
secret, the fear of the secret—so clearly close to Faulkner, who all his
life sought the company of Heroes (pilots, hunters, horsemen)—goes
far to explain the cluttered and irrationally disarranged shape of the
brief lean story which *Pylon* contains, barely bones enough for a lyric
poem.

Perhaps *Pylon* is not a novel. Surely a good deal of irritation with
its shape and language proceeds from our own—perhaps even Faulkner's—misconception of its form. It is called a novel, has the size of a
novel. But east and west, the novel, as distinguished from the poem,
has traditionally been an instrument of reason intended for discovery
and comprehension and then, of necessity, forgiveness—in fact, the supremely Christian form, the new dispensation which rose to augment,
if not supersede, older pagan forms (the psalm, epic, lyric, drama)
which were hymns to mystery, human and divine. Faulkner's great books
have other aims—or achieve other ends, whatever their aims. *The Sound
and the Fury, As I Lay Dying, Light in August*—all end as examples of
that older chthonic art, the icon which both portrays and worships the
unseen god; and their form and tone are shaped (often tortured, wrenched)

by the posture of worship, of muffled awe at the sight of darkness. *Pylon* approaches a lesser darkness than those three great books—a private darkness, though real and hurtful, and a frightened, rapt and willful approach—but it makes all the same, if we struggle to watch, a moving obeisance.

1968

A REASONABLE GUIDE
THROUGH PERILOUS SEAS*

WILLIAM FAULKNER'S Nobel Prize was the rock that tripped a slide of journalistic and critical attention unequaled (for the span—fourteen years) in irrelevance, fantasy, sheer bad-mannered unhelpfulness. Even Shakespeare can barely have been so badly, uncomprehendingly, used. And to mention Shakespeare is to suggest possible reasons for the unique bulk and opacity of most Faulknerian criticism; for surely Faulkner more than any great artist except Shakespeare was silent to the world's curiosity and comment, scornful of seeking its fame, scornful of fame finally, belatedly, offered. Late in his life, for instance, he said that he wrote novels for years before it occurred to him that anyone might read them. And since an appetite for Fame (as end or means) has been one of the few constants in the declared motives of ancient and modern artists, despised Fame has taken a heavy toll of Faulkner for being of all great novelists the one least willing to prepare an audience, explain to an audience, clarify or dilute for an audience. Fielding, Dickens, Tolstoy, Stendhal, Twain—all were deeply conscious of writing for *someone* (one or millions); and they agonizingly adjusted their private visions, not to soothe or please but to be merely visible, audible, to that someone. And Fame's toll is the volumes of nonsense, barnacled to the huge books *because* Faulkner would not explain, justify, adjust, not think of readers —who after all were hardly there for the first twenty-five years.

This indifference of Faulkner's was perhaps, like so much about him, peculiarly Southern, a form of fierce hauteur. Now another Southerner, Cleanth Brooks, has given us the first half of his study of Faulkner (a second volume is planned); and at once it is the most courteous, modest, sensible and helpful of existing guides. For a guide is most nearly what it is, a handbook for strangers. There are introductory chapters on Faulkner's province and people (full of the information that only a native could

* *William Faulkner: The Yoknapatawpha Country* by Cleanth Brooks (Yale University Press, 1963).

possess, information productive of calm understanding), a chapter on Faulkner as nature poet, separate chapters for each of the novels set in Yoknapatawpha County, eighty pages of notes which often and convincingly refute previous (sometimes hilarious) misreadings, genealogies and chronologies of fictional families, a full character-index with page numbers to the stories and novels, an index to Brooks himself, and Faulkner's own map of the county.

In many ways, then, the book one might have expected from Brooks as Southerner and distinguished teacher but curiously not the book expected of Brooks as New Critic, author of *The Well-Wrought Urn*, the relentless verbal inquisitor. Perhaps such fine combing will come in the second volume in which Brooks promises to

> concentrate on Faulkner's development as an artist—his beginnings, the forging of his style, and the working out of the special fictional techniques associated with his name. . . . to examine some of the earlier drafts of his novels and to discuss his process of revision with reference to style and structure.

But, for now, Brooks has cast a broad loose net and landed, not the inert mass of symbols, parallels, archetypes which are the usual Faulknerian catch (which Brooks himself denounces as "symbol-mongering") but any number of separate attentions, insights and understandings. His method—if not infallible, surely the safest for dealing with an apparent genius—is to assume from the start that Faulkner knew what he meant, that the finished book is that meaning, that the *form* is the meaning, and that the central question to ask of form, characters, accidents is "Why are you built as you are?" It is a method which now seems almost shockingly naive (In fact, I can think of only one other living critic who employs it—H. D. F. Kitto, whose studies of Greek drama are among the handful of great illuminations of tragedy); but it leads Brooks into fresh, relevant and—most valuable—unifying discoveries, apparently modest perceptions around which a whole work suddenly arranges its baffling elements. For instance:

—that in *Light in August* "Faulkner has given us a kind of pastoral—that is, he has let us see our modern and complex problems mirrored in a simpler and more primitive world." (This is braced throughout with numerous comparisons to Wordsworth.)

—that the mode of *Light in August* "is that of comedy. To say so in the light of some of the terrible episodes may seem perverse. But Faulkner's comedy is frequently a makeweight to the terrible. . . . Its function is to maintain sanity and human perspective in a scene of brutality and horror."

—that "The only people in Faulkner who are 'innocent' are adult males; and their innocence amounts finally to a trust in rationality—an overweening confidence that plans work out, that life is simpler than it is."

Perhaps, to employ his own terms, it is the innocence of Brooks' own method (however richly yielding) which has restrained him from the kind of final simple revelations of Faulkner which, say, Coleridge and Bradley gave us of Shakespeare—revelations of the *use*, the good, of reading Faulkner. The virtue of his method is also its vice—its almost undoubting confidence that all Faulkner's plans worked out, that to have uncovered his intentions is to have confirmed his achievement of those intentions and the worth of all those intentions (even in *Sanctuary*, of which Brooks thinks a good deal more highly than Faulkner did). Such innocence leads him to argue for instance that *Absalom, Absalom!* is "the greatest of Faulkner's novels." He supports the claim with a stunning apparatus of clarification, with elaborate ratiocinative tables for the weighing of evidence in the separate accounts of Sutpen's folly and fall; but he does not face Faulkner's nearly total refusal to handle the story (and so many other stories) in the way it begs to be handled, in the way Faulkner worked most revealingly—scenically, pictorially.

In short, Brooks finally makes common cause with most other Faulknerian critics by dangerously underestimating the extent to which Faulkner was not so much the great undisciplined novelist of our time as the most willful, *playful* great novelist since Fielding. Faulkner himself often said that he wrote "for fun" and that "Fun is to accomplish something which I thought that perhaps I couldn't."*

The imagined memory of that small beautiful head bowed alone in a room in Oxford, Mississippi, stroking down volume after volume—like the plays of Hamlet's players, "tragedy, comedy, history, pastoral, pastoral-comical, historical-pastoral, tragical-historical, tragical-comical-historical-pastoral, scene individable or poem unlimited"—because finally it *amused* him to do so, unchecked, unconcerned for the negligent present world or the solemn hierophants-to-be, unconcerned to be universal, to tell more than private truths about what he had seen and thought he knew (one has only to talk with any literate French- or Englishman to discover that half of Faulkner is as exotic to them as any Byzantine gold-enameled bird; by refusing to compare Faulkner's aims and achievements with those of other great novelists, Brooks has obscured this vital fact)—that image surely, nailed-up in our minds, would be the safest rudder through the

* Faulkner in Gwynn and Blotner, *op. cit.*, p. 257.

perilous sea he poured us. Mr. Brooks' second volume may well clarify that image by examining the secret trails—manuscripts, drafts. But for now he has given us more than sufficient gifts for gratitude—the Baedeker of Faulkner guides, all that reason can give and money buy.

1964

AN EMPTY TOMB*

JOSEPH BLOTNER, then in his thirties and an assistant professor of English at the University of Virginia, met William Faulkner in February 1957 when Faulkner was in his first term as writer in residence there. Five and a half years later, Faulkner was dead; and Joe Blotner's was the last hand to relinquish the cypress coffin as it sank. During those years, Blotner served Faulkner with loyal affection. He transcribed Faulkner's responses to student questions and coedited the useful *Faulkner in the University*; with his wife he provided for the Faulkners the kind of quiet care which is scarce in academic communities. Above all he seems to have absorbed a good deal of the increasingly fluid warmth of Faulkner's last years and to have returned it with a welcome filial generosity (Faulkner said of him, "He's my spiritual son. He loves me better than he does his father").

Now twelve years after the death, Blotner provides these enormous volumes—more than two thousand pages, with notes—which he calls a *biography*. The final two hundred pages are unquestionably a *memoir*— warm though heavy on worship and, in the description of death and burial, genuinely eloquent in feeling and prose—but is the total a biography, the recoverable data of an interesting human life filtered through the screens of an intuitive intelligence and passed to readers as a useful compound of fact and comprehension, a book about a life? I'm afraid it isn't; and the reasons why seem to me complex and typical of the general failure of recent American literary biography.

First is the large fact that Faulkner's life—the visible actions of his days—may not have been interesting. Few creative artists have had interesting lives; they haven't had time. The passionate action (peril and victory) is in their work, work achieved in solitary and stationary labor. Faulkner knew the fact well; and his understanding of it explains a part of his violent objection to scholarly and journalistic attempts on his private life. Blotner records (dangerously) Faulkner's exact statement of the problem, cast oddly in the third person which he so frequently used of

* *Faulkner: a biography* by Joseph Blotner (Random House, 1974).

himself—" 'Faulkner himself has already milked his private life of any or all interesting literary matter so anything in this mss. that is true will be dull and what is not dull probably wont (*sic*) be true, and therefore the mss. will belong to the scavenger school of literature.' " The books then consume and become the life; the daily actions are of no more interest to a witness than those of other citizens who live and die in small towns, have wives and daughters, the financial problems of middle-class workmen, and a serious involvement with alcohol.

Second is the fact that Blotner's technical strategy has committed him to a chronological presentation of the visible events of Faulkner's days, with almost no comment or mediation between event and audience. Even at the distant end, there is no summation—only the statement of the preface that "to me he seems America's greatest writer of prose fiction. The narrative will perhaps reveal more clearly how he seemed to me as a man. I cannot hope to look upon his like again." The narrative claims to be virtually complete in its offerings and to contain the apparatus for its own interpretation and understanding. Since a narrative is—by etymology and usage—a piece of shaped knowledge, what does Blotner's narrative know?

I think this is a fair if drastic summary. A boy is born in 1897 into a middle-class Mississippi family of Scottish stock. The family can be shown to have possessed for several generations both the usual Gaelic-Southern tendency to violence in the face of life's most ordinary conundrums and the equally usual blend of wit, eloquence, and obfuscating rhetoric. The boy has a normal childhood, though he shows signs of either proud self-sufficiency or serious self-entrapment. He is devoted to his lively mother, affectionate with his three brothers and family servants; and he develops an early attachment to a neighbor-girl, slightly older than he. He is an indifferent student but a good reader, a meticulous sketcher, and an adolescent poet. His verses win him the friendship of an intelligent older man, Phil Stone, whose encouragement will be crucial in the years of early manhood.

Those years include the baffling marriage of his sweetheart to another man, his own retreat into four months of RAF training in Canada (the source of much subsequent mythmaking), the publication of his first poem, a smattering of courses at Ole Miss; odd jobs at home, in New York and New Orleans (where he samples the local versions of postwar bohemia, heavily spiritous). Through those years, the informed encouragement of Stone, the blind faith of his own mother, and the kindness of Sherwood Anderson result in the publication of a first volume of frail poems and then, in quick succession, three immature but vigorous novels.

Now he is past thirty, a joke in his own town, and more withdrawn than ever. His sweetheart divorces her husband; he marries her, contracting to support a readymade family (she has two children). And though he takes a menial job, he pins his hopes on writing. In the next four years, in a conflagration of brilliance, he publishes four novels—*The Sound and the Fury, As I Lay Dying, Sanctuary, Light in August*. His stories appear in national magazines. He is highly praised if little read and is able to buy an antebellum house for his family, which now includes a daughter, his only child. Financial necessity soon takes him to Hollywood where he is to spend miserable periods through the next thirteen years, writing fruitless screenplays. During those years—the early forties —he continues to publish a diminishing but marvelous flow of fiction. His reputation remains high; his always tentative commercial success has evaporated. The drinking has hardened into cyclical bouts of black intensity; his wife is now alcoholic; finances are perenially desperate; his attempts at repair in Hollywood are more wretched than ever; most of his friendships have atrophied or chilled (especially the one with Stone).

Then the luck begins to turn—Malcolm Cowley edits the famous *Portable Faulkner*; there is a sale of film rights; he wins the Howells Medal and then the 1949 Nobel Prize for Literature. He lives another twelve years, is as celebrated as he was ignored, travels to Asia and Europe as a successful if mercurial cultural ambassador, has several May-December affairs with young women; continues to drink at any sign of trouble; then with his wife, he gradually settles into a warmer life in Virginia near his married daughter, the university, and the hunt clubs. He publishes four extraordinary final novels; dies of the apparent effects of a horse fall, exacerbated by age and continuing drink; and is acknowledged the first American novelist of his time.

That, I think, is Blotner's outline, fleshed with thousands of incidents and anecdotes. What it claims to know are those visible events—and the unexamined triumph of the work (the fiction like the life is considered only as *event*). But the invisible remains, as it does in any life, preeminently a creator's; and Blotner gives it almost no attention—aside from the opening bow to genetic heritage, a brief description of the pattern of his drinking, and an acknowledgement of the inexplicable nature of the genius, the two volumes give no explicit attention to the numerous mysteries which almost certainly nourished or starved the work. To name only the most insistent—

What was the nature of the shaft of ice near the heart of Faulkner's adult character? Was it really a core of frigidity or fear (as many of the facts of his relations with family and helpful friends suggest) or was it a thin protective sheath? If it is not central in him, why does family love seem to alternate so unpredictably with revulsion? What were the origins of his wife's long battle with drink, begun apparently after their marriage; and what of the disintegration of the marriage in its middle years? How can he tell his young daughter, when she attempts to forestall a bout by saying "Think of me," "—Nobody remembers Shakespeare's children"? Why must he invent elaborate myths of physical prowess? Most puzzling of all, why did the work bring him so little relief from the terrors of life? (A serious probe with that single question might be the richest means of examining and winnowing the work, now in danger from academic fans hungry for a universal American genius.)

But Blotner has relentlessly hewed to his premise, the blighting premise of Carlos Baker's *Hemingway*—that by the long recital of facts, he can restage the once-visible life before the eyes of us who never witnessed it; that we will then understand at least as much of its shape and meaning as the actual witnesses (more, since none of them knew as many facts as we). Not a book *about* a life then but the life itself—that seems the intent.

I'm sorry to say it fails—sorry not because I'm convinced that a biography of Faulkner is possible or desirable (I'm not) but because Blotner's intent was clearly a loving one; and given its premise, it was pursued with mammoth industry, care, and apparent accuracy in the hope of homage to a lost friend and his body of work, work which is after all its own monument. Sorry too because—if the unexplored silences of Faulkner's life do contain substance for a book, and they well may—Joseph Blotner seems qualified by labor and love and intelligence to write it.

Now that he has published his vast archive (surely the fullest chronology of any artist's days) could he think of turning back to the start again—the lonely boy, the lonely man who died, the great books between—and making a smaller but large thing (distilled, useful, heartening): a book about a life, the map of a heart?

1974

NEWS FOR THE MINESHAFT

AN AFTERWORD TO
A GENEROUS MAN

I DON'T intend mystery or mischief in saying that the meaning of *A Generous Man* is itself—its physical shape, which is both the product of its meaning and the container, limiter, protector; the shell of the crab (though the crab can slough its shell and grow). I say it in order to start with a minimal accuracy; and I'd expand first by claiming that anyone who has chosen to read it at all can discover its full content in how-it-looks—not in what it says, least of all in "what it says to you" (that bloodless scrap so often flung by exhausted artists to the gaining wolves). The famous little girl in Graham Wallas' *Art of Thought,* warned to think out her meaning first, says, "How can I know what I think till I see what I say?" And Wallas says she has the makings of a poet. The makings, granted— her crucial verb is *see*; but had she been a poet, she would certainly have substituted *you* for the first and third *I*. Tolstoy said it impersonally, "This indeed is one of the significant facts about a true work of art—that its content in its entirety can be expressed only by itself." I labor what may seem a thundering cliché because it is not honored in spirit—as any American novelist will affirm who has skimmed his potential two-hundred reviews or has had the hair-raising experience of looking into the quarterly fiction studies. In fact, I can think of only one contemporary critic, since the death of Erich Auerbach, who has made it his steering principle (any critic who is not himself a novelist or poet)—H. D. F. Kitto, in *Greek Tragedy* and *Form and Meaning in Drama*—and he has quietly proceeded through Greek drama, producing startling illumination from a single assumption which, though he applies it only to drama, he holds valid for all other forms—"If the dramatist had something to say, and if he was a competent artist, the presumption is that he has said it, and that we, by looking at the form which he created, can find out what it is."*

The meaning therefore, for the audience or the artist himself, cannot be complete until the work is complete. This is not to say that the artist works automatically, unconsciously, without plan or continuous con-

* *Form and Meaning in Drama* by H. D. F. Kitto (Methuen, 1956), p. v.

scious control. It does say, though, that the plan for any work of the necessary length and complexity of a novel will (and must, for the sake of truthfulness and vivacity) undergo an elaborate and apparently uncontrollable bombardment of accident, accretion, whim—in addition to the more astonishing and satisfying discoveries of secret relations, the secret autonomous life of the story itself, its concealed fecundities (which will proceed in part from those accidents).

That process of continuous growth in the idea and shape of A *Generous Man* is, for me, most nearly recoverable now in the progressive titles which I find in the manuscript. The first page is dated 21 January 1964; the title is A *Mad Dog and a Boa Constrictor*. I kept no orderly notes for the story, as I had done—voluminously, a year in advance—for A *Long and Happy Life*; but my memory is that the story surfaced as I lay in bed, insomniac, one night in January '64, still beached like many others by the backwash of John Kennedy's murder. What in fact had been beached was not so much me as the novel I had worked at for two years before, a story of waste and panic in which I had personal stakes, suddenly harmonious with recent events yet doomed by them, inaudible now as a clavichord note in a *Wozzeck* fortissimo. And what arrived that sleepless night—clicked up instantly formed in my head—was a story which seemed an antidote, a way back to work. The given was two tales, till then unrelated, which I had known for years—a runaway circus-snake and a mad dog whose rural owners set it free to rave (they could neither kill it nor watch it die slowly and would not pay a vet)—and my immediate grateful decision, seconds later, was that both tales were comic (the snake would be caught, the dog not actually mad); that both could be yoked into a single story by the Mustian family, the central family of A *Long and Happy Life* (1962) and of my second short story "A Chain of Love" (1955); and that the central figure now would be the elder Mustian son, Milo. The story, I thought, would be brief—eighty pages—and essentially a farce for my own good cheer. It would also, I thought, be easy work.

So within the next day or two I began, with very little more forethought than I've mentioned—the bones of a story, a set of characters ready-made and well-known for ten years. The title was as simple as the impulse seemed—A *Mad Dog and a Boa Constrictor*—and I rattled along through the early pages at, for me, a brisk clip (twenty-three pages in the first thirty days; a finished page a day is good speed). My initial aim was being fulfilled—for the first time in more than ten years of writing, I was working with pleasure; without the reluctance, the neurotic obstacles which all craftsmen (Mozart and Handel excepted, apparently) strew between themselves and the desk (obstacles whose absence I have now come to fear, they being the surest danger signs that I'm nearing a center which shrinks from touch, the flesh puffing madly around the sore). I should have been apprehensive but I wasn't. In my gratitude to be at work at all, I was only delighted.

And the first eighty pages exhibit that delight, in their larger shape (the quick tumbling of scenes; scene hitched to scene more tightly than appears, by outrageous surprise); in a quality of action (the literal movement of characters through space) balletic and clear-lined, whose faith is that, in the young characters at least, gesture and movement is revelation, that they cannot *lie* so long as they move (a quality of course which is at the mercy of each reader's sight, his willingness to yield to coercion from me and make his own sights from the actions offered); in the archeology of character (the creation of pasts for characters whose futures I had long since fixed); the guying of as many as possible of the sacred solemnities of Southern fiction, my own included (from the bow to *Tom Sawyer* in the opening sentence on through the humble but noble dog, the pathetic idiot, the sanctity of blood and name—"We use the names they give us, that's all. They called me Milo so that's how I act"—the hunters who think they are chasing bear or boar but end with nothing more edible than Beauty and Truth in their gassy bags, the young stud watering some parched lady's life); most intensely, in the rhythm and rate of language, the conversion of mid-South farm-dialect into forms and meters which appear, I think, natural but are thoroughly made from the inside by pleasure—a sentence in the meter of the *William Tell* Overture (so far undetected, page 4);* scenes as on pages 11–15, which have both a mirror-accuracy to this family's life and a striking resemblance, in form at least, to Rossini's scenes of comic confusion (the sextet in *L'Italiana in Algeri*) or the swirl of *ariette* in Verdi's *Falstaff*—three lines of passionate fun per man, which lay his life open to public view.

Yet there seems to me now, in those early pages, a high almost desperate pitch to the playfulness. Quite early, rifts begin to yawn in the farce; and the buried strata are slowly revealed—though I did not know it, the theme was *loss*. My old abandoned impulse was asserting itself, humping up beneath the surface glaze—waste and destruction in their homeliest forms (the apparent loss of a dog to disease, remembered loss of a son-and-father to alcohol, the sudden separation by roaring adolescence of brother and sister, a drunk vet's drowning in loneliness, a woman's snake and chief means of support vanished, a middle-aged sheriff still panting to catch what he'd never had or earned—the love of his wife—and more). And the forms are progressive, dogs to men.

My working-title had changed by then (the end of part one). The

---

* All pages references are to be the first American and British editions of *A Generous Man* (Atheneum, 1966; Chatto & Windus, 1966).

manuscript does not show a date for the change, but it must have occurred between pages 48 and 67; for by page 67, I have twice used the phrase "clear day." The first time, without apparent intention of special weight for a common phrase—

> Eyes still shut, his mouth burst open on the surge of his joy, the sudden manhood that stood in his groin, that firmed the bones of his face and wrists as the truck bore him on through this clear day among his family, his first known girl, toward his life to come, his life he would make for himself as he wished. (p.48)—

but at its recurrence, twenty pages on, in Rosacoke's dream of Milo's new manhood, with a sense, for me at least, of gravity, freight—

> She said, "You will die and ruin us, Milo." He said, not looking, "I am almost a man. I must fall to rise." He jumped and he rose and the last she saw—before she woke—was him rising not falling as he had foretold, above limbs and leaves into steady light, a single figure in clear day alone, no thought of when that day might end. (p.67)

By then or within the next few pages (six months after the candid beginning), I had made the phrase my title—*Clear Day*, to which I added a protective description, *an escapade*. That remained my title, through the end—October '65—and the book was announced thus by Atheneum, though by early that fall, I had begun to face the need for a change. A musical play had been announced for New York, called *On a Clear Day You Can See Forever*. The papers were calling it *Clear Day*; and I know exactly the spot where I heard, on my car radio in the voice of Robert Goulet, its title-song—"On a Clear Day"—and admitted to myself that I was cornered and must change or risk confusion as "the book of the show."

Few readers understand the importance of titles and names to writers. It is difficult to discuss them at all without sounding precious or fraudulent; but surely what is involved is no stranger than the ancient and continuing magic of names—our names are organic to us, handles to our lives, vulnerable heels; chosen for us before we were born and our surest survivors, in an age of records. We all spent solitary hours as children, saying our names aloud until they metamorphosed from familiarity through abstract sound to final mystery, essence—so with a novelist who has spent two years or longer with a carefully named set of characters and with a satisfying title on his manuscript. The prospect of change is the threat of loss—name is essence and can be lost. A changed name will be a diminished name. (I remember my confusion and revulsion when, as a child, I learned the true names of several famous film stars. The apparent ease with which they had shed them seemed then—and now—a frightening display of gleeful self-hatred. And one of the real crises of my career was the discovery, after years of use, that the male hero of A *Long and Happy Life* shared names with an elderly citizen of my town and that I might be required to change the name of a character I'd invented six years before—the man, approached, cheerfully gave permission for the use.)

Why had *Clear Day* insisted upon itself so early in the work and why at the end was I so reluctant to discard it? Habit—after eighteen months, I was used to the name. But also a weakness for its easy attractiveness of connotation. A clear day is a welcome experience. So is *calm sleep* or *steady love*. (So, supremely, is *a long and happy life*, though that bears a crippling sting in its tail.) And when I began to search for new titles, I at first turned up a series of approximations—A *Full Day*, *First Light*, *Morning Light*, A *Given Day*, A *Perfect Day*, *Fair Day*—and was near to settling on *Morning Light*, only to discover that H. M. Tomlinson had preempted the title. None of the others chimed. I was worried and since I was deep in revising the text, I tried to discover the meanings which *Clear Day* had collected, for me and for the story. This is not to say that I had not known its meaning since at least page 80—sixteen months before—nor that the phrase, once chosen as title, had not exerted its own control, tunneling always only just out of sight, surfacing at moments of intensity as sign and reminder, almost warning—to the characters, to me, to the future reader—that this story was steered, not hauled or pushed; and steered by a steady vision of Milo, the boy at the center, the pitch of his youth.

But more than his youth—I saw, looking back. The pitch of his life.

A consecutive list of the chief passages, beyond the two already given, which contain the phrase *clear day* (with its related words—*morning, afternoon, night, day* or the adjective only) would reveal—I saw, with some surprise—the spine of the story, the linked control:

> Rooster said "What's the time?"
> "Maybe eleven twenty-five."
> "And you think it's morning?"
> "For half an hour—sure."
> Rooster said "What's your age?"
> "I told you—fifteen."
> "And you think that's young?"
> "Well, I've met one or two older people through the years."
> Rooster said it to the road. "It is eleven twenty-five, a clear broad morning that will be noon soon. You are fifteen, a man and the

Lord has hung gifts on you like a *hatrack*. . . . Don't think it's morning when it's late afternoon." (pp. 85–86)

[Milo] did not hear (he was whirling on down), but blinded and weak, he did feel her gaze, accept her hopes and turn them in his mind to a momentary dream—Lois at last, clear in perfect nakedness, waiting on a porch as he moved towards her, answered her smile, extended his open hands to hers and heard her say, "I have been afraid, waiting in the dark. I have kept my promise. Why have you failed? You said you would come to me long before night." He answered, "Night? It is still clear day" but looking up, saw it was really night, that the light was from her, her readiness, so he said, "I am sorry. I was tending to duties but now I am here and look, I am ready." (pp. 160–161)

[Rooster] thumbed towards Milo. "He's had his day." (p. 211) "But don't stop with taking," Mr. Favro said.

"I ain't," Milo said. "I been learning things—but I told you that. These past three nights, these two clear days. I been handing out stuff like the whole Red Cross, like loaves and fishes to people on the hills." (pp. 254–255)

So Rosa looked to Rooster—"Maybe this is the end?" But Rooster looked to Milo, answered to him. "Could be I guess. What could *keep* it from being? You've had *your* day. Maybe I've had mine—maybe never will." (p. 256)

But Milo paused above her on arms as straight as what stood ready beneath to serve, looked at her eyes—only them, nothing lower—and said unsmiling, "I have heard that the saddest thing on earth is to love somebody and they not love back."

"So have I," she said and by smiling fully, forced him to smile, then rocked the heel of her own tough hand in the pit of his neck (where nerves pierce the skull) and drew him forward, welcomed him down, and the rest was giving—pure gift for both, no thought of receipt though receipts poured in so long as they worked, as if fresh joy could flood your thighs, stream down through your legs, drown your heart, gorge throat and brain, offer (even threaten) a new clear life (so long as you moved) and yet roll on, roll past, leave you spared. (pp. 265–266)

But Rato turned, faced Milo, grinned. "Morning," he said. "Morning," Milo said. Then they both looked up to the lifting sky—Lois followed their eyes—and found they were right. It was

morning (clear, cloudless, the oldest gift), would be morning oh six
hours yet. (p. 275)

The phrase had become, since its first uncalculated appearance, both
a controlling and a fertilizing device. It had become—without, I am
almost sure, conscious knowledge by me—the emblem of the fullness of
the impulse. Whether it was an initial fullness or a gradually gathering
one, I cannot say. It was certainly one which I neither anticipated nor
understood when I began the story. And an emblem of more than its
fullness—its truthfulness. Truth to the final seriousness, even grimness,
of a story I had thought was farce and to the shape of a quickly changing
character—the boy Milo's—as he reaches (in three days) the height of
his manhood, poises in clear broad day, descends (descends, not falls).

I had seen what I had not quite seen before, in the nearly two years
since beginning the book (two years which include a ten-month gap at
the comma in the penultimate line of page 172)—that the story had made
itself, and well (clearly, economically), in response to its own impulse
and needs. What must go without saying is that it responded also to needs
of mine; to observation of life around me in those two years; to personal
bafflements, pleasures, and defeats; family deaths. I do not mean to play
hierophant in barring the entrance to that one cave. It still contains matters
of the greatest force and urgency for my daily life. I only confess my
inability to talk sense—truthful usable sense, anyhow—about a process
so gradual, complex and irrecoverable. Inability, and lack of curiosity.
The *story* exists, is the thing that matters—existed, whole, as I searched
it for a title. And the things which I saw it saying most strongly of Milo's
life were in Rooster's voice. First, his early warning, "Don't think it's
morning when it's late afternoon"; then his grim summation almost at
the end, "You have had *your* day."

So he had—Milo—and the sense is heavy at the end (the final passage
above is the end) that it was his last day, that—in Donne's use of the
same metaphor—"His first minute, after noon, is night." The final light
of the book is still morning, but morning for only "six hours yet." A
limited sentenced strip of day is what is left him as he turns from his
vision, vague as it is, of a new clear life toward his home again, his
ravenous duties at his old—and future—mill, which in nine years' time
will have left him the charred and raucous figure of A *Long and Happy
Life*.

But, ended as it is, it had *been* day at least (three days in fact, Saturday
to Monday). A number of witnesses realize that—the sheriff, his wife,
Rosacoke, Lois, Selma. And what a day—the single moment when Milo
stood ready to offer freely, with rushing plentitude, the virtues he had

earned or had laid upon him; virtues called from him by the shape of the story, the demands of every event and meeting. It had been, I saw, his manhood, not his "coming to manhood" as might appear.

So my search for a title was colored now by my retrospective findings; and the list of prospects lengthened—*The End of Day, First Dark, The Midst of Day, A Generous Man*. That the last was best, I would still maintain—as the fullest flag for the whole—though I didn't see a notice of the book which actually considered the title, and only a few which accepted its clear offer of news. (How many readers accept and use the fairly indispensable help offered by such titles as *The Great Gatsby* and *Rabbit, Run?* An attempt to measure the degree of irony, if any, contained in that *Great* or the realization that the title of Updike's novel is an imperative, almost a plea, by author to hero, would carry a serious reader a good deal farther than he might otherwise go toward the core of the books. So, conversely, might an attempt to rename a supreme but mis-leadingly named book, like *Anna Karenina*. Maybe *Happy Families?* or Tolstoy's early title for it, *Two Marriages?*—either of them considerably more accurate and helpful than his final eloquent choice.)

I had called *Clear Day* an escapade, when I thought it was one. Perhaps I should have called *A Generous Man* a romance. If I had ended at what might appear a possible point, on page 244, the end of part two (with a further phrase to clarify that Milo had fainted, not died), then I would have had a story that answered the classical tests for prose ro-mance—a mode common from the first century to the present, deriving apparently from the *Odyssey* and New Comedy, in which stylized char-acters capable of allegorical expansion move through "strange adventures, separations, wanderings across seas and lands, rescues miraculously ef-fected, dangers overcome and trials passed, until the final triumph of reunion with loved relatives."*But surely the minimal requirement for romance is a happy ending—Daphnis and Chloe married and bedded; Prospero restored to his dukedom a wiser, more merciful man; Ishmael alive in the wreck of the *Pequod*, planning his book; Catherine and Heath-cliff joined in death on their rightful moors; the curse of the Pyncheons laid.

Hawthorne's own definition of romance, in his preface to *The House of the Seven Gables*, is disappointingly exterior—

---

* Ernest Schanzer, introduction to Shakespeare's *Pericles* (New American Library, 1965), p. xxxi.

When a writer calls his work a Romance, it need hardly be observed that he wishes to claim a certain latitude, both as to its fashion and material, which he would not have felt himself entitled to assume, had he professed to be writing a Novel. The latter form of composition is presumed to aim at a very minute fidelity, not merely to the possible, but to the probable and ordinary course of man's experience. The former—while, as a work of art, it must rigidly subject itself to laws, and while it sins unpardonably so far as it may swerve aside from the truth of the human heart—has fairly a right to present that truth under circumstances, to a great extent, of the writer's own choosing or creation.

But whatever a writer's reasons for choosing the form *romance* or, more probably, for producing one and then discovering he has done so, his basic strategy in prose romance will have been wish-fulfillment; or more exactly, the arousal and examination of a number of our oldest fears—that we are not the children of our parents, that lovers may be permanently parted, that nature is indifferent if not hostile—and then at-least-partial allaying of those fears, a granting of our deepest needs: Here is your long-lost father / wife / daughter / beloved. All is well. The gods are not mocked.

All that could be said of *A Generous Man* at the end of part two. The dead have worked through their blood-relations—and beasts and extraordinary events—to right their wrongs; old debts are paid by a golden boy who never incurred them; relations are clarified through recognitions; forgiveness, comprehension, gratitude abound. They sometimes do in life—and to that extent the romance is "realistic." There is however a third part, thirty pages. Renunciations, further (and final) separations, a grim future seen, a grim present faced, its demands obeyed—and all that, not nailed on by a willfully sadistic author but inherent in the characters, their actions, the world.

So perhaps not *romance*, despite a passage in Northrop Frye's *Anatomy of Criticism* which tends my way (and the ways of Alain-Fournier, Kafka, Ralph Ellison)—

Certain elements of character are released in the romance which make it naturally a more revolutionary form than the novel. The novelist deals with personality, with characters wearing their *personae* or social masks. He needs the framework of a stable society, and many of our best novelists have been conventional to the verge of fussiness. The romancer deals with individuality, with characters *in vacuo* idealized by revery, and, however conservative he may be, something nihilistic and untamable is likely to keep breaking out of his pages.

Yet A *Generous Man* is not a novel—its resemblance to Japanese Noh drama or to *The Magic Flute* is closer than to most twentieth-century fiction—and permitting it to appear as a novel only confirmed some readers in their suspicions that I had intended to write the previous history of the Mustian family in the realistic mode of A *Long and Happy Life* and had, early in the job, lost all control. A python capable of conceptual thought; a ghost who assists at a flat-tire change, then attempts a murder, then repents and leads the way to a lost fortune; a teenage palmist who foretells the plot of A *Long and Happy Life*; all accepted as apparently unexceptional by characters observed "realistically," recognizably the cast of an earlier sane novel—the man's lost hold.

Not this time. The form of the theme was new and different, and had taken hold. (The Milo of A *Generous Man* stands in roughly the same relation to Milo of A *Long and Happy Life* as Stephen Dedalus in *Ulysses* to Stephen in *Portrait of the Artist*). The theme, I have said, was—for its own reasons and mine—*loss*. But loss in the midst of plenty or at the sudden end of plenty; loss-in-*time* too (three days' time)—absence before he had realized *presence*. The presence—of all Milo's resources and his use of them—had been, as their counterparts are in any person, miraculous; that is, inexplicable in terms of our present knowledge of heredity, environment or training. The form of his story is therefore miraculous. Laws are suspended, laws of the European and American realistic novel and those physical laws which, in fiction or in life, are our most elegant walls against the large world—that terrible, perhaps even benevolent world which turns huge, around and beneath our neater world which agrees to forbid it. The dead, incompletions, the past which is future. And A *Generous Man* proceeds under no law except its own—the demands of its meaning, demands of the large world to deal with ours. Demands which are met by the shape of the story; the resistance and yielding of character; finally, by language, the irreducible medium and servant and guide of the meaning.

There are, strangely, many readers who respond to the language of an elaborate work of fiction with considerable bluster and attempts at suppression. In fact, the long history of art and manners might be seen —and not entirely misleadingly—as an endless knock-up between the plain style and the elaborate. The good old days when men were men, could say what they meant in ten puffs of smoke and wore linsey-woolsey against all weather—Aeschylus vs. Euripides, Athens vs. Alexandria, Giotto vs. Bernini, Hemingway vs. Faulkner. Surely it might have been clear by now that, in serious verse and fiction, the language (in its atomic structure of syllable, meter, order) proceeds from the pressure of the entire given impulse as it shoulders upward through one man (his unconscious mind, his conscious, his training, his *character*) and will therefore bear the marks, even the scars, of its unique journey. When Shakespeare writes, in *Pericles,*

> *She speaks,*
> *My lord, that, may be, hath endured a grief*
> *Might equal yours, if both were justly weighed.*
> *Though wayward fortune did malign my state,*
> *My derivation was from ancestors*
> *Who stood equivalent with mighty kings:*
> *But time hath rooted out my parentage,*
> *And to the world and awkward casualties*
> *Bound me in servitude,*

and when Milton writes, in *Samson,*

> *Great Pomp, and Sacrifice, and Praises loud*
> *To Dagon, as their God who hath deliver'd*
> *Thee, Samson, bound and blind into thir hands,*
> *Them out of thine, who slew'st them many a slain,*

what is at issue is not clarity vs. murk, sincerity vs. artifice, but fidelity to an impulse, a willingness by the poet to display language which bears whole strips of his skin and entrails (because they are *his* entrails for good or bad, what he has to offer), and a refusal to contract with readers-on-horseback, racing by.

Or—another way—lines like

> *non sapei tu che qui è l'uom felice?*

or

> Before Abraham was, I am

simple as they sound, may express even more complicated realities than

> *But ah, but O thou terrible, why wouldst thou*
>   *rude on me*
> *Thy wring-world right foot rock? lay a lionlimb*
>   *against me? scan*
> *With darksome devouring eyes my bruisèd bones?*

But the clear terror was produced by Dante and Jesus, the turbid by Hopkins. You may have strong reasons for thinking that the first two achieved larger, worthier ends; but you cannot therefore dismiss Hopkins as obscure, mannered, self-intoxicated, any more than you can dismiss a turtle for failing to win the Kentucky Derby. *You* staged the race and entered the turtle against his will and his nature. Your duty—if you mean to read at all and not just clock winners—is to discover the exact race which Hopkins has entered, the goal he approaches, and only then to judge his performance over his own course.

That is not to claim that all language produced by all artists is equally acceptable and could not admit change. The implicit threat to plain-style is oversimplification; to the elaborate, fancification—both, forms of lying; the only error in art. And, more particularly, any process which is both so sudden and slow, and still so mysterious as inspiration is vulnerable to any number of accidents, from flu to madness, along the chain of transmission—accidents which will be almost impossible to hide. The weaknesses of Shakespeare's character are as clearly on show in every hundred lines (for all his track-covering) as Rimbaud's in all the *Saison en enfer* or mine in *A Generous Man*.

For the language of *A Generous Man*, so far as it differs from the "language really used by men" (what men? and when?— you? now?) in complexity, density and compression, is neither a style nor a manner as either is generally understood nor a series of calculated effects nor the appliqué of decoration (raising the rural tone a notch). It is the literally reflexive response of all my available faculties to the moment at hand— a boy's first drunk, a girl's nightmare, the boy's sudden possession by an unfinished past—and to my vaguer sense of a total vision and structure, the story. The voice of the story is—with all faults of intonation and detail—the vision of the story.

This is not to say that I take no conscious care of language. It is the largest care I take (the other things, for better or worse, occurring beyond care); but—aside from obvious editings, omission of repetitions; the choice of a monosyllable here, a disyllable there, for sinew or speed—it is not a care directed toward elegance or memorability of diction. I never think, "This is a Price story and had better start sounding like one." What I think is roughly this (and it is really never a conscious thought)—my job is to make a language which is as faithful as my gift and craft permit to the complexity of knowledge and experience, the mystery and dignity of characters and objects, unearthed by this story; and finally, as clear and as quickly communicative as those prior fidelities will allow. (If you object that my argument rests on examples from verse and proves nothing for prose, which is traditionally the plainer medium, I'd want you to show me, on the hinges of the world, the law which says that prose cannot respond, like verse, to the full demands of its subject and the nature of its author.)

A Generous Man—read through now for the first time since passing proof three years ago—stands for me, at a possible distance, as a story told, an object made. Another three years might well bring it down around my ears (so they might the world); but now, though I don't claim perfection for it, I can say that I do not find a sentence I would cut or change. I think it is right, in the way it needs to be; and the question, I suppose, for a serious reader—who has somehow decided to spend several hours of his life going through it and has got to the end—is then, *So what?* What was it doing? Did it do it well, in terms of its aim? Then, did it seem worth doing at all, with such care, in a world already choking on books (warehouses stuffed with Lord's Prayers on heads of pins)? You realize of course that it means to change your life? Has it made you begin? Would anything, anyone?

There are smaller questions which might follow those. How difficult is it for a reader not familiar with rural life in the American South to respond with serious attention to characters who speak and act in a dialect and manner which is simultaneously the manner—however coarsened —of a long and continuing tradition of comedy now most visible in Li'l Abner and the Beverly Hillbillies? Has "the South" been fouled beyond use, for now—and not merely by caricature but by its own follies—as a source of serious comedy? Aristophanes in Athens? (My faith is that existence is—or will prove to have been—comic and that a serious writer can use any matter which he knows and needs to know, in which he imagines a whole design.) Was it, on balance, an error to use the Mustian family in a work whose conventions are so nearly incompatible with earlier work in which they appear? (I hope I have answered that. Milo's early life—his quick manhood—was different in kind, not merely in degree, from the rest of his life. So is the youth of most men—in all times and countries known to me, at least. Teach for a few years if you doubt that. Watch a group of students be eighteen, then twenty-two. *A Generous Man* may have been my "college novel.") Was it an error to call the snake *Death* and send the symbol-hounds howling down dark trails that ended blankly?—not however before they had raced past, or over, the sense of the book? (Maybe it was. Maybe I should change the name. I meant it first as a joke-in-character. What would you call a twenty-foot python that you showed for a living at county fairs?—what better than

Death? Then other jokes followed—"Death is dead" etc.—and I let the name become one more nail in the coffin I was building for the great Southern hunt: what are you boys hunting? Death, what else? I trusted the wit of the audience.)

The final question, from reader to writer, might be, "There you stand with a smile on your face (or writhing at my feet). Explain and justify. Just what have you achieved that cheers (pains) you so?"

Today's answer might be, "The smile is of puzzlement, not satisfaction, and will not wipe off." Mr. Ramsay thinks in *To the Lighthouse*, "The very stone one kicks with one's boot will outlast Shakespeare." Quite possibly—though with the bomb on stock since Virginia Woolf's death, Shakespeare's chances are considerably improved. You could store him safely in an Arizona mineshaft; the stone's in trouble, though, like you and me. So the smile (if not the writhing) is apparently for that—that *A Generous Man* will clearly outlast me and everyone alive as I write this line (so will my cufflinks). What else will it outlast and what will it say to whoever lasts with it or oars through drowned space to find it in the rubble? Would it be enough?—a jawbone sufficient to remake the old ass, and plan a new?

1968

THE ONLOOKER, SMILING

AN EARLY READING OF
THE OPTIMIST' S DAUGHTER

IN MARCH 15, 1969, *The New Yorker* published an issue half filled with a story by Eudora Welty called *The Optimist's Daughter*. The story is some thirty thousand words long, a hundred pages of a book—much the longest work published by Miss Welty in fourteen years, since her fourth collection of stories, *The Bride of the Innisfallen* in 1955. In those years, in fact, fewer than twenty pages of new fiction by her have appeared (two extraordinary pieces rising from the early civil rights movement, "Where is the Voice Coming From?" and "The Demonstrators"). Now there is this novella—and, close behind it, news of a long comic novel, more stories, a collection of essays.

A *return*, in our eyes at least (Miss Welty could well ask "From where?"); and some eyes (those that haven't raced off after the genius-of-the-week) have got a little jittery with time. Returns in the arts are notorious for danger—almost always stiff-jointed, throaty, short-winded, rattled by nerves and ghosts of the pressures which caused the absence. There have been rare and triumphant exceptions—among performers in recent memory, Flagstad and Horowitz, grander than ever. But who among creators? American arts are uniquely famous for silent but audibly breathing remains—novelists, poets, playwrights, composers. The game of naming them is easy and cruel, and the diagnoses multiply. Yet I think back eighty years to Verdi's return with *Otello*, thirteen years after *Aïda* and the Requiem, for an ample precedent to Miss Welty's present achievement.

I have known the new story for less than a month and am straining backward to avoid instant apotheosis; but I don't feel suspended over any fool's precipice in saying this much—*The Optimist's Daughter* is Eudora Welty's strongest, richest work. For me, that is tantamount to saying that no one alive in America has yet shown stronger, richer, more useful fiction. All through my three readings, I've thought of Turgenev, Tolstoy, Chekhov—*First Love, The Cossacks, The Steppe*—and not as masters or originals but as peers for breadth and depth.

And an effortless power of *summary*, unity (of vision and means).

For that is what I have felt most strongly in the story—that Miss Welty has now forged into one instrument strands (themes, stances, voices, genres) all present and mastered in various pieces of earlier work (many of them, invented there) but previously separate and rather rigidly compartmented. I'm thinking especially of "comedy" and "tragedy." In her early work—till 1955—she tended to separate them as firmly as a Greek dramatist. There is some tentative mingling in the larger works, *Delta Wedding* and the linked stories of *The Golden Apples*; but by far the greater number of the early stories divide cleanly—into rural comedy or farce, pathos or tragic lament, romance or lyric celebration, lethal satire. This is not to say that those stories over-select to the point of falsification (fear and hate lurk in much of the laughter, laughter in the pain) but that the selection of components-for-the-story which her eye quickly or slowly made and the subsequent intensity of scrutiny of those components (place, character, gesture, speech) exhibited a temporary single-mindedness as classical as Horace's, Vermeer's.

But now in *The Optimist's Daughter* all changes. If the early work is classic, this might be medieval—in its fullness of vision, depth of field, range of ear. Jesus *and* goblins, Macbeth *and* the porter. There is no sense however of straining for wholeness, of a will to "ripeness," no visible girding for a major attempt. The richness and new unity of the story— its quality of summary—is the natural image produced by *this action* as it passes before Miss Welty's (literal) vision—look at a room from the perfect point, you can see it all. She has found the point, the place to stand to see this story—and we discover at the end that she's seen far more than that. Or perhaps the point drew her—helpless, willing—toward it, her natural pole?

For it is in this story that she sustains most intensely or has the fullest results extracted from her by the stance and line-of-sight which, since her first story, have been native to her—that of the onlooker (and the onlooker's avatars—the wanderer, the outsider, the traveling salesman, the solitary artist, the bachelor or spinster, the childless bride). Robert Penn Warren in his essay "Love and Separateness in Eudora Welty" defined the stance and theme as it formed her early stories—

> We can observe that the nature of the isolation may be different from case to case, but the fact of isolation, whatever its nature, provides the basic situation of Miss Welty's fiction. The drama which develops from this basic situation is of either of two kinds: first, the attempt of the isolated person to escape into the world; or second, the discovery by the isolated person, or by the reader, of the nature of the predicament.

And a catalogue of her strongest early work and its characters is a list of onlookers, from R. J. Bowman in "Death of a Traveling Salesman" (her first story) and Tom Harris in "The Hitch-Hikers" (both lonely bachelors yearning for the richness which they think they glimpse in the lives of others—mutual love, willful vulnerability), to the young girl (a would-be painter) in "A Memory" and Audubon in "A Still Moment" (the artist who must hole-up from life, even kill it, to begin his effort at description and comprehension), to the frightening and hilarious spinsters of "Why I Live at the P.O." and *The Ponder Heart* or the more silent but equally excluded Virgie Rainey of *The Golden Apples,* to the recently orphaned Laura who visits her Fairchild cousins in *Delta Wedding* as they plunge and surface gladly in their bath of proximity, dependence, love.

You might say—thousands have—that the onlooker (as outsider) is the central character of modern fiction, certainly of Southern fiction for all its obsession with family, and that Miss Welty's early stories then are hardly news, her theme and vision hardly unique, hardly "necessary," just lovely over-stock. Dead-wrong, you'd be.

In the first place, her early onlookers are almost never freaks as they have so famously been in much Southern, and now Jewish, fiction and drama. (Flannery O'Connor, when questioned on the prevalence of freaks in Southern fiction, is reported to have said. "It's because Southerners know a freak when they see one.") They have mostly been "mainstream" men and women—in appearance, speech and action at least. These visions and experiences have been far more nearly diurnal—experiences comprehensible at least to most men—than those of the characters of her two strong contemporaries, Carson McCullers and Flannery O'Connor, whose outsiders (often physical and psychic freaks) seem wrung, wrenched, from life by a famished special vision.

In the second place, the conclusions of Miss Welty's early onlookers, their deductions from looking—however individual and shaped by character, however muted in summary and statement—are unique. Their cry (with few exceptions, her salesman the most eloquent) is not the all-but-universal "O, lost! Make me a *member*" but something like this—"I am here alone, they are there together; I see them clearly. I do not know why and I am not happy but I *do* see, and clearly. I may even understand— why I'm here, they there. Do I need or want to join them?" Such a response—and it is, in Miss Welty, always a response to vision, literal eye-sight; she has the keenest eyesight in American letters—is as strange as it is unique. Are we—onlookers to the onlookers—moved to sympathy, acceptance, consolation? Are we chilled or appalled and, if so, do we retreat into the common position?—"These people and their views are maimed, self-serving, alone because they deserve to be. Why don't they have the grace to writhe?" For our peace of mind (the satisfied reader's), there is disturbingly little writhing, only an occasional moment of solemn panic—

"She's goin' to have a baby," said Sonny, popping a bite into his mouth.

Bowman could not speak. He was shocked with knowing what was really in this house. A marriage, a fruitful marriage. That simple thing. Anyone could have had that.

Somehow he felt unable to be indignant or protest, although some sort of joke had certainly been played upon him. There was nothing remote or mysterious here—only something private. The only secret was the ancient communication between two people. But the memory of the woman's waiting silently by the cold hearth, of the man's stubborn journey a mile away to get fire, and how they finally brought out their food and drink and filled the room proudly with all they had to show, was suddenly too clear and too enormous within him for response.

Or a thrust through the screen, like Lorenzo Dow's in "A Still Moment"—

He could understand God's giving Separateness first and then giving Love to follow and heal in its wonder; but God had reversed this, and given Love first and then Separateness, as though it did not matter to Him which came first. Perhaps it was that God never counted the moments of Time. . . . did He even know of it? How to explain Time and Separateness back to God, Who had never thought of them, Who could let the whole world come to grief in a scattering moment?

But such moments are always followed by calm—Bowman's muffled death or Dow's ride onward, beneath the new moon.

Yet in those early stories the last note is almost invariably rising, a question; the final look in the onlooker's eyes is of puzzlement—"Anyone could have had that. Should I have tried?" Not in *The Optimist's Daughter* however. The end clarifies. Mystery dissolves before patient watching— the unbroken stare of Laurel McKelva Hand, the woman at its center. The story is told in third person, but it is essentially seen and told by Laurel herself. At the end, we have not watched a scene or heard a word more than Laurel; there is not even a comment on Laurel which she, in her native modesty, could not have made aloud. That kind of secret first-person technique is at least as old as Julius Caesar and has had heavy work in modern fiction, where it has so often pretended to serve Caesar's own apparent aim (judicial modesty, "distancing") while in fact becoming chiefly a bullet-proof shield for tender egos, an excuse for not confronting personal failure (Joyce's *Portrait* is the grand example), a technical act of mercy. But Laurel Hand is finally merciless—to her dead parents, friends, enemies, herself; worst, to us.

This is what I understand to be the story—the action and Laurel's vision of the action.

Laurel Hand has come on sudden notice (and intuition of crisis) from Chicago, where she works as a fabric designer, to a New Orleans clinic where her father Judge McKelva, age seventy-one, is being examined for eye trouble. (The central metaphor begins at once—vision, the forms of blindness; the story is as troubled by eyes as *King Lear*; and our first exposure to Laurel's sensibility suggests youth and quivering attentiveness.) In a clinic she has time to notice this—

Dr. Courtland folded his big country hands with the fingers that had always looked, to Laurel, as if their simple touch on the crystal of a watch would convey through their skin exactly what time it was.

Laurel's father is accompanied by his new wife Fay; and at the diagnosis of detached retina, Fay's colors unfurl—hard, vulgar, self-absorbed, envious of Laurel and, in Laurel's eyes, beneath the McKelva's and Laurel's dead mother. The doctor advises immediate surgery, over Fay's protests that nothing is wrong. The judge declares himself "an optimist," agrees to eye-repair; the surgery goes well, and Laurel and Fay take a room in New Orleans to spell one another at the Judge's bedside—their important duty, to keep him still, absolutely motionless with both eyes bandaged through days of recovery. Friction grows between the two women but with no real discharge. Fay shows herself a kind of pet, baby-doll—her idea of nursing consisting of descriptions of her new shoes or earrings, her petulance at missing Mardi Gras whose time approaches loudly through the city. Laurel watches quietly, reading Dickens to her father, oppressed by his age and docility—

He opened his mouth and swallowed what she offered him with the obedience of an old man—obedience! She felt ashamed to let him act out the part in front of her.

Three weeks pass, the doctor claims encouragement, but the Judge's deepening silence and submission begin to unnerve Fay and to baffle Laurel. (It is only now—nearly fifteen pages in—that we learn Laurel's age. She is older than Fay and perhaps Fay is forty. We are, I think, surprised.

We had felt her to be younger—I'd have said twenty-four and only now do I notice that she bears a married name; yet no husband has been mentioned and will not be till just before the midpoint of the story. There is no air of caprice or trick about these crucial withholdings, only quiet announcement—"Now's the time for this.") Then on the last night of Carnival, Laurel in her rooming house senses trouble and returns to the hospital by cab through packed, raucous streets. (Inevitably, a great deal of heavy holy weather will be made over Miss Welty's choice of Carnival season for this opening section and the eve of Ash Wednesday for the first climax. So far as I can see, she herself makes almost nothing of it—the revelry is barely mentioned and then only as a ludicriously inappropriate backdrop to death. Even less is made of the city itself, almost no appeal to its famous atmosphere—it is simply the place where a man from the deep South finds the best doctors.) At the hospital, Laurel finds her foreknowledge confirmed. Fay's patience has collapsed. She shakes the silent Judge, shouts "enough is enough"; and Laurel enters to watch her father die—

> He made what seemed to her a response at last, yet a mysterious response. His whole pillowless head went dusky, as if he laid it under the surface of dark pouring water and held it there.

While Laurel and Fay await the doctor's confirmation in the hospital lobby, they watch and listen to a Mississippi country family come to oversee their own father's death—the Dalzells, family of the Judge's deranged roommate. (Their sizable appearance is not, as might first seem, a chance for Miss Welty to ease tension and pass necessary clock-time with one of her miraculously observed country groups. Funny and touching as they are—

> "If they don't give your dad no water by next time round, tell you what, we'll go in there all together and pour it down him," promised the old mother. "If he's going to die, I don't want him to die wanting water."

—the Dalzells make a serious contribution toward developing a major concern of the story. They are, for all their coarse jostling proximity, a *family* of finer feeling and natural grace than whatever is constituted here by Fay and Laurel; and they will soon return to mind, in sweet comparison with Fay's Texas kin who swarm for the funeral.) At final news of the Judge's death, Fay lunges again into hateful hysterics; but Laurel tightens—no tears, few words. Only in the ride through revelers toward the hotel does Laurel begin to see, with a new and steelier vision, meanings hung round people, which she does not yet speak—

Laurel heard a band playing, and another band moving in on top of it. She heard the crowd noise, the unmistakable sound of hundreds, of hundreds of thousands, of people *blundering*.

Part II opens with the train ride home to Mount Salus, Mississippi. (Laurel's view from the train of a single swamp beechtree still keeping dead leaves begins to prepare us for her coming strangeness, her as yet unexpected accessibility to ghosts.) Mount Salus is a small lowland town and is now home only to the dead Judge—Fay will inherit Laurel's childhood home but is Texan forever; Laurel will return to Chicago soon. But two groups of her friends survive in the town—her dead parents' contemporaries and her own schoolmates—and they rally to her, ambivalent hurtful allies, as Fay's kin—the Chisoms—arrive for the funeral. Led by Fay's mother, they cram the Judge's house like a troupe of dwarfs from a Goya etching, scraping rawly together in a dense loveless, shamingly vital, hilarious parody of blood-love and loyalty—"Nothing like kin. Yes, me and my brood believes in clustering just as close as we can get." It is they—Fay's mother—who at last extract from Laurel what we have not yet known, that Laurel is a widow:

"Six weeks after she married him. . . . The war. Body never recovered."

"*You* was *cheated*," Mrs. Chisom pronounced. . . . "So you ain't got father, mother, brother, sister, husband, chick nor child." Mrs. Chisom dropped Laurel's finger to poke her in the side as if to shame her. "Not a soul to call on, that's you."

So the Chisoms stand at once—or pullulate—in Laurel's sight, as a vision of the family and of love itself as horror, hurtful, willfully vulnerable, parasitic. Yet one of them—Wendell, age seven, viewing the corpse— also provides her with a still point for temporary sanity, for "understanding" Fay and her father's love for Fay—

He was like a young, undriven, unfalsifying, unvindictive Fay. His face was transparent—he was beautiful. So Fay might have appeared to her aging father, with his slipping eyesight.

That emergency perception and the cushioning care of friends prop Laurel through Fay's last hysterical kiss of the corpse and on through the burial. —Propped but stunned, and open on all sides—especially the eyes—for gathering menace to her saving distance. Above the graveyard, she sees a flight of starlings—

black wings moved and thudded in perfect unison, and a flock of migrant starlings flew up as they might have from a plowed field,

still shaped like the grounds of the cemetery, like its map, and wrin-
kled in the air.

And afterwards, at the house again, she numbly accepts more insults from
Fay and waits out the slow departure of the Chisoms—taking Fay with
them for a rest in Texas.

    Part III is the longest of the four parts, both the story's journey through
the underworld and the messenger of what the story learns there. It has
four clear divisions. In the first, Laurel entertains four elderly ladies,
friends of her parents, who raised a question so far unasked (among the
signs of mastery in the story, one of the surest is the patience, the un-
defended gravity with which Miss Welty answers—or asks—all the reader's
questions in her own time, not his; and finally makes him admit her
justice). The question is, why did Judge McKelva marry Fay?—"What
happened to his judgment?" One of the ladies flatly states that Laurel's
to blame; she should never have married but stayed home and tended her
widowed father. Laurel makes no defense, barely speaks at all till the same
lady weakens and begins "forgiving" Fay—

    "Although I guess when people don't *have* anything. . . . Live
so *poorly*—"
    "That hasn't a thing to do with it," Laurel said.

This new ruthlessness (a specific defeat of her own attempt to forgive Fay
through the child Wendell) calms in the following scene—Laurel alone
in her father's library. Here, because of a photograph, she thinks for the
only time in our presence of her own marriage—"Her marriage had been
of magical ease, of *ease*—of brevity and conclusion, and all belonging to
Chicago and not here." But in the third scene—Laurel's contemporaries,
her bridesmaids, at drinks—she bristles again, this time to defend her
parents against affectionate joking—"Since when have you all thought
my father and mother were just figures to make a good story?" Her friends
retreat, claim "We weren't laughing at them. They weren't funny." (Laurel accepts the clarification; only at the end, if faced with "They weren't
funny," might she offer correction, huge amplification.) The fourth scene
is longest, strangest, the crisis—from which Laurel, the story, all Miss
Welty's earlier onlookers and surely most readers emerge shaken, cleared,
altered. On her last night in Mount Salus before returning to Chicago
and before Fay's return, Laurel comes home from dinner with friends to
find a bird flying loose indoors, a chimney sweep. She is seized at once
by an old fear of birds (we are not reminded till the following morning
that a bird in the house means bad luck ahead), and in panic shuts herself
into her parents' bedroom—now Fay's—against its flight. Here, alone

and silent except for sounds of wind and rain, among her parents' relics, she endures her vision—of their life, hers, the world's. Her initial step is to calm herself, to examine the sources of her recent angers, her present terror—

What am I in danger of, she wondered, her heart pounding. Am I not safe from *myself?*

Even if you have kept silent for the sake of the dead, you cannot rest in your silence, as the dead rest. She listened to the wind, the rain, the blundering, frantic bird, and wanted to cry out, as the nurse cried out to her, "Abuse! Abuse!"

What she first defines as the "facts" are these—that her helpless father had been assailed and killed by his own senseless self-absorbed young wife and that she (his only child) was powerless to save him but can now at least protect his memory. Protect—and flush her own bitterness—by exacting justice from Fay, extracting from Fay an admission of her guilt. Yet Laurel knows at once that Fay, challenged, would only be baffled, sealed in genuine blind innocence. Balked in advance then by invincible ignorance, is Laurel to be paralyzed in permanent bitterness? She can be, she thinks, released and consoled by at last telling someone—the facts, the names. But tell who? Her own mother, long since dead. To tell her mother though—should that ever be possible—would be an abuse more terrible than Fay's. Laurel can only go on telling herself and thereby through her perpetual judging becomes a new culprit, another more knowing Fay. That is—and can go on being—"the horror." At that moment, desperate with rage and forced silence, she makes the only physical movement open (the bird still has her trapped in the room). She retreats into an adjoining small room. It had been her own nursery, where she'd slept near her parents; then the sewing room; now a closet where Fay has hidden Laurel's mother's desk. Here, memory begins—a long monologue (yet always in third person) which bears Laurel back through her parents' lives, her life with them. (The structure and method of these fifteen pages at first seem loose, old-fashioned. No attempt is made through syntax or ellipsis to mimic the voice or speed of Laurel's mind, to convince us that we literally overhear her thoughts. Yet the process of memory proceeds with such ferocious emotional logic to an end so far beyond Laurel's imagined needs or desires—Laurel's and ours—that we are at last convinced, as shaken as she.) The memories begin warmly—here are things they touched, relics of their love, a family desk, a small stone boat carved with her father's initials, his letters to her mother (which Laurel will not read, even now), a photograph of them in full unthreatened youth. In the flood of affection, Laurel begins to move from her old stance of onlooker to a conviction of having shared her parents' lives, been a corner of their love. She continues backward through memories of summers in the West Virginia mountains with her mother's family. (Both her parents' families were originally Virginian; and it would be possible—therefore someone will do it—to construct a kind of snob-machine with these genealogies: Virginians are finer than Mississippians are finer than Texans. The story says no such thing; only "This is what happened"—Miss Welty's own mother was from West Virginia, her father from Ohio). Those summers, recalled, seem made of two strands—her mother's laughing immersion in family love and her own childish bafflement: tell me how much and why they love you, your mother and brothers. This early bafflement is focused for Laurel in her first sight of her grandmother's pigeons. Without claiming a mechanical connection which Miss Welty clearly does not intend, it is worth noting that this sight is the beginning (so far as we know) of Laurel's present personal distance, her stunned passivity in the face of the Chisoms feeding on one another—

> Laurel had kept the pigeons under eye in their pigeon house and had already seen a pair of them sticking their beaks down each other's throats, gagging each other, eating out of each other's craws, swallowing down all over again what had been swallowed before: They were taking turns. . . . They convinced her that they could not escape each other and could not be escaped from. So when the pigeons flew down, she tried to position herself behind her grandmother's stiff dark skirt, but her grandmother said again, "They're just hungry, like we are."

It was a knowledge and revulsion which her mother had seemed to lack —until her long final illness at least. The terms of that illness are not fully explained—Laurel's mother went blind, lay in bed for years, growing slowly more reckless and condemnatory, more keensighted in her observation of husband and daughter as they hovered beside her helpless. As the illness had extended through five years (just after Laurel's widowhood) and as Laurel now recalls it, her mother had at last endured the awful knowledge in its simple killing progression—that we feed on others till they fail us, through their understandable inability to spare us pain and death but, worse, through the exhaustion of loyalty, courage, memory. In the pit of her illness, Laurel's mother had said to the Judge standing by her—

> "Why did I marry a coward?" . . . Later still, she began to say— and her voice never weakened, never harshened; it was her spirit speaking in the wrong words—"All you do is hurt me. I wish I might

know what it is I've done. Why is it necessary to punish me like this
and not tell me why?"

Then she had sunk silent toward her death, with only one last message
to Laurel—"You could have saved your mother's life. But you stood by
and wouldn't intervene. I despair for you." In the teeth of such judgment,
Laurel's father—the optimist—had married Fay; had chosen to submit
again to need, and been killed for his weakness. What had been betrayed—what her mother like a drugged prophetess had seen and condemned before the event—was not his first love but his first wife's
knowledge, the dignity and achievement of her unanswerable vision. Fay's
the answer to nothing. Then can love be?—Answer to what? Death and
your own final lack of attention doom you to disloyalty. You're killed for
your cowardice. With that news, the scene ends. Laurel sleeps.

> A flood of feeling descended on Laurel. She let the papers slide
> from her hand and put her head down on the open lid of the desk
> and wept in grief for love and for the dead.

—Grief surely *that* love had not saved but harrowed her parents, a love
she had not shared and now can never.

Part IV is a quick hard, but by no means perfunctory, coda. Laurel
wakes in early light, having slept at her mother's desk. Now unafraid, she
leaves her parents' room, sees the exhausted bird perched on a curtain.
Mr. Deedy, the blundering handyman, calls by to peddle spring chores.
Laurel asks him in to catch the bird. He declares it bad luck and scares
it around from room to room but only succeeds in making a nosey tour
of the house. Then Missouri, the maid, arrives and she and Laurel gingerly
arrange the bird's escape in the only passage of the story where the touch
seems to me to press a little heavily, uneasily—

> "It's a perfectly clear way out. Why won't it just fly free of its own
> accord?"
> "They just ain't got no sense like we have. . . . All birds got to
> fly, even them no-count dirty ones."

Laurel burns her mother's papers, saving only the snapshots and the carved
stone boat. She calls herself a thief—the house and contents are Fay's
now—but she justifies herself:

> It was one of her ways to live—storing up to remember, putting aside
> to forget, then to find again—hiding and finding. Laurel thought it
> a modest game that people could play by themselves, and, of course,

when that's too easy, against themselves. It was a game for the bereaved, and there wasn't much end to it.

Her calm seems complete, her departure foregone and unprotested; but in a final look through kitchen cupboards, she finds her mother's breadboard—its worn polished surface inexplicably gouged, scored and grimy. Her numb peace vanishes, her rejection of revenge. She knows that, in some way, this is Fay's work, Fay's ultimate murder of Laurel's mother, the house itself, that she has "conspired with silence" and must finally shout both "Abuse!" and "Love!" And indeed Fay arrives at this moment, her return from Texas timed for Laurel's departure (the bridesmaids by now are waiting at the curb to drive Laurel to Jackson). Laurel challenges Fay with the ruined breadboard—

> "It's just an old board, isn't it?" cried Fay.
> "She made the best bread in Mount Salus!"
> "All right! Who cares? She's not making it now."
> "Oh, my mother could see exactly what you were going to do!"

Laurel has judged at last, in rage, and in rage has discovered the order of experience, the mysterious justice of time and understanding, her mother's final accurate desperation—

> Her mother had suffered every symptom of having been betrayed, and it was not until she had died, had been dead long enough to lie in danger of being forgotten and the protests of memory came due, that Fay had ever tripped in. It was not until then, perhaps, that her father himself had ever dreamed of a Fay. For Fay was Becky's own dread. . . . Suppose every time her father went on a business trip . . . there had been a Fay.

So memory itself is no longer safe, no "game for the bereaved." The past is never safe because it is never *past*, not while a single mind remembers. Laurel requires revenge. She accuses Fay of desecrating the house, but in vain—as she'd known the night before, Fay does not understand and will not ever, least of all from Laurel (she had used the board for cracking nuts). Fay can only resort to calling Laurel "crazy," to hurtful revelation, an anecdote of Laurel's mother's last wildness—throwing a bedside bell at a visitor. Laurel raises the breadboard to threaten Fay. Fay has the courage of her ignorance, stands and scornfully reminds Laurel that her friends are waiting outside—"You're supposed to be leaving." Then Fay goes on to claim she'd intended reconciliation, had returned in time for that—"we all need to make some allowance for the cranks." Laurel abandons the weapon, one more piece of Fay's inheritance, and hurries to leave, escorted away by her own bridesmaids.

I have summarized at such length because it's my experience, both as writer and teacher, that even a trained reader (especially trained readers) cannot be relied on to follow the action, the linked narrative, of any long story, especially of a story whose action is interior. (Ask ten trained readers what happens in *Heart of Darkness*—not what are the symbols or controlling metaphors but, simply, who does what to whom and why? Who knows what at the end? Then you'll see some darkness.) Also because to summarize *The Optimist's Daughter* is to demonstrate how perfectly the meaning inheres in the form and radiates from it. Nothing is applied from outside or wrenched; the natural speed of the radiation—action into meaning—is never accelerated (with the possible exception of the trapped bird's escape); and no voice cries "Help!" at its lethal rays—lethal to illusion, temporary need.

But the length of a summary has left me little space to discuss important details—to mention only two: first, the language (which in its stripped iron efficiency, its avoidance of simile and metaphor, bears almost no resemblance to the slow dissolving impressionism, relativism, of the stories in *The Bride of the Innisfallen*; that was a language for describing what things are *not*, for intensifying mystery; this is a language for stating facts) and, second, the story's apparent lack of concern with Mississippi's major news at the time of the action—the civil rights revolution. Its apparent absence is as complete as that of the Napoleonic wars from Jane Austen. And for the same reason, surely—it is not what this story is about. When Judge McKelva's old law partner says of him at the funeral, "Fairest, most impartial, sweetest man in the whole Mississippi Bar," no irony seems intended or can honestly be extracted. (I've stressed *apparent* absence because any story which so ruthlessly examines blindness is "about" all the forms of blindness; and if any reader is unprepared to accept the fact that in all societies at all times good and evil coexist in all men and can, under certain conditions of immense complexity, be compartmentalized, quarantined from one another within the same heart, then this story's not for him. So much the worse for him—neither will most art be.)

What I cannot skimp is my prior suggestion that the puzzlement or contented suspension of onlookers in Miss Welty's earlier fiction vanishes in *The Optimist's Daughter*, that the end clarifies. The stance of the onlooker—forced on him and/or chosen—is confirmed as the human stance which can hope for understanding, simple survival. The aims of participation are union, consolation, continuance—doomed. Laurel (who might well be the adult of the girl in "A Memory" or even of Laura in *Delta Wedding*) might so easily have left us with a last word fierce as her mother's. She might have said, "Show me a victor, an *actor* even." Or worse, she might have laughed.

For there is at the end, each time I've reached it, a complicated sense of joy. Simple exhilaration in the courage and skill of the artist, quite separate from the tragic burden of the action. Joy that a piece of credible life has been displayed to us fully and, in the act, fully explained (I take Laurel's understanding to be also the author's and ours; there can be no second meaning, no resort to attempts to discredit Laurel's vision). And then perhaps most troubling and most appeasing, the sense that Laurel's final emotion is joy, that she is now an "optimist" of a sort her father never knew (if not as she drives away from her home, then tomorrow, back at work)—that the onlooker's gifts, the "crank's," have proved at last the strongest of human endowments (vision, distance, stamina—the courage of all three); that had there been any ear to listen, Laurel would almost surely have laughed, abandoning her weapon (as Milton's God laughs at the ignorance and ruin of Satan, only God has hearers—the Son and His angels). For Laurel has been both victim and judge—who goes beyond both into pure creation (only she has discovered the pattern of their lives—her parents', Fay's, the Chisoms', her friends', her own) and then comprehension, which is always comic. All patterns are comic—snow crystal or galaxy in Andromeda or family history—because the universe is patterned, therefore ordered and ruled, therefore incapable of ultimate tragedy (interim tragedy is comprised in the order but cannot be the end; and if it should be—universal pain—then that too is comic, by definition, to its only onlooker). God's vision is comic, Alpha and Omega.

1969

POSTSCRIPT

IN THE fall of 1971 Miss Welty revised the story on which this essay was based; and the new version was published in the spring of 1972, still as *The Optimist's Daughter* though longer by a third. Despite the additions and changes, it is much the same story—so nearly so that I have not rewritten the essay. It was the result, glad but considered, of renewed contact with Miss Welty's work after some fourteen years of silence; and to revise now would be to compromise that shock of pleasure. In any case, the story described above—both what happens and what is meant —seems to me intact in the new version and virtually identical with it. Miss Welty has said, "I hope it's simply more what it was meant to be."

Yet the addition of ten thousand words to a previous thirty thousand—and the consequent adjustments of pace, texture, emphasis— provide the opportunity to watch a powerful hand at work, refining, defining (occasionally over-defining perhaps), inventing credible irrefutable life in spaces which no reader can have noticed as blank. Since such a detailed comparison would require a long essay of its own, I'll point only to the two sets of additions which seem most substantial.

Laurel's stepmother Fay Chisom McKelva has acquired, early in the story, a refusal to admit to Laurel the existence of a living family (the numerous Chisoms who materialize crucially at Judge McKelva's funeral)—a refusal which lends human credibility to the nearly monstrous Fay and eventually casts new light on the story's love-and-horror of kin, duty, company. Laurel herself has acquired memories of and reflections upon her own long-distant love, marriage and widowhood; and those thoughts are now triggered in her by a new scene as powerful as any in the first version. At the end of her night's vigil in the room of her dead parents, among the debris of their love, her dead husband appears—

> Now, by her own hands, the past had been raised up, and *he* looked at her, Phil himself—here waiting, all the time, Lazarus. He looked at her out of eyes wild with the craving for his unlived life, with mouth open like a funnel's.
>
> What would have been their end, then? Suppose their marriage had ended like her father and mother's? Or like her mother's father and mother's? Like—
>
> "Laurel! Laurel! Laurel!" Phil's voice cried.
>
> She wept for what happened to life.
>
> "I wanted it!" Phil cried. His voice rose with the wind in the night and went around the house and around the house. It became a roar. "I wanted it!"

Strong as that is, my initial reaction to it—and especially to the dream and morning reflections which it evokes from Laurel—was that it diluted the true harshness of Laurel's own widowhood. (In the first version her marriage and its brief happiness was mentioned, but hardly more; and Laurel indulges in no memories of it. The reader was allowed to deduce, from Laurel's own present and her natural forgetfulness, the harsh justice of her pure condemnation of Fay and the swarming Chisoms, her own friends, even her father.) But after several readings, the additions seem to me clearly aimed at keener definition of Laurel's belated discovery, growth and endurance; and while (as with the additions to Fay) they were not strictly required, why should they be omitted, once they have occurred to a writer in a form as rich as this?—

As far as Laurel had ever known, there had not happened a single blunder in their short life together. But the guilt of outliving those you love is justly to be borne, she thought. Outliving is something we do to them. The fantasies of dying could be no stranger than the fantasies of living. Surviving is perhaps the strangest fantasy of them all.

What Miss Welty has done seems to me to stand as an instructive parallel to the practice of those ancient tragedians who told, and retold several times, a single story vital not only to their own individual continuance as men and artists but also to the health of the state. She described once an initially tragic, ultimately comic action of apparent personal urgency; and now, for her own reasons, she has described it again with slightly altered eyes (a changed name or two, occasionally variant reports of the ways in which characters proceed from one event and its burdens to the next). My own conviction that the story is the masterpiece till now of her short fiction and that it has not only use for readers but urgent news, the force and mutability of universal myth, is strengthened by the new version (as is my pleasure in its challenge to a tenet of post-Flaubertian fiction—the vision of a single perfect telling of a given story). Any serious reader who will read both *The New Yorker* version of March 15, 1969 and the Random House version of 1972 will be rewarded with that news and—in its two forms—with the chance for intimate encounter with the feeling, thought and procedure, the astonishing power for both summary and continuous growth of a writer as sizable as any in modern letters and certainly as deep.

1972

FRIGHTENING GIFT*

EUDORA WELTY'S new novel (her first in sixteen years) is a frightening gift—because it hands us, after so long a wait, an offering of such plenitude and serene mastery as to reveal with panicking suddenness how thin a diet we survive on—little dry knots of fashion, self-laceratation; windy flights from "plot and character" into bone-crushingly dull (and ancient and easy) "experiment" and, throughout, a growing and maiming attachment to the modern city as the only scene for fiction. Reading it, one is reminded that liberated prisoners of war in 1945 often succumbed to shock on receiving full rations.

Not that *Losing Battles* has gone unheralded. Miss Welty's admirers have heard of its growth for well over ten years; and any of them who backslid into doubt (would it ever appear and, if so, would it be one more arthritic mastodon of the sort that generally lumbers out in response to long waits?) were firmly rescued last year by a new long story, *The Optimist's Daughter*, her strongest work till then.

But here it is, full and finished—more than twice the length of *Delta Wedding*. As that (her first novel, 1946) was secreted around a wedding (and the final section of *The Golden Apples*, 1949, around a funeral) so *Losing Battles* grows from and eventually around a family reunion in northeast Mississippi in the mid-1930s, Depression-time. The family are the children—at least five generations—of Elvira Vaughn; and the occasion of their gathering is Elvira's ninetieth birthday and the simultaneous end of a prison term by her great-grandson Jack Renfro—nineteen, a golden boy and the family's one hope in the face of destitution, a lovable hope but clearly doomed.

Hope for what and why doomed? First, for the continuation and perpetuation of Elvira's line, of the chance for reunion, the chance for love, dependence, personal hate (as opposed to urban anonymous hate); then for rescue, the raising of a crop, simple salvation from the welfare rolls. And doomed because we have already seen or heard Jack lose every battle he has entered, except the struggle to retain sweetness, patience,

* *Losing Battles* by Eudora Welty (Random House, 1970).

self-confidence, green hope—but who and what will Jack be in, say, 1945? Defeated like his kin—but embittered? dried? hating? Those are responses which most of them have escaped. How? Miss Welty shows—through obsession with blood-ties, the duties of family regardless of "love."

Doomed also because Jack (before his sentence for "aggravated battery") has married his schoolteacher Gloria, who has borne him a daughter in his eighteen-month absence. Gloria is an orphan, a foundling whose paternity becomes a matter of deepening mystery as the novel proceeds; and though she may or may not be Jack's cousin (and thus a blood-member of the reunion), she urges Jack from the moment of his return to take her and their child and leave the ganging family, "afloat in night, and nowhere, with only each other."

Gloria's vision is simple and touching ("If we could stay this way always—build us a little two-room house, where nobody in the world could find us"); and her persistence has been such as to suggest that she may eventually succeed in separating Jack from his family (and hers?) or, if not that, then in poisoning the well of affection by her objecting presence. Yet even if they were to go now into isolation, against Jack's will and nature, and love only one another, they would carry their own doom, palpable as their baby. All Elvira's descendants, except Jack's mother, have left—but to return, with their own loud families, their own lives submerged in dozens of others, diluted, finally lost. Lost for lack of sense—the knowledge of how to flourish, even survive, alone. (Jack's grandparents fled years ago—abandoning home, Elvira, children—only to drown in the nearest river.)

But so are all the novel's solitaries lost—the spinsters and bachelors descending into viciousness (Miss Lexie, a hateful but hilarious practical nurse to invalids) or guilty madness (Uncle Nathan, an uncaught murderer) or the grander balked but lucid rage of Miss Julia Mortimer, the schoolteacher who fought vainly for years to show her pupils (most of the reunion) some of the forms of freedom.

It is Miss Julia's rage and death which, though only reported (with appalling, again comic, power), radiate from the center of the novel with unstoppable power, the unanswerable truth to which the reunion and the human family itself are attempts at defiant answers—that solitude is, first and last, man's condition, his home, his loyal companion who will always turn lethal when its claims are ignored. As of course they must be ignored, if recognizable human life is to proceed. But should it proceed?

As beautiful, as rich in pleasure and laughter, as this novel shows the natural world to be and many of the lives in that world, it is urgent to see that *Losing Battles* finally raises such questions (they have always been the central questions of Miss Welty's work) in forms as complex and massive as in any earlier novel in English. I am not indulging in literary-couturier's hyperbole in saying that Miss Welty's new novel is comparable, for depth and breadth and stamina, not with other American novels but with larger things—*The Tempest, The Winter's Tale, War and Peace.* And—lest the above suggest a tragedy—like them, it is comic (more, it is funny—perhaps the funniest novel since *Huckleberry Finn*). Its faith is clearly that the world is ordered, that life—even a Renfro's—unfolds to messages contained in its seed and that any man's efforts to misread the commands, even decipher them, must only end in laughter. And if only God laughs—well then, only He was watching.

But Eudora Welty has seen at least the seed and the codes packed in it, and has shown us what she sees. No one writing sees more. And no one else's writing—the actual surface of the language, the bones of the novel—says more fully and clearly, yet with more justice to the multiplicity of experience and vision, what is seen and known, what in fact is partly discovered for her and for us *by* the language this story has produced in her mouth, a language almost entirely devoted to human speech and supported on literally thousands of metaphors and similes. Everything is and is not what it seems; is itself but slides as we watch and listen, into some other thing (now its brother, now its enemy), a metamorphosis which grips not only objects (trees, houses, dishes) but people and their actions, all created beings, good itself and evil, and comes to rest in only one mind, the maker's.

1970

ANSWERABLE CALLS*

AMERICAN LETTERS may still lack a novelist whose life-work matches in weight the achievement of Dickens or Tolstoy, but it's famous that our twentieth-century masters of the short story bow to no one for stylistic elegance or emotional penetration. The past decade has brought in stout collections from three of the best—Flannery O'Connor, John Cheever, Paul Bowles—and of the certified living masters of the form, only Eudora Welty has resisted collection (though all but two of the stories were continuously available in separate volumes). A change of publisher stymied the project for several years; but here finally they are—forty-one stories, the entire contents of her four individual collections plus two stories previously uncollected.

The best news is the handy availability in a single package of stories as good in themselves and as influential on the aspirations of other stories as any since Hemingway's. Second best—a quick check indicates that Welty has avoided the worst temptation of collectors, the revision of old work in hindsight. Thus some of the early stories are still clouded by a compulsively metaphoric prose (virtually everything is compared to, equated with, some other thing). And even an untypically hollow story like "The Purple Hat" or a misfire like "A Visit of Charity" has been perpetuated with the successes. Far better though to have them in the forms of their initial occurence than obscured by a forged technical gloss or suppressed uselessly.

Only one sizable question may be asked. Would it have been better to break up the sequence of the original volumes and print the stories in order of composition (with an exception for *The Golden Apples*, whose stories are connected)? Such an arrangement would at least have made possible the inclusion of a few never-collected early stories as viable as two or three now canonized, and it would have clarified the reader's legitimate search for evolving themes and repetitions in a writer whose concerns have dived and surfaced in unusually patient cycles. But Welty presumably chose in favor of her first, chiefly musical placement; and she

* *The Collected Stories of Eudora Welty* (Harcourt Brace Jovanovich, 1980).

of all contemporary writers since Auden has spoken out most sternly against the bald historical-biographical curiosity of readers and critics. In any case, the original appearances of the components of the four volumes were closely grouped. Those in A *Curtain of Green* were published in magazines from 1936 to '41, those in *The Wide Net* from 1941 to '43, *The Golden Apples* from '47 to '49, *The Bride of the Innisfallen* from '49 to '54, and the two latest stories in '63 and '66. (Each of the volumes was followed by a novel—*The Robber Bridegroom* in 1942, *Delta Wedding* in '46, *The Ponder Heart* in '54, and the two late stories by *Losing Battles* in 1970 and *The Optimist's Daughter* in 1972.)

A long performance then and one which, though it has never lacked praise and devoted readers, has presented critics with the kind of fearless emotional intensity, the fixed attention to daily life, and the technical audacity that have mercilessly revealed the poverty of scholastic critical methods. In the forties the lucid early stories and *Delta Wedding* were automatically accused of Gothicism and indifference to the plight of Southern blacks. The connected stories of *The Golden Apples* set off a dismal and apparently endless hunt for mythological underpinning (a curse that the stories innocently brought on themselves). The internalized experiments of the long stories of the fifties met with general bafflement. Though prizes descended and though a handful of stories were rushed into most anthologies while Welty fans round the land stood ready to burst into recitations from "Petrified Man" or "A Shower of Gold," it was only with Ruth Vande Kieft's discerning *Eudora Welty* in 1962 that the size of the achievement began to be acknowledged and mapped—the size and the peculiar pitfalls of the stories as objects for contemplation, guides to action.

The difficulties are big, both of matter and manner. As the center of critical power shifted in the fifties from the South to the Northeast, a vestigial resistance to Southern fiction quickly enlarged and hardened. The South had had too long an inning as Literary Central; its writers were obsessed with the ruling classes of a society rotten with greed and racist inhumanity (as though Tolstoy, Flaubert, or Bellow had more exemplary subjects). Thus Welty's Christian-White-Ladies and their ineffectual mates, her resigned fieldhands and maids, her garrulous white-trash, were obstacles for a high proportion of trained readers. And no native Southern critics of distinction rose in succession to Ransom, Tate, and Warren to mediate such work to the nation.

But even more daunting than the unabashed Southern grounding of the work was the statement at its center, a quiet reiterated statement that declared two polar yet indissoluble things. Most disturbing of all, the statement proved itself by locating characters and actions of recognizable solidity and pursuing them with a gaze that occasionally seemed serpentine in its steadiness—or angelic (as in angel of judgment). On first acquaintance one might be tempted to link the Welty of the stories with an apparent progenitor and paraphrase the statement by quoting D.H. Lawrence's essay on Poe—"A ghastly disease love. Poe telling us of his disease: trying to make his disease fair and attractive. Even succeeding."

If we substitute *Homo sapiens* for *Poe* there, we do have a crucial beam for the scaffolding of any of Welty's stories. That fact was realized in other terms in Robert Penn Warren's important early essay, "The Love and the Separateness in Miss Welty." For the stories from first to last do say this clearly, "Human creatures are compelled to seek one another in the hope of forming permanent bonds of mutual service, not primarily from an instinct to continue the species" (children are only minor players in her cast) "but from a profound hunger, mysterious in cause, for individual gift and receipt of mutual care." (*Tenderness* is Welty's most sacred word.) "So intense is the hunger however that, more often than not, it achieves no more than its own frustration—the consumption and obliteration of one or both of the mates." (The words *bitter* and *shriek* occur as frequently, and weightily, as *tenderness*.)

To that extent, Poe or even Strindberg is a truer ancestor to the stories than Virginia Woolf or E. M. Forster, who have often been mentioned. But such whimsical genealogies are of interest only to literary historians. They give little help to a reader whose aim is the enjoyment of and kinetic response to fiction that is so obviously the report of a particular pair of eyes on a particular place. For the dense matrix of observed life—mineral, bestial, human—which surrounds Welty's statement of the doomed circularity of love is the source of her originality, the flavor which quickly distinguishes a stretch of her prose from any other writer's.

She knew that now at the river, where she had been before on moonlit nights in autumn, drunken and sleepless, mist lay on the water and filled the trees, and from the eyes to the moon would be a cone, a long silent horn, of white light. It was a connection visible as the hair is in the air, between the self and the moon, to make the self feel the child, a daughter far, far back. Then the water, warmer than the night air or the self that might be suddenly cold, like any other arms, took the body under too, running without visibility into the mouth. As she would drift in the river, too alert, too insolent in her heart in those days, the mist thin momentarily and brilliant jewel eyes would look out from the water-line and the bank. Sometimes in the weeds a lightning bug would lighten, on and off, on and off, for as long in the night as she was there to see.

Out in the yard, in the coupe, in the frayed velour pocket next to the pistol, was her cache of cigarettes. She climbed inside and shielding the matchlight, from habit, began to smoke cigarettes. All around her the dogs were barking.

Welty's monitoring senses record two main strands of data—the self-sufficient splendor of the natural world (in a number of American and European places) and the enciphered poetry of human thought and speech which rises, sometimes through fits of laughter, to moments of eloquently plain truth-telling. The first-written of the stories provides a pure example. In "Death of a Traveling Salesman," the lost itinerant shoe-salesman comes suddenly to understand the fertile union of a couple in whose home he was harbored after an automobile accident.

Bowman could not speak. He was shocked with knowing what was really in this house. A marriage, a fruitful marriage. That simple thing. Anyone could have had that.

Somehow he felt unable to be indignant or protest, although some sort of joke had certainly been played upon him. There was nothing remote or mysterious here—only something private.

Such yearning for love is found in numerous other mouths in the stories, as character after character (male and female indifferently) reaches the boundary of illusion. But the second half of their repeated discovery is almost never spoken, by character or author. Only at the solitary ends of fated action do the characters perceive an inexorably closing circle. Having earned his vision, the salesman flees the scene of care and continuance and dies of heart failure, literally felled by his knowledge. Virgie Rainey at the end of "The Wanderers" is driven from her home and all she has known by the collapse of her dream of transcending love; and her first stopping place—perhaps her final destination—is a heightened awareness of the gorgeous nonhuman world that coils round our species (the only species, so far as we know, capable of contemplating that world). The casual pair who nearly connect in "No Place for You, My Love" are actually prevented by a watchful and judging world, the sun-struck land below New Orleans.

In peopleless open places there were lakes of dust, smudge fires burning at their hearts. Cows stood in untended rings around them, motionless in the heat, in the night—their horns standing up sharp against that glow.

At length, he stopped the car again, and this time he put his arm under her shoulder and kissed her—not knowing ever whether gently or harshly. It was the loss of that distinction that told him this was now. Then their faces touched unkissing, unmoving, dark, for a length of time. The heat came inside the car and wrapped them still, and the mosquitoes had begun to coat their arms and even their eyelids.

Later, crossing a large open distance, he saw at the same time two fires. He had the feeling that they had been riding for a long time across a face—great, wide, upturned. In its eyes and open mouth were those fires they had had glimpses of, where the cattle had drawn together: a face, a head, far down here in the South—south of South, below it. A whole giant body sprawled downward then, on and on, always, constant as a constellation or an angel. Flaming and perhaps falling, he thought.

(Similar ambush awaits the characters in her novels, though the greater length of a novel generally results in a more ambiguous, if not truer, statement. The stories preserve the naked cry—as sane, inevitable, and unanswerable as the evening call of a solitary beast from the edge of a wood.)

No wonder that admirers of Welty's fiction have concentrated most of their scrutiny and affection on comic stories like "Why I Live at the P. O." or the numerous others that richly summon atmospheres of serene nature and the warm conglomerations of family life—weddings, funerals, reunions. The choice has been instinctive, a normal reflex of narrative hunger (which craves consolation, with small side-orders of fright or sadistic witness).

The favorites are certainly worthy. In previous American fiction only Mark Twain shows as skillfully poised a comic gift, poised on the razor that divides compassion and savagery (Faulkner's comedy is oddly gentler). Her power over loving and tussling groups of kin gathered on magnetized family-ground is matched only by the nineteenth-century Russians, as is her courage for the plain declaration of loyalty and duty. A story like "A Worn Path" is unimaginable in any hands but hers or Chekhov's (and it is only illustrative of my point that this uncomplicated tale of duty has evoked a blizzard of nutty mytho-symbolist explications). And her effortless entry into masculine minds as various as the traveling salesman, the younger salesman in "The Hitch-Hikers," the young husband of "The Wide Net," the black jazz-pianist of "Powerhouse," and the majestically thoughtless King McClain of *The Golden Apples* is a sustaining assurance (in the presently gory Gender Wars) that the sexes can occasionally comprehend and serve one another if they choose to.

But such selective attention—and the popular antholgies have been as monotonous as her admirers—has resulted in a partial, even distorted sense of Welty as the mild, sonorous, "affirmative" kind of artist whom

America loves to clasp to its bosom and crush with belated honors (Robert Frost endured a similar reputation, but he had handmade it assiduously). It is one of the qualities of genius to provide wares for almost any brand of shopper—it has taken ages to wrestle Jane Austen from the chaste grip of the Janeites or Dickens from the port-and-Stilton set–and Welty's stories have, without calculation, stocked most departments. But such an embarrassment of choice endangers understanding.

One can hope then that this first display of the whole supply in a single place will encourage readers not only to sample the random colors and harmonies of twenty-odd masterpieces but to read all forty-one in the roughly chronological order of their arrangement. I've already suggested the chief discovery or rediscovery to be made—a contemporary American genius of range as well as depth (we've specialized in depth, narrow depth with few exceptions).

The breadth of Welty's offering is finally most visible not in the variety of types—farce, satire, horror, lyric, pastoral, mystery—but in the clarity and solidity and absolute honesty of a lifetime's vision. That it's a Janus-faced or Argus-eyed vision, I've also suggested—even at times a Gorgon stare. Yet its findings are not dealt out as one more of the decks of contradictory and generally appalling Polaroids so prevalent in our fiction and verse. A slow perusal here—say a story a night for six weeks —will not fail to confirm a granite core in every tale: as complete and unassailable an image of human relations as any in our art, tragic of necessity but also comic (even the latest story, a chilling impersonation of the white assassin of a black civil-rights leader, jokes to its end). As real a gift in our legacy as any broad river or all our lost battles.

1980

THE WINGS OF THE DOVE

A SINGLE COMBAT

T OLSTOY, in the blind lucidity of his age and conversion, consigned all his own fiction to the category of bad art, exempting only two short stories, "God Sees the Truth But Waits" and "A Prisoner of the Caucasus." No sane reader has ever believed him (five years before his own death, drowned in *Finnegans Wake*, Joyce wrote of one of Tolstoy's late fables, "In my opinion *How Much Land Does a Man Need* is the greatest story that the literature of the world knows");* but a large share of the agony of Tolstoy's old age boils steadily through him from that conviction— *Most of my work is worthless, even wicked*. Pain on that scale commands at least respect. And we might have considered more carefully his awful self-multilations; grappled with his aesthetic, not merely dismissed it as puritan crankery.

Henry James has not been believed either—not by his admirers; his detractors are hungry for any concession—when in his preface to *The Wings of the Dove*, written nearly ten years after the novel, he calls it a failure. Not in so many words of course—

> Yet one's plan, alas, is one thing and one's result another; so that I am perhaps nearer the point in saying that this last strikes me at present as most characterised by the happy features that *were*, under my first and most blest illusion, to have contributed to it. I meet them all, as I renew acquaintance, I mourn for them all as I remount the stream, the absent values, the palpable voids, the missing links, the mocking shadows, that reflect, taken together, the early bloom of one's good faith.

And notice that he does not concede a failure of conception or vision, only of execution. All his examples of failure (all of them just; almost all of them ignored by those who think *The Wings of the Dove* his masterpiece) are essentially failures of technical economy—this or that character is skimped, this part is disproportioned to that and (worst, he implies) the latter half of the novel is "false and deformed. . . . bristles with 'dodges.' "

---

* Stuart Gilbert, ed., *Letters of James Joyce* (Viking, 1957), p. 364.

Well, a declaration—I admire James more than many, less than some; but I believe him about this novel. He was no masochist, professed no fake humility; years after finishing *The Wings of the Dove*, he saw that it failed. I believe he was right.

But failed to do what?—and how? How might he have succeeded? My own strong feeling is that his sense of failure is intuitive, muffled, not understood, and that his list of mere technical errors, while accurate, is no more than a screen, one more screen erected between himself and his subject. And the screen, as so often, is built of near-chatter. In fact, his own diagnosis of the major technical error seems to me the reverse of true—the first half is the distended, time-serving half; only in the second does he begin to edge toward the buried subject, to accept the force of the magnet of his interest, his helpless obsession (the second half suffers from omissions, starvations).

What did he conceive his subject to be? In the preface he defines what he calls his *motive* or *idea*—

> a young person conscious of a great capacity for life, but early stricken and doomed, condemned to die under short respite, while also enamoured of the world; aware moreover of the condemnation and passionately desiring to "put in" before extinction as many of the finer vibrations as possible, and so achieve, however briefly and brokenly, the sense of having lived.

Then he summarizes—a little tidily and unconvincingly, as always—the metamorphosis of that given into his final plan, his pattern:

> My young woman would *herself* be the opposition—to the catastrophe announced by the associated Fates, powers conspiring to a sinister end and, with their command of means, finally achieving it, yet in such straits really to *stifle* the sacred spark that, obviously, a creature so animated, an adversary so subtle, couldn't but be felt worthy, under whatever weaknesses, of the foreground and the limelight.

He never, in the preface, mentions a fact which he freely owned in letters and implied in his memoirs and which has since become one of the most famous facts of his life—the relation of *The Wings of the Dove* to the death of his beloved cousin Minny Temple at twenty-four of consumption. It is possible to trace through his letters, notebooks and scenarios his lifelong intention to memorialize Minny in a novel; but for all Leon Edel's cautious and credible suggestion that James felt relief and therefore permanent guilt at Minny's death—now he would not have to marry her, only love her—nothing is explained. *The Wings of the Dove* intends, secretly if not consciously, to be a good deal more than an elegy to Minny

Temple, more than a lovely pavan on the death of a beautiful girl, a princess who yearned to live. (James had said of Minny, "Death, at the last, was dreadful to her; she would have given anything to live"; and perhaps more revealingly to his brother William, "I can't put away the thought that just as I am beginning life, she has ended it.")*

The book itself—the finished book—yearns. And it is that sense of yearning—in James; in the material itself, plot and character—to be the last word on something other than poor Minny Temple (or Milly Theale) which raises the richest questions about it and hints at least at their answers. *The Wings of the Dove* struggles—against James himself—to be the full, perhaps final, statement on James' central lifelong obsession—betrayal, treachery. Graham Greene was among the first, and is still the most eloquent, to have tracked the theme. In 1936 he suggested, "It is possible that through Wilky and Bob we can trace the source of James's main fantasy, the idea of treachery which was always attached to his sense of evil." † (Wilky and Bob were the two James brothers who served in the Civil War; and Greene suggests that Henry's own mysterious avoidance of service may be the seed of his fantasy—there two persons are betrayed by one.) And again in 1947, Greene returns to the theme, with no theory now of its genesis—

> what deeply interested him, what was indeed his ruling passion, was the idea of treachery, the 'Judas complex'. . . . We shall never know what it was at the very start of life that so deeply impressed on the young James's mind this sense of treachery; but when we remember how patiently and faithfully throughout his life he drew the portrait of one young woman who died, one wonders whether it was just simply a death that opened his eyes to the inherent disappointment of existence, the betrayal of hope. The eyes once open, the material need never fail him. He could sit there, an ageing honoured man in Lamb House, Rye, and hear the footsteps of the traitors and their victims going endlessly by on the pavement.**

Granting the passion, I would suggest that the treacheries in James' fiction do not generally take a one-to-one form (Judas vs. Christ or, say, Henry vs. Minny Temple or Constance Woolson) or the form of one-betraying-two (as in Henry vs. Wilky and Bob). No, doesn't the theme burn most intensely, writhe most painfully, when there is a *gang-up* (secret at first but later revealed—because intended to be revealed; therefore

---

* Leon Edel, *Henry James: The Untried Years* (Lippincott, 1953), pp. 332, 326.

† Graham Greene, "Henry James: The Private Universe," *Collected Essays* (Viking, 1969), p. 35.

** Graham Greene, *"The Portrait of a Lady,"* op. cit., p. 60.

hurtful, even lethal)?—two against one. The tutor and the pupil against his parents, Miles and Flora (and the ghosts) against the governess, Kate and Densher against Milly, Amerigo and Charlotte against Maggie (and her father). In fact, if betrayal is at the center of *The Wings of the Dove*, isn't Kate after all the most terribly betrayed? Milly merely triumphs.

And in all those examples, the treachery is—in some degree—sexual. Some character is always brought to an agonized moment which might be spoken thus—*Those others there—those two in shadow—are having together the thing I require, which they refuse me. But look, they are moving into light to show me!* James' recognition of the degree of sexuality involved ranges from apparent and embarrassing blindness in "The Pupil" (1892) through the teasing, near-coyness of *The Turn of the Screw* (1898) to the veiled, subaqueous yet brutal thrusting of *The Golden Bowl* (1904). Yet it is a continuously growing recognition, an almost straightline journey toward fullness and daring until, in *The Golden Bowl*, he manages a treatment of adult sexual hunger, fulfillment, damage and regret as complete as any in Western fiction before, say, Lawrence. Only Tolstoy in *Anna Karenina* and perhaps Stendhal (certainly not Flaubert or Hardy, who badly needed to be) were as successful in working round the restrictions of censorship, public and personal. The triumph of all three— including James in *The Golden Bowl*—is that they supply for us, but entirely by implication and indirection, all that we require to know about the sexual needs, behavior (the actual techniques) of their protagonists. Their methods are similar—their lovers are, first of all, beautiful (therefore desirable to the reader), relatively "healthy" in relation to their sexuality (therefore readily followable, as opposed to Bovary or Tess or the women of Dickens); and great technical care is taken to impress upon us, early and throughout, their visible physical presence, their animal odor, so that when the necessary veils descend, we can by simple extension penetrate them and watch. It is entirely relevant to see that a reader of *The Golden Bowl* can take this paragraph (preliminary to the first adultery of Amerigo and Charlotte) and extend it through the next half-hour of unrecorded action. Not only can but must, for a full reading of the joy, offense and pain James intended—

> "It's sacred," she breathed back to him. They vowed it, gave it out and took it in, drawn, by their intensity, more closely together. Then of a sudden, through this tightened circle, as at the issue of a narrow strait into the sea beyond, everything broke up, broke down, gave way, melted and mingled. Their lips sought their lips, their pressure their response and their response their pressure; with a vi-

olence that had sighed itself the next moment to the longest and deepest of stillnesses they passionately sealed their pledge.

But that is later than *The Wings of the Dove*—though since it is by only two years, we can safely assume one of two reasons to explain James' far greater reticence in the earlier novel on the crucial matter of Merton Densher's passion for Kate, the hold over him of which she is conscious and which she manipulates coldly—either James considered a fuller treatment of their union and decided against it for some technical reason, relevant to the novel only, or he feared it. Since the suppression results in a serious thinness in his fabric, I assume that—in this story, with these characters—he feared their sexuality, this particular set of acts. Imagine what an extraordinary flood of light (not necessarily lethal or even corrosive) might have been shed upon Densher's bondage to Kate and upon Kate as an even more complex and powerful (and frightened) tiger than she now appears—if James had only chosen, or been able, to *see* and dramatize for us, the hour of their first intercourse in Venice. Or of how Densher would have been complicated if James could have occupied all of his head, dramatized the daily workings, ravages, of his hunger—a little coarsened, no doubt, but so much more credibly humanized and comprehensible in his subservience to Kate, in his otherwise unexplained inability to do a stroke of work in the novel (he talks of wishing to write) and in his growing, unwilling entanglement with Milly, a dying body.

It is impossible to guess now—even if we possessed the concluding volume of Edel's biography—at the reasons, in 1902, for James' flight from the sexuality which stands so centrally in *The Wings of the Dove* (it would not be untrue of the *story* to say that it is a murder story, as lurid in its own way as that of Sir Thomas Overbury, in which the motive and fuel is sexual lust). I've mentioned Graham Greene's early suggestion that James' obsession with treachery may have sprung from his conviction of having malingered his own way out of the Civil War while permitting two of his brothers to go and be psychically (at least) destroyed; we still read occasionally claims of his impotence, his mysterious early accident (though Edel has convincingly laid those to rest: he injured his back); and there are increasing suggestions (especially in Edel's fourth volume and in surviving second-hand oral tradition) that James accepted only very late in life the fact of his own homosexuality (therefore, treachery to all women, above all his mother—for among the paradoxes of the thoughtful homosexual is a realization that should the Oedipal dream be granted, father removed and mother led bedward smiling, he would alas fail her; he would no longer want her); but it would be ignorant and falsely reductive to accept any or all these as explanations for a permanent personal demon of such strength as this one that rode James into his work. (My own tentative observation would be that, however strong the obsession, James is capable of "identifying" now with the betrayer, now with the victim. In *The Wings of the Dove*, for instance, he inhabits, almost entirely, Densher and Kate; but in *The Golden Bowl*, he inhabits Maggie—we never "understand" the feelings of Charlotte or Amerigo. And I might, in justice, record the casual and quasi-disastrous question of a friend of mine—"Aren't all novels secreted round a betrayal?")

No, but what is important is to recognize that something has apparently forbidden James to tell his given story in *The Wings of the Dove*—to tell it in the only way it could have been told and in the way he seems to have intended to tell it—dramatically, scenically. I've read a number of the eloquent defenses of the novel which claim that it is precisely that—entirely dramatic (see Percy Lubbock's in *The Craft of Fiction* for the most ingenious case); but a quick glance through the pages will show what a majority of burdened readers know—that for any one page treated scenically, with the hieratic intensity which is entirely James' own and one of the most impressive gifts acquired in his later years (though subject, often, to deflating guffaws—*Come, ladies, this is only a tennis match; the world is unmoved by your little game!*), there will be a number of those gray unparagraphed pages which, whether they intend to inhabit a character's head or (in pursuit of James's blessed economy) to summarize a sequence of ungiven scenes, remain so often inert and obscuring—the monologue of an artist who has locked himself out of his subject and, to pass the time till he dares re-enter, must lurk on the stoop (but must never cease talking, dictating this day's stint). He recognized the error himself. He writes in the preface,

> I haven't the heart now, I confess, to adduce the detail of so many lapsed importances; the explanation of most of which, after all, I take to have been in the crudity of a truth beating full upon me through these reconsiderations, the odd inveteracy with which picture, at almost every turn, is jealous of drama, and drama (though on the whole with a greater patience, I think) suspicious of picture.

Given my own understanding of James' understanding of his subject and characters then, what might have been his way of writing the novel? First, I should state what I take to be his story. Kate Croy, a beautiful young woman made desperate by an uncertain and impoverished childhood, has simultaneously come to live with her wealthy, vulgar and imperious Aunt Maud and fallen in love with a handsome and almost equally poor young journalist, Merton Densher. In the teeth of Aunt

Maud's intentions of a better match, the lovers pledge a permanent but secret troth as Densher prepares to depart for America, on his paper's business. There he meets, casually and with no great interest, Milly Theale, a young New Yorker, orphaned and the heiress to immense wealth, who is about to depart for Europe with an older companion, the widowed short-story writer Susan Stringham whose heart Milly has won. (There are hints that Milly is seriously ill.) While Densher continues his American tour, the ladies sail to Italy, cross the continent slowly (with further omens of Milly's condition) and arrive in London—where Milly becomes the immediate toast of Aunt Maud's tacky circle (Aunt Maud is an old schoolmate of Susan's). As quickly, Milly and Kate become intimates (neither knowing of the other's acquaintance with Densher). But soon Milly, accompanied by Kate, is consulting Sir Luke Strett, a famous physician. He is at once fascinated by her—her person, her case, her solitude and freedom (there is some suggestion that he may be infatuated with Milly)—but though he soon tells Susan of the gravity of Milly's condition (we are never told the disease but, despite Kate's denial, consumption seems implied), he never prescribes more to Milly than that she *live*, seek happiness. It is a prescription which she seriously attempts to take. But now Aunt Maud has learned of Milly's meeting with Densher and asks Milly to discover if Densher has returned to England and is again seeing Kate. (Aunt Maud intends Kate for Lord Mark, a member of her circle, who has however begun to eye Milly.) Milly has no sooner said that she believes Densher still absent when—on the morning of Sir Luke's talk with Susan—she surprises Densher and Kate in the National Gallery. Fascinated, Milly still does not fathom the extent of the relation (she assumes that Densher loves Kate but is unreciprocated); and soon Kate is proposing that Densher capitalize on Milly's clear infatuation with him to permit them—Kate and Densher—to meet more openly. Further, Kate knows that Milly is ill and offers Densher the excuse that he can console Milly. So intense by now is Densher's sexual fascination with Kate that he cannot refuse; and he calls on Milly, who—attempting to follow Sir Luke's advice—complicatedly welcomes him, as the occasion for "living." She has assumed, without asking, that Sir Luke has told Susan of the gravity of her illness. She knows, at least, that he has ordered her to leave London for three months. She goes to Venice, takes a palazzo and—attended by Susan, Kate, Aunt Maud, Lord Mark (who soon departs, refused by Milly), Densher and a staff—accepts the role of princess urged on her by all. She knows by now that she is "very badly ill." It is there, at last, in his rented rooms (where he has hoped to write but cannot) that Densher persuades Kate to bed with him—only after Kate, now certain of Milly's approaching death, has forced him to promise to marry Milly, for her money and their freedom. Densher does permit Milly to believe that he loves her, remains in Venice (unable to work) because of that love; but he has not brought himself actually to propose ("It was on the cards for him that he might kill her") when he finds himself, after six weeks, without explanation, no longer received by Milly. Immediately thereafter, he discovers Lord Mark (balked of both Kate and Milly) in the Piazza and realizes that he—freshly returned to Venice—is somehow the cause of Densher's exclusion from Milly. After three solitary days, he is visited by Susan, who tells him that Milly is worse, has not so much as mentioned his name in three days—and then that Lord Mark has informed Milly of Densher's secret engagement to Kate. Susan asks him to deny it, true or not, to save Milly's life. Densher responds only with a baffled "Oh!," and they await the arrival of the urgently summoned Sir Luke. After more days of silence, Sir Luke, departing, conveys to Densher a message from Milly that he call on her and that Milly is "better." That visit is not directly communicated to us. We see Densher next in London, where he has waited two weeks before contacting Kate. Kate at once informs him that Milly is dying, that Sir Luke has rushed again to Venice. Densher explains the reason for Milly's haste—Lord Mark's revelation. Kate accepts, ambiguously, a share of the guilt for Milly's knowledge but asks why Densher could not have denied the story. He replies that he could not; that in any case it would not have helped Milly now, sick as she is. He even adds, ominously, that had he made the denial, he would also have made it true—broken their engagement. Only then do we get from Densher any hint of the final interview with Milly—and then only that she merely, and pleasantly and without signs of disease, asked him not to stay in Venice any longer. Kate's satisfied vision is that Milly is dying in peace, with the knowledge "of having *been* loved"; that therefore her own deceit and Densher's is blessed. But Milly's wings hover too closely over Densher now. He feels his relation to her to be beautiful, sacred, and that he is now "forgiven, dedicated, blessed"; and though he feels both able and compelled to marry Kate at once, she refuses—her plan is incomplete; Milly still lives. But Milly dies at Christmas and Densher, knowing that, receives a letter from her, which he cannot bring himself to open. He carries it to Kate, who announces without opening it, that she knows the contents—Milly has made him rich. Then she burns the letter. Two months later, her guess is confirmed—Densher learns from New York of a large bequest to him. But in a final meeting with Kate, in his rooms, Densher refuses to accept it—Kate may have it if she likes and go her way. Or, without it—as they were—he will marry her "in an hour." The unacceptability—impossibility—of either choice expels Kate from the rooms, and his life, forever.

That is, I think, a summary of the action which would be acceptable to the finished novel's warmest admirer, give or take a detail. Now again I suggest that the story is untold—or is *only* told (recited at us) in a number of places and, in several crucial places, not told at all. A glance back through the summary suggests a number of baffling omissions, figures hastily sketched and demanding fuller work—what is the full nature of Sir Luke's interest in Milly (he appears to be unmarried)? What is the background of Densher's agonizing case of sexual rut?—is he virgin before Kate? How exactly does Kate act in their one embrace? What is its meaning to her? Was she a virgin? What is the meaning to Densher of his work? Is he a *good* writer? Why do we have no samples? What is the source of his income when he is idle? What is the full nature of Lord Mark and his interest in Milly, Kate and Densher (there is a hint of his homosexuality)? How does he learn of the betrothal? What is the full atmospheric, sensory role of Venice in the action (there is extraordinarily little detailed scene-painting)? Doesn't a great deal of Densher's moral evolution in Venice (his solitary thinking) need to be scenic?—thought can be scenic. Why may we not see fully the final interview between Milly and Densher? Why are we given nothing of the thoughts and actions—the awful sights—of Milly's last days and death? (In the preface, James says, "Heaven forbid that we should know more"—I'd think Heaven required it.) Isn't a great deal of the famous difficulty of the late prose produced not so much by the convolutions of the method, the complexities of the subject, but simply by haste in composition and the fact that the novel was dictated to a typist, not written by hand? And to name only two of the other matters which are hinted, then abandoned, their effects forbidden—what is the background of Kate's passionate hatred of illness ("I'm a brute about illness. I hate it.")? What of the undertones of lesbian love in almost all the numerous female relations?

If you grant that even a small number of those questions are valid, then you must return me to the postponed question—what other fictional method might James have employed? —Only, I suspect, that method which he is often credited with developing or at least perfecting but which comes to an earlier and richer growth in writers who offended his passion for form and economy—Tolstoy, Dostoevsky. It might be called the Dramatic-Cerebral or the Thinking Dramatic—that is, a method whose faith is in the dignity and visual comprehensibility of objects (people, rocks, buildings) and whose conviction is that if all the objects relevant to a given action can be clearly and truly shown (literally pictured in language), heard (through dialogue) and overheard (through a conventionalized rendering of the relevant thoughts of characters), then the given story, so long as it concerns essentially sane men and women in a recognizably

organized society, will be told, so far as it is possible to tell. *Anna Karenina,*
The Brothers Karamazov.

This is not to beat James with other men's sticks, even geniuses'. It
is only to say that—faced with the action, characters, themes, the secret
impulses and pressures of *The Wings of the Dove* and James' own admission
of failure—I can imagine no alternative. If he could have forced himself
to face every turn of his story as *scene,* to trust in the rendering of action
and speech (and ruthlessly to reduce his own hovering authorial presence,
a presence he had deplored in "The Art of Fiction"), to do the full work
of imagining and conventionalizing the individual thoughts of characters
(notice that, so often, such thoughts as he renders *sound* only like—
James), to say "Heaven forbid!" to no necessary horror—then we'd feel
his purpose, his pattern would be wrought. We would have learned it,
not been told. (It is this almost ceaseless *telling* which combines with his
abandonment of all but a few explicit visual effects—Milly's clothes—to
make him seem, in the late novels, like one of the great blind poets—
Milton, Joyce.) Wouldn't this, you say, produce a novel far longer than
the existing novel? Yes, thousands of pages—Tolstoy again, Proust, Dostoevsky, Samuel Richardson: no expendable page; no whole scene, at
least. But surely it would not result in a novel which diminishes, not
intensifies, the complexity of experience. For, by so steadily diminishing
the literal visibility of his figures in *The Wings of the Dove,* James has
diminished our interest in them either as "human beings" or as ciphers
in his game. He has also (and by no means incidentally) diminished their
own threat to him, their creator. The late method so often risks earning
the description which James himself applied to puppet shows—"What an
economy of means—and what an economy of ends!" It can be meager,
even easy.

But is this more than an exercise in futility? Was such an alternative
conceivably open to James in 1902? I have glanced at his scorn of an
entirely scenic method, as practiced by the great Russians. Here is a full
statement, from a letter to Hugh Walpole, written in 1912—

> Don't let any one persuade you—there are plenty of ignorant and
> fatuous duffers to try to do it—that strenuous selection and com-
> parison are not the very essence of art, and that Form is [not] sub-
> stance to that degree that there is absolutely no substance without it.
> Form alone *takes,* and holds and preserves, substance—saves it from
> the welter of helpless verbiage that we swim in as in a sea of tasteless
> tepid pudding, and that makes one ashamed of an art capable of such
> degradations. Tolstoi and D.[ostoevsky] are fluid puddings, though
> not tasteless, because the amount of their own minds and souls in

solution in the broth gives it savour and flavour, thanks to the strong, rank quality of their genius and their experience. But there are all sorts of things to be said of them, and in particular that we see how great a vice is their lack of composition, their defiance of economy and architecture, directly they are emulated and imitated; *then*, as subjects of emulation, models, they quite give themselves away. There is nothing so deplorable as a work of art with a *leak* in its interest; and there is no such leak of interest as through commonness of form. Its opposite, the *found* (because the sought-for) form is the absolute citadel and tabernacle of interest. *

So it would be difficult enough to imagine James choosing a method (or returning to it; he'd employed it earlier, extensively) which seemed to him now so unshapen and wasteful. (And yet—even granting James a temperamental aversion to the Russians, couldn't he have seen that their method, scorning charges of its inimitability, was a bow for Odysseus, an instrument usable only by precisely what James claimed to be—an artist, the high-priest of the sanctity of appearances, the visible world?) And there were other pressures directing him forcefully elsewhere—the increasing importance of sexuality in his late work (or his increasing consciousness of its importance; it had always been there, though often embarrasingly ignored) clearly drove him, technically and personally, toward the methods of indirection; then, urgently (but not really discussibly), language was now arriving in his mouth (for unrecoverable reasons—he had had *his* life) in more and more complex, writhing and opaque forms (and the mouth was the page, as we've seen—a fact which suggests that the best hope of reading the late novels is *aloud*, to say them back to him); there was the matter of habit and the necessity of speed (he had always worked rapidly—several books a year in many years—and the prospect of a five or ten year effort may have been literally unthinkable to him; he lived by writing, he needed cash, which the late books hardly made); finally—and I'd guess most powerfully—there was the matter of his subject, the past of his theme, its potential for killing raids on his psyche.

That returns me to my earlier suggestion that this particular subject (for whatever reasons—his relations with Minny Temple, with his brothers, his parents, whomever) was one which James, at this time, was prevented from treating fully—not by the literary conventions and repressions of his time (he circumvented them brilliantly, and shockingly, earlier and later) but by personal fears. James' last completed novels—*The Wings of the Dove* and *The Golden Bowl*—cast a strong backward light on all his

* Percy Lubbock, ed., *The Letters of Henry James* (Scribner's, 1921), II, pp. 237–238.

previous work and show him to stand, not where he wanted us to think
he stood (with Turgenev and Flaubert, lucid and aware) but with Kafka
—as lurid and mad in his own quite private way, as desperate in his efforts
at comprehension and self-healing and often as helpless. Not in *The
Golden Bowl*—that triumphs, but triumphs in turning on the threats,
staring them all into basilisk stone; the method works, both reveals and
heals, though both operations are monstrous—but certainly here in *The
Wings of the Dove*. He knew it, of course, long before us.

Then—so what? Should the novel not exist? Should James never
have attempted it or, at least, never published it? Should it not be read?
On the contrary, strongly. I'd call it his second most interesting novel
(first, *The Golden Bowl*) and the richest source of all for a study of the
workings of his final manner, its relation to his life as both enemy and
shield. There is a whole category of deeply flawed works by masters which,
literally through their rifts, permit us to see more deeply toward their
centers of origin than do any number of sealed perfections—the last *Pietàs*
of Michelangelo, Shakespeare's *Tempest*, Milton's *Samson*, Beethoven's
Fidelio, Tolstoy's *Resurrection*, *The Wings of the Dove*.

Without yielding any of the foregoing, I can still understand, and
all but agree with, F. O. Matthiessen's assessment of it—

> In a more restricted but very relevant sense one may also look for
> the essential design, not through the successive stages of an artist's
> whole development, but in his masterpiece, in that single work where
> his characteristic emotional vibration seems deepest and where we
> may have the sense, therefore, that we have come to 'the very soul.'
> Such a book in James' canon is *The Wings of the Dove*.*

It is most of that. And it has real splendors, scenes as powerful as
any in all his work, as any west of Moscow—the last gathering at Milly's
palazzo with Kate like a bronze python coiled loosely round the room
but waiting, ready and competent; the destruction of Milly's unopened
letter, an act so large in its forward and backward revelation as to surpass
any ordinary notion of "symbol" and become pure action, any novelist's
greatest dream, where a single hand moving from here to here lays open
whole lives; the final meeting of Densher and Kate where their stored-up
acts march inward to meet them with the crushing tread of an ending
Bach fugue; the many scenes in which two characters stand alone in a
room, cubes of air between them, and say to one another, not what any
imaginable "human being" might have said but the awful monosyllables
of what they *mean* to say, a secret language of hate and longing which

---

* F. O. Matthiessen, *Henry James: The Major Phase* (Oxford, 1944), pp. 42–43.

was how James had come to hear the language of men, as strange to him now, as unresonant, as Martians.

It isn't, though, "his masterpiece." He made that clear himself; no one would have known better (his own candidate seems to have been *The Ambassadors*). Too often it is best described by a passage from itself—

> an impenetrable ring fence, within which there reigned a kind of expensive vagueness made up of smiles and silences and beautiful fictions and priceless arrangements, all strained to breaking.

But I don't know another work of his—of any great novelist, for that matter—which demonstrates more intensely, movingly, maddeningly, frighteningly and rewardingly the dilemma of an artist whose subject has seized *him* and will not relent, will neither free him nor permit his success, will inflict awful wounds for every infidelity—every flinch or flicker—yet will maim him at last for his helpless devotion. Again, I think of Kafka, his spiritual brother—

> You do not need to leave your room. Remain sitting at your table and listen. Do not even listen, simply wait. Do not even wait, be quite still and solitary. The world will freely offer itself to you to be unmasked, it has no choice, it will roll in ecstasy at your feet. *

That contains, in full terror, the dilemma of James in *The Wings of the Dove*. His subject came—his old loyal subject, the world he knew, rolled grinning on his floor. If he—being himself, having weathered his life— was forced to rise, move farther away and (far from being silent) was compelled to talk at its uninvited ecstasies, I can still see courage in his being there at all, his struggle to watch. The novelists of my own generation—most of whom ignore him, an irrelevant spinster—might learn from the sight, the uneven combat, invaluable lessons in stamina and courage. So might Hemingway, say—whose own combat, set down beside James', seems often conducted under lights, before cheering fans. So might any reader. Courage is honored in proportion to the threat, to the victory won.

1970

---

* Franz Kafka, *The Great Wall of China* (Schocken, 1946), p. 307.

MERE WITNESS*

THE FERVENT JAMESIAN REVIVAL of the 1940s and 50s has ebbed, but readers of fiction continue the debate that raged in his own lifetime. They divide neatly into three camps. First are those for whom he is the greatest of all American novelists and literary theoreticians. Second are those who see his early work as thin and bloodless, his late work as the intolerably mannered chatter of a spinster. The third are those who think both things—they admire his work selectively, acknowledging the intellectual and linguistic grandeur of the late novels but regretting their unnecessary difficulty.

No one, however, who has read the five original volumes of Leon Edel's biography can deny that James's life—begun in New York City and ended in London, after forty years of exile—was his grandest production. Or a grand gift, which he had the wit to accept from Fate and to shape toward a final serene comprehension and peace. Now that James's contemporaries are dead, Edel has taken the opportunity to condense his five volumes into one and, in the process, rewrite large portions—expanding candidly on the nature of James's severely repressed and compressed homosexuality, a trait whose long-delayed demands James ultimately came to understand (if only in letters and balked gestures—even Edel cannot guess at the extent of the old James's overt ventures, if any).

The five-volume life was supreme among American biographies, and the new edition is better still. The long arc of the life and work is now more clearly visible, and our emotional response is therefore guided with greater speed and force. If there is any significant loss, it would be only that the immense length of the original gave the patient reader a fuller sense of the vast difficulty of the hour-by-hour ordeal of a man who labored ceaselessly and heroically to identify, expel, and then confront in art the Medusa-life. The condensation, however, will be accessible to legions who would never have tackled the original; and the revisions will provide former readers with sizable rewards for a new trek.

I've just awarded the original highest rank in American biography,

* *Henry James* by Leon Edel (Harper & Row, 1985).

and I must explain my choice. First, Edel has a long-lived, productive, and innately fascinating subject. Among Americans, only Washington, Jefferson, Lincoln, and Lee (among nonliterary figures) and Whitman and Hemingway (among writers) offer equally diverse, consequential, and compelling possibilities for contemplation. All but Hemingway have by now been dealt with honorably and, in some cases, brilliantly in biographies. But in no case was the biographer better suited for the task than Edel. His supreme quality is a broad gift for clear-eyed sympathy—in the literal sense of *feeling with* his subject. In greater calm than was ever available to James, Edel has unearthed the precise long path of a life and ennabled others to experience the path as endured and mastered. He never errs on the side of positive bias toward a man who often worked mightily to blind himself and his colleagues to the heart of his own dilemmas; neither does he condescend or judge. He merely watches.

But, to echo James, *merely*! The life was long by any standards—seventy-three years—and the visible work is enormous: novels, stories, plays, essays, travel books, a boatload of letters. Edel has mastered it all and, in a brisk but inclusive prose, leads us to a gradual understanding of the relation of work to life, the dual importance of the work both as public art and private struggle for continuance as a functioning civilized human being in a particular time and world. Commencing his study only a few years after James's death, he was also able to question most of the chief surviving figures in the story. Thus the strong particular odor of an actual person haunts the pages, the presence of an enormous body and mind, a presence afflicted by more than ordinary fears and indecisions but steadily at war with those demons—a war which ended in victory for the man, a life subject to no final enemy but death.

In a time when literary biographies have degenerated into appalling catalogs of daily folly—with no consideration of those creations which redeem folly—Edel's *Henry James* is a sovereign example of industry, fairness, and clarity. It is—what few biographies manage to be—a large and truthful work of art. If the living James would have roared at the exposing eye of candor, the immortal James can only be grateful, proud, and appeased.

1985

POEM DOCTRINAL
AND EXEMPLARY TO A NATION

A READING OF
SAMSON AGONISTES

> A *little onward lend thy guiding hand*
> *To these dark steps, a little further on.* . . .*

SO BLIND SAMSON gropes into the scene, the prison yard at Gaza, entreating a silent unnamed guide. That Milton—visualizing for the stage, despite his denial in the preface—must have seen the guide as one of the mutes common in Greek tragedy (a prison guard or a boy) only darkens the irony. Whose hand?—God's. Samson prays unknowingly and, in the first two lines, casts his own fate and predicts the final achievement of his life—the reflection to his people, through the Chorus of Hebrews, of God's light on him. The reeling-in of Samson has begun—he would not come freely—and half of the action of the play will be that catch, that battle on the line of angler and prey; the other half, the lessons that battle deposits in its audience.

But Samson has not yet felt the hook. His first speech, the prologue, begins low, half-numb, monosyllabic, not an outpouring of immediate agony, present despair (his response in lines 9–10 to "The breath of Heav'n fresh-blowing, pure and sweet" is hardly that of a man in despair)—more nearly a narrative, a scroll of the spiritual adventures which have brought Samson to this point in time, this place in relation to God, slowly unrolled for himself (and conceivably for the mute guide; when does he depart? is Samson's command "Yet stay" at line 43 delivered to the guide as well as himself?). Why unrolled?—for another try at reading and comprehension, at piercing his night. Why understand?—so that rest can descend. He's wrong—so he'll move, swim freely toward the ship, the line in God's hand. But soon he is circling, fighting, the first passionate flight, first aria of grief—

> *Retiring from the popular noise, I seek*
> *This unfrequented place to find some ease;*

---

* All quotations from Milton's verse (and those from the note to *Paradise Lost* and the preface to *Samson*) are given in the text of Merritt Y. Hughes, *John Milton: Complete Poems and Major Prose* (Odyssey, 1957).

> *Ease to the body some, none to the mind*
> *From restless thoughts, that like a deadly swarm*
> *Of Hornets arm'd, no sooner found alone,*
> *But rush upon me thronging, and present*
> *Times past, what once I was, and what am now*

—and has brought himself to his old obsessive questions—

> *O wherefore was my birth from Heaven foretold*
> *Twice by an Angel*

> *Why was my breeding order'd and prescrib'd*
> *As of a person separate to God,*
> *Design'd for great exploits; if I must die*
> *Betray'd, Captiv'd, and both my Eyes put out. . . .*

Samson seems on the edge of hurling questions at God; but it is soon clear that he will not even permit himself the relief of indictment. All the questions return to himself; and their answer—"O impotence of mind, in body strong!"—is his surest instrument of self-torture. If any question is put to God, it is implied in the lines on blindness—"Why am I thus bereav'd thy prime decree?"—yet, though the weight of the question breaks the very structure of the verse itself (from consistent decasyllables to hexasyllables pressed from him like sobs), Samson can quickly subsume even blindness under the wings of his own guilt in the awful grave image, one which has haunted Milton since the days of *Comus* and will soon be turned against Samson by the Chorus:

> *Myself my Sepulcher, a moving Grave,*
> *Buried, yet not exempt*
> *By privilege of death and burial*
> *From worst of other evils, pains and wrongs. . . .*

He is stopped in the tracks of his self-loathing by the sound of approaching feet, and he ends with the speculation that Philistines are coming to "insult" and "afflict" him. He does not know that these are well-meaning Hebrews (who will nonetheless afflict him more seriously than Philistines); oddly, he has not recognized that any human being, friend or enemy, is a reproach to him now, that to the self-condemned all fingers point.

So the Chorus enter—presumably fifteen Hebrew elders, men of Dan, Samson's tribe. (Though Milton calls the Chorus simply "Danites," there is no classical precedent to suggest that he may have visualized the mixture of sexes employed in some modern productions; and the later speeches of the Chorus on women make such a mixture ludicrous.) Maybe little use can be made of the fact; but it is grotesquely touching to notice that these austere prison-visitors enter on an echo from the perfumed world of pastoral masque. Their first words—"This, this is he"—recall the first song of *Arcades*, addressed by Milton at age twenty-three to the Countess Dowager of Derby:

> *This, this is she*
> *To whom our vows and wishes bend,*
> *Here our solemn search hath end.*

The first nine lines of the parodos are a reflex picture. The Chorus stand unannounced for a moment to look at their former champion, their hope—to them, an isolated ruin and apparently a despairing one—

> *As one past hope, abandon'd,*
> *And by himself given over. . . .*

The fact that we know him to be in better state than the Chorus does not intrude upon their thrill of horror at the chance to diagnose total disaster. Samson does not hear their words, only their steps, which is as well for him, since they move into the second part of the ode and ask their own many-edged questions—

> *Can this be hee,*
> *That Heroic, that Renown'd,*
> *Irresistible Samson?*

The questions reveal the depth of Samson's fall by reflecting the degree of shock in the Chorus; they suggest a genuine sympathy for Samson and, by tripping them into jubilant memories of the days of his glory, the questions permit the Chorus to give us useful past narrative while simultaneously revealing themselves as men who resort to this brand of self-cheer in the teeth of shock, this savage affirmation of community, as though to say, "We are the men who remember *this*, for whom it was done"—eloquent if not lovable. Beneath their sympathy, however (though closely related to their sense of self), run strains of bitterness, an ambiguity of purpose in the prison visit (is it possible to visit prison otherwise?), of morbidity in their desire to stare at the fate of a man who might have been their deliverer but failed through his own voluptuousness, and of a contempt (the belly of their pity) for strength without virtue. By the naked ferocity of language and rhythm in their memory of Samson's physical adventures (as contrasted with the spiritual adventures of the prologue)—

> *Who tore the Lion, as the Lion tears the Kid,*
> *Ran on embattled Armies clad in Iron,*

> *And weaponless himself,*
> *Made Arms ridiculous, useless the forgery*
> *Of brazen shield and spear*

—they again take a measure of Samson's fall and affirm the reasons: strength without virtue, force without limit. And in their next movement, falling into Samson's own hexasyllabic grief, they repeat his image of the buried soul and complicate it by seeing his imprisonment as three-fold— Philistine prison, prison of blindness, prison of soul in body. Only in the fourth and last movement of the parodos do they hint at their own involvement in Samson's tragedy. The hint is oblique, glancing, its sharp edge pressed against Samson—"O mirror of our fickle state"—and they end with a return to their cruel theme:

> *But thee whose strength, while virtue was her mate,*
> *Might have subdu'd the Earth,*
> *Universally crown'd with highest praises.*

It might be said in objection that the whole parodos is an aside whose purpose is past-narration and that the real function of the Chorus as friends "who seek to comfort him what they can" (Milton's description from the prose Argument) does not begin until they are in direct communication with Samson. But the objection cannot face certain problems implied in the tone of the parodos—by the scurrying dactyls of "Let us not break in upon him," which C. S. Lewis has called the sort of verse mice might write, if mice wrote verse; and by the heavy presence of rhyme to the point of jingle. If we recall Milton's note of 1667 on the verse of *Paradise Lost* with its dismissal of rhyme—

> as a thing of itself, to all judicious ears, trivial and of no true musical delight; which consists only in apt Numbers, fit quantity of Syllables, and the sense variously drawn out from one Verse into another, not in the jingling sound of like endings, a fault avoided by the learned Ancients both in Poetry and all good Oratory

—then we are left with three choices: that Milton had changed his mind in the intervening years and was here employing rhyme in a relatively simple ornamental or musical sense; or that *Samson* was written before 1667; or that in *Samson* Milton was making dramatic use of assonance, rhyme, jingle as instruments of plotting and characterization. In any case, it would hold Milton to an absurd consistency (he changed his mind in *Samson* about more important matters than rhyme—such as human will) to insist that rhyme in the choruses marks them as "bad Oratory"; but it is important to state the problem now and, farther on, to attempt a decision.

The first episode begins as Samson announces that he can hear disjointed speech. The Chorus approach and address him in terms which, however typical of Hebraic lament, are hardly apt as consolation—

> *Matchless in might,*
> *The glory late of* Israel, *now the grief.* . . .

Yet they identify themselves as friends, counselors, who come with "apt words" to console. And Samson responds with a definition of friendship —loyalty in adversity—which seems unironic but which has, for us who heard the parodos, its edge. Like a speaking sphinx, he displays his misery to them—the sight they have come to see—and offers them a view of his blindness different from that in the prologue. There he had exclaimed, "O loss of sight, of thee I most complain!" But, faced by his people, he calls blindness a blessing—how could one self-wrecked bear to see the world? That this new tack hints at remnants of self-regard—even traces of mirror-gazing—is clear from his first question to the Chorus. He does not ask about his aged father but about his own reputation in Israel; and he implies a dreaded but desired answer in—

> *Am I not sung and proverb'd for a Fool*
> *In every street; do they not say, "How well*
> *Are come upon him his deserts?"*

Samson's obsession with earned guilt suggests, throughout the early episodes, an inverted egotism; but it never seems self-pity. He prevents that, as here, by returning always to the seed of his folly—

> *Immeasurable strength they might behold*
> *In me, of wisdom nothing more than mean.* . . .

But now—and for the first time—he goes beyond his own guilt to imply a questioning of God:

> *This with the other should, at least, have pair'd,*
> *These two proportion'd ill drove me transverse.*

More trained than we at spotting heresies, the Chorus pull him up at once—"Tax not divine disposal"—but they feel no need to proceed to a defense of Mysterious Providence. Not yet. They grant, with brisk near-cheeriness, that voluptuouspess is no rare crime; and they advise Samson to spare himself self-blame. They cannot resist, however, employing a famous camouflage device to ask him why he married foreign wives. Such choral questions are common enough in Greek tragedy, especially in

Prometheus and *Oedipus at Colonus* where they are technical conveniences to trigger an actor into narrative or the justification of past action. But Milton is already passing every ancient device through the prism of his needs; and his Chorus do not say, "Tell us why you married Philistine women." They detour—

> *Yet truth to say, I oft have heard men wonder*
> *Why thou shouldst wed* Philistian *women rather*
> *Than of thine own Tribe fairer, or as fair,*
> *At least of they own Nation, and as noble*

—and add a small firm stroke to their own growing picture.

Samson replies that his foreign marriages were prompted by God to speed Israel's deliverance and again returns to his own weakness (and by now, 220 lines in, Milton has firmly established the crushed density of syntax which will eventually be shared by all characters except perhaps plain Manoa—a language discriminating, distancing them from us— another of his many attempts at a kind of sane historical fidelity and at shielding us, sparing us the threat of direct contact with his own full vision). The Chorus, for the first time, attempt consolation. They ignore his spiraling guilt and indulge in another homely tactic—this time for raising-the-tone, changing-the-subject—but their good intention can only fuel three lines; then the air of Samson's presence and their own deep divisions force from them the severest condemnation they can make:

> *In seeking just occasion to provoke*
> *The* Philistine, *thy Country's Enemy,*
> *Thou never wast remiss, I bear thee witness:*
> *Yet* Israel *still serves with all his Sons.*

For once, in a flash that hints at fire under ashes (there are guilts that even he will not shoulder), Samson refuses the condemnation and transfers it to Israel's leaders who refused him support when he, single-handed, slew a thousand Philistines; then he moves into thoughts on corrupt peoples who refuse God's heroes and prefer easy bondage to "strenuous liberty."

It is not clear at first that Samson includes the Chorus among those who failed him; but their response shows at least a dodging discomfort (he is still far more dangerous than they'd planned). They ignore the present ungrateful rulers of Israel and turn back in history for a terse and eloquent memory of similar ingratitudes to Gideon and Jephtha. By its look on the page—studded with italic names—the speech may at first appear decorative or another link between *now* and *then*; but if we recall how often, in any life, memory is a refuge from the present, a harbor from error, and if we notice that the intensity with which they hurl their eloquence backward finally lands them in a jingle—

> *Had not his prowess quell'd thir pride*
> *In that sore battle when so many died*
> *Without Reprieve adjudg'd to death,*
> *For want of well pronouncing* Shibboleth

—then we may suspect that what they say, that all they say, becomes a mirror before them.

Samson's reply is produced by his own ruling masochism and by his, as yet, fairly uncomplicated gratitude for company. He accepts without irony the historical comparisons, denies his personal importance and again laments his inability to fulfill God's purpose. All his earlier questions and hints of questions rest now, torpid.

But the Chorus refuse the pause and burst into their first stasimon —"Just are the ways of God." The beginning looks abrupt, an unheralded eruption; but gradually they show the trail of their movement—they are lecturing, homilizing, themselves. They are replying to (not *answering*) the question which has swelled hideously, lethally before them since their first glimpse of blind Samson, the question which they have forbidden Samson to ask—"Why has God so degraded Samson and Israel, and Himself?" Even now, they do not ask the question; but it stands in their midst (and ours) throughout the ode, huge, the pole round which they dance. Their reply, which begins with a firm assertion of the justice and reason of God's ways and proceeds through confident-sounding old-man platitudes on atheism—

> *Unless there be who think not God at all:*
> *If any be, they walk obscure;*
> *For of such Doctrine never was there School,*
> *But the heart of the Fool,*
> *And no man therein Doctor but himself*

—curves, veers as it grows in their throats. The surface of their confidence is uncracked until they attempt a specific defense of God in the matter of Samson; then all their confidence in reason crumbles. They can only say, "Down Reason then, at least vain reasonings down." Their answer to the great *Why?* is that the question must not, cannot be asked—an answer which is often the last redoubt of the shaken and doubting pious. How shaken, how doubting, we have yet to discover. Samson's father Manoa is seen in the distance; and they break off—rescued—to announce his arrival.

Manoa enters and begins the second episode by asking the Chorus to direct him to Samson. When they have pointed the way, Manoa breaks into cries of disbelief and recollections of past glory which come more naturally from a father than, earlier, from the Chorus. It would be possible to think of these lines as repetition—signs of the play's senility or, conversely, its early lack of finish—but surely it is adequate and useful to notice that Milton, far from carelessly repeating the parodos, alters the material to the character of the old father. For instance, Manoa reduces to nine lines (340–348) the substance of twenty-seven lines of the parodos (124–150). A chorus obviously are expected to be lyrical, expansive; but the compressed grief of Manoa is more moving than all the rhetorical sheen of the Chorus, though his motives soon appear as complex as theirs, tangled in a specially paternal way. Yet Manoa himself is soon approaching the questions which Samson approached in the prologue. In fact, by line 356 (addressing whom?—Samson? the Chorus? the surrounding air? he does not specifically address his son until 362), Manoa has come nearer than Samson or the Chorus to a direct interrogation of God, bitter and with no trace of rhetoric—

> *Why are his gifts desirable; to tempt*
> *Our earnest Prayers, then, giv'n with solemn hand*
> *As Graces, draw a Scorpion's tail behind?*

And though he sheers off, retains the third person, asks questions *about* God (no one has yet said *You!* to God) Manoa goes on into thoughts that sound very much like orders to the Almighty—

> *Alas! methinks whom God hath chosen once*
> *To worthiest deeds, if he through frailty err,*
> *He should not so o'erwhelm, and as a thrall*
> *Subject him to so foul indignities,*
> *Be it but for honor's sake of former deeds.*

Manoa goes so far toward explicit indictment of God that Samson stops him with a line the Chorus have used against him—"Appoint not heavenly disposition, Father." The Chorus had actually warned Samson, "Tax not divine disposal"; Samson's own wording—with the sense of "Don't give God orders, Father"—lends the warning a filial tone and is the first flash of a warm wit that will color and deepen the relations of Samson and Manoa (and which, not incidentally, provides another secret sign of hope in Samson). But Samson quickly accepts full responsibility for his misery, testifies to the justice of his punishment, gives a long account of his surrender to both his Philistine wives, then declares that his present degradation is not so ignoble as his early servitude—"foul effeminacy"—to women.

Manoa replies with a paternal gravity so understated as to have its own no doubt intentional wit, "I cannot praise thy marriage choices, Son." He agrees to the tragedy of all Samson's mistakes but, in his eminently practical way, reminds Samson that he need not overpay his debt of penitence. Yet for all his healthy expedience, he will not ignore or obscure the greatest of Samson's crimes; indeed, he understands the crime in a way not previously advanced, and with no clear reason, he mentions it now (is the reason, again, paternal?—"I told you so"?)—Samson is responsible for the degradation of Jehovah and the magnification of Dagon in the eyes of the Philistines (and, perhaps, we may wonder, among some of the notoriously fickle Hebrews?). Samson again accepts the charge; he is especially stricken to have caused "doubt / In feeble hearts," but he is confident that God will triumph over Dagon and without the aid of Samson.

Manoa receives the confidence with such enthusiasm that he seems, as he often does, on the edge of a lyric outburst—

> *these words*
> *I as a Prophecy receive: for God,*
> *Nothing more certain, will not long defer*
> *To vindicate the glory of his name*
> *Against all competition, nor will long*
> *Endure it, doubtful whether God be Lord,*
> *Or* Dagon

—but he stops short and reveals that he has already made overtures to Philistine lords for Samson's release. He, at least, has worked to help his son in the only way he thinks practical. He has understood nothing of the "Prison within Prison / Inseparably dark" which is Samson's announced vision of his own soul (and Manoa will prove righter than anyone in the play now knows).

Samson expresses his preference for prison, his need for punishment, his shame at the thought of returning to his people to be "avoided as a blab." The ugly and comic colloquialism starts out of the, by now, luxuriant and monotonous coils of Samson's self-obsession—the direct hit of a lifelong narcissist who has had time, and the resources, to become the world's authority on some aspects of himself; and who knows himself a blab.

Manoa again urges moderation in all this self-affliction—a little unselfish self-mercy. (Alfred Adler said late in life that the sum of his psychology was "All neurosis is vanity"—a truth available for clear enunciation to these two old Jews; for *Samson* is the most profoundly Jewish of great extra-Biblical poems.) Perhaps, he says, God will forgive; perhaps

God intends that Samson return now to Israel to seek forgiveness. But Samson again refuses; he will seek pardon but not freedom. He recalls the obnoxious pride of his free days when he walked Israel "like a petty God"; he remembers himself in the lap of Dalila (*sees*—all Samson's memories are intensely visual; and the most obtuse of Eliot's charges against Milton is a lack of visual acuity) as "a tame Wether"—a castrated sheep—and in this ultimate image of his physical degradation, Samson aligns himself with Oedipus and Cornwall (in blinding Gloucester) by viewing blindness as a surrogate castration.

At this new depth, the Chorus rush into six lines on Samson's temperance in respect to wine. The tack seems abrupt to the point of authorial awkwardness (and is one of the passages exhibited by those who think the play unfinished); but in fact the few lines do considerable work—work which is both in-character and which further reveals character. For instance, Samson and Manoa have catalogued exhaustively all Samson's betrayals of God. The Chorus, silent but attentive for two hundred lines, remember the one vow which Samson never broke—the central command that a Nazarite should separate himself from wine and strong drink—and they rush in with it now, a gift, at the first opening. And at first they appear to have succeeded, at least in changing the subject. Samson follows them with six lines on his exclusive use of water; and the pleased Chorus expand into a more general condemnation of strong drink, a thumping Prohibition tract in five lines.

But Samson cannot be diverted for long. With the consummate skill of his narcissism, he employs the diversion itself as a pivot back into self-blame—

> But what avail'd this temperance, not complete
> Against another object more enticing?

—and he meditates upon the possible *use* of his returning home to be "A burdenous drone; to visitants a gaze,/Or pitied object." He seems to say that here in prison he at least has work—the drudgery which earns his bread and pays on his debts of guilt. It will be a thousand lines—moments before the catastrophe—until Manoa affirms that God will not leave Samson "Useless, and thence ridiculous"; but the Chorus have already hinted at the equation *useless* = *ridiculous* in the parodos—

> weaponless himself,
> Made arms ridiculous, useless the forgery
> Of brazen shield and spear

—and Samson begins here dimly to share an article of Milton's lifelong faith that the truly ridiculous is the useless. It is an article which will become a cornerstone of Samson's reconstruction. Samson, though, is a failed judge, not a prophet. He cannot see that foundations are present on which God is building, that the hook is in his mouth; so he delivers now the nine lines which, for all the calm of their surface, are Samson's—the play's, Milton's—deepest gaze toward despair, its ultimate nadir, the crisis of the disease of being Samson, to be followed by death or recovery:

> *All otherwise to me my thoughts portend,*
> *That these dark orbs no more shall treat with light,*
> *Nor th' other light of life continue long,*
> *But yield to double darkness nigh at hand:*
> *So much I feel my genial spirits droop,*
> *My hopes all flat, nature within me seems*
> *In all her functions weary of herself;*
> *My race of glory run, and race of shame,*
> *And I shall shortly be with them that rest.*

Manoa briskly but accurately diagnoses false despair, the product of less than fatal mental anguish; he urges his son to wait calmly and hear "healing words" from the Chorus (who, a third of the way in, have hardly offered healing) while he goes off to argue a ransom.

Alone again with the Chorus, Samson rouses from his brief calm (why now?—surely a response to his father's presence, now that presence is safely withdrawn) and attempts to dive still deeper in a long aria, a monody on psychic torment which is as authoritative a report as any in literature—

> *Thoughts my Tormentors arm'd with deadly stings*
> *Mangle my apprehensive tenderest parts,*
> *Exasperate, exulcerate, and raise*
> *Dire inflammation which no cooling herb*
> *Or med'cinal liquor can assuage,*
> *Nor breath of Vernal Air from snowy* Alp

—but is firmly doomed, if its purpose is death, a rush toward self-destruction. The bottom, as Eliot said, "is a great way down"; but Samson has reached bottom some thirty lines before—the bottom of himself, at least, beyond which lies silence—and is now being lifted, with ghastly slowness, on the shards of his old vices: self-esteem, narcissism, the eloquence of the two—toward what he cannot imagine (*we* know). He implies a last tired questioning of God; then, sure of his total isolation, ends in a simple prayer, "speedy death."

Except for their brief sally on temperance, the Chorus have stood silent for more than three hundred lines. In reading, it is easy to forget their mute presence; but they have stood throughout, listening, absorbing, responding impotently as they wait. And the content of their second stasimon, which they now launch, is a clear delayed-action graph of their continued responsiveness. Their previous ode had brought them dangerously near an abyss; and since then they have witnessed the agonized exchanges between Samson and Manoa—Manoa's hard-headed practicality and cruel paternal accuracy circling, powerless, round Samson's growing voluptuous despair. They have just heard Samson rending his inner horror, as with nails at a fresh scar, and trailing into the spent prayer for death.

So the ode begins calmly, taking its first note from Samson's weariness, with a movement on patience, commended by the wise "as the truest fortitude." It seems for a while that they are working themselves into the sort of stoic comfortless advice which might be expected of a Chorus, especially of the Chorus who delivered the parodos of this play —a swatch of plain-dull. And just as it seems that they are indeed knuckling-under for a siege of masochism, trouble threatens—

> But with th'afflicted in his pangs thir sound
> Little prevails

—and the dam falls, an outpouring which is the first great shout in a play that has, till now, been conducted in a prison-hush, a shout at first of wonder more than anger, printed as an exclamation not a question:

> God of our Fathers, what is man!
> That thou towards him with hand so various,
> Or might I say contrarious,
> Temper'st thy providence through his short course,
> Not evenly, as thou rul'st
> Th'Angelic orders and inferior creatures mute,
> Irrational and brute.

They are thinking of great men—Samsons—not themselves; and it is their first completely sympathetic speech (in both senses—the first in which they are feeling *with* Samson as friends and in which they are entirely likable as men). The ordeal of the last few hundred lines has brought them a long way from their early two-edged "consolation"; and they stand stripped of selfishness and petty sadism, of delusion, and contemplate God's visible use of His great men—

> Yet toward these, thus dignifi'd, thou oft,
> Amidst thir height of noon,

> Changest thy count'nance and thy hand, with no regard
> Of highest favors past
> From thee on them, or them to thee of service.
>   Nor only dost degrade them, or remit
> To life obscur'd, which were a fair dismission,
> But throw'st them lower than thou didst exalt them high,
> Unseemly falls in human eye. . . .

—"Unseemly falls in human eye": there is a moving delicacy of fairness in their choice of adjective (throughout the ode, they are kept from hysteria chiefly by their struggle to be fair). They do not call God unjust or evil; but they call some of his visible acts "unseemly." They come this near the brink—and Samson must know that it is he, the spectacle of his life, who has brought them this near to "diffidence of God, and doubt"—but they stop. It is among their oldest reflexes, that they hesitate to make explicit accusation of God. They have drawn their general picture of the miseries of the debased great; but they have not forced themselves (or allowed themselves to race) to the final connection, to point to Samson and say to God, "Here is the man." And it seems that they cannot; for now they begin a chastened, hedging prayer—

> So deal not with this once thy glorious Champion,
> The Image of thy strength, and mighty minister.

Even here, at their most sympathetic, they ask for the wrong gift—that God comfort Samson, not that He again use Samson. Then they plunge to the point—

> What do I beg? how hast thou dealt already?
> Behold him in this state calamitous, and turn
> His labors, for thou canst, to peaceful end.

So Samson has brought them—they have let themselves be brought, "heads without name"—not perhaps to doubt of God's existence but surely to literal "diffidence," lack of trust in His promises of justice, a retreat to the mean, demeaning (though, for all we know, accurate) ethics of their first stasimon: "Who made our Laws to bind us, not himself." If the Chorus were forced by events to continue speaking now or to make the play's next action, it is not possible to predict where they might end—at the mill with Samson? or as suicides? or (far more likely) back home at their chores, the bitterer for their trip, the more "useless" thence "ridiculous" (to whom?—to God, at least). And if Samson were forced now to fill a silence, could he do more than exhale?

Rescue again arrives—the Chorus can break off to announce an arrival, and in a tone radically, almost ludicrously, new:

> *But who is this, what thing of Sea or Land?*
> *Female of sex it seems,*
> *That so bedeckt, ornate, and gay,*
> *Comes this way sailing*
> *Like a stately Ship*
> *Of Tarsus, bound for th' Isles*
> *Of Javan or Gadire*
> *With all her bravery on, and tackle trim,*
> *Sails fill'd, and streamers waving,*
> *Courted by all the winds that hold them play,*
> *An Amber scent of odorous perfume*
> *Her harbinger, a damsel train behind. . . .*

—Dalila, of course; and the tired wit of the initial description (a full-rigged ship is a common metaphor for an overdressed woman) and their references to her as a "thing," as "it," are meant to tell us more about the Chorus than Dalila, though the fact that they move in fifteen lines from ridicule to implied tribute is one index to Dalila's beauty (and another elaborately visualized stage-direction; still another is often ignored—Dalila comes with "a damsel train," a silent chorus of beauties who stand in reinforcement of her power and meaning throughout the episode):

> *Yet on she moves, now stands and eyes thee fixt,*
> *About t' have spoke, but now, with head declin'd*
> *Like a fair flower surcharg'd with dew, she weeps*
> *And words addrest seem into tears dissolv'd,*
> *Wetting the borders of her silk'n veil. . . .*

Her first words—"With doubtful feet and wavering resolution/I came"—raise the central question about this third episode: why is Dalila here? The question has parts—first, why does Dalila think she is here? (the others are, why does Samson think she is here?; why the Chorus?; and why God?). And that is unanswerable, overall (though more or less answerable at any given moment); for Dalila herself does not know all her reasons for coming and, like the Chorus', they are both good and bad. Goethe interrupted Crabb Robinson, who was reading the scene to him, to say, "See the great poet! he *putt* her in right!"—to which W.P. Ker added, a century later in *The Art of Poetry*, "Dalila . . . is so far in the right that Samson cannot be thoroughly in the right when he argues against her."

The question, again, is not, "Is Dalila right?"—it will be fatal to God's purpose if Samson accepts her offer—but "Is Dalila sincere in her offer to care for Samson 'At home in leisure and domestic ease' "? If we answer No (and No throughout the scene)—and if Milton's answer is No—then Dalila becomes a simple flat character, a monster of nearly incredible proportions who wants Samson in her power again to torture as everyone has tortured damaged beasts. If we answer Yes—with Goethe and Ker—then she becomes instantly a richer, more mysterious character, a truer woman (and incidentally throws further light on the silliness of the choral bluster at her exit). The nearest approach to accuracy would be to answer, "Both." Surely her initial offer is "sincere"—sincere as she can make it. She feels some remorse for her part in the ruin of her husband; she would like to make recompense in the only way she knows—in bed (and her sense of Samson as superb *rider* is rank throughout):

> *Here I should still enjoy thee day and night*
> *Mine and Love's prisoner, not the Philistines',*
> *Whole to myself, unhazarded abroad*

and

> *Life yet hath many solaces, enjoy'd*
> *Where other senses want not their delights*
> *At home in leisure and domestic ease. . . .*

But what she has not reckoned with—and never understands—is that she is simultaneously both herself and a pawn to a foreign God. She comes as Dalila (who might conceivably have been accepted with honor and with good results for the subjected Israelites) and as the Old Temptress to Body (who must now be repelled to prove old weakness dead and to exercise new strength, new grace); and when that unconscious complexity of role collides with Samson's own new seething complexities—old vices being made new strengths through contact with the cruelty, stupidity, pathos and desperate need of the Chorus—she loses grip on all her various mounts and rides off in several reckless directions at once, though she retains to the end the courage and splendor of her own multiplicity:

> *At this who ever envies or repines*
> *I leave him to his lot, and like my own.*

It is her final display of mixed motives that provokes the flood of abuse poured on her by the Chorus and Samson as she departs. Samson declares, "God sent her to debase me"—and the inaccuracy of the second half of the claim does not destroy the truth of the first, that Dalila was literally a minister from God and that her ministry has worked or is working—but the Chorus, having first dismissed her as "a manifest Serpent," acknowledge the power of Dalila:

> *Yet beauty, though injurious, hath strange power,*
> *After offense returning, to regain*
> *Love once possest, nor can be easily*
> *Repuls't, without much inward passion felt*
> *And secret sting of amorous remorse.*

That they attribute her power simply to her "beauty"—presumably her physical allure, though they call it "strange"—does not conceal their new confusion in the face of the rapidly complicating spectacle of Samson's fate, a spectacle more complex at the start than they were equipped to watch or comprehend. And the truthful ambiguity of these lines is a credible preparation for the quick and ludicrous resolution which they achieve in the following ode, the third stasimon.

To call their resolution ludicrous is to announce, before examining, a solution to the problem—what are we to make of the attitude to women and marriage which the Chorus express? The ode was customarily cited, into the early twentieth century (and in the face of the triumphant salvatory femininity of Eve in *Paradise Lost* and of the strong, not entirely defeated, armaments granted to Dalila), as one of the prime texts on Milton's own misogyny. But here, if ever, we must remember Milton's statement on the understanding of drama—

> we must not regard the poet's words as his own, but consider who it is that speaks in the play, and what that person says; for different persons are introduced, sometimes good, sometimes bad, sometimes wise men, sometimes fools, and they speak not always the poet's own opinion, but what is most fitting to each character.*

That, and a study of what is on paper, the irreducible words, seem to license if not require a procedure like this. Assuming that *Samson* was written, or at least finished, after *Paradise Lost* and that Milton still held to the strictures on rhyme pronounced in the note to the epic, then it would be difficult to imagine a passage more guilty, under these strictures, of "wretched matter," injudiciousness, triviality: the opening eight lines with their six repetitions of the *it* rhyme—which is complicated and recalled in "gifts," "mix'd" and "infix'd"—and the nine closing lines with

---

* Milton, *Defensio Prima*, S. L. Wolff, trans., in F. H. Patterson, ed., *The Works of John Milton* (Columbia, 1931–38), VII, 307.

their heavy tolling. So, remembering that few things in literary study are more dangerous than the identification of humor in relatively old material, especially material in which humor is not normally expected (how many laughs has, or had, the *Oresteia?* the book of *Job?* the Gospels?), we might decide that a reading like this is as plausible as any. The ode is purely dramatic; it expresses sentiments, obeys codes proper to a group of Hebrew elders—the general Old Testament view of women and marriage; in fact, the prevailing view in the world today. (Whether they are also the sentiments of John Milton in the 1660s is another, not particularly relevant, question; they were certainly not his sentiments twenty years earlier when, in his divorce tracts, he elaborated a vision of marriage as mutual love, the profoundest courtesy, which is only soiled and diminished, though not obliterated, by the present voice of the Chorus.) It is possible, however—and this is where the jingling and thudding of the third stasimon, its rhythmic anticipations of Gilbert and Sullivan, define its tone —that the Chorus themselves do not really believe all they say, that they overstate their scorn of women's wiles and over-assert their marriage rights in the attempt to strengthen Samson against any remaining desire to follow Dalila, to confirm him in his violent treatment of her—and to do the same services for themselves (they have, after all, seen and briefly succumbed to Dalila; and the very violence of Samson's final rejection confirms his own awareness of danger). Whatever the case, there is again a playful tone of relief as another arrival permits a change of subject; and in the brief exchange which follows, Samson loses patience with the still-pedantic Chorus for the first and only time—

CHORUS   *But had we best retire, I see a storm?*
SAMSON   *Fair days have oft contracted wind and rain.*
CHORUS   *But this another kind of tempest brings.*
SAMSON   *Be less abstruse, my riddling days are past.*

The newest visitor is Harapha, a Philistine giant who gives us some notion of the awfulness of Samson in his own strongman "petty God" phase. The episode is built as a shouting-match between Samson and Harapha—Samson repeatedly challenging the bully to single combat, with all the odds to Harapha, and Harapha weaseling. The scene, and most of its verse, are as deadly for modern readers as similar matches in Homer, Shakespeare or on the playgrounds of their childhoods—no one could wish it a syllable longer (though serious actors might clarify its points)— and a close reading here would be tedious, windy and unrewarding. But the results of such a reading would show that Samson has experienced, early in the episode or before it, a radical revival of confidence in self and in God. When Harapha accuses Samson of having fought of old with magic power and protection, Samson replies—

> *I know no spells, use no forbidden Arts;*
> *My trust is in the living God who gave me*
> *At my Nativity this strength, diffius'd*
> *No less through all my sinews, joints and bones,*
> *Than thine, while I preserv'd these locks unshorn,*
> *The pledge of my unviolated vow*

—and when Harapha observes that the living God hardly seems to live here, has abandoned his chosen hero, Samson can accept a part of the charge and revise it—

> *All these indignities, for such they are*
> *From thine, these evils I deserve and more,*
> *Acknowledge them from God inflicted on me*
> *Justly, yet despair not of his final pardon*
> *Whose ear is ever open; and his eye*
> *Gracious to re-admit the suppliant;*
> *In confidence whereof I once again*
> *Defy thee to the trial of mortal fight,*
> *By combat to decide whose god is God,*
> *Thine or whom I with Israel's Sons adore.*

Harapha of course avoids the fight and departs, still huffing, eighty lines later, with Samson's even healthier, grislier challenges ringing at his heels; but the question about the episode remains—why and how has Samson moved from the despair of the ghastly monody through the clenched near-hysteria of his rejection of Dalila to this sane vigor, this lip-curled smiling excitement? —For two reasons and in two ways: he is drawn now, reeled-in rapidly by God who is ready to end *this* story; and he has comprehended for the first time through the action of the day—and specifically through the choral response to that action (the various odes)—the already disastrous effect he has had upon his own people, the Chorus. Not simply the fact that now they are vassals of the Philistines but that they are spiritually stunned, perhaps lost, and that they lack his own heroic resilience to rescue themselves. There is, almost certainly, a third reason, wild and loose—with all the fresher inspirations that arise in Harapha's wake comes also a knowledge of the old black chance, Harapha might kill him:

> *But come what will, my deadliest foe will prove*
> *My speediest friend, by death to rid me hence,*
> *The worst that he can give, to me the best.*

But if Milton is aware of the rattling of that, like seed in a gourd, the Chorus are not. Their own response to Harapha, and Harapha's effect on Samson, is whole and simple. They were roused by the sheer noise of the episode and its indications of rebirth in Samson; and after a few quick exchanges with Samson (including their only successful levity in the play, "His Giantship is gone somewhat crestfall'n"), they launch impulsively into a praise of heroic action, the impulse being surely the great smile registered in the opening movement, that of parched ground bathed by rain—

> *Oh how comely it is and how reviving*
> *To the Spirits of just men long opprest!*
> *When God into the hands of thir deliverer*
> *Puts invincible might*
> *To quell the mighty of the Earth. . . .*

In the one verb "puts" they flash a moment of perception (they still see Samson as a largely passive receptacle of God's strength, used or abandoned at His mysterious will); otherwise, the first nineteen lines of their fourth stasimon are, minus expected ferocity, the sort of song appropriate to the early days of Samson's glory. But the sentiments clang brassily now. Samson has not yet *acted*—not an act visible to his waiting people—and the chances for significant action are apparently all but non-existent. So their excitement has pushed them past hard fact; they have not caught up (how could they?) with the changes rapidly occurring in, arriving in, Samson's soul; and they soon realize the tactlessness of their paean to "invincible might." The change to sobriety and decorum is signaled by a "but"—"But patience is more oft the exercise/Of Saints." They think it likely that Samson's blindness may finally force him to resignation and the company of martyrs "Whom Patience finally must crown." But they are not sure—their prediction is not a prediction but a guess; does their tentativeness throughout the ode, even in the over-confident opening, explain the relative absence of rhyme?—and their doubts are strengthened by sight of the approaching Public Officer.

The Officer orders Samson to come to the Philistines' solemn feast. Samson refuses on two grounds—Hebrews are forbidden to attend pagan rites, and he will not perform blind for the sport of his captors. The old pride, again, is not broken but is now *used*, not abused; it has a new face—no longer the narcissism of a strongman but the offended dignity of one who still values the shards of honor remaining to him.

The Officer departs, lowering; and the Chorus urge Samson to reconsider. It is a long-delayed return to their promised offer of "counsel" and a curious one—they want Samson to go to the feast; why? It has been suggested that the Chorus are again attacking Samson's sense of his own specialness, his chosen-ness; but two simpler (and more likable) forces seem stronger—the Chorus, like Samson, are drawn now by God's plan (as satellites to Samson or as the central body?) and they fear for their own safety if Samson refuses. Samson, in argument with them, continues to refuse until they exclaim in what sounds more like parental exasperation than anger, "How thou wilt here come off surmounts my reach."

But Samson dimly knows. In the most difficult lines of the play, he reverses his decision—

> *Be of good courage, I begin to feel*
> *Some rousing motions in me which dispose*
> *To something extraordinary my thoughts.*
> *I with this Messenger will go along,*
> *Nothing to do, be sure, that may dishonor*
> *Our Law, or stain my vow of Nazarite.*
> *If there be aught of presage in the mind,*
> *This day will be remarkable in my life*
> *By some great act, or of my days the last.*

For any reader who can accept the idea of divine inspiration, no convincing will be needed—Samson has been inspired, and *now*. The only question is, how specifically inspired?—does Samson know the details of the rest of his fate? And that is unanswerable. For a reader who cannot —how has he read this far?—these lines, this moment, will no doubt seem dramatically unacceptable. We might argue for Samson that no sudden change of heart is involved, that the entire beginning and middle of the play (all his encounters, and chiefly that with his only constant human companions throughout—the Chorus) have constituted an education for Samson, long-delayed but successful; in the silence between lines 1380 and 1381, he accepts the logical (though probably still dark) demands and duties of that education. He is truly passive, a listener not a speaker; he is caught. And, laying aside for now any question of afflatus, how else could Milton have treated such a turn?—through a multiplication of visitors and episodes? a longer episode here with the Chorus in which they and Samson might specify the nature of their now-clarified mutual dependence and duties? In fact, Samson now knows what he needs to know; the Chorus do not, but they will have more time to learn than Samson (because a large part of what they learn will *be* Samson). What we as readers do not know (or will not learn in the next four hundred lines) or will refuse to accept is, Milton might say, the fault of our weakness—that will hurt us ("All wickedness is weakness"); but Milton never promised safety. In short, Samson has detected, or suspected, the "guiding hand" which he had implored (of a mute) in the first line of the play and has surrendered to the suspicion. The one thing which he cannot doubt is that he is guided, pulled, toward *rest*—his goal from the first: any direction from here lies rest. The hand of grace—God's hand—seems paternal again or (disturbingly) maternal.

So when the Officer returns as expected with a sterner command, Samson obeys with lines that build quickly to a comic near-fawning— who could have imagined, even ten lines before, that such a response would be both credible, acceptable and right?:

> *Because they shall not trail me through thir streets*
> *Like a wild Beast, I am content to go.*
> *Masters' commands come with a power resistless*
> *To such as owe them absolute subjection;*
> *And for a life who will not change his purpose?*
> *(So mutable are all the ways of men). . . .*

But that is for the Philistines, in his office as their "Mummer." The Officer, pleased with compliance, guesses that Samson may now indeed earn his freedom and gives him time for words with his friends.

For them both it is farewell. Despite mutual hedgings, the loopholes left for survival, their last exchange has the already-posthumous calm of many final partings. Samson does not allude to his suspicion of Providence in the summons. He prepares them instead for the possibility of his death at the hands of the Philistines and warns them that, come what will, they may find themselves in danger for his sake—that he gives them no more definite warning, or command to flee, seems to confirm the vagueness of his inspiration, the totality of his surrender. His people, like himself, he leaves in the hands of God, not even troubling to remind them of the fact. His last direct word, to them and us, rightly concerns his honor—

> *Happ'n what may, of me expect to hear*
> *Nothing dishonorable, impure, unworthy*
> *Our God, our Law, my Nation, or myself;*
> *The last of me or no I cannot warrant.*

But the Chorus, always an observer of forms, send benediction with, and after, him (does he exit abruptly at line 1426 or slowly enough to hear them?). This fifth, and briefest, stasimon reveals that the Chorus are also apprehensive of some divine act. They do not dare to be explicit; they only commend Samson to God (Whom they again, and calmly, affirm deserving of glory), invoke the angel of his birth to guard him, and again recall his past. In relation to their own capacities, they have had to come as far as Samson—from their ambivalent parodos, their untested but tub-thumping certainties, their desperate collapses—to this hushed expectancy. Samson has led, or at least brought, them. That he may have led them to the brink of a pogrom does not scatter them now; the mice of the parodos have stoutened and stand. They can end now—the first ode they really finish—to meet the return of Manoa.

He enters "With youthful steps," full of his day's work; Samson's ransomed freedom appears to be at hand—two-thirds of the Philistine lords have agreed (one group for "Private reward," another "having reduc't/ Thir foe to misery beneath thir fears"). The Chorus express their joy in the hope. Then the dialogue is broken by a noise—which the Chorus accurately identify as a Philistine shout of pleasure at the sight of their famed enemy. The exchange continues with Manoa's slightly self-congratulatory affirmation of willingness to bankrupt himself for his son. To which the Chorus respond generously and without irony in lines that, though a simon-pure example of "choric comment" (the only such in the play), are transformed by their new calm and passionate sympathy—

> *Fathers are wont to lay up for thir Sons,*
> *Thou for thy Son art bent to lay out all;*
> *Sons wont to nurse thir Parents in old age,*
> *Thou in old age car'st how to nurse thy Son,*
> *Made older than thy age through eyesight lost.*

And their praise ignites Manoa to a further vision of his role—as attendant to the freed Samson whom he now sees powerfully, seated at home:

> *And on his shoulders waving down those locks,*
> *That of a Nation arm'd the strength contain'd*

—and to an ironic wager on Samson's future utility to God which crystallizes at last the ideas of *use/uselessness, esteem/ridicule* which have hung suspended since the beginning of the play—

> *And I persuade me God had not permitted*
> *His strength again to grow up with his hair*
> *Garrison'd round about him like a Camp*
> *Of faithful Soldiery, were not his purpose*
> *To use him further yet in some great service,*
> *Not to sit idle with so great a gift*
> *Useless, and thence ridiculous about him.*

The Chorus again second the hopes and explain their participation in Manoa's hopes and joy, "In both which we, as next, participate." "As next" implies "of kin"—the Chorus, who introduced themselves as "friends and neighbors," are now moved to go even beyond the tribal bond and claim *relation*.

At that moment—and surely with the full knowledge and intent of both God and Milton—the catastrophe occurs. Manoa begins a thankful reply but, after six words, breaks off to register a second noise—"Horribly loud, unlike the former shout." In the thirty lines before the arrival of the Messenger, Manoa and the Chorus speculate on the nature of the catastrophe and the safest course of action for themselves; and it is worth noticing that this Chorus stands its ground—it is they who advise Manoa to "keep together here." In place, they indulge again the gift, so visible in the parodos, for depiction of events which they have not witnessed— events, in this case, have not occurred as they imagine, and will not—

> *What if his eyesight (for to Israel's God*
> *Nothing is hard) by miracle restor'd,*
> *He now be dealing dole among his foes,*
> *And over heaps of slaughter'd walk his way?*

But a witness arrives. It is important to remember a fact of which little is made in the lines but which would presumably be clear, through costuming, onstage—the Messenger is, as the Chorus announce him, "An *Ebrew*, as I guess, and of our Tribe." For many urgent reasons Milton could not have sent the Chorus itself to the doomed arena; but the survivor and testifier, the witness and historian of Samson's triumph and death, is another kinsman, a man (or boy) of Dan. He begins his report, the longest speech of the play, with a few facts about himself—that he had come to Gaza on business early this morning but, the business hardly begun, had heard rumors of Samson's appearance and, though piteous of his state, "minded / Not to be absent at that spectacle." Then he tells the famous story, adding numerous pictorial details to the Biblical account which tell us more about Milton's vision than the Messenger's, especially in his account of Samson's last words. In *Judges* they are given (after a brief prayer that he be strengthened to avenge his eyes), bare and awful —"Let me die with the Philistines." Milton's Messenger heard them thus—

> *"Hitherto, Lords, what your commands impos'd*
> *I have perform'd, as reason was, obeying,*
> *Not without wonder or delight beheld.*
> *Now of my own accord such other trial*
> *I mean to show you of my strength, yet greater;*
> *As with amaze shall strike all who behold."*

(—"As reason was." What reason? We partly know; will be told more by the next hundred lines, the end of the play; part will be secret shared by Samson and God—or kept by God.) And the Messenger's expansion of *Judges* 16:23—"Then the lords of the Philistines gathered them together for to offer a great sacrifice unto Dagon"—suggests a specific desire by Milton to stress Samson's success in creating the conditions for the freedom of his people:

> *Upon the heads of all who sat beneath,*
> *Lords, Ladies, Captains, Counsellors, or Priests,*
> *Thir choice nobility and flower, not only*
> *Of this but each* Philistian *City round. . . .*

Indeed, when the Messenger concludes four lines later—with a final reminder that Samson has "inevitably" destroyed himself—it is to the previous spectacle of dead overlords (and, presumably, Dalila?) and potential freedom that the Chorus respond initially. For nine lines the full Chorus define this "dearly bought revenge" as the fulfillment of Samson's work—"The work for which thou wast foretold to *Israel*." In the hundred remaining lines of the play, they will learn—or come to understand— that Samson's "work" was neither so simple nor so simply achieved; but for now, their joy volts through them, flinging them into their final full ode, which for the first time they sing antiphonally—Milton indicating their division into Semichoruses. And the division seems designed to point their development from hateful joy to calmer discovery.

The first Semichorus, in perhaps the most extraordinary language of the play (arguably, of Milton's work), sings a hymn of victory, ferocious and exultant, as has often been suggested, with the old Hebraic joy of the songs of Miriam and Deborah. So impressive is it in its bald utter power—

> *Among them hee a spirit of frenzy sent,*
> *Who hurt thir minds*

—that readers have generally failed to ask an urgent question, intended by Milton: are the Chorus "right"? (or the seven or eight men who constitute the half)? Not that Milton intends us to import later notions of pity and mercy into material which he has struggled to keep chronistic; but aren't we meant to see, as the play and the joy wind down, that the tone of the reaction is mistaken, inaccurate?—that exultation is an imprecise response to Samson's victory, a defamation of its nature, committed innocently, no doubt, but committed? In fact, Samson himself is barely thought of in the first Semichorus; and then only as "thir destroyer."

The second Semichorus, to point the omission, begins with

Samson—"But he though blind of sight"—and upon that builds an elaborate mythopoeic meditation. Enormous amounts of commentary now exist which attempt to chart the image as it metamorphoses through snake and eagle to phoenix—

> *His fiery virtue rous'd*
> *From under ashes into sudden flame,*
> *And as an ev'ning Dragon came,*
> *Assailant on the perched roosts,*
> *And nests in order rang'd*
> *Of tame villatic Fowl; but as an Eagle*
> *His cloudless thunder bolted on thir heads.*
> *So virtue giv'n for lost,*
> *Deprest, and overthrown, as seem'd,*
> *Like that self-begott'n bird*
> *In the Arabian woods embost,*
> *That no second knows nor third*

—but even the most restrained comments have only pointed to the function of the ode for us, the audience of the play. T. R. Henn in *The Harvest of Tragedy* has seen it as "designed to provide this slowing down expansion and realignment of Samson's death into a mythology of its own." Certainly that is a part of the function for the Chorus as well (and Manoa will make similar efforts in his last speech); the Chorus of Sophocles' *Antigone* make a parallel effort as Antigone is led off to death—

> *Such was the fate, my child, of Danae*
> *Locked in a brazen bower,*
> *A prison secret as a tomb,*
> *Where was no day.* *

But its main function, *for them*, is further expression—and discovery in expression, of their total final attitude to Samson and his work. And if their ornate resort to dragons and the phoenix seems too quickly formalized and frigid, then that is not simply because they are Semitic tenants of a Greek-controlled building but because *that is what they feel*, and are coming to know—Samson was always a man apart, chosen before his birth by God to liberate His people, isolated from those people by his boisterous pride and excess and by their ancient indifference, isolated still further from all humanity by blindness, imprisonment and obsessive guilt, and now in death rapidly thrust backward into the safety of history, fable, poetry; never truly their kinsman at all, however recently they have wished

* Sophocles, *The Theban Plays*, translated by E. F. Watling (Penguin, 1947), p. 151.

to claim him. So, though the divided ode is a number of remarkable things, it is not a lament. They never lament Samson nor does his father; and this human and dramatic omission has misled a number of readers into an assumption that the play ends "gloriously" not tragically (*gloriously for whom?* we will have to ask later).

In fact, so little does the ode resemble any of the numerous types of traditional lament that Manoa's interruption—"Come, come, no time for lamentation now, / Nor much more cause"—seems a last example of the brisk and often obtuse "practicality" of the old man. The first lines of his last speech are given over—after the quick "*Samson* hath quit himself / Like *Samson*"—to a catalogue of the practical results of Samson's death: "years of mourning" to the Philistines, to Israel conditional "Honor . . . and freedom." Manoa is doing a sum, and the answer which he reaches is the most famous lines of the play—

> *Nothing is here for tears, nothing to wail*
> *Or knock the breast, no weakness, no contempt,*
> *Dispraise, or blame, nothing but well and fair,*
> *And what may quiet us in a death so noble.*

Armed with that, he can then give orders—they must find Samson's body, wash off its "clotted gore," bear it silently home (*silence* for safety? or because lament would be meaningless?) where he can raise over it a fitting tomb and monument. Only now does he grant himself (and us) a moment's mercy, in his last old-man prophecy—

> *Thither shall all the valiant youth resort,*
> *And from his memory inflame thir breasts*
> *To matchless valor, and adventures high:*
> *The Virgins also shall on feastful days*
> *Visit his Tomb with flowers, only bewailing*
> *His lot unfortunate in nuptial choice,*
> *From whence captivity and loss of eyes.*

The Chorus end the play, as a chorus does in all but three of the surviving Greek tragedies. Initially, they seem to respond to Manoa, affirming that "All is best"; and as they proceed and end the play, they construct a stanza, their first—fourteen lines, rhyming A B A B C D C D E F E F E F—which might seem, in its order (nearly a sonnet), an obeisance to tradition: that Greek tragedies end with hieratic choral formulae which state calm wisdom, or at worst, a dignified take-it-or-leave-it. But all Greek tragedies don't—*Prometheus* and *Agamemnon*, for instance, end in terror (admittedly provisional endings as the first or second parts of trilogies)—

and a study of this last song in *Samson* will show that, while formally resembling its ancient originals, it attempts, and performs, more elaborate work—on-going not summary—than any single speech in surviving Greek drama: it defines the degree to which the play is what Milton said it was, a tragedy and a dreadful one; it defines the spiritual progress of the Chorus; defines at last their use as the central character of the play; and sums the full potential of meaning which Milton saw inherent in the Greek dramatic form—a potential that had drawn him like magnetic-north since his college years.

What they sing is—

> *All is best, though we oft doubt,*
> *What th' unsearchable dispose*
> *Of highest wisdom brings about,*
> *And ever best found in the close.*
> *Oft he seems to hide his face,*
> *But unexpectedly returns*
> *And to his faithful Champion hath in place*
> *Bore witness gloriously; whence* Gaza *mourns*
> *And all that band them to resist*
> *His uncontrollable intent;*
> *His servants he with new acquist*
> *Of true experience from this great event*
> *With peace and consolation hath dismist,*
> *And calm of mind, all passion spent.*

What they seem to say are four things—God moves so mysteriously that we often fear His complete abandonment; but always He returns (or *has* always returned) and vindicates Himself and His people (His servants by choice not merit); and from such a vindication as we have witnessed today, we learn new things, discover that by watching we acquire "true experience" (the hero acquires the same, plus death)—we learn to take consolation in the faith that events are "ever best found in the close"; and our dying heroes are our means of seeing a close, a finished action; we learn the meaning of patience. And this much we know we have learned (for this one time, if not permanently) from a given and finished act— the hand and line of God revealed in Samson's last struggle and surrender, to answer our dark questions.

What questions?—all those summed in the second stasimon and answered through the play: what is man that God should use him so? (use him *how?*—as He has used Samson and his Danite neighbors). Part of God's answer is to split the question—"Which man? There are kinds and My interest in them varies." So they restate the question—"Why use

Samson thus?" God says, "Three reasons—for My good, his good, your good." They say, "What did he do for each of us three?" God says, "Helped to perfect us." They say, "Please explain." God says, "He fulfilled My will, his own (which had come to coincide with mine); and he taught you who you are." They say, "Who are we?" God says, "My servants." They say, "What service then?" God says, "Faith and patience to wait till the close."*

So the Chorus are happy, and with sufficient cause (though the darkness in some of those answers is more threatening than they seem now to notice). But is Samson? No—dead, crushed, "Soak't in his ene- mies' blood," in the prime of life, saved only through physical and spiritual humiliation, and destroyed by his salvation. A wiser, saner, more obedient servant, he might have lived for decades and judged his people well, rearing sons as heirs (how odd that he, a whoremonger, should be barren, both in *Judges* and Milton). Now he must leave them with nothing but memory and what they can make of it, a complex example and the *conditions* for political freedom. For all the questions that are answered, then, a huge one remains, unasked by the Chorus or any actor—the minimal question which the audience, at least, of any tragedy must ask before full comprehension can begin: "What does this tragic action cause to happen; what is its end result, what, in the world, is changed because of this action? Often in Greek tragedy—*Seven Against Thebes, Oedipus the King, Antigone*—the terrible answer is, "Nothing is changed." The tragedy occurs in a vacuum; we see a great catastrophe—the self- mutilation of Oedipus, the deaths of Antigone and Eteocles—but we do not *hear* it. The Chorus encircle the suffering hero, witness his agony, perhaps lament—but they are ultimately untouched, unchanged. And it is that silence at the heart of such tragedies—as though great rocks had fallen into gorges, silently for lack of hearers—which makes them so nearly unbearable.

Yeats seems to have investigated only one of the potential aspects of his "emotion of multitude" when he said (in the essay of that name)—

> The Greek drama has got the emotion of multitude from its chorus, which called up famous sorrows, even all the gods and all heroes to witness, as it were, some well-ordered fable, some action separated but for this from all but itself. . . . The Shakespearean Drama gets the emotion of multitude out of the sub-plot which copies the main

---

* I am aware of imputing to Milton the heretical notion of a perfectible God and can only say that I feel in the play a powerful undercurrent in that direction—that God Himself learns, grows through His heroes. Milton had, after all, studied Aeschylus all his life and a perfectible growing God is the cornerstone of both the *Prometheia* (as generally conjectured) and the *Oresteia*.

plot, much as a shadow upon the wall copies one's body in the firelight.

He speaks only of what might be called positive multitude—that audience which absorbs the hero's drama, takes his shock, conducts the current onward to us, surrogate witnesses but learners like them. Surely, though, there is negative multitude as well—which witnesses and rejects. And it is the chief measure of Milton's originality in *Samson* (for it really does not resemble any Greek play, except in form), and almost certainly his chief reason for choosing the Greek receptacle, that he found he could achieve positive and negative multitude by his unprecedented use of the Chorus. (Why should he have wished to achieve both kinds?—because, whenever he wrote the play, the relations of such polarities were the urgent burden of his curiosity and his knowledge: the relations of a great man, vertical and horizontal, with heaven and earth.)* We have already noticed his achievement of positive multitude—Samson's tragedy causes the last speech of the Chorus and, more, the restoration of faith and patience which shines through the speech. But there is something left over, the unviolated isolation of Samson to the end and the hard fact that he was required to give eyes, freedom, life, for men like this—

> *the common rout,*
> *That wand'ring loose about*
> *Grow up and perish, as the summer fly,*
> *Heads without name no more remember'd*

—men who may "sympathize," who may even come to perceive and make partial and temporary use of the great action done for them but who cannot accompany him on his awful journey or reach him with their intermittent jingling sympathy, only with their wavering hostility and the desperation to which his spectacle drives them.

It is that *left-over*, the bitter residue of waste at the end that keeps

---

* I have studied, I think, all the arguments against the traditional dating of *Samson* as Milton's last finished work (from A. H. Gilbert who would have Milton begin it just out of college, to W. R. Parker, who spreads it through Milton's late thirties and early forties, well before the start of *Paradise Lost*); and I was once attracted by their audacity. But the weight of my particular nineteen years' reading of the poem has not let me accept, for long, a theory which sees *Samson* as anything but the final product of Milton's maturity, begun and finished after the two epics. I could give, and elaborate upon, a number of reasons—its unprecedented and unfollowed verse, its architecture (which bears no resemblance to his early Italianate-operatic ideas of drama as sketched in the Trinity manuscript), its extraordinary view of human will (an *impaired* will, I think; by no means totally free) —but the strongest for me is the most personal, therefore least defensible: that it stands so alone—from all his other work, however grand—in finality of mastery, in perfect identity of thought and form and language as to set it unmistakably last, a terminus.

the play a tragedy. It settles so heavily, for all the song, that we do not need to see Samson's body again, borne in state toward home, mutilated far past the ghastly norm we accepted at the start; or to be reminded that no word is said in the length of the play about heaven or hell or any other afterlife in which Samson might join Damon and Lycidas in laving his locks to the choiring of saints (at best, he rests in the brown air of Sheol—"The dead praise not the LORD, neither any that go down into silence." Psalm 115:17); or to guess from past history or the sequel in *Judges* and Josephus that Samson's people will again not seize the chance for freedom. (Is the end of *Lear* heavier?—lighter, surely; a relief by comparison.) And, with all that, the sense that to win even so much, God had to rig the match, hook Samson against his will by brutal grace and draw him cruelly in through the monstrous deeps of his past.

Yet Milton, in his preface, claimed catharsis for his ending and laid over Aristotle's definition his own hope and vision—

> Tragedy, as it was anciently compos'd, hath been ever held the gravest, moralest, and most profitable of all other Poems: therefore said by *Aristotle* to be of power by raising pity and fear, or terror, to purge the mind of those and such like passions, that is to temper and reduce them to just measure with a kind of delight, stirr'd up by reading or seeing those passions well imitated.

Still, a purge, though it may palliate, cannot erase or cancel. God's name is I AM; tragic man's, I HAVE BEEN. In his *Form and Meaning in Drama*, H. D. F. Kitto has offered an expansion and correction of Aristotle which coincides wholly with the burden of *Samson*. He devotes most of his argument to a distinction between the tragedy of character (which was Aristotle's Macedonian misapprehension of Athenian art) and what Kitto calls "religious drama" and is able at last to make this summary—

> In fact, what this religious drama gives us is rather Awe and Understanding. Its true Catharsis arises from this, that when we have seen terrible things happening in the play, we understand, as we cannot always do in life, *why* they have happened; or, if not so much as that, at least we see that they have not happened by chance, without any significance.

Awe and understanding—they seem unarguable as the products, the effects, of *Samson*, both the play and the man. And the effects are exerted over two distinct audiences—the Chorus and us. For one of the supreme achievements of Milton was at last to have made a perfect object (the last previous approach had been *Lycidas*, thirty-odd years before), one requiring no external audience, fit *or* few—the audience exists in the play itself: the Chorus. No other tragedy in the Greek form—with the possible exceptions of the *Suppliants* and *Prometheus* of Aeschylus and the *Bacchae* of Euripides—contains a Chorus so involved in the action, with so much at stake in the fate of the hero, so nearly the "hero" itself. Not only does the Chorus in *Samson* speak a fourth of the lines—27%—but its urgent role is implied in the title. *Agonistes* is a noun descriptive of an athlete contending in public games (an *agon* being a contest)—freely, but accurately, a wrestler.

Samson Wrestling. Both history and poetry are filled with secret wrestlings—the grandest of all is the oldest, *Genesis* 32—and Samson's bout might well have been secret, he and Jehovah in a cell alone. That loneliness is clearly implied in *Judges.* But in Milton's vision, he wrestles before an audience—and like all athletes, partly because of, partly for, the audience (there are always private motives and issues). If Samson is Milton's subject, the Chorus is his object—God's object. The Chorus and us; for the play strives to serve us as Samson serves his people, to show us how enormously and darkly but indubitably, unanswerably, God "made our Laws to bind us, not himself." That we can sit—a second audience, much like the first—and also watch the contest and deduce again its rules (announced at Creation) is one of the privileges and dangers of having survived Milton. That we—nations of men—have not heard and answered his play, the delivery of his promise at age thirty-three to write a poem "doctrinal and exemplary to a nation," is the heaviest stone on the body of Samson, only the latest of centuries of proof that a part of his final victory was ridiculous, because partly useless. Old Manoa hoped God would not leave Samson "Useless, and thence ridiculous." God, and man, partly did.

1957, 1971

FOUR ABRAHAMS, FOUR ISAACS BY REMBRANDT

(NOTES BEFORE A NOVEL)

THE TEXT - GENESIS 22

GOD TESTED ABRAHAM. He said to him "Abraham!"

Abraham said "Sir."

God said "Take Isaac the son you love and go to Moriah. There burn him to me on the hill I will show you."

The next dawn Abraham saddled his ass, took two of his slaves and his son Isaac and, chopping wood for the fire, set off toward the place God was showing.

Three days out Abraham saw the place still far ahead. He said to his slaves "Wait here with the ass. I and the boy will go up and worship and then come back."

Then Abraham took the wood and loaded it on Isaac. The flint and the cleaver he carried himself in his own hands. The two of them climbed on together.

At last Isaac spoke. "Father."

"Here, Son."

Isaac said "You have wood and flint but no sheep."

Abraham said "Son, God will furnish the sheep."

The two of them climbed on together and came to the place God was showing Abraham. Abraham built an altar there. He stacked the wood. He bound his son Isaac. He laid him on the altar on the firewood. He reached for the cleaver to kill his son.

But an angel of God spoke from heaven. "Abraham! Abraham!"

"Here," he said.

The angel said "Do not touch the boy. Now I know you fear God since you did not grudge me the son you love."

Abraham looked up and saw a ram, horns caught in briars. He went and took the ram and burned it instead of his son to God. Then Abraham called the place *Yahweh Yireh*, God provides.*

---

* Translation by Reynolds Price.

1. ABRAHAM AND ISAAC

AN ETCHING. CIRCA 1638

If the boy is five, the man is a hundred and five. He looks eighty.
The boy's name *Isaac* signifies *Laughter*. His mother Sarah laughed when
she overheard God tell her husband, over lunch by the terebinths of
Mamre, that she—old she, barren all her life and now bone-dry—would
conceive a son in pleasure and bear him safely. Laughed in derision but
bore the son and—seeing him, knowing the joke was on her—had the
grace to say "God has brought me laughter" and name the boy that. The
man's name *Abraham* signifies *The Father is Exalted.*

This morning—mid-morning by the westward shadows—they both
think they're doing that. Exalting the father—the man exalting God by
living his life, the boy his father by trusting him with laughter as he lolls
on his lap, the pit of his small arm above his father's sex. The man smiles
slightly. Exalting, laughing, trusting, waiting. They both think they're
waiting.

The man waits in total ease, in winter velvets, in stifling sun. It
cannot touch him. He is not on guard, not cocked for ambush. No visible
slaves and he's not even armed. He thinks he is waiting for his future—
generations thick as stars (nations, kings) to swarm onward through this
boy's trimmed sex toward endless time, a blessing to the earth, all sons
of Abraham, exalting the father. It has all been promised, sealed by
Abraham with a sacrificial heifer, she-goat, ram, dove, pigeon; and cir-
cumcision of himself and all his men. Sealed by God with the tardy gift
of this boy, growing Laughter.

The boy in his fancy dress—almost a jester's: cut sleeves, belled
tassels—is oblivious as all boys are to heat. He already knows the news
(every camp slave knows it; wears it as livery). He does not know precisely
that the very seeds are waiting in the dry tight buds of his fork, only that
he waits to become the promised funnel who will pour the future. He
has heard of no conditions or reservations—none have been expressed,
no fine print in the contract—so he laughs toward the east and the sun,
holds his apple.

And so the old man has brought an artist to etch them, to honor
their calm waiting, preserve it for their sons. And both have taken this
natural pose outdoors at the southwest corner of the house on a bench
near flowers. The pose is the essence of their patient assurance. *History
by the tail, an apple in the hand—and a joke, at that.* The man and the
artist both think—no cause to doubt—that the man's right hand rings the
boy's throat in love, to turn him toward the image growing on the plate.

The light of day doubts. Negeb sun, pounding yards of Dutch velvet, has laid behind the man a shadow like stain, with a mindless blind face. It cannot offer warning—would alter its message if they turned to see. It has come from God and knows He is stoking up to speak again.

He has changed His mind—His awful prerogative—thinks the boy a bad idea, too successful a rival, a giggling vessel for a giggling eternity. He thinks He will say "Burn the boy to Me"—enough of she-goats, pigeons—then have the old fool to Himself again for another few years of lunches by the terebinths, mutton and dates. Then cancel history, stop laughter. Silence.

The high flowers also know what waits, but also don't warn. Their forward lean is for better hearing—they strain to catch the news, early waves of the silent world for which they've yearned. A few vipers, scorpions. The news is launched.

At the edge of the picture, edge of day, He is speaking—"Abraham." The sound rushes toward them, arrives.

2. ABRAHAM AND ISAAC ON MORIAH

AN ETCHING. 1645

If the boy is eleven, the man is a hundred and eleven. He looks ninety—bent shoulders, swollen fingers and though (by the shadows) it is clearly mid-morning and (by the foliage) summer, his right hand is drawing a shawl tighter round him. He is cold though his clothes are the same as before. Only three changes—a turban not a cap, a neck chain of authority, a short sword on his right. The boy wears his childhood jester's dress—or a new larger copy—cut sleeves, bottom tassels (though the bells are gone) and soft boots that can't have been right for the trip. Whoever dressed him didn't know his destination.

He is strong. He holds the wood he's borne up the mountain and he does not pant. He has watched his father set the firepot down and turn and has asked the question that has grown these three days—"Father, you have wood and flint but no sheep." Not a question, a statement, final inventory that reveals him a victim—to himself, last to know. Eleven years old. Not old enough even to enter the Temple (when there'll be a Temple, eight hundred years hence on this same rock). The tight dry balls still high in his loins, a year from working. The seed not only not waiting but not there.

The man answers now—"Son, God will furnish the sheep"—pointing skyward, home of trouble. (Or is trouble condensing in the dark behind

1. "Abraham Caressing Isaac," an etching by Rembrandt,
circa 1638
(*Courtesy of The Pierpont Morgan Library*)

2. "Abraham and Isaac on Moriah," an etching
by Rembrandt, 1645
(*Courtesy of The Pierpont Morgan Library*)

3. "The Rescue of Isaac," an oil by Rembrandt, 1635
(*Courtesy of The State Hermitage Museum*)

4. "The Sacrifice of Isaac," an etching by Rembrandt, 1655
(*Courtesy of The Pierpont Morgan Library*)

the boy, a complicated shadow made by nothing in sight, not cast by sun? God in a smoke, watching?) The gesture up is the only apology the old man can make. Neither of them looks to the handy altar—stone at the left, garlanded with weeds, as ready as all natural objects to witness, assist if needed in a death.

The boy knows however. His eyes have clouded, crouched backward darkly. *The sheep is me.* He had finally hoped that it might be a slave, till they left the slaves.

The man knows the boy knows, thinks he'll surrender. He has not even posted slaves as guards.

The boy is going to run. About-face and run. The way is just behind him, a quick trail down. He will, and will escape. He is seeing, this instant, that his father offers it—his only chance—that his father is too old to hold even him; that his father has worn too many clothes; that his own jester's dress is full and light, designed for speed; that the slaves, if they see him at all, will not care.

The old man would see it if he'd pipe-down and look—the boy's face dark as the growing shape behind him. If he'd ever done more in his life than listen—inner voices, upper voices, shunting whole shoals of kin round the Middle East like herring.

In a moment though he'll see. Or feel. The boy will have thrown the sticks against his old thin ankles and be halfway down Moriah. He will see, feel, know—that one victim's gone and will not be caught. Not by him, his slaves, his God. That this boy, lost, will die in the desert, food for kites. But that he—old man—must swear two slaves to silence, then shuffle home, dodder out a tale for Sarah and the whole grieving camp; must mumble it the rest of his time, day and night, to any idle passer, while he dreads the arrival of the vision in his head—a saved savage Isaac: grown, able, armed, strengthened by another God and bent on the death of his ancient father. His heart's blood, drained by night into sand, Sarah sleeping beside him oblivious, untouched, re-awarded motherhood in morning light.

But Isaac will be bones—the son he loved, Laughter.

3. THE RESCUE OF ISAAC

AN OIL. 1635

The boy is fifteen, the man a hundred and fifteen. He looks a fairly hearty eighty-five. And is fairly sensibly dressed for the scene. The boy has agreed to strip to his drawers, has agreed that his hands be tied behind him, and freely reclines on a bed made of sticks and his folded clothes. He spreads trusting knees on loins that function quite adequately now, though only for himself a year or so yet. A long hippy high-naveled boy who knows two things—that the man's palm is hot; that his own narrow chest is broadened, flattered, by the brown gold light of late afternoon. He writhes up to catch it, pour it round on his throat, tits, belly.

The two have been waiting.

For what?

The sticks for the pyre know the game is rigged. They've been carefully fire-proofed by offstage hands. Even the landscape northward is green and expects gentle rain to lay the dust for their smooth trip home; expects smiling passengers, loose with relief, who'll pause for wayside snacks from arbors, drinks from springs.

The man and the boy had performed their scene and were awaiting an entrance—angel rescue. The boy had drawn four breaths through those fingers wet with nerves and had thought "My face is covered for the picture." His brief unpleasantness, the man's arthritic lurch, are responses to nothing more dangerous than bad timing. The old man had churned to the climax prematurely. No thunderclap of rescue. So he (Frank Morgan? Ethel Barrymore?) had thought "What now? Hone the knife again?" (a lovely knife that will not cut butter; a set in fact—note the dagger still sheathed) and was sawing the air, his old ticker pounding, when the winged youth fell in through the backdrop—"Halt!"

Saving, stunning, both cast and audience—of whom, the painter wears the biggest grin, having most to gain. Guilders.

4. THE SACRIFICE OF ISAAC

AN ETCHING. 1655

The boy is seventeen, the man a hundred and seventeen. He looks a strong ninety. Both are in earnest. The man has removed his turban and coat, thrown them down on the ledge at his right (at the end will he stand and assume them slowly or, howling, abandon them; flee in his smock?). The boy, having watched the man disrobe and roll back sleeves on arms appallingly strong for his age (wrists like thick cocks), has taken the scent of the day at last. Three days' silent mystery ended this morning—morning light—ended by sight of the old man's arms. More of his father's body than he's ever seen, and now will see no more. He has not wasted breath asking after a sheep but has silently stripped to his plain loose drawers, laid his robe on the man's right knee as an apron, then knelt on the man's gapped loins, above the man's sheathed knife so oddly there (what is in the man's belt, at the boy's mouthlevel?—a second knife?). The loins he was promised to perpetuate—and now is able, fuller of life than he'll ever be again—but won't.

He is choosing this. The boy is choosing to die—silent, uninformed, not sentenced even. He is trying still to think of a reason, not for his father's will but his own. *Why do I let him?*—but he cannot think. Old enough to pass on his father's seed, to found whole nations, he is too young to know an answer to his question.

His picture knows, his chin, neck, arms—*I want to die at my father's hands.* Otherwise, lean as he is—runner's calves, runner's ankles and feet—he could have drawn the offered knife, killed the madman, killed the slaves eavesdropping on the next ledge down (set there as guards), killed the ass, killed the two men strolling in middle distance. Or killed the man, vaulted the overdressed slaves and sought rescue from the two men strolling who stand a fair chance of being angels at least, if not God and an angel, and will promptly congratulate, award him his lineage, full birthrights, perquisites. Or maybe kill him instantly where he stands, panting, pleading (shade trees just beyond them). Kill him with a look as He killed the boy's Cousin Lot's wife for less.

The boy is choosing this—against his will, he still thinks.

The old man was not sure until this moment. The command, four days ago, had stove him in; the three days' silent trip had seemed total agony, each step toward scalding duty. And each movement till now. The ritual placing of slaughter tools—firepot, bloodbasin, triangle of sticks (are the tongues on the lower left fire or weeds?). Disrobing, sitting, arranging the sheath, witnessing the boy's quick peel to white flesh. He had thought this would be the moment he'd feel—that sight of the boy's flesh, *his,* made by him, would still his arm, freeze it, strengthen him to set his own face against God, say No and die. Or survive and retrace the steps of forty-two years back to Haran, assume his old worship of the frozen moon goddess in his own father's tracks. The promise refused.

But he bore the sight, bore the feel of the boy when the boy spread his robe as a kindness on his lap and knelt dumbly forward on the withering seed. Bore the brush of the boy's dry lashes on his palm as he reached out to blind him. Then felt himself locked into will, not refusal; knew the boy was lost. Thought as he drew the razor knife in silence, "His will not mine," meaning God's. Promise canceled. He looked only down, could watch the ready boy. No sound but the wheezing slaves below, the ass's munch. Hum of the boy's blood in loins, throat. He moved the knife forward, knew at last—*My will, mine.*

Then slashes of hard light, rush of wings, calm hands on his arms, a face pressed toward him, "Abraham! Do not touch the boy." More slashes of light—typical harsh mercy.

Another angel, no flaming minister, young himself, the face of a farmer (and a farmer's foot, dark, beneath the armed hand), concerned, gentle, restraining him gently.

Useless. Too gently. The strong two want this.

The man is going to kill the boy.

1972

FOR ERNEST HEMINGWAY

Iᴀ I ʜᴀᴅ ʙᴇᴇɴ conscious of caring enough, as late as the spring of 1970, to check the state of my own feelings about the work of Hemingway (nine years after his death and at least five since I'd read more of him than an occasional story for teaching purposes), I'd probably have come up with a reading close to the postmortem consensus—that once one has abandoned illusions of his being a novelist and has set aside, as thoroughly as any spectator can, the decades of increasingly public descent into artistic senility (dosing those memories with the sad and sterile revelations of Carlos Baker's biography), then one can honor him as "a minor romantic poet"* who wrote a lovely early novel, *The Sun Also Rises*, and a handful of early stories of the north woods, the first war, postwar Americans in Europe which are likely to remain readable and, despite their truculent preciosity, leanly but steadily rewarding. But I don't remember caring enough to come up with even that grudging an estimate.

Why?—partly a participation in the understandable, if unlikable, international sigh of relief at the flattening of one more Sitting Bull, especially one who had made strenuous attempts to publicize his own worst nature; partly an attenuation of my lines to the work itself; partly a response to the discovery that, in my first three years of teaching, A *Farewell to Arms* had dissolved with alarming ease, under the corrosive of prolonged scrutiny, into its soft components (narcissism and blindness) when a superficially softer looking book like *The Great Gatsby* proved diamond; but mostly the two common responses to any family death: forgetfulness and ingratitude.

Then two reminding signals. In the summer of '70, I visited Key West and wandered with a friend one morning down Whitehead to the Hemingway house, tall, square and iron-galleried with high airy rooms on ample grounds thick with tropic green, still privately owned (though not by his heirs) and casually open, once you've paid your dollar, for the

* Patrick Cruttwell, "Fiction Chronicle," *The Hudson Review*, XXIV (Spring 1971), p. 180.

sort of slow unattended poking-around all but universally forbidden in other American Shrines. His bed, his tile bath, his war souvenirs (all distinctly small-town Southern, human-sized; middle-class careless well-to-do—the surroundings of, say, a taciturn literate doctor and his tanned leggy wife just gone for two weeks with their kin in Charleston or to Asheville, cool and golfy; and you inexplicably permitted to hang spectral in their momentarily cast shell). But more—the large room over the yard-house in which Hemingway wrote a good part of his work between 1931 and 1939 (six books) at a small round table, dark brown and unsteady; the small swimming pool beneath, prowled by the dozens of deformed multi-toed cats descended from a Hemingway pair of the thirties. Green shade, hustling surly old Key West silent behind walls, a rising scent of sadness—that Eden survived, not destroyed at all but here and reachable, though not by its intended inhabitants who are barred by the simple choices of their lives and, now, by death (Hemingway lost the house in 1939 at his second divorce). The rising sense that I am surrounded, accompanied by more than my friend—

> *I am moved by fancies that are curled*
> *Around these images, and cling:*
> *The notion of some infinitely gentle*
> *Infinitely suffering thing.*

The center of my strong and unexpected response began to clarify when I discovered, at home, that I had recalled Eliot's first adjective as *delicate*—"some infinitely delicate / Infinitely suffering thing." What thing?

In October, the second signal. *Islands in the Stream* was published and received, with one or two enthusiastic notices, a few sane ones (Irving Howe, John Aldridge) and a number of tantrums of the beat-it-to-death, scatter-the-ashes sort. In fact, the kinds of notices calculated to rush serious readers to a bookstore (such response being a fairly sure sign that a book is alive and scary, capable of harm); and no doubt I'd have read the book eventually, but a combination of my fresh memories of Key West and a natural surge of sympathy after such a press sent me out to buy it, a ten-dollar vote of—what? *Thanks*, I suddenly knew, to Hemingway.

For what? For being a strong force in both my own early awareness of a need to write and my early sense of how to write. Maybe the strongest. A fact I'd handily forgot but was firmly returned to now, by *Islands in the Stream*.

A long novel—466 pages—it threatens for nearly half its length to be his best. And the first of its three parts—"Bimini," two hundred pages—is his finest sustained fiction, itself an independent novella. Finest, I think, for a number of reasons that will be self-evident to anyone who can bury his conditioned responses to the Hemingway of post-1940, but chiefly because in it Hemingway deals for the first time substantially, masterfully and to crushing effect with the only one of the four possible human relations which he had previously avoided—parental devotion, filial return. (The other three relations—with God, with the earth, with a female or male lover or friend—he had worked from the start, failing almost always with the first, puzzlingly often with the third, succeeding as richly as anyone with the second.)

It would violate the apparent loosehandedness of those two hundred pages to pick in them for exhibits. Hemingway, unlike Faulkner, is always badly served by spot-quotation, as anyone will know who turns from critical discussions of him (with their repertoire of a dozen Great Paragraphs) back to the works themselves. Faulkner, so often short-winded, can be flattered by brief citation, shown at the stunning moment of triumph. But Hemingway's power, despite his continued fame for "style," is always built upon *breath*, long breath, even in the shortest piece—upon a sustained legato of quiet pleading which acts on a willing reader in almost exactly the same way as the opening phrase of Handel's *Care selve* or *Ombra mai fù*. What the words are ostensibly saying in both Hemingway and Handel is less true, less complete, than the slow arc of their total movement throughout their length. Therefore any excerpt is likely to emphasize momentary weakness—artificiality of pose, frailty of emotion—which may well dissolve in the context of their intended whole. The words of *Ombra mai fù* translate literally as "Never was the shade of my dear and lovable vegetable so soothing"; and any three lines from, say, the beautifully built trout-fishing pages of *The Sun Also Rises* are likely to read as equally simple-minded, dangerously vapid—

> He was a good trout, and I banged his head against the timber so that he quivered out straight, and then slipped him into my bag.

So may this from part I of *Islands in the Stream*—

> The boys slept on cots on the screened porch and it is much less lonely sleeping when you can hear children breathing when you wake in the night.

But in the last novel, the love among Thomas Hudson, a good marine painter, and his three sons is created—compelled in the reader—by a slow lateral and spiral movement of episodes (lateral and spiral because no episode reaches a clear climax or peaks the others in revelation). All the episodes are built not on "style" or charged moments, though there are lovely moments, or on the ground-bass hum of a cerebral dynamo like Conrad's or Mann's but on simple *threat*—potentially serious physical or psychic damage avoided: the middle son's encounter with a shark while spearfishing, the same boy's six-hour battle to bloody near-collapse with a giant marlin who escapes at the last moment (the only passage outside *The Old Man and the Sea* where I'm seduced into brief comprehension of his love of hunting), the boys' joint participation in a funny but sinister practical joke at a local bar (they convincingly pretend to be juvenile alcoholics, to the alarm of tourists). Threats which delay their action for the short interim of the visit with their father but prove at the end of the section to have been dire warnings or prophecies (warnings imply a chance of escape)—the two younger boys are killed with their mother in a car wreck, shortly after their return to France. Only when we—and Thomas Hudson—are possessed of that news can the helix of episodes deliver, decode, its appalling message, to us and to him. The lovely-seeming lazy days were white with the effort to speak their knowledge. *Avoid dependence, contingency.* The rest of the novel (a little more than half) tries to face those injunctions (restated in further calamities) and seems to me to fail, for reasons I'll guess at later; but the first part stands, firm and independent, simultaneously a populated accurate picture and an elaborate unanswerable statement about that picture. Or scenes with music.

For in that first two hundred pages, the junction of love and threat, encountered for the first time in Hemingway within a family of blood-kin, exact from him a prose which, despite my claims of its unexcerptibility, is as patient and attentive to the forms of life which pass before it (shark, marlin, men) and as richly elliptical as any he wrote, requiring our rendezvous with him in the job—and all that as late as the early 1950s, just after the debacle of *Across the River and Into the Trees*. Take these lines of the son David after his ordeal with the marlin—

> "Thank you very much, Mr. Davis, for what you said when I first lost him," David said with his eyes still shut.
> Thomas Hudson never knew what it was that Roger had said to him.

Or this between Hudson and young Tom, his eldest—

> "Can you remember Christmas there?"
> "No. Just you and snow and our dog Schnautz and my nurse. She was beautiful. And I remember mother on skis and how beautiful she was. I can remember seeing you and mother coming down skiing through an orchard. I don't know where it was. But I can remember the Jardin du Luxembourg well. I can remember afternoons with the boats on the lake by the fountain in the big garden with trees."

(That last sentence, incidentally, reestablishes Hemingway's mastery of one of the most treacherous but potentially revealing components of narrative—the preposition, a genuine cadenza of prepositions set naturally in the mouth of a boy, not for exhibit but as a function of a vision based as profoundly as Cézanne's on the *stance* of objects in relation to one another: a child, late light, boats on water near shore, flowers, shade.)

Such prose, recognizable yet renewed within the old forms by the fertility of its new impetus—family love—is only the first indication, coming as late as it does, of how terribly Hemingway maimed himself as an artist by generally banishing such passionate tenderness and emotional reciprocity from the previous thirty years of his work (it is clear enough from A *Moveable Feast*, the Baker biography, and private anecdotes from some of his more credible friends that such responses and returns were an important component of his daily life). The remaining 260 pages suggest—in their attempt to chart Hudson's strategies for dealing with external and internal calamity, his final almost glad acceptance of solitude and bareness—an even more melancholy possibility: that the years of avoiding permanent emotional relations in his work left him at the end unable to define his profoundest subject, prevented his even seeing that after the initial energy of his north-woods-and-war youth had spent itself (by 1933), he began to fail as artist and man not because of exhaustion of limited resource but because he could not or would not proceed from that first worked vein on into a richer, maybe endless vein, darker, heavier, more inaccessible but of proportionately greater value to him and his readers; a vein that might have fueled him through a long yielding life with his truest subject (because his truest need).

Wasn't his lifelong subject *saintliness*? Wasn't it generally as secret from him (a lapsing but never quite lost Christian) as from his readers? And doesn't that refusal, or inability, to identify and then attempt understanding of his central concern constitute the forced end of his work —and our failure as his readers, collusive in blindness? Hasn't the enormous and repetitive critical literature devoted to dissecting his obsession with codes and rituals, which may permit brief happiness in a meaningless world, discovered only a small (and unrealistic, intellectually jejune) portion of his long search? But doesn't he discover at last—and tell us in *Islands in the Stream*—that his search was not for survival and the techniques of survival but for goodness, thus victory?

What kind of goodness? Granted that a depressing amount of the work till 1940 (till *For Whom the Bell Tolls*) is so obsessed with codes of behavior as to come perilously close to comprising another of those deadest of all ducks—etiquettes: Castiglione, Elyot, Post (and anyone reared in middle-class America in the past forty years has known at least one youth, generally aging, who was using Hemingway thus—a use which his own public person and need for disciples persistently encouraged). Yet beneath the thirty years of posturing, his serious readers detected, and honored, great pain and the groping for unspecific, often brutal anodynes—pain whose precise nature and origin he did not begin to face until the last pages of *For Whom the Bell Tolls* and which, though he can diagnose in *Islands in the Stream*, he could not adequately dramatize: the polar agonies of love, need, contingency and of solitude, hate, freedom.

What seems to me strange and sad now is that few of his admirers and none of his abusers appear to have sighted what surfaces so often in his last three novels and in *A Moveable Feast*—the signs that the old quest for manly skills (of necessity, temporary skills) became a quest for virtue. The quest for skills was clearly related to *danger*—danger of damage to the self by Nada, Chance, or Frederic Henry's "They": "They threw you in and told you the rules and the first time they caught you off base they killed you." But the quest of Col. Cantwell in *Across the River* (which metamorphoses from obsession with narcotic rituals for living well to the study of how to die), the unconscious quest of Santiago in *The Old Man and the Sea* (too heavily and obscurely underscored by crucifixion imagery), the clear fact that the subject of *A Moveable Feast* is Hemingway's own early failure as a man (husband, father, friend), and the fully altered quest of Thomas Hudson in *Islands in the Stream* (from good father and comrade in life to good solitary animal in death)—all are related not so much to danger as to mystery. No longer the easy late-Victorian "They" or the sophomore's Nada (both no more adequate responses to human experience than the tub-thumping of Henley's "Invictus") but something that might approximately be described as God, Order, the Source of Vaguely Discernible Law. The attempt not so much to "understand" apparent Order and Law as to detect its outlines (as by Braille in darkness), to strain to hear and obey some of its demands.

What demands did he hear?—most clearly, I think, the demand to survive the end of pleasure (and to end bad, useless pleasures). That is obviously a demand most often heard by the aged or middle-aged, droning through the deaths of friends, lovers, family, their own fading faculties. But Hemingway's characters from the first have heard it, and early in their lives—Nick Adams faced on all sides with disintegrated hopes, Jake Barnes deprived of genitals, Frederic Henry of Catherine and their son, the Italian major of his family in "In Another Country," Marie Morgan of her Harry, and on and on. Those early characters generally face deprivation with a common answer—activity. And it is surprising how often the activity is artistic. Nick Adams becomes a writer after the war (the author of his own stories); Jake Barnes is a journalist with ambitions (and, not at all incidentally, a good Catholic); Frederic Henry, without love, becomes the man who dictates to us A *Farewell to Arms*; Robert Jordan hopes to return, once the Spanish Civil War is over, to his university teaching in Missoula, Montana and to write a good book. But, whatever its nature, activity remains their aim and their only hope of survival intact—activity as waiting tactic (waiting for the end, total death), as gyrostabilizer, narcotic. In the last novels, however—most explicitly in *Islands in the Stream*— deprivation is met by *duty*, what the last heroes see as the performance of duty (there are earlier heroes with notions of duty—Nick, Jake—but their duty is more nearly chivalry, a selfconsciously graceful *noblesse oblige*).

The duty is not to survive or to grace the lives of their waiting-companions but to do their work—lonely fishing, lonely soldiering, lonely painting and submarine-hunting. For whom? Not for family (wives, sons) or lovers (there are none; Cantwell knows his teenage contessa is a moment's dream). Well, for one's human witnesses then. Why? Cantwell goes on apparently, and a little incredibly, because any form of stop would diminish the vitality of his men, his friend the headwaiter, his girl—their grip upon the rims of their own abysses. Santiago endures his ordeal largely for the boy Manolin, that he not be ashamed of his aging friend and withdraw love and care. Thomas Hudson asks himself in a crucial passage in part III (when he has, disastrously for his soul, stopped painting after the deaths of his three sons and gone to chasing Nazi subs off Cuba)—

> Well, it keeps your mind off things. What things? There aren't any things any more. Oh yes, there are. There is this ship and the people on her and the sea and the bastards you are hunting. Afterwards you will see your animals and go into town and get drunk as you can and your ashes dragged and then get ready to go out and do it again.

Hudson deals a few lines later with the fact that his present work is literally murder, that he does it "Because we are all murderers"; and he never really faces up to the tragedy of having permitted family sorrow to derail his true work—his rudder, his *use* to God and men as maker of ordered reflection—but those few lines, which out of context sound like a dozen Stoic monologues in the earlier work, actually bring Hudson nearer than any other Hemingway hero toward an explicit statement of that yearning for goodness which I suspect in all the work, from the very start—the generally suppressed intimation that *happiness* for all the young sufferers, or at least *rest*, would lie at the pole opposite their present position, the pole of pure solitude, detachment from the love of other created beings (in the words of John of the Cross), and only then in work for the two remaining witnesses: one's self and the inhuman universe. "There is this ship and the people on her and the sea and the bastards you are hunting"—brothers, the Mother, enemies: all the categories of created things. Hudson, and Hemingway, halt one step short of defining the traditional goal of virtue—the heart of God. And two pages before the end, when Hudson has taken fatal wounds from a wrecked subcrew, he struggles to stay alive by thinking—

> Think about the war and when you will paint again. . . . You can paint the sea better than anyone now if you will do it and not get mixed up in other things. Hang on good now to how you truly want to do it. You must hold hard to life to do it. But life is a cheap thing beside a man's work. The only thing is that you need it. Hold it tight. Now is the true time you make your play. Make it now without hope of anything. You always coagulated well and you can make one more real play. We are not the lumpenproletariat. We are the best and we do it for free.

But again, do it for whom? Most of Hudson's prewar pictures have been described as intended for this or that person—he paints for his middle son the lost giant marlin, Caribbean waterspouts for his bartender, a portrait of his loved-and-lost first wife (which he later gives her). Intended then as gifts, *from* love and *for* love, like most gifts. But now, in death, the reverberations threaten to deepen—Thomas Hudson's paintings (and by intimation, the clenched dignity of Nick Adams and Jake Barnes, Robert Jordan's inconsistent but passionate hunger for justice, Cantwell's tidy death, Santiago's mad endurance—most of Hemingway's work) seem intended to enhance, even to create if necessary the love of creation in its witnesses and thereby to confirm an approach by the worker toward goodness, literal virtue, the manly performance of the will of God. *Saintliness*, I've called it (*goodness* if you'd rather, though *saintliness* suggests at least the fierce need, its desperation)—a saint being, by one definition, a life which shows God lovable.

Any God is seldom mentioned (never seriously by Hudson, though Jake Barnes is a quiet Catholic, Santiago a rainyday one—and though Hemingway himself nursed an intense if sporadic relation with the Church, from his mid-twenties on, saying in 1955, "I like to think I am [a Catholic] insofar as I can be" and in 1958 that he "believed in belief").* Isn't that the most damaging lack of all, in the life and the work?—from the beginning but most desperate toward the end, as the body and its satellites

* Carlos Baker, *Ernest Hemingway, A Life Story* (Scribner's, 1969), pp. 530, 543.

dissolved in age and the abuse of decades? I mean the simple fact that
neither Hemingway nor any of his heroes (except maybe Santiago and,
long before, the young priest from the Abruzzi who lingers in the mind,
with Count Greffi, as one of the two polar heroes of A *Farewell to Arms*)
could make the leap from an enduring love of creatures to a usable love
of a Creator, a leap which (barring prevenient grace, some personal experience of the supernal) would have been the wildest, most dangerous
act of all. Maybe, though, the *saving* one—leap into a still, or stiller,
harbor from which (with the strengths of his life's vision about him, none
canceled or denied but their natural arcs now permitted completion) he
could have made further and final works, good for him and us. That he
didn't (not necessarily *couldn't*, though of modern novelists maybe only
Tolstoy, Dostoevsky and Bernanos have given us sustained great work
from such a choice) has become the single most famous fact of his life
—its end: blind, baffled.

But he wrote a good deal, not one of the Monster Oeuvres yet much
more than one might guess who followed the news reports of his leisure;
and there remain apparently hundreds of pages of unpublished manuscript. What does it come to?—what does it tell us; do to us, for us,
against us?

I've mentioned the low present standing of his stock, among critics
and reviewers and older readers. Young people don't seem to read him.
My university students—the youngest of whom were nine when he
died—seem to have no special relations with him. What seemed to us
cool grace seems to many of them huffery-puffery. But then, as is famous,
a depressing majority of students have special relations with only the fayest
available books. (Will Hemingway prove to be the last Classic Author
upon whom a generation modeled its lives?—for *classic* read *good*.) Even
his two earliest, most enthusiastic and most careful academic critics have
lately beat sad retreat. Carlos Baker's long love visibly disintegrates as he
tallies each breath of the sixty-two years; and Philip Young nears the end
of the revised edition of his influential "trauma" study (which caused
Hemingway such pain) with this—

> Hemingway wrote two very good early novels, several very good stories
> and a few great ones . . . and an excellent if quite small book of
> reminiscence. That's all it takes. This is such stuff as immortalities
> are made on.

The hope is that the good books will survive a depression inevitable
after so many years of inflation (Eliot is presently suffering as badly;
Faulkner, after decades of neglect, has swollen and will probably assuage
until we see him again as a very deep but narrow trench, not the Great

Meteor Crater he now seems to many)—and that we may even, as Young wagers gingerly, come to see some of the repugnant late work in the light of Hemingway's own puzzling claim that in it he had gone beyond mathematics into the calculus (differential calculus is defined, for instance, as "the branch of higher mathematics that deals with the relations of differentials to the constant on which they depend"—isn't his constant clarifying now, whatever his reluctance to search it out, his failures to dramatize its demands?).

But since no reader can wait for the verdict of years, what can one feel now? What do I feel?—an American novelist, age thirty-eight (the age at which Hemingway published his eighth book, *To Have and Have Not*; his collected stories appeared a year later), whose work would appear to have slim relations, in matter or manner, with the work of Hemingway and whose life might well have had his scorn? (he was healthily inconsistent with his scorn).

I have to return to my intense responses of a year ago—to the powerful presence of a profoundly attractive and needy man still residing in the Key West house and to the reception of his final novel. I've hinted that these responses were in the nature of neglected long-due debts, payment offered too late to be of any likely use to the lender. All the same—what debts?

To go back some years short of the start—in the summer of 1961, I was twenty-eight years old and had been writing seriously for six years. I had completed a novel but had only published stories, and those in England. Still, the novel was in proof at Atheneum—*A Long and Happy Life*—and was scheduled for publication in the fall. I had taken a year's leave from teaching and was heading to England for steady writing—and to be out of reach on publication day. On my way in mid-July I stopped in New York and met my publishers. They had asked me to list the names of literary people who might be interested enough in my book to help it; and I had listed the writers who had previously been helpful. But as we speculated that July (no one on the list had then replied)—and as we brushed over the death of Hemingway ten days before—Michael Bessie startled me by saying that he had seen Hemingway in April, had given him a copy of the proofs of *A Long and Happy Life* and had (on the basis of past kindnesses Hemingway had done for young writers) half-hoped for a comment. None had come. But I boarded my ship with three feelings. One was a response to Bessie's reply to my asking "How did you feel about Hemingway when you saw him?"—"That he was a wounded animal who should be allowed to go off and die as he chose." The second was my own obvious curiosity—had Hemingway read my novel? what had he thought? was there a sentence about it, somewhere, in his hand or had he, as seemed likely, been far beyond reading and responding? The third was more than a little self-protective and was an index to the degree to which I'd suppressed my debts to Hemingway—what had possessed Bessie in thinking that Hemingway might conceivably have liked my novel, the story of a twenty-year-old North Carolina farm girl with elaborate emotional hesitations and scruples? My feelings, close on a death as they were, were so near to baffled revulsion that I can only attribute them to two sources. First, the success of Hemingway's public relations in the 40s and 50s. He had managed to displace the unassailable core of the work itself from my memory and replace it with the coarse useless icon of Self which he planted, or permitted, in dozens of issues of *Life* and *Look*, gossip-columns, *Photoplay*—an icon which the apparent sclerosis of the later work had till then, for me at least, not made human. Second, emotions of which I was unconscious—filial envy, the need of most young writers to believe in their own utter newness, the suppression of my own early bonds with Hemingway. In short, and awfully, I had come close to accepting his last verdict on himself—forgetting that he laid the death-sentence on his life, not the work.

Yet, a month later, I received a statement which Stephen Spender had written, knowing nothing of the recent distant pass with Hemingway. It said, in part that I was a "kinetic" writer of a kind that recalled certain pages of Hemingway, and Joyce. I was pleased of course, especially by Joyce's name ("The Dead" having long seemed to me about as great as narrative prose gets—certain pages of the Bible excepted); but again I was surprised by the presence of Hemingway. Spender had known my work since 1957. He was the first editor to publish a story of mine, in *Encounter*; and in his own *World Within World*, he had written briefly but with great freshness of his own acquaintance with Hemingway in Spain during the Civil War (one of the first memoirs to counter the received image of Loud Fist). So I might well have paused in my elation to think out whatever resemblance Spender saw. But I was deep in a second book—and in the heady impetus toward publication of the first—and a sober rereading of Hemingway (or a reading; I'd read by no means half his work) was low on my list of priorities.

It should have been high; for if I had attempted to trace and understand Hemingway's help in my own work, I'd have been much better equipped for dealing with (in my own head at least) a comment that greeted A *Long and Happy Life* from almost all quarters, even the most sympathetic—that it sprang from the side of Faulkner. It didn't; but in my resentment at being looped into the long and crowded cow-chain that stretched behind a writer for whom I felt admiration but no attraction, I expended a fair amount of energy in denials and in the offering of alternate masters—the Bible, Milton, Tolstoy, Eudora Welty. If I had been able to follow the lead offered by Bessie and Spender, I could have offered a still more accurate, more revealing name.

So it was ten years before my morning in the house in Key West and my admiration for *Islands in the Stream* reminded me that, for me as a high-school student in Raleigh in the early fifties and as an under-graduate at Duke, the most visible model of Novelist was Hemingway (*artist* of any sort, except maybe Picasso, with whom Hemingway shared many external attributes but whose central faculty—continuous intellec-tual imagination, a mind like a frightening infallible engine endowed with the power of growth—he lacked). For how many writers born in the twenties and thirties can Hemingway not have been a breathing Mount Rushmore?—though his presence and pressure seem to have taken a far heavier toll on the older generation, who not only read Hemingway but took him to war as well. Not only most visible but, oddly, most universally *certified*. Even our public-school teachers admired him, when they had been so clearly pained by Faulkner's Nobel—the author of *Sanctuary* and other sex-books. In fact, when I reconstruct the chronology of my intro-duction to Hemingway, I discover that I must have encountered the work first, at a distant remove, in movies of the forties—*The Short Happy Life of Francis Macomber, For Whom the Bell Tolls.* It was apparently not until the tenth or eleventh grade—age fifteen or sixteen—that I read any of him. As the first thing, I remember "Old Man at the Bridge" in a textbook. And then, for an "oral book-report" in the eleventh grade, *A Farewell to Arms*. (I remember standing on my feet before forty healthy adolescents—it was only 1949—and saying that Hemingway had shown me that illicit love could be pure and worth having. I don't remember remarking that, like water, it could also kill you—or your Juliet—but I must have acquired, subliminally at least, the welcome news that it made Frederic Henry, a would-be-architect, into a highly skilled novelist.)

It was not till my freshman year in college, however, that the effect began to show (in high school, like everyone else, I'd been a poet). My first serious pieces of prose narrative have a kind of grave faith in the eyes, the gaze of the narrator at the moving objects who are his study—a narrowed gaze, through lashes that screen eighty percent of "detail" from the language and the helpless reader, which seems now surely helped onward, if not grounded in, early Hemingway. Here, for example, is the end of the first "theme" I remember writing in freshman English, a five-hundred-word memory of the death of my aunt's dog Mick—

It was still hot for late afternoon, but I kept walking. Mick must have been getting tired; but she bounced along, doing her best to look about as pert as a race horse. My head was down, and I was thinking that I would turn around and head home as soon as I could tear that auction sale sign off the telephone pole down the road. A car passed. It sounded as if it threw a rock up under the fender. I looked up at the highway. Mick was lying there. The car did not stop. I went over and picked her up. I carried her to the shoulder of the road and laid her down in the dry, gray dust. She was hardly bleeding, but her side was split open like a ripe grape, and the skin underneath was as white and waxy as soap. I was really sorry that it had happened to Mick. I really was. I sat down in the dust, and Mick was in front of me. I just sat there for a long time thinking, and then I got up and went home. It was almost supper time.

The fact that I'd read *The Catcher in the Rye* a couple of months earlier may account for the *about* in the second sentence and the *I really was*, though they are normal in the context; but it would be hard to maintain now, in the face of the elaborate syntax required by my later work, that this early sketch wasn't actually a piece of ventriloquism—the lips of my memory worked by Hemingway, or by my notion of Hemingway. This was remarked on, and mildly lamented, by my instructor, an otherwise helpful man who would probably have been better advised to wonder "Why is this boy, visibly so polar to Hemingway or Hemingway's apparent heroes, nonetheless needful of lessons from him, and lessons in vision not behavior?" (strangely, the man shot himself three years later). Maybe it's as well that he didn't. I suspect now that I was responding, at the butt-end of an adolescence perceived as monstrously lonely and rejected, to the siren song in the little Hemingway I'd read and that I heard it this way—"If you can tell what you know about pain and loss (physical and spiritual damage, incomprehension, bad love) and tell it in language so magically bare in its bones, so lean and irresistible in its threnody as to be instantly audible to any passerby, then by your clarity and skill, the depth and validity of your own precarious experience, you will compel large amounts of good love from those same passers, who'll restore your losses or repair them." And if I'd been conscious of the degree of self-pity involved in that first exchange, I might have been revolted and turned from narrative (as I'd turned, two years before, from drawing and painting). But I was only warned that I "sounded like Hemingway"; and since I knew perfectly well that everyone in America sounded like Hemingway, that was no obstacle. So I had written several sketches and my first real story, "Michael Egerton"—all under the tutelage of Hemingway's voice and stance—before I had read more than one or two of his stories and *A Farewell to Arms*. An "influence" can be exerted by the blinking of an eye, the literal movement of a hand from here to there, five words spoken in a memorable voice; and the almost universal sterility of academic-journalistic influence-hunting has followed from a refusal to go beyond merely symptomatic surface likenesses toward causes and the necessary question "Why was this writer hungry for this; what lack or taste was nourished by this?"

I did go on. One of the exciting nights of my life was spent in early September, 1952, reading *The Old Man and the Sea* in *Life* magazine, straight through by a naked light bulb, in the bed in which I was born (reread now, after years of accepting second-hand opinions on its weakness, it again seems fresh and dangerous, and though a little rigid, one of the great long stories). I remember reading, admiring, and—better—feeling affection for *The Sun Also Rises* during a course at Harvard in the summer of 1954; and I still have my old Modern Library edition of the first forty-nine stories, with neat stern notes to less than half the stories in my college-senior's hand—the notes of a technician, and as knowing and disapproving as only a young technician can be, but so unnaturally attentive as to signal clearly that some sort of unspoken love was involved, exchanged in fact —the exchange I began to define above, and to which I'll return. But, oddly, that was it—after 1955, I don't recall reading any more Hemingway till 1963, *A Moveable Feast*, well after I'd written two books of my own —and then not again till 1971 when I reread all I'd covered and the two-thirds I hadn't.

Why? Not *why was I rereading?* but why had I read him in the first place, more than twenty years ago; and why had he helped so powerfully that I felt last summer—and still—this strong rush of gratitude? And why did I put him down so soon? Maybe another piece of Spender's comment will crack the door. He suggested that *A Long and Happy Life* advanced the chief discovery of Joyce and Hemingway, "which was to involve the reader, as with his blood and muscles, in the texture of the intensely observed and vividly imagistic writing." Assuming what I hope is true— that I needn't drown in self-contemplation if I think that out a little, and that I'm not pressing to death a comment made in kindness—what can Spender have meant? I remember, at the time, being especially pleased by his calling the prose "kinetic" which I took to mean concerned with and productive of movement. I don't recall telling Spender, but it had been my premise or faith before beginning *A Long and Happy Life* that by describing fully and accurately every physical gesture of three widely separated days in the lives of two people, I could convey the people— literally deliver them—to you, your room, your senses (I considered *thought* a physical gesture, which it is, though often invisible to the ordinary spectator). That faith, consciously held, guided the book through two years of writing and seems to me still the motive force of its claim on readers.

Isn't it also Hemingway's faith, in every line he wrote? Isn't it Tolstoy's, Flaubert's? Doesn't it provide the terrible force of the greatest narratives of the Bible?—*Genesis* 22, *John* 21. I'd read those as well, long before my discovery of Hemingway; and from the ninth grade, after *Anna Karenina*, I'd had my answer to the question "Who's best?" But as a tyro, I clearly took light from Hemingway. He was there, alive in Cuba, nine hundred miles from the desk in my bedroom, still writing—ergo, *writing was possible*. The texture of his work, his method, was apparently more lucid than Tolstoy's, unquestionably more human than Flaubert's (at least as I knew them in translation); and everything was briefer and thus more readily usable. But far more important—again I don't remember thinking about it—was what lay beneath that apparent lucidity. He said more than once that a good writer could omit anything from a story—knowingly, purposely—and the reader would respond to its presence with an intensity beyond mere understanding. There are striking examples—the famous one of "Big Two-Hearted River" which is utterly silent about its subject, and now *Islands in the Stream* which has a huge secret embedded in its heart, its claim against love, against life (as terrible as Tolstoy's in *The Kreutzer Sonata* or Céline's, though entirely personal and, like theirs, not dramatized). But what I discovered, detected with the sensing devices no one possesses after, say, sixteen, was both more general and more nourishingly specific—the knowledge that Hemingway had begun to write, and continued, for the reasons that were rapidly gathering behind me as my nearly terminal case of adolescence was beginning to relent: write or choke in self-loathing; write to comprehend and control fear. Loathing and fear of what? Anyone who has read my early fiction will probably know (they are not rare fears), and in the only way that might conceivably matter to anyone but me; nor is it wise-guy reductive to say that any sympathetic reader of Hemingway has possessed that knowledge of him since *In Our Time*—and that such knowledge is precisely what Hemingway intended, knowledge acquired from the work, not directly from the life. But the magnetic fields of fear in both cases—or so I felt, and feel —are located in simultaneous desperate love and dread of parents, imagined and actual abandonment by one's earliest peers, the early discovery that the certified emotions (affection, love, loyalty) are as likely to produce waste, pain and damage to the animal self as are hate, solitude, freedom—perhaps more likely.

But Hemingway's work, at least, is complete and no damage can be done him or it by one more consideration of his technical procedures and their engines, their impetus (harm to a dead writer could only be the destruction of all copies of his work). And, oddly, in all that I know of the vast body of Hemingway criticism, there is almost no close attention to the bones of language, of the illuminating sort which Proust, for instance, gave to Flaubert. This despite the fact that most of his readers have always acknowledged that he gave as passionate a care to word and rhythm as Mallarmé. The most interesting discussion of his method is in fact by a writer—Frank O'Connor in his study of the short story, *The Lonely Voice*—and though it is finally destructive in its wrongheadedness and envy, it is near enough to insight to be worth a look. O'Connor feels that Hemingway studied and understood Joyce's early method and then proceeded to set up shop with Joyce's tools—"and a handsome little business he made of it." And regardless of the justice of that (it's at least a refreshing alternate to the usual references to Gertrude Stein and Sherwood Anderson), it is in O'Connor's description of the Joyce of *Dubliners* that he casts indirect light on Hemingway—

> It is a style that originated with Walter Pater but was then modeled very closely on that of Flaubert. It is a highly pictorial style; one intended to exclude the reader from the action and instead to present him with a series of images of the events described, which he may accept or reject but cannot modify to suit his own mood or environment.

The following, however, is as far as he goes toward an attempt at understanding the motive for such procedure, in either Joyce or Hemingway—

> By the repetition of key words and key phrases . . . it slows down the whole conversational movement of prose, the casual, sinuous, evocative quality that distinguishes it from poetry and is intended to link author and reader in a common perception of the object, and replaces it by a series of verbal rituals which are intended to evoke the object as it may be supposed to be. At an extreme point it attempts to substitute the image for the reality. It is a rhetorician's dream.

And finally—

> in neither of these passages [from Joyce and Hemingway] is there what you could call a human voice speaking, nobody resembling yourself who is trying to persuade you to share in an experience of his own, and whom you can imagine yourself questioning about its nature—nothing but an old magician sitting over his crystal ball, or a hypnotist waving his hands gently before your eyes and muttering, "You are falling asleep; you are falling asleep; slowly, slowly your

eyes are beginning to close; your eyelids are growing heavy; you are falling—asleep."

Despite the fact that *I* feel strong bonds with the voice in early Hemingway at least, the core of that seems roughly true of both writers —Joyce in the cold dexterity of A *Portrait of the Artist* and Hemingway all his life, though in an entirely different way. Why true? Surely the motives are different and infinitely complex in each case (though one might suspect, especially after Ellman's biography, that Joyce's production of such a distancing method was only one more cast skin of an essentially reptilian nature). If I attempt my own description of Hemingway's procedure (a description largely coincident with what I *felt* as a student and what drew me to him as I began to write), then I can guess more legitimately at motives.

Hemingway's attempt, in all his fiction, is *not* to work magic spells on a reader, locking him into a rigid instrument of vision (in fact, into a movie) which controls not only what he sees but what he feels. The always remarked absence of qualifiers (adjectives, adverbs) is the simplest and surest sign here. Such an attempt—and one does feel and resent it often, in Flaubert and Joyce—is essentially the dream of achieving perfect empathic response, of making the reader become the story, or the story's emotional center at any given moment: Emma Bovary, Gabriel Conroy. And it is the dream not only of a few geniuses but of a large percentage of readers of fiction—the hunger for literally substitute life. Doomed of course, for the sane at least. But while Hemingway attempts as unremittingly as anyone to control his reader—to station him precisely in relation both to the visible and invisible actions of the story and to the author himself, and finally to trigger in him the desired response (again, to both story and author)—his strategy is entirely his own, and is in fact his great invention (the pure language itself being older than literature). Look at the famous opening of A *Farewell to Arms*—

> In the late summer of that year we lived in a house in a village that looked across the river and the plain to the mountains. In the bed of the river there were pebbles and boulders, dry and white in the sun, and the water was clear and swiftly moving and blue in the channels.

—As classical as Horace—in the sense of generalized, de-localized, deprived of native texture. What size house and what color, built how and of what? What village, arranged how around what brand of inhabitants, who do what to live? What river, how wide and deep? What kind of plain, growing what; and what mountains? Later—considerably later—he will tell you a little more, but very little. If you have never traveled in northern

Italy in late summer—or seen the film of the book—you'll have no certainty of knowing how the earth looks above and beneath the action, in this or any other of his works. Or, in fact, how anything or anyone else *looks*. But by the audacity of its filterings, it demands that you lean forward toward the voice which is quietly offering the story—only then, will it begin to yield, to give you what it intends. And the gift will be what you *hear*—the voices of imagined characters speaking a dialect which purports to be your own (and has now convinced two generations of its accuracy). His early strategy is always, at its most calculated, an oral strategy. If we hear it read, it seems the convincing speaking-voice of this sensibility. Only on the silent page do we discover that it is as unidiomatic, as ruthlessly intentional as any *tirade* of Racine's. For behind and beneath all the voices of actors (themselves as few in number as in Sophocles) rides the one real voice—the maker's. And what it says, early and late, is always this—"This is what I see with my clean keen equipment. Work to see it after me." What it does not say but implies is more important —"For you I have narrowed and filtered my gaze. I am screening my vision so you will not see all. Why?—because you must enact this story for yourself; cast it, dress it, set it. Notice the chances I've left for you: no noun or verb is colored by me. I require your senses." What is most important of all—and what I think is the central motive—is this, which is concealed and of which the voice itself may be unconscious: "I tell you this, in this voice, because you must share—*must* because I require your presence, your company in my vision. I beg you to certify my knowledge and experience, my goodness and worthiness. I mostly speak as *I*. What I need from you is not empathy, identity, but patient approving witness —loving. License my life. Believe me." (If that many-staged plea is heard only intermittently in Hemingway's work after 1940—broken then by stretches of "confidence"—I'd guess that the cause would be the sclerosis consequent upon his success, the success of the voice which *won* him love, worship, a *carte blanche* he lacked the power to use well. Goethe said, "Beware of what you want when young; you'll get it when old." And the memory of the famished face of the deathbound Hemingway, quilted with adoration and money, is among the saddest and most instructive memories of Americans over twenty-five; his last gift to us.)

I've suggested that a final intention of Hemingway's method is the production of belief in the reader—belief in his total being and vision. Remember that he always spoke of the heavy role of the Bible in his literary education. The role has been generally misunderstood; seen as a superficial matter of King James rhythms, the frequent use of *and*, narrative "simplicity." But look at a brief though complete story from *Genesis*
32—

In the night Jacob rose, took his two wives, the two slave girls and his eleven sons, and crossed the ford of Jabbok. When he had carried them all across, he sent his belongings. Then Jacob was alone, and some man wrestled with him there till daybreak. When he saw that he could not pin Jacob, he struck him in the pit of his thigh so that Jacob's hip unsocketed as they wrestled. Then he said "Let me go; it is daybreak."

Jacob said "I will not let go till you bless me."

The man said "What is your name?"

He said "Jacob."

The man said "You are Jacob no more but Israel—you have fought gods and men and lasted."

Jacob said "Tell me your name please."

He said "Why ask my name?" and departed.

So Jacob called the place *Penuel,* face of God, "For I have seen God's face and endured"; and the sun struck him as he passed Penuel, limping. *

—and then at Erich Auerbach's description of Old Testament narrative:

the externalization of only so much of the phenomena as is necessary for the purpose of the narrative, all else left in obscurity; the decisive points of the narrative alone are emphasized, what lies between is nonexistent; time and place are undefined and call for interpretation; thoughts and feelings remain unexpressed, are only suggested by the silence and the fragmentary speeches; the whole, permeated with the most unrelieved suspense and directed toward a single goal . . . remains mysterious and "fraught with background."†

There is, give or take an idiom, a profound likeness between the account of Jacob's struggle and any scene in Hemingway; and Auerbach might well be describing Hemingway, not the Bible. I have already implied the nature of the likeness, The specific hunger in Hemingway which was met by Biblical method. Both require our strenuous participation, in the hope of compelling our allegiance, our belief. Here are three passages chosen at random from a continuous supply—the opening of "A Very Short Story":

One hot evening in Padua they carried him up onto the roof and he could look out over the top of the town. There were chimney swifts in the sky. After a while it got dark and the searchlights came

---

* Translation by Reynolds Price.
† Erich Auerbach, *Mimesis* (Doubleday Anchor Books, 1957), p. 9.

out. The others went down and took the bottles with them. He and
Luz could hear them below on the balcony. Luz sat on the bed. She
was cool and fresh in the hot night.

a moment from Thomas Hudson's Nazi-hunt in the Cuban keys:

They called to the shack and a woman came out. She was dark as
a sea Indian and was barefooted and her long hair hung down almost
to her waist. While she talked, another woman came out. She was
dark, too, and long-haired and she carried a baby. As soon as she
finished speaking, Ara and Antonio shook hands with the two women
and came back to the dinghy. They shoved off and started the motor
and came out.

and—curiously analogous to Jacob's ordeal with "some man"—the almost
intolerably charged and delicate exchange between Frederic Henry and
his friend the young Italian priest who has visited him in hospital with a
gift of vermouth:

"You were very good to come, father. Will you drink a glass of
vermouth?"
"Thank you. You keep it. It's for you."
"No, drink a glass."
"All right. I will bring you more then."
The orderly brought the glasses and opened the bottle. He broke
off the cork and the end had to be shoved down into the bottle. I
could see the priest was disappointed but he said, "That's all right.
It's no matter."
"Here's to your health, father."
"To your better health."

Given the basic narrative strategies of the Old Testament and Hemingway,
only the tone of the motives is different—and in the third-person Old
Testament the voice is plain command; in Hemingway, a dignified pleading: *Believe!* and *Please believe.* Believe what? *The thing I know.* What
do you know? In one case, the presence of the hidden hand of God; in
the other, that his life is good and deserving of your witness, will even
help your life. Then, why believe? In one case, simply and awfully, so
that God be served; in the other, so that the voice—and the man behind
it—may proceed through his life. That is the sense in which both styles
are almost irresistibly kinetic. And the reason why they have been two of
the most successful styles in the history of literature.

Why did it fail him then?—his work, the literal words in their order
on the page. In one sense, it succeeded too brilliantly—won him millions

of readers willing to exert the energy and certify the life, some of them willing even to alter their own lives in obedience to what they, understandably though ludicrously, took to be injunctions of the work (there are certainly injunctions, though not to noise and bluster). But for nothing—or too little. In the only sense that can have mattered to him, his vision and its language failed him appallingly. It won him neither the relatively serene middle working-years of a Conrad or a Mann nor the transcendant old age of a Tolstoy, a James, Proust's precocious mastery of a silly life. Nor did it, with all its success in the world, allay even half his daily weight of fear. Immense time and energy were thrown elsewhere in flagging hope—sport, love, companions, drink, all of which took dreadful cuts of their own. Maybe it's permissible to *ask* why the words failed him; but to dabble in answers if one did not at least share a long stretch of his daily life and witness the desperate efforts in their long mysterious complexity is only a game, though a solemn game which can be played more or less responsibly and one which can no longer harm him or the work.

I've indulged already in the early pages of this with a guess, from the gathering evidence of his last four books, about his submerged subject which he found and attempted to float too late, when the search itself— or flight from the search—had dangerously depleted his senses and, worse, prevented the intellectual growth which might have compensated. But the words themselves? and the vision and needs which literally pressed words from him?—were they doomed from the start to kill him? A language fatally obsessed with defending the self and the few natural objects which the self both loves and trusts? A vision narrowed, crouched in apprehension of the world's design to maul, humiliate? Insufficiently surrendered to that design? Whatever the answers (and I'd guess that each is a mysterious Yes), it's clear that he was never capable of the calm firmfooted gaze of the godlike Tolstoy, who at twenty-six was producing from his own military experience, in a story called "The Wood-Felling," narrative so sure of its power as to be a near-lethal radiation—

> The wounded man lay at the bottom of the cart holding on to the sides with both hands. His broad healthy face had completely changed during those few moments; he seemed to have grown thinner and years older, his lips were thin and pale and pressed together with an evident strain. The hasty and dull expression of his glance was replaced by a kind of bright clear radiance, and on the bloody forehead and nose already lay the impress of death. Though the least movement caused him excruciating pain, he nevertheless asked to have a small *chérez* with money taken from his left leg.

The sight of his bare, white, healthy leg, when his jack-boot had been taken off and the purse untied, produced on me a terribly sad feeling. *

Or even of the constitutionally hectic D. H. Lawrence, who in fragments from an unfinished novel could see and speak in a language of open trust in man and nature which promises the stamina of his death—

Quickly the light was withdrawn. Down where the water was, all grew shadow. The girl came tramping back into the open space, and stood before the holly tree. She was a slim, light thing of about eighteen. Her dress was of weathered blue, her kerchief crimson. She went up to the little tree, reached up, fingering the twigs. The shadow was creeping uphill. It went over her unnoticed. She was still pulling down the twigs to see which had the thickest bunch of berries. All the clearing died and went cold. Suddenly the whistling stopped. She stood to listen. Then she snapped off the twig she had chosen and stood a moment admiring it.

A man's voice, strong and cheerful, shouted: "Bill—Bill—Bi-ill!"

The donkey lifted its head, listened, then went on eating.

"Go on!" said the girl, waving her twig of holly at it. The donkey walked stolidly two paces from her, then took no notice.

All the hillside was dark. There was a tender flush in the east. Away among the darkening blue and green over the west, a faint star appeared. There came from far off a small jangling of bells—one two three—one two three four five! The valley was all twilight, yet near at hand things seemed to stand in day.

"Bill—Bill!" came the man's voice from a distance.

"He's here!" shrilled the girl.

"Wheer?" came the man's shout, nearer, after a moment.

"Here!" shrilled the girl.

She looked at the donkey that was bundled in its cloth.

"Why don't ye go, dummy!" she said.

"Wheer is 'e?" said the man's voice, near at hand.

"Here!"

In a moment a youth strode through the bushes.

"Bill, tha chump!" he said.

The donkey walked serenely towards him. He was a big boned, limber youth of twenty. His trousers were belted very low, so that

* Leo Tolstoy, *Tales of Army Life*, translated by Louise and Aylmer Maude (Oxford, 1935), p. 66.

his loins remained flexible under the shirt. He wore a black felt hat, from under which his brown eyes gazed at the girl.

"Was it you as shouted?" he said.

"I knowed it was you," she replied, tapping her skirt with the richly berried holly sprig.*

Yet Hemingway's work—its damaged tentative voice, for all its large failures, its small ignorances and meannesses—did a great deal, for him and us. Beyond carrying him through an after all long life and conveying an extraordinary, apparently usable portion of that life's texture of pleasure and pain to millions of contemporary strangers, it has left live remains—a body of fourteen volumes which, in my guess, will winnow to eight and then stand as an achievement so far unexcelled in American letters, certainly by no one in his own century.† For what?—the intensity of their gaze, however screening, at a range of men and dangers which, with the inevitable allowances for private obsession, are as broadly and deeply representative as any but the great masters' (we don't yet possess one); for the stamina of their search, however veiled, through four decades for the demands and conditions and duties of human goodness in relation to other men, beasts and objects, and finally God; and then (strongest but most unprovable, most primitive and mysterious) for the language in which the search externalized itself, his optics and shield, weapon and gift. Gift to whom?

Me, as I've said, who have responded over twenty-five years to what I took to be an asking voice with what I now see was apprenticeship, neither exclusive nor conscious and quickly renegade but clearly the gravest homage I can offer. Useless to him but profound nonetheless. The profoundest—for I also see that I loved his voice and studied its shapes, not for its often balked and raging message but because I, balked and enraged, shared the motives at which I've guessed and, stranger, its two subjects: freedom and virtue. Polar heights, inaccessible maybe to climbers more intent on self-protection (footholds, handholds) than on the climb itself, the route and destination.

Gift also to all other living American writers as obsessed as he with defense of what the self is and what it knows, any one of whom seems to me more nearly brother to him—in need and diet, dream and fulfillment, vision and blindness—than to any other artist in our history, or anyone else's (and, oddly, our avatar of Byron, the proto-American artist). Like

* The surviving fragments are printed in Edward Nehls, ed., *D.H. Lawrence, A Composite Biography*, I (University of Michigan, 1957), pp. 184—195.

† My own list, now, would be—*The Collected Stories, The Sun Also Rises, A Farewell to Arms, Green Hills of Africa, For Whom the Bell Tolls, The Old Man and the Sea, A Moveable Feast, Islands in the Stream.*

it or not, our emblem and master whose lessons wait, patient and terrible.

Gift especially to the young. For it is almost certainly with them that his life now lies. It is easy enough to patronize Children's Classics— Omar, Mrs. Browning, Wolfe, lately Hesse—but any writer's useful survival is in heavy danger when the young abandon him entirely; it is only on them that he stands a chance of inflicting permanent damage (are Milton and Dante effectively alive? can they yet be saved in some form they'd have agreed to?—not by schools, apparently). In all Hemingway's work, until *The Old Man and the Sea* and *Islands in the Stream*, the warnings, if not the pleas, are for them; the lessons of one master, diffidently but desperately offered—*Prepare, strip, divest for life that awaits you; learn solitude and work; see how little is lovely but love that.*

—Half the lesson of the desert fathers, and given in language of the desert, bleached, leached to essence. The other half—an answer to *Why?*—is withheld until the last, and then only muttered. Surely there are young people now, readers and writers—children when he died—to whom he is speaking his dark secret language of caution and love, help and beggary, in the lean voice of an infinitely delicate, infinitely suffering thing. No shield, no help at all of course, to him or us (he never said it would be); yet more—a diamond point that drills through time and pain, a single voice which moves through pain toward rest and presses forward shyly with its greeting and offer, its crushing plea, like that of the hermit Paul when St. Antony had tracked him through beasts and desert and begged for instruction:

> Behold, thou lookest on a man that is soon to be dust. Yet because love endureth all things, tell me, I pray thee, how fares the human race: if new roofs be risen in the ancient cities, whose empire is it that now sways the world; and if any still survive, snared in the error of the demons.*

1972

---

* St. Jerome, "The Life of St. Paul the First Hermit" in Helen Waddell, ed. and trans., *The Desert Fathers* (Henry Holt, 1936), pp. 47–48.

THE BEST KIND OF MONUMENT*

 HE TWO MOST FAMOUS American novelists of the twentieth century
are in grave need of rescue. If the fictions of William Faulkner and Ernest
Hemingway were intended in part as rudders through life, as justifications
of lives endured, as prayers for comprehension, then their lives are in
greater danger now, nearly fifteen years after their deaths, than ever before.
The threats to both life and work are strong—Faulkner lies flat beneath
the midden of misconstruction and indiscriminate praise heaped on him
by tardy academic critics in eternal quest of an American World-Genius
and by Joseph Blotner's admiring but undiscerning biography; Hemingway
suffers the opposite, critical deflation and the subtly hostile biography of
Carlos Baker.

Rescue would consist of the understanding for which their work
asked, the absolution their hard lives craved, their generous offers accepted
and used. And the wave of response to their crashes has not lacked occasional straws, even rafts—Cleanth Brooks's discussion of Faulkner, Malcolm Cowley's of Hemingway, the attentions of a few younger novelists
to both—but the only real rescue-parties in sight have come from directions which neither man might have foreseen or felt he deserved: from
family, blood-kin. Two of Faulkner's brothers, John and Murry, have
published affectionate memoirs which go some way toward warming the
chill figure, impotent yet bristling, whom Blotner offers (and there is a
daughter from whom word may be hoped). Hemingway's elder sister
Marcelline and his younger brother Lester have provided valuable accounts of the young Ernest—gentle, considerate, and vulnerable—and
of their difficult parents whose own mental complexities predicted so many
of Ernest's. His first wife Hadley has cooperated with Alice Sokoloff in
an account of that marriage, and his fourth wife Mary has completed an
autobiography.

Now Gregory Hemingway, a physician and the youngest of Ernest's
three sons, has published a brief memoir; and while it stops short of giving
what it might have (a richly explicit view of Hemingway as more than

---

* *Papa: A Personal Memoir* by Gregory Hemingway (Houghton Mifflin, 1976).

father), it provides the first trustworthy testimony that the man was not
—or not only—what he sometimes seemed from the late thirties on: a
monster of self-absorption and self-deception, insanely destructive of his
own brain and body and of those around him.

The form and tone of this memoir are the best witnesses to its own
credibility. In my second reading of it, I found that some of my initial
objections—to careless prose, to moments of the old "Papa-bluster," to
the obvious absence of an editor—largely dissolved in a realization of its
form and voice: the book and its tale are an oral performance; a late-night
unearthing of childhood joy and adolescent regret toward a discovery of
manly love and pardon, all extended tentatively in a low monologue, half
for the silent confidant (us) and half for the speaker. It is the form in fact
of many of his father's most affecting pages—the solo voice which seems
to describe but ultimately pleads.

Here the voice opens with a circling statement of the worst it has to
tell—the pain of being that man and woman's child (Gregory was the
second son of Pauline Pfeiffer, who died ten years before Ernest and
cannot answer but who increasingly and maybe unjustly appears a disaster
in his life—luring him from the splendid Hadley, habituating him quickly
to the pleasures of her money and her chattering covey of friends), the
pain which a neglected but rich son inflicted on his father and mother,
the collapse into a drunken interval of elephant slaughter in Africa when
the weight of the guilts and hatreds exceeded a young man's strength. Yet
in that sad opening, the voice says the chief thing it wants us to hear—
"In his youth, my father was not a bully, a sick bore, or a professional
celebrity. . . . The man I remembered was kind, gentle, elemental in his
vastness, tormented beyond endurance, and although we always called
him papa, it was out of love, not fear."

The remaining movements (chapters) illustrate and attempt to vali-
date that claim with a procession of memories—childhood in Key West;
custody-summers in Bimini, Sun Valley, and Havana when Ernest had
moved on to Martha Gellhorn and then Mary Welch; the needless break
which kept father and son apart for the last decade of Ernest's life; the
reunion with brothers at Ernest's funeral in Idaho; Gregory's "relief when
they lowered my father's body into the ground and I realized that he was
really dead, that I couldn't disappoint him, couldn't hurt him anymore";
and his final self-canceled hope for his father: "I hope it's peaceful, finally.
But, oh God, I knew there was no peace after death. If only it were
different, because nobody ever dreamed of, or longed for, or experienced,
less peace than he."

The illustrative memories work, at one level. While a good deal that
charmed a preadolescent son is not likely to charm a reader today—the

killing of animals, the boxing and drinking, the cake-walk of women, Nazi-sub chasing in a forty-foot boat (Dr. Hemingway speaks of his own disenchantments), the episodes accumulate to convince that the man did need love and loyalty *and* compel them from sane and sensitive companions by his huge vitality of beauty, strength, and wit. Two finely described episodes demonstrate what the fiction occasionally suggests— that not only paternal duty but a sustained and serious delicacy of respect could inform Ernest's relations with a young son. In Cuba in the summer of '42, Ernest alone nursed Gregory with constant attention and nocturnal stories through a mysterious attack which resembled polio; and he later managed cooly to save the boy from three twenty-foot sharks who threatened him while spearfishing (that account is especially welcome since it was transformed into one of the important scenes of the beautiful "Bimini" section of *Islands in the Stream*).

Even Dr. Hemingway's cautious first response to the memory—"I guess almost any man would have waited for a child"—doesn't diminish its total radiance on any available chart of human values; and he knows that: "he was a reserved man, somewhat incapable of expressing his affection in the conventional way, and I hadn't realized how much he really cared until he hoisted me on his own shoulders, which were barely out of water, and swam back across that reef with most of his own body still exposed under the surface."

At a deeper level though, hard questions begin. Was the steady diet of love steadily repaid, or was it merely one of several kinds of fuel which the dynamo extorted to produce the next million volts of charm? Dr. Hemingway examines such questions in only one too-brief passage and then at a remove, in discussing his father's divorces—"He would feel himself beginning to stagnate after he had been married to one wife for a while [but]. . . . The periodic injection of high-octane creative energy left more of a hangover of contrition and remorse each time . . . it takes something out of you to look back at your wife and your children by the side of the road and see that dazed look on their faces." To have gone further would have carried Dr. Hemingway into territory he mostly avoids—his father's novels and stories. Did they ever seem to him—and do they seem to him now—sufficient transportation for the heavy tolls taken?

It's a potentially silly question—did Karl Beethoven feel amended by the *Missa Solemnis* and the Sonata, Opus 111, for his uncle's outrages? Well, Karl was a dull boy and left us no sign, beyond a suicide attempt. But Gregory Hemingway is a man of insight and proven forbearance; and he broaches the matter himself by saying that, faced with the choice of a career, "What I really wanted to be was a Hemingway hero." He then makes it plain that, at eighteen, his understanding of the Hemingway hero was the popular understanding—the mobile adventurer of grace, dignity, and stoic courage who is able to record his own true story. A boy may be excused for failing to notice other and strong kinds of heroes in the books—the young priest or old Count Greffi in *A Farewell to Arms*; the patient father of "Fathers and Sons"; even Robert Jordan of *For Whom the Bell Tolls*, whose ambition is to return from the war, teach at the University of Montana, and write a book. And certainly Dr. Hemingway acknowledges having grown into attitudes which seem close to those of the men his father admired ("I can even feel the life in a great tree now, and I wince when I see one girdled and know it must die").

But my own curiosity, as an admirer second-to-none of his father's fiction and a man now willing to trust his own witness, is to know the extent to which Ernest Hemingway's lifelong and deepening quest for a nearly hermetic but generous virtue—for sanctity even—was communicated to the companions of his life, as it clearly has been to thousands of readers who never touched the man. The question has not been faced in public by any friend or kinsman. Dr. Hemingway writes a chapter called "Lessons," but he doesn't face that head-on anywhere. Did the message often get delivered, then and there?

The question is personal and presses too hard. Read with less urgency and with an ear for the fuller story packed into pauses and skips, the *book* becomes his answer; a son's slow soliloquy of regret, love, thanks. And more—there are revealing childhood responses that couldn't have been guessed (Gregory's reaction to his parents' divorce was not dismay but delight in the realization that now he would have his previously intermittent father to himself every summer, shared only with his brothers and the next two wives, both of whom he liked); and the valuable remarks of a physician on some of the diseases which contributed to bringing his father down (especially on the role of liver damage in impotence, the fear of which seems to have haunted Ernest most).

With all its omissions and silences then, it stands as the best kind of monument, his father's best hope till now of stripping off the gorgon "Papa" mask—the impacted ravening for death and harm; all the pilotfish and suckfish who steered him from his course, his actual life—and of standing again where at first he meant to stand: quietly behind the work itself.

The work awaits him like a nearly perfect place—a temple, tall and light, calming and lifting for long days of contemplation and rest till we see what it lacks: a visible, honorable icon of God; a guess at the face behind mountains, streams, seas which commands us to live. Gregory Hemingway has made his own guess now to fill that void in his father's great place, a hard-won guess—the face is devotion, continuance, mercy; the love of kin and fellows and the earth. The place seems whole at least, rescued and safe.

1976

DODO, PHOENIX
OR TOUGH OLD COCK?

Whither the southern novel? Anyone who has lived and tried to write fiction within the bounds of the old Confederacy in the last ten years has heard that question, and been asked to answer it, only slightly less often than "Whither race?" No one imagines that the first question is more urgent than the second—though even in the deepest South there are sane men who suspect the two questions to be intimately and secretly related, perhaps symbiotic—and few serious novelists have the time or need to answer such idle, hilariously unanswerable questions as the first, knowing, like artists in any art, that *the novel* has never existed, only *novels*, and that Southern novels will proceed, if at all, not by anyone's diagram or battle-plan—there are whole careers, whole magazines devoted to making nothing else—but as they always have: by miracle. By the unpredictable, so far unmanageable but apparently not accidental births of babies who will in their teens and twenties—because of the specific weight of their experience upon certain cerebral and coronary tendencies (genetic? or even more directly God-given?)—begin to produce long works of narrative prose fiction. Any plans or diagnoses which advance beyond that bedrock, however sane and studious the planner, are no more than sibylline mutterings-amongst-the-offal (or self-justifications, screwings-up of courage or face: *whither me?* or *whence my silence?*).

So—my own answer (or a sketch for this week's answer), my own justification, quick calisthenics as I poise at the brink of a sixth book of fiction (Southern: by a Southerner; set in the South and about the South, among other places). But first a little brush-clearing to state at least an intelligent question. I've suggested that there never was a Southern novel (though there are already sober-looking guides to The Novel in North Carolina or Mississippi or Georgia). I'll go further—there was never a flood of good novels out of the South, though there was and still is a thick torrent of prose fiction, no better than most—and my question will be something like this: will strong fiction (attentive, passionately perceived, freshly and honestly built, useful beyond the Mason-Dixon) continue to trickle out of a geographical region defined as the old Confederacy, a country larger than France? If so, will it come from natives and long-term inhabitants or, indiscriminately, from writers who, in an increasingly mobile population, happen to pause there?

First answer: why wouldn't it?

—Two strong reasons maybe: (1) that the old South is used-up, worked-out, as a vein for novelists and (2) that the new South will prove unworkable, not a vein at all but a Medusa.

To consider the question of exhaustion—and for a change, from the point of view of a novelist, not a reader or a literary journalist: I've never heard a Southern novelist, good or bad, speak more than momentarily about the South-as-exhausted-vein. (I've spoken of it momentarily myself, usually after a bout of reading journalists on the subject, journalists who assume that because *they* are exhausted, with a quantity of reading which they have after all volunteered to do, therefore the South is—or the midwest or urban Jewry or, tomorrow, the black ghetto.) But I do hear the lament from everyone but writers—"Oh, you're a Southern novelist. How brave!" (and, *aside*, "How sad! how touching!"). But then how brave to have been a painter in fifteenth-century Rome, a composer in nine-teenth-century Vienna.

For surely what is exhausted is the *reader* of Southern fiction of the past forty years, not the South or its novelists. And exhausted by what? —as always, by quantity not quality. The publicists of any renaissance— especially among an oppressed people (ex-Confederates, Jews)—can hardly be blamed for their early delirium; but any publicity is doomed to sate an audience very quickly—and in our case, to sate it with what amounted to a serious inaccuracy: that the South swarmed with genius. It didn't, though considering its size, the length and range of its history, the South can come honorably out of a cool examination of its fiction in the past forty years. In fact, its record as a country can stand with the simultaneous record of any other country—with France, Britain, Germany, the rest of America. For since 1930 the South (as literal cradle and crucible) has contained the careers of three novelists of world stature—William Faulkner, Robert Penn Warren, Eudora Welty—and of two masters of the short story—Katherine Anne Porter, Flannery O'Connor. Three women, two men—four of them from or concerned with the deep South, one from Texas.

Unquestionably there have been in the same period other distin-guished Southern novelists and story-writers, not to speak of poets and dramatists; and in another ten years the list may well bear another two or three names (there are strong visible candidates). But I think my point is clear. Insofar as there is any sense of exhaustion with the South-as-literature, that exhaustion is felt only by readers (and by professional readers, at that) who have forced themselves to consume large quantities of the fiction—first-rate or fifth—emerging from so peculiar, so high and gamy a culture as that of the old South.

The situation is radically different for young Southerners who think of themselves as novelists and are beginning their work now. If they have read widely in the fiction of their region (by no means a certainty; I hadn't until I had written two books of my own), they may indeed feel that certain objects and themes have been handled so frequently and obsessively, well and badly, as to be dangerously worn, the comic-Southern stereotypes— odorous ladies with memories of the War in mansions by swamps hung with moss and moccasins where dead blacks are dumped for misde- meanors. And yet, and yet—most Southerners my age (b. 1933) and thousands born in 1971 have had or will have early, intense and formative encounters with a number of living originals of the types. And more— bellied sheriffs, beloved and loving retainers, revival preachers, claustro- phobic families, tottering rhetorical childhoods drowned in lonely back- waters fed by books (not Southern) and dreams of escape.

If these Southerners have had their very educations as writers deter- mined in part by realities which now arouse conditioned boredom in a small over-read audience, what are they to seize as their themes and subjects when their experience requires, compels the order of fabu- lation? —Their experience, of course; the matter on which they can speak with authority, their lives, their literal visions, the mysterious inventions and combinations which their imaginations extract from, force into, that experience. For any serious novelist who is sane enough to ignore book- journalism will know, as cornerstone of his work, that if the compulsion to write fiction continues in any one organism, then the exhaustion of a portion of a given decade's journalists with a given subject or region is precisely meaningless since it is produced by the unavoidable plethora of lesser work summoned by a local genius' call and promoted by the huck- sters of a free economy, work whose memory and force will survive (twenty years hence) only in the author's family and in graduate English depart- ments. The man who can and must merely proceeds, trusting the heat of his own vision to vaporize accretions, dissolve patinas, reveal the thing itself. In any case, time—if time continues—will winnow the products. Whoever wrote for less than time?

And no one maintains that the past forty years have seen no changes in the old South—its look, sound, smell, the charge in air and objects. Enormous changes, apparently, though most of them so recent (since 1945) as to be beyond measurement or tests for permanence, influence, direction. Industrialization, urbanization, integration, uglification. Yet however great their threat to all that has been meant by "South"—and the first two would seem the great threats, as they did to the Agrarians in

1930—the fact remains that vast stretches of the old South remain untouched by the twentieth century. *Survive* is perhaps more accurate, but
surviving as opposed to *flourishing* has always been the supreme Southern
specialty, black and white.

When Eudora Welty's *Losing Battles* was published in 1970, several
of the more serious reviewers (I saw a handful of the old "What?-more-
hillbillies?" groans; my own two earliest novels got a fair amount of hill-
billying when in fact they dealt with characters who live two hundred
miles east of the nearest hill and are as distinct from hillfolk as from
Brooklyn cabbies) suggested that, strong as it was, this was clearly the last
Southern novel, since the South that had fueled Faulkner and Miss Welty
was gone and good-riddance.

Nonsense. The old South—the Confederacy, still spiritually intact,
with the difference only that the slaves were called servants—continued
in alarming good-health into the late 1950s and throughout the whole
huge region, Mississippi to Virginia, country and town. And today I can
leave my house, midway between Duke University and Chapel Hill, walk
five hundred yards and be in houses and among people, white and black,
who could today conduct mutually intelligible, agreeing dialogues with
their resurrected great-grand-parents and who, for all that, do not see
themselves as isolated islands of the past but as typical of the world around
them. I can drive sixty miles to the house where I was born, in a town
of two hundred; visit my aunts (whose mother—my grandmother whom
I clearly remember—was kissed by General Lee in 1870), submerge with
them gladly in days of memory—the sacred hilarious appalling past reeled
through us again in the sacred forms (each word as rigid in its place and
function as a phrase of the Mass, as productive of promise, release, joy).
And not only I—my niece, age three, already listens closely to the same
ceremonies; and though she is a visitor, how can I guess what strata are
slowly, immovably depositing in her? Or the millions of children who
live, not visit, in the rural/small-town South and turn from television
to the oral tradition many times each day, who are fighting again this
afternoon in hundreds of public schools the final lost battles of the Civil
War, a gray line of six-year-olds in the van? If such encounters do not,
in fifteen years or so prove to have been intense, mysterious, scarring
enough to produce their own novelists (whose work will feed at the same
dugs as Faulkner's or Warren's or Welty's), then claim that Southern
fiction is dead. For whatever new subjects, new forms of life the new
South is offering (and to me they seem either developments of the old or
copies of standard American types), the old South will go on offering its
life as subject for another fifty years at least—the working life of those
who are children in it now. Not *offering* but *imposing*, and those apprentice

novelists upon whom it imposes itself must invent new tools for seeing and controlling its intent on their lives or smother in silence—or turn to the fiction of game and puzzle which is presently cranking-up in younger regions already gone to desert.

But these children, like their parents, are also experiencing various kinds of new South—almost half of them are chiefly if not exclusively experiencing an urban South (North Carolina plans to have a 51% urban population by 1980); and while neither Atlanta nor New Orleans yet vies seriously with New York, Chicago, Los Angeles as irreclaimable disaster-sites, they are trying hard and cheerfully, and, given time, may well succeed. Birmingham is nearly as difficult to breathe in as Gary; and dozens of smaller cities—green and clean ten years ago: Raleigh, Richmond, Charleston, Savannah—are imploring not so much their own ruin as their mortal trivialization, drowning in a sea of carwashes, burger-stands, pennanted gas pumps. So the next question is, as I said at the start—will the new South prove unrelated to the old, a petrifying gorgon quite literally?

Unanswerable of course, and in any case not a peculiarly Southern question—though a look at simultaneous American fiction of other regions gives serious pause. Insofar as the twentieth-century novel in this country has consisted of the South and the Jews (with the odd midwesterner), it has been the product of two profoundly similar cultures—God-and-family centered, oppressed and oppressing (the old ghetto Jew being his own Negro), gifted with unashamed feeling and eloquence, supported by ancient traditions of sorrow and the promise of justice, a comic vision of ultimate triumph. But with one large difference—the classical Southern novel is rural; the Jewish, urban. I can think of no exception (maybe Malamud's *A New Life*? Roth's *When She Was Good*?). And while the moral resources of Judaism have irrigated the work of Malamud, Bellow and Roth, a great many other specifically Jewish novels have suffered the predictable pressures of their scenes—frayed nerves, self-absorption (through urban isolation), ghetto smugness, *noise*.

Surely, in fact, the great dilemma of an American Jewish novelist now is not, again, exhaustion (the unimaginableness of certain repetitions after *Portnoy*, say) but the far more daunting fact that the modern novel, from its eighteenth-century origins till 1922 (*Ulysses*), was a bilocal form—city and country. It is difficult to think of any great European novelist before Joyce whose every novel is not intricately strung between the mutually nourishing poles of city and country—Fielding, Stendhal, George Eliot, Tolstoy, James, Proust, Lawrence, Mann. Dickens and Dostoevsky (the supreme urban novelists, the first and richest students of city-nerves) send their plots and people for frequent and indispensable visits to the country; and I'm not the only man who thinks that *Wuthering Heights*, entirely rural, is the greatest single novel of a nineteenth-century England already locked in the mania of urbanization, nor the only one to notice that not one of the classic American novels through Hemingway and Faulkner is exclusively, even largely, urban in setting.

Why this oscillation?—a simple reflection of earlier life when populations were mostly rural and writers could afford villas, cottages, *dachas* for clearing-the-head, flushing-the-pipes? The remnants of nineteenth-century nature worship? All that and a good deal more. Chiefly this—such a range of geographical movement has, until the past ten years, been the novelist's technical strategy for expressing what was an early and strengthening perception of the occidental novel: that the European and American city of stone, asphalt, traffic, harassed parks cannot provide an *anima* of imagery sufficiently rich or varied to support long fictions concerned with emotions other than hate, rage, anxiety. Why?

Wordsworth knew, in 1800, the preface to *Lyrical Ballads* (and the fact that he speaks of conditions for poetry seems to me no objection)— "Humble and rustic life was generally chosen . . . because in that condition the passions of men are incorporated with the beautiful and permanent forms of nature." *Permanent*. You might argue that a city is a form of nature (even that, as recently as ten years ago, a few of them were beautiful forms); and I'd join you in affirming that the suggestiveness-to-art of a Rome or an Athens is largely a function of its longevity, its *apparent* permanence, the long scale it offers for the measurement of our brevity; but even the most resigned city-dweller would not contend that permanence is a feature of any American city—oh, a few square blocks of Charleston, Savannah, a few other "heritage-squares" in chloroform. The deepest principle of American cities as opposed to European or Oriental is precisely their impermanence, mutability (and surely one explanation of the present state of horror of our cities is that our premise has always been, "It's awful; never mind; we'll get it right next time"). Now, add to that basically economic impermanence a new and perfectly feasible threat—nuclear destruction—and anyone can see that, for the first time in history, a city the size of greater New York is literally easier to destroy, to vaporize in every stone, than any one man within the city. Given five minutes' warning, the man can take shelter; the city cannot. Neither can the country of course; but the threat of destruction against, say, the Appalachians or any given rock, field or tree has thus far seemed less credible than that against clustered buildings. (The current revival of fear for the environment, overdue as it is, is essentially a fear for man—man may succeed in destroying himself, the tuna, the plankton; but does anyone seriously suppose that nature—the earth—would not survive us? The earth has been hell and desert several times before.)

So rocks and trees condemn our folly and our virtue, chasten our fret as buildings never can—scratch a farmer and find the tragic sense of life—yet they still can console us because they will submit to the pathetic fallacy, will absorb all our emotions, not simply our destructive emotions. Or—if consolation is impossible or irrelevant—illumination, clarification; because they offer us the only objects of meditation in the presence of which the literally human qualities of man can be distanced, comprehended, calmed, controlled. That is not merely the experience of Wordsworth and all the novelists of the world till 1922 but of Aeschylus, Jesus, Oedipus at Colonus, King Lear.

Will Southern novelists then—undaunted by their native horrors, unintimidated by general misapprehension—be finally silenced by urban din? or galvanized into nerves and jitters? or forced into cave art (the scared cottage-industries mentioned above)? Maybe. Why not? Maybe I've answered that already. Literally because many more than half of the people of the South still live in close proximity with a nature that beautifully, grandly asserts its permanence. If that nature—its organic killable members—is killed, as it may be, then its memory may well survive in a few of the human survivors and work for generations (the Garden of Eden has lingered nicely—as dream, implied condemnation, blueprint). And if, in twenty or fifty years, Southerners all huddle like the rest of the nation in cities of dreadful night, there will still be what there has always been (often all there has been for the South, always all there has been for the novelist)—the past, as dream, condemnation, cause of the present. The past which, for all the stunning raids upon it, all the muffled hobbling obeisance to it, refuses to die or yield for more than the space of one novel in one man's life but grows, proliferates in each new life and demands early treatment, desperate remedy. Perhaps, indeed, as readers we *have* had the Civil War, the lavendered ladies, preachers and sheriffs, bare-souled adolescents; but as the stuff of life in a huge and long-inhabited country, they have no more been plumbed than the Marianas Trench. And other central traumas and figures are untouched—the great Depression (my father's Civil War), the manless years from 1941–45 when many of us grew up in the midst of a war three thousand miles away yet hooked into our hearts, the black-rights struggle of the 50s and 60s, the present agonies of school and housing integration, another war; thousands of others unknown to me; and Southern blacks (having given us our best poetry) have only begun to write their pasts, their visions of self and of us, into novels that may yet tell us, and in time, so much we need to know. And what Jeremiahs we could make among the ruins. Our credentials are impeccable—the only people in the nation who have claimed from the start that graceless man, even *homo Americanus*, was damned and doomed, would botch all jobs, and that we in the South were the damnedest of all.

So—given an imaginably livable world and the survival of memory—the next fifty years seem as safe as years get for anyone born in the South whose life here demands control in the form of what we have agreed in the past two centuries to call fiction. Beyond that—well into the twenty-first century—even I won't peer. First, children must be born with the genes, the senses (though maybe all that will prove manageable). Then the world must remain an observable world, one that human eyes and ears can bear to study, can conceive reasons for wishing to portray, a world that will hold pose long enough. If these conditions vanish, so probably will the novel. Forms with longer lives and achievements as grand are dead as pterodactyls—epic, pastoral, dramatic tragedy. And not only the American Southern novel—all fiction, everywhere. Not to speak of organisms far more gravely threatened, of far greater weight in the life of the race.

And yet, and yet. If the race survives in some recognizable form, if language is employed to communicate emotion and acquired experience, if men spend large tracts of time in one place (however man-ruined or man-made) and if one of those places remains the ground we now call the South, it is all but inconceivable that one man at least (white, black, red, yellow; whatever new mixtures) won't be compelled to retire to private space and, helpless to do otherwise, invent some means of saying what he knows, having had his life. The novel, for instance. A Southern novel.

1972

A VANISHED WORLD*

THIS ENORMOUS VOLUME is a selection from the letters and journals of the family of Charles Colcock Jones of Liberty County, Georgia, in the fourteen years from 1854—1868 (the years of impending crisis, Civil War, Reconstruction). But more than a volume, it is a book, with a calm proud beginning, a terrible middle, a desolate peaceful end; a book shaped round its many meanings—and the best book known to me which is concerned with the lives and minds of upper- and middle-class white Southerners during the War. It is richer than its only rival, the *Diary* of Mary Boykin Chesnut, in that it gives us the letters and voices of a number of people—a rich slaveholding Presbyterian minister, his well-fed kindly wife, their educated and respectful but lively and independent children, their gathering inlaws and grandchildren; their numerous kin and, by report, a huge cast of white employees, tradesmen, soldiers of both armies, slaves and freedmen.

So smooth is the operation of selection and abridgement by which this scattered mass of miscellaneous papers is finally made to reveal both the minutiae of a vanished life and the controlling, extraordinarily complex moral vision which created that life (and which, though brutally assaulted, continues to shape our history—thus the world's—to this day) that a reader may well forget another of the central facts of the book: the inherent news and shapes of the material have been coaxed from it by a single man, the editor, Robert Manson Myers. And his labors have been not only superbly tactful but apparently staggering; for the Joneses were compulsive savers, devoting large parts of their time to recording the surfaces of their days and then to insuring that their casual and remarkably spontaneous records would survive (Myers' preface and epilogue, detailing the wanderings of the papers and his own work with them, are nearly as interesting and instructive as the body of the book). In fact, it would be a good deal more accurate to say that, unlike the usual quasi-hysterical human packrat, the

---

* *The Children of Pride: A True Story of Georgia and the Civil War*, edited by Robert Manson Myers (Yale University Press, 1972).

Joneses were calm believers in the importance of their daily lives and ultimate destinies.

Why? Many reasons, most of which are already familiar to any student of aristocracies; and while all those reasons operate in the lives of the Joneses (their wealth, their power over numerous human beings whom they literally own, their intelligence), there is one which may come as a shock to many readers: they trusted in the importance and meaning of their lives because they trusted that their lives were intended and witnessed and sternly judged by a God. And, for me at least, the most richly yielding of all the multiple themes and stories of the book is the theme of Providence—their own view of the nature of their relation to God, family, neighbors, dependents, the earth itself; their view of liberty and duty.

I say *view*, in the singular, because there is near-perfect unanimity of vision among all the correspondents. The first premise of their slightest note is that they are bringing one another news. And yet they almost never offer real news—any idea or demand to or upon the recipient which is likely to cast new light on his assumptions or behavior. Their only demand (aside from the endless and no doubt maddening favors asked— send me so many yards of cheap calico, sell a family of slaves for me) is that the recipient lead a Christian life. This, for instance, is the ground bass of the fullest and most important correspondence in the book—that between Dr. and Mrs. Jones and Charles their elder son who, despite a good deal of apparently sincere piety, quietly ignores their demand, even refuses to discuss it and (for the period of the book at least) is unable to "become a Christian." But it is important to see, with no patronage at all, that even such a crucial demand often seems to mean *Live like me*.

And that stultifying unanimity, that readiness to spend one's entire life in the warm bath of family (and in the safety of the family's defenses against alien thought), explains as fully as can be explained the inevitable tragic destiny of the old South—and incidentally shows us the chief vehicle of that doom, a vehicle for the perpetuation of an entire status quo (above all, slavery): family piety, ancestor worship. That it is a vehicle in excellent repair in the South in 1972 gives further edge to a study of these particular vanished lives.

But is all their news for us tragic, mere unbroken folly? It would be easy to think so—worse than tragic: trivial—and a number of the readers who might learn most from the book (politicians; social planners, especially young ones) will find it difficult not to be quickly and violently repelled by the racial relationships described; the constant views of slaves as either amusing, gratifying pets or ineducable unforgivable ingrates. But—beyond what may be gained from a close look at a world through its own eyes, and once we have removed our own hypocrisy-glasses—there is other news, messages which are not simply important but urgent.

To mention only two: that while the family is the most dangerous of human institutions, it is also the only specifically human institution and may be revised or flouted at great peril; that, whatever the moral crimes of the South, its voice was the single powerful voice in American history which spoke against the literal destruction of the earth, the voice which asserted that there were objects more important than men, black or white (and the fact that the South has long since silenced its own claim makes a recovery of it, in its original form, imperative).

The highest recommendation then—both to students and to casual readers (the book is, as Myers claims, "akin to an epistolary novel"; and its story—both in setting, incident, types of character, and vision—is surprisingly reminiscent of *Gone with the Wind*, a novel much despised of late but which, as a document of the past at least, gets strong confirmation from *The Children of Pride*). My only reservations—aside from a brief suspicion, in this season of hoaxes, that the survival of so many papers from such a universally articulate family was all but too good to be possible—are that the six hundred pages which precede the outbreak of the war might well have been pruned (I see that Myers is establishing, by his leisurely pace, the complexity of leisurely lives; but the Joneses, like other humans, are a great deal more interesting in trouble than out; and such scenes as those surrounding Sherman's raids on the family home and the heroic response of the women would come more powerfully if they had not been held from us so long) and that Yale might have made the book considerably more comfortable for readers by breaking it into two volumes. Its nearly two thousand thin pages weigh some five pounds on my bathroom scales; but I've hazarded them on my lap for a month now with a growing awareness that their ponderousness was more than weight—a burden, which we should attempt to bear.

1972

A LUCID VALOR*

THE DRUGGED DEMENTIA of Tennessee Williams's last twenty years was more than adequately noted by the press. And there are now many young readers and playgoers who think of him only as a raucous and pathetic ruin. The unalterable fact of his immense contribution to dramatic literature—from *The Glass Menagerie* in 1944 through *The Night of the Iguana* in 1961—is presently all but sunk in the closer reality of his disastrous late plays and the public spectacle of a runaway life. If the great plays are inadequately remembered and honored, how much more so the stream of related work that Williams published or left—two interesting eccentric novels, a disordered but hilarious and often touching memoir, and this surprisingly enormous volume of short stories.

Stories were, from the time of his St. Louis boyhood, an important strand of what Williams saw as his unified life work—a nearly endless filament spun from an existence tormented from the beginning by grotesquely incompatible parents, a schizophrenic sister, and numerous parasitic lovers. His battlecry always was "Valor!" And few artists' lives offer a memory more valiant than that of the Tennessee Williams who sat down at dawn most mornings and, for hours, *wrote*—wrote literally to stay alive, sane and useful. That many of the dawns were miserable makes it all the more a wonder that so much of the work is lucid, firmly built, compassionate, and compelling—with a charge like no other dynamo's.

Even his greatest admirers have condescended to the stories, finding them of interest only insofar as they foreshadow characters, plots and themes from later plays. Any reader's tally will be different. But faced with this chronologically arranged and presumably ultimate collection, any fair account of Williams's fiction must surely agree that six or eight pieces are of an invigorating individual mastery. For me, "Portrait of a Girl in Glass", which foresees the plot and the entire cast of *The Glass Menagerie*, is as self-contained and piercing as the later play. And the

* *Collected Stories* by Tennessee Williams (New Directions, 1985).

novella, "Three Players of a Summer Game," which invents Brick and Maggie Pollitt of *Cat on a Hot Tin Roof*, is a more complex and profound achievement than the ensuing play. Admittedly, pieces like "Man Bring This up Road," even the long "Night of the Iguana," are little more than unsatisfactory sketches for eventual large plays. But the chief pleasure that this collection offers so abundantly is specifically the pleasure of brief mastery.

The short story is, above all, *short* (the reason for its present unpopularity with the size-hungry American reading public). And plays are short—relative to epics or novels. An uncut performance of, say, *Hamlet* requires a good deal fewer minutes of our waking lives than *Anna Karenina*, not to mention Lady Murasaki or Proust. Williams's genius—and it was as large a genius as America has produced—was for condensed and pressurized experience and expression. Stories and plays, which seldom ask more than three hours of our lives, were natural functions of his understanding, his essential metabolism (inexplicably, his brief poems seldom jell).

How good are they? How likely to give present and enduring pleasure and guidance "In this dark march toward whatever it is we're approaching" (Blanche DuBois)? First, as in most lifelong compendia, there is the expected portion of botched apprentice work—though the first piece, "The Revenge of Nitocris," published when he was seventeen, may prove a genuine (though lengthy) hoot for party performers. Even in the awkward early prose, however, there are almost always moments of startling power—radiant fragments of the explosive vision which Williams will eventually mold into incandescent bombs.

The apprenticeship slides almost imperceptibly into mastery with the stories of the late 1930s-early 40s—"The Field of Blue Children," "The Mysteries of the Joy Rio," and "Portrait of a Girl in Glass." The first successes, we now know, proceeded more or less directly from events of his own youth and early manhood. By the late forties-early fifties he attempted stories that, while still grounded in personal experience, proliferated in the kind of magical realism so widely believed to have originated in Latin America—stories like the outrageous but dead-serious "One Arm" and "Desire and the Black Masseur." But the large masterpieces of this middle period, and of the entire collection, are still those grounded in Williams's own gypsy youth—"The Resemblance between a Violin Case and a Coffin" (another story about his tragic sister Rose) and "Three Players of a Summer Game" (from his boyhood in Mississippi and Tennessee). They move with a leisurely, even archaic, nobility of pace and tone through unblinking scrutiny of those few tendencies of human nature which empowered him—the irreparable damage one person can inflict on his or her companions, the tyranny and persistence of physical desire, the pathos and peculiar grace of the walking wounded.

The scrutiny continued with no pause through his remaining harried years—the latest story is from 1980—but by the 1960s the careful grave stride had changed to an often frantic, occasionally hilarious, surreal dash through bizarre unearthly landscapes peopled by cartoon-bold but empty allegorical types. The novella "The Knightly Quest" is the most nearly successful example of this final manner. But the promise of a Kafkaesque parable set in a secret weapons factory is quickly sabotaged by its air of reckless and random invention. Something has come loose in the writer's life and gaze; a still-comic but now desperate cry of rage at human folly flaps wildly through the jagged actions and generally drowns whatever communication was intended—though perhaps none was. As with so many aging artists, the late work is far more nearly a dialogue with the self than with an audience. Perhaps the public and critical rejection of his last plays had convinced Williams that he no longer commanded an audience beyond his own ears and hands. The final vision then is desperate, incommunicable, sealed.

But the youthful and middle years are here before us now, in deep and dignified plenty. Even at the sad rejected end, Williams knew his own worth—he'd made a whole world. These stories, fruits of labor in the mouth of Hell, confirm him unanswerably and give the strong lie to his loud detractors.

1985

NEW TREASURE*

$\mathbf{S}$IMPLICITY OF MEANS and lucidity of results may not be the universal aim of art throughout the world, but they're very nearly so. The brute suavity of French cave-paintings, the mathematically sophisticated but visually spare shapes of Greek temples, the calligraphic and encoded elegance of Oriental scroll-painting, the Bach Prelude in C, a William Blake lyric, the final movement of Beethoven's last piano sonata (opus 111), an Appalachian ballad. Who doesn't love them all? Millions may resist the polyphonic magnificence, wit, and ecstasy of Bernini's Saint Teresa; but who has not surrendered to Michelangelo's youthful Virgin of the Pietà?

Yet how to describe, or discuss, any such masterpiece? How—in Chesterton's joke—to play the Venus de Milo on a trombone? It is a famous and lamentable limitation of modern aesthetic criticism—whether of the graphic and plastic arts, literature, music, or performance—that such orderly verbal analysis has proved generally helpless in the presence of apparent "simplicity," the illusory purity of means and ends toward universally comprehensible results. Where is there a genuinely illuminating discussion of Blake's "Tyger," Gluck's "Dance of the Blessed Spirits," or Joan Baez's traversals of the Child ballads?—one that helps us understand *how* and, above all, *why* such complex but supremely satisfactory ends are achieved in such small and evidently transparent vehicles. As readers' minds are most engaged, in narrative fiction, by wicked or at least devious characters, so the mechanistic methods of modern critics require complexity of means before their intricate gears can begin to grind.

Thus (since I'm here to celebrate three plays) Shakespeare is the critic's darling among dramatists. Apart from questions of relative depth and durability of interest, he provides the critic an apparently infinite parade of artifice—one which anyhow shows no sign of exhausting in their multitudinous hands.

In Europe at least, other dramatists—Racine, Ibsen, Strindberg, Chekhov, and Shaw—have elicited memorable and still useful studies.

---

* Preface to *Courtship, Valentine's Day, 1918* by Horton Foote (Grove Press, 1987).

But what American dramatist has yet received similar treatment? Admittedly, our first great playwright has been dead fewer than forty years. But again, Eugene O'Neill worked with sufficient awkwardness of means toward his broad and deep effects to make him unattractive to a tribe of critics energized primarily by technical adroitness. An almost identical assertion might be made for our second internationally significant dramatist, Tennessee Williams. The straightforward urgency and eloquence of his best early work—the lean balladic lament of *Glass Menagerie* or the arpeggiated rising howl of *Streetcar*—have yet to receive sustained helpful attention from critics.

Any sympathetic viewer of the recent films and plays of Horton Foote is likely to share the critics' dilemma. Were you as deeply moved as I by his film *Tender Mercies* (1983)? Then can you tell me why? Explain to me how even actors as perfect as those he found, even so resourceful a director, could employ so few and such rhetorically uncomplicated speeches toward the brilliant achievement of such a calmly profound and memorable face-to-face contemplation of human degradation and regeneration. I confidently suggest that even St. Augustine in his *Confession* goes no farther toward the heart of that luminous dark mystery than Horton Foote. And I—a novelist, poet, playwright, and critic—cannot hope to begin to tell you how he has made that longest and hardest of journeys. I can only urge you to look and then agree or disagree. (One of the film's prominent early reviewers said that watching it was about as diverting as watching paint dry; I plainly agreed with a majority of critics and thought it one of the most successful films, in all ways, of recent decades.)

In the case of *The Orphans' Home*, his recent and monumental cycle of nine related plays, I'm in better luck—though only to this extent. The plays are now being published by Grove, and the volume I introduce here is the first of a proposed three. Though two of the plays have been filmed and several others performed on-stage, no one has yet seen all of them in coherent productions; and given the scattered disorganization of the American commercial theatre and the poverty of the lively regional companies, no one is likely to see all nine any year soon. But soon all will be readable; and the black-and-white outlines of Foote's large scheme will be at least discernible.

For what these texts—and his recent films—demonstrate is how unquestionably Foote is the supreme musician among our great American playwrights. More even than with Tennessee Williams, Foote's method (and his dilemma) is that of the composer. His words are black notes on a white page—all but abstract signals to the minds of actor and audience, signs from which all participants in the effort (again all those at work on both sides of the stage or camera, including the audience) must make their own musical entity.

Take the case of *1918*, the third play here. A careful reading of its printed text will provide the pleasures we expect of well-made and intensely felt drama—the gracefully attenuated line of suspense, the nearly devastating crisis, the unexpected but credible and warm resolution. Despite the scarcity of stage descriptions or directions to the actors, we can (if we're ideally cooperative) construct our own series of pictures of small-town early twentieth-century Texas, not that different from small-town America anywhere else—or small-town bourgeois France of the same time, for that matter. But nowhere can we point to speeches of an extraordinary or heightened eloquence, language of an "unreal" intensity or rhythm. Memory is allowed to flow and blossom (for all the plays are loosely based on the history of Foote's own families) into universal emotion but only within the strict verbal channels of the quotidian, the daily norm. Language is pruned and shaped but not visibly transformed.

See the film of *1918* though. And there, within the physical confines of a modest budget, a small company of beautifully restrained and emotionally transparent players perform the minimal text with such grave musical skill as to achieve a final effect of genuinely transcendent volume. From the bare lines of Horton Foote's original text—and from nowhere else really, except the voluble faces of the actors—there pours finally a joyful and unanswerably powerful psalm of praise: suffering (to the point of devastation) is the central human condition and our most unavoidable mystery. Yet we can survive it awhile and sing in its face. The only tonal parallels that come easily to mind—for similar findings, wisdom, and credibility—are the conclusion of *A Long Day's Journey Into Night* or the rapturous final claim of Chekhov's *Uncle Vanya*. Yet even they, for all their grandeur of human love and pardon, are not bolstered by such a glacial weight of evidence as Foote provides in the prior and succeeding plays of his cycle, rich as it is in all the emotions from farce to tragedy to transcendence.

Courtship and *Valentine's Day* are parallel achievements, traveling through their chronology with as little baggage as a bone-poor spinster aunt but always with an unexpectedly prolonged final resonance. Indeed, the three are grouped as numbers six, seven, and eight in the cycle of nine. When all three volumes of the series have appeared, and *The Orphans' Home* can then be studied and seen whole and entire, I'm confident it will take its rightful earned place near the center of our largest American dramatic achievements—a slowly generated, slowly won, apparently effortless, surprisingly wide vision of human life that flowers before our patient incredulous eyes with an opulent richness of fully communicated pleasure, comprehension, and usable knowledge: a permanent gift.

1986

DODGING APPLES

T HE MAKING of any work of art is as mysterious as making a child and likely to remain so longer. But the human mind, at least since the eighteenth century, has abhorred mystery. Or maybe not abhorred; our relation to mysteries is far more ambiguous—we love and dread them, therefore strain to solve them in the generally desperate hope of controlling them, of shielding our faces at least from their threats, their claims on us. So hot have men felt these threats to their stability, their continuance as men, that one could write a reasonably full history of the race simply by charting men's raids on and retreats from, their inching victories over and permanent defeats at the hands of such mysteries as invisible God, the visible bodies of outer and inner space, and darkest of all (because most visible)—other men, our daily fellows.

Only very late in the history of man's curiosity however is there evidence of any substantial investigation into the specific mysteries offered by works of art. Mystery was affirmed as the essence of art. Art was a function of God—man's completion of a gesture begun by Him, the gesture of His will that we know Him—and like God, art was acknowledged to be now consoling, now killing, by unpredictable turns. The young Milton, just turned twenty-one (and in the same month as his Nativity Ode), wrote in his *Elegia Sexta*—

> *Diis etenim sacer est vates, divumque sacerdos,*
> *Spirat et occultum pectus et ora Iovem.*

[Indeed a poet is sacred to the gods, a priest to gods, And from his secret heart and mouth breathes Jove.]

—not only wrote it but believed it all his life, his literal credentials (far older than the *Ion* of Plato); and no one has ever demonstrated he was wrong.

There must have been isolated pioneers from the first who envied and wondered—sullen watchers crouched in hair against the walls of caves, wondering how that one there in the firelight (a figure like themselves) could transcribe with only his fingers, ground earth, juice of berries, a likeness of the awful world, a vision in which that world of savage beasts, fragile men, was reduced to visible size, held, even yoked. Then Aristotle, Longinus, the Alexandrian rhetoricians, the critics of the Italian renaissance; and always artisans were passing their discoveries to young apprentices (often with elaborate secrecy) in manuals of rhetoric, directions for the mixing of pigments, cutting of marble. But serious investigation by laymen of the methods of artists, as opposed to response to the arts as quasi-divine phenomena, began only in the late eighteenth century, in Germany and England where the scientific method, so newly won, promised to light all dark corners, and was first directed at works of sculpture and painting. Only in the twentieth century did any number of critics turn their attention to the problems of the production of literature, the processes that ended in prose and verse. (Again, I'm referring to laymen, omitting the essays of Dryden, Coleridge, Wordsworth, Baudelaire, James, Valéry, Conrad—which, however much light they release, always deprive us of final revelation, always refuse to make us poets.)

But to break off this simplified, and arguable, history—my point is that the study of methods of literary creation began with the first touching flush of faith in Physical Law and has attempted to continue for the past two centuries as a scientific study—the attempt to apply scientific method to the understanding of works which have continued to deny that they were created in obedience to the laws of that method. (What has not been widely noticed is that the "scientific" method of literary study has often been more nearly theological-expository. A number of the New Critics, for example, were sons of ministers or were reared in strict Protestant-Jewish traditions of scriptural scrutiny—and some of their more extreme techniques resemble nothing so much as the ruthless squeezings given to the book of *Revelation* in thousands of fundamentalist churches today.)

Most scientific investigation has been, at least until the past thirty years, devoted primarily to answering the central question of any onlooker, any creature—How?—to the discovery through observation of how particles behave under various conditions, of how mass achieves effect. And the great majority of students of literary creation since the eighteenth century, and virtually all teachers (certainly in America), have reasoned by seductive analogy and imported the scientist's How? into hostile country. Virtually every serious critic of the past thirty years has devoted himself to one of two questions—"How is this thing built?" and "How does it work?": this tragedy of Shakespeare, ode of Keats, novel of Joyce? And hilariously often their answers imply, "Thus I demonstrate that, given time, I could have made it myself."

Admitted: the question How? is often a possible question, admitting an infinity of answers varying in interest, validity, usefulness; but at best it is a preliminary question; and any reader content to rest in its answers has done little more than roll out an apple in the path of Atalanta (the poem is Atalanta)—to halt the poem, take it off his tracks, his back, to tame it, defuse it. Readers rest in How? only when they have silently, maybe unconsciously, admitted that Why? would open the gates of their lives to the poem.

For Why? is the thing to dare to ask. Several critics have specifically denied that valid answers to Why? can be provided for any poem, least of all by the given poet. No doubt the question can lead so far into speculation about intention as to leave one finally mired in silliness as deep as any encountered by pure structuralists; but the great theoreticians of physics have never avoided the question, have even (Newton and Einstein) acknowledged the apparent irrationality of the methods which ended in their own discoveries (if they are "discoveries" and not, say, poems); so its avoidance by structuralists seems all the odder, a willful self-maiming (self-maimings being generally meant as self-protections).

So, *how* is a poem made (I'm calling all works of literature poems); what kind of machine is it? Then, *why* was it made? Why is it this sort of machine, not some other? Why was it launched at all into a world gagging on five thousand years of accumulated poems? Why launched at this time, down these specific ways, at this specific speed? Then maybe How? again; for once having dealt with Why?, a reader is likely to find early answers to How? irrelevant. Until a reader asks that forked question—however unanswerable—he has not even begun the trek into the heart of a poem, the guarded room in which the poet left his unchained monster, his secret design upon our lives. For the design, the diet of the monster, is the secret of a poem, not its mechanics (any trained mechanic can diagram those)—the poet's design and the poem's design (often they are different) for altering the life of the reader, the world, by his sonnet, novel, story, his *act*. A poem is an act, as much as a parting wave, a welcoming kiss, the signing of a sentence—life or death.

I believe those things because I believe that all works of art of all sizes—from the Parthenon and *King Lear* to the briefest Elizabethan lyric, the whisk in the Japanese tea ceremony—have kinetic intent. They came into existence in order to change something (or a number of things)— the actions of a friend, the hatred of an enemy, the savagery of man, the course of poetry, the sounds in the air. So—again—do all acts, maybe all atoms.

I believe that for two reasons. First, it is clear from a reading of the life and letters of any great artist (though there is presently a good deal of smiling at the fervent statements of purpose of, say, Beethoven) and, most directly and powerfully, from a study of the works themselves. The "purpose" of Michelangelo's Sistine frescoes is, first, to do a job; fulfill a

promise. After eighteen months of agonizing work on the ceiling, he wrote
to his father,

October 1509

I've finished that chapel I was painting. The Pope is quite
satisfied. *

Beyond that, at least one more purpose is clear and usable and demands
our response—to bring us, and the painter, to our knees in awe of the
beauty and power of man and in dread of the unimaginably greater power
of the God who made man and will someday cancel or remake him, to
prepare us as fully as possible for that day when the Son will come flinging
Judgment from the skies. Beyond that, the chance that the frescoes are
one immense petition to a human being, a friend or lover (maybe pictured
there?)—a petition for love, a certificate of worthiness. However specu-
lative, such guesses—as long as they touch base with known facts of
life—are not so useless to a witness as they might seem, are on the contrary
among the richest lessons any act can provide; and a refusal by witnesses
to return to works of art a measure of the response which the artist has
demanded (explicitly, implicitly) is an act of betrayal. Like all betrayals,
easy and cowardly. Far better abandon the witness and study to better-
equipped—tougher, wilder, more vulnerable—men who at least volun-
teer, however hopelessly, to change their lives.

Second, I believe in the kinetic intent of works of art from long and
necessarily close observation of my own motives and purposes as a writer.
I'll risk discussing those. The risk is multiple, for you and me. I risk
most—pomposity, solemnity, self-delusion. But then I am what I know,
of all things in the world (any writer—any person—who is not the world's
authority on himself is in serious trouble); and a conviction of the wide
validity of his own knowledge is the final myth upon which any artist
builds his work, any person builds his life. (The central myth of the artist
is surely not Narcissus but Perseus—with the artist in all roles, Perseus
and Medusa and the mirror-shield.) I wouldn't speak, not publicly, if I
didn't believe in the value and urgency of what I see and think I know.
And then I risk lying, not so much willfully (however much more amusing
that might be) as by simplification, by reducing to bare formulae motives
of considerable and unrecoverable complexity. Lying unconsciously also,
for obviously I don't know all the reasons why I write a given story, scene
or sentence. I'm worked, like you, by masked puppeteers. Yet there are
many motives and intentions of which I am conscious and have been,

---

* Robert J. Clements, ed. and trans., *Michelangelo, A Self-Portrait* (Prentice-Hall,
1963), p. 144.

more or less from the start—age ten or eleven. I think I know why I write—the publicly usable reasons and a number of the central private ones which can be communicated, if at all, only by the work itself—and I think I can discuss a few of those motives, sanely and honestly if a little simplistically.

I write, first, because that seems to be the intention of all my faculties. It is what I can do, as a diver can dive, through grace and practice. Then, given the bent (or is the "bent" produced by the need?), I employ it to understand what is mysterious—in the behavior of the visible world, the behavior of God, of my friends and enemies, strangers, finally of myself. For I've written nothing which is not in its way an attempt to understand something which has happened to me, by me, or through me—something of a certain size, a certain apparent or threatened importance, not only in my life but in the world's. (Aristotle said in the *Poetics* that

> beauty consists in magnitude and order; therefore an exceedingly small animal cannot be beautiful, because the vision is confused when it is applied to an object so small as to be almost invisible; nor can a very large animal . . . be beautiful, for the eye does not take it in at once, but it presents no unity and completeness of view to those who look at it. Hence, as it is necessary for bodies and animals to have magnitude, but such as can properly be embraced in one view, so it is necessary for stories to have size, but such that they can be easily remembered. *

—a more useful passage for a writer to consider than Henry James' famous command to be one of those people "upon whom nothing is lost." Most of what happens should be lost, if not on an artist then certainly in his art—lost or buried, as of no size, no meaning, no truthful, comprehensible magnitude.)

But to say that I write to understand the mysteries impinging upon my life is not to say that I write autobiographically. I generally don't. Some enormous writers have—Tolstoy, Dickens, Proust. But I—! (I set myself beside them for the point)—I've usually found it necessary to study, attempt to circumnavigate, then dissect the mystery which I needed to understand by distancing it, setting it outside my own chaotic life, imagining a set of credible characters, a characteristic action (people and acts most often quite different from me and mine), then lobbing the mystery like a bomb into their midst, witnessing the results and recording them. If that implies cool calculation—me facing a Mystery, then seeking my

---

* Aristotle, *The Poetics* in Allan H. Gilbert, ed. and trans., *Literary Criticism: Plato to Dryden* (American, 1940), p. 80.

people and plot by abstraction—then it's misleading. The sense of mystery occasionally comes first—an amorphous curiosity—but much more often, a simple picture in the head: he here, she there; his name is Milo; why does he move thus?

The next intention is joined to the last and has always been for me the most complex and secret intention and (better) the happiest—to offer to explain what I think I've learned about a given mystery, not to "readers but to one particular person. It's literally true to say that everything I've written till now was written first for an audience of one (occasionally two or three) and offered to that person for at least two reasons—to communicate the results of my investigation into some mysterious relation or experience we shared; second, to justify my life to that friend or relation, to earn what that friend had already given. This is nearly impossible to discuss. I'll quote a relevant passage from Stephen Spender then pass on, but not because this motive is less important than any other. On the contrary, of all my conscious motives this is the strongest and most productive of joy. Spender says in his essay "The Making of a Poem,"

> Why are writers so sensitive to criticism? Partly, because it is their business to be sensitive, and they are sensitive about this as about other things. Partly, because every serious creative writer is really in his heart concerned with reputation and not with success. . . . I suspect that every writer is secretly writing for *someone*, probably for a parent or teacher who did not believe in him in childhood. The critic who refuses to "understand" immediately becomes identified with this person, and the understanding of many admirers only adds to the writer's secret bitterness if this one refusal persists.

—To attempt understanding then; to offer explanation (or progress-reports). Finally, to change. I've said, at length, that I know of almost no considerable work of art which does not intend to cause some action (response to *its* action), to work some change. Maybe the only exceptions are works of praise, pure adoration—the psalms of David to God, those sonnets of Shakespeare which seem only still praise of the young friend. But are they, however beautiful, pure and static? Can any adoration ever be? Surely David—beyond all personal needs for exercising a skill, for maintaining a singer's reputation, for stunning his wives and the dangerous court—intends to convert us, the unbelieving world, to the worship of Yahweh. And such a sonnet as number twenty-six—

> *Lord of my love, to whom in vassalage*
> *Thy merit hath my duty strongly knit,*
> *To thee I send this written ambassage,*

> *To witness duty, not to show my wit.*
> *Duty so great, which wit so poor as mine*
> *May make seem bare, in wanting words to show it,*
> *But that I hope some good conceit of thine*
> *In thy soul's thought, all naked, will bestow it;*
> *Till whatsoever star that guides my moving*
> *Points on me graciously with fair aspect,*
> *And puts apparel on my tattered loving*
> *To show me worthy of thy sweet respect.*
> > *Then may I dare to boast how I do love thee;*
> > *Till then, not show my head where thou mayst prove me.*

—lean as it is in its humility, surely it exists in all its only half-veiled firmness to win, or fasten, a love withheld or toyingly given.

My own stories, then. What actions do they seek? Again I've brought you to the brink of my life, to information which even if I could give it, and you could remain awake to hear, would be of no use to the stories or you. The stories, for better or worse, are yours; the life is mine. But I can say truthfully if unspecifically that, so far as I understand my conscious intentions and those of my numerous puppeteers, I have always written in the hope of altering, literally causing movement in, one or two of three possible things—myself, that person for whom I was writing, or the world at large (though I don't recall ever thinking of the *world* till a piece was done). Whatever my swarm of private dreams, the hope of making the world a better place has not surfaced often enough for recognition. My own life, yes. The lives of a few friends and enemies, though I'd seldom ask them except in stories. Then if anyone else looks in—welcome to whatever meal is laid, if meal at all.

"But," you're thinking, "he conceals more than he says." I do. I said I would. But I also undertook to lie as little as possible. Maybe, though, I can make partial amends by discussing a particular story, one which has an intense but typically distant relation to my life—the first serious story (as opposed to sketch, or mess) I ever wrote and one which has had considerable life in American and foreign anthologies since I began it at age eighteen. I can discuss it largely because it is my first story and because I remember clearly the events of its composition and because I think I know why it was written—some of the usable reasons, at least. I don't know how (I've never known a serious writer who didn't subscribe fairly literally to some notion like Plato's or Milton's of inspiration, uncontrollable or uninvocable afflatus); I never will and don't mind.

There are two kinds of reasons why I wrote "Michael Egerton"—private and public. Public first. I wrote it over a period of four years, my undergraduate years at Duke; and I wrote both the first and final drafts to fill class assignments at the last legal moment. The first version was written in the fall of 1951. The late Philip Williams, my instructor in an especially free section of freshman English, had given me rein to write my next theme in narrative. I'd previously done him a sketch or two which he'd praised with the sort of invigorating salt I'd craved through years of distrusted total approval; he pointed out, for instance, the odd resemblance between the end of my first theme and the end of A *Farewell to Arms*. I had rearranged my memories of an aunt's dog's death and concluded with this departure from the scene—"I just sat there for a long time thinking, and then I got up and went home. It was almost supper time."

Now, in November, I was to produce a double-length narrative (one thousand words). For Monday. On Sunday night I was of course sitting in a freshman dormitory that rocked with the now healthy-seeming violence of the early fifties—firecrackers cannoning in the halls, lighter-fluid conflagrations on the terrazo, whole rooms of furniture being transported to the quad and erected there in place to greet hapless returning weekenders—and I had no narrative, no serious idea. I must have clutched at various moments-from-my-life—I'd had eighteen years of it—but I don't recall the false starts now. What I do recall is mounting despair as the night moved on, the awful sense of a head which has vacated when needed most. Then—on the vacancy and in the midst of firecrackers and scattering buffoons—a picture. That dramatically—lo. A literal image in my head, visible and complete as a lantern slide—an eleven-year-old boy, blond, large and complete for his age, standing between two windows, his arms extended cruciform, bound at the wrists with the exposed cords of window sashes, ten-pound pig-iron weights excluding blood from his fingers.

That much—the picture—was inspiration. But that implies arrival from the exterior. This picture was only the surfacing of a monster whose presence I had forgotten, certainly had not specifically implored, would not in fact (as I came to understand him) have wanted to call. The picture and its fragmentary story had lain in my unconscious mind for seven years. It was literally "true," had happened in the summer of 1944, the one summer I was sent to camp. The boy in the picture had slept in the bunk above me and had begun the two weeks as my sudden friend and the pride of our cabin, our golden boy who, as suddenly, retreated from me and our cabinmates into private passive grief which he would not or could not explain and which finally aroused our sadism and provoked the final act of punishment—the punishment which had deposited its picture in me, a participant; then had bided its time, its curious revenge.

But that night in 1951, it seemed a plain story, one which I could tell by morning and (being me then) could tell in three pages. So I wrote the pages, described the boy as the glistening friend he'd been, then as the silent victim he became. When Philip Williams read it, he saw at once, and said, that what I'd stated was no story but a mystery, and an unsolved mystery. I had described only what I knew, the visible before-and-after of what had happened. Mystery remained—why had the boy changed utterly in such little time?—and to both Williams and me that seemed the central mystery. If I wanted to make a story, as opposed to telling the limited facts, I must solve the mystery, discover (that is, invent) a reason for the change in the boy. Simple enough. But next week's theme was nearly due; and in any case my energies then were invested in love and the soft-centered poems love was pressing from me, so I set the sketch aside, gladly buried the memory—which insisted on returning. I still have the opening of a second version which I attempted the following summer, more talkative and visually detailed than the first but aborted after three pages, well short of encountering mystery; and two summers later I worked as a camp counselor in the North Carolina mountains, hopeful that the final necessary particles might accrue to the magnet of my untold story. But the story remained untold. In my junior year, Elizabeth Bowen visited Duke, asked to meet some student writers and see their work. I was one of the called, for my poems presumably; but suspecting that Miss Bowen would rather see prose, I rooted out my fragmentary sketch and offered that. Her response was almost the same as Philip Williams'—the difference being that she stated the problem in technical terms: my sketch lacked a middle. It had a firm beginning and a strong end but no middle; by then I'd read enough Aristotle to remember that "A complete thing is what has a beginning, a middle, and an end" and that "a middle is that which comes after something and has something after itself."* And I seemed on the edge of revelation, of being handed a complete thing—again from my unconscious—but again I waited. The middle didn't come and I didn't call it.

Not till the next fall, 1954. I was then a senior and enrolled in William Blackburn's course in prose narrative (the one such course I ever took); but I was also deep in other things—editing the local literary magazine, applying for graduate fellowships, beginning my history honors-thesis on Milton and other course work—so when the first story was due for Blackburn, I obeyed one physical law at least (conservation of matter) and found my first sketch, now three years old, and set out to make it a middle. It was not called "Michael Egerton" then but by the name of the real boy. I changed the name first, knowing I was on my own now, that

---

* Aristotle in Gilbert, *op. cit.*, p. 79.

if I was going to make a *thing* out of my memory, I must imagine the
middle of those summer weeks, invent the boy's dilemma and grief (Egerton is a name in my mother's family and one of which I was proud
then—the Egerton family having commissioned *Arcades* and *Comus* from
the young Milton). In fact, to discover and control the nature of this event
in my life, to attempt to lay its returning ghost—and to pass my prose
course—I was going to have to lie about it, complete it in my head by
the addition of what probably never occurred, not to my mysterious friend
at least. So I did it one night, beginning without a clear plan for the
middle but working as I always have when revising—by beginning to copy
my previous draft in longhand. Something in the act of physically forming
words has always been my own best prod—ink against paper—and has
often made me think that writing is a manual art as surely as sculpture.
The hand, writing, balks at the uncompleted (or decorated, obscured)
gesture, invents its full plain arc, pauses at the lip of holes in one's early
sight and attention. And what mine invented to order that night (or at
some prior point in the ten years' waiting) to complete this story was a
witnessed encounter—the narrator ("I") sees from a distance and is later
informed of a meeting between Michael his friend, Michael's mother and
her new husband. My middle was divorce then—and Michael a common
victim, the child as shuttlecock. Nothing galvanizing, to a reader at least,
but credible and a sufficient stimulus for Michael's scorched response (I've
wondered occasionally, hearing the story, if the mother's only speech is
impossibly cruel—"Michael, this is your new father. How do you like
having two fathers?" —In a country where any morning paper is apt to
carry news of one more child-beating, scalding, maiming? In any case,
the narrator hears the speech filtered through Michael; what *he* says she
said). A complete thing, beginning, middle, end; of a certain contemplable
size. My first story—or the first I'd finished in the expectation of seeing
in print, of reading years hence without shame.

Why did I have it? At the time, of course, I wasn't asking (I only
wanted to hear, from someone who indubitably knew, precisely how strong
it was, how sizable, what it portended for my life and work; and by great
luck I heard that spring, when Eudora Welty came to Duke and read it).
And maybe I shouldn't be asking now—I've already implied here a number
of my more public motives—but I have the time and am interested and
am asking, and am now so far from the summer of '44 or its writing in
'51 and '54 that I see "Michael Egerton" with the sort of double vision
which in this one case no one else on earth possesses (not that any of
them minds): maker and audience.

As soon as I had finished that second draft, I knew something I hadn't
known before—that the story was not about Michael but the narrator,

therefore me. I learned that from the middle which volunteered itself—divorce. Not that I had experienced divorce at close range; I hadn't. But I knew very well at age twenty-one that the central conscious terrors of my own childhood had been dual and related—destitution and abandonment (knew as forcefully and freshly as ever since my father had died nine months before). In the years from my birth till the age of ten ('33–'43), destitution had been a genuine threat, the hand of the Depression. Abandonment wasn't, though I feared it, fantasied frequently about life in orphanages (there were several nearby with real Dickensian orphans—dutchboy haircuts, patched clothes, the steady gaze of the betrayed) and entered passionately into the near-universal child's suspicion that I had already been abandoned, was the child of unknown parents, merely adopted by the Prices whose lives I now greatly complicated—all experienced so intensely as to suggest a positive yearning for abandonment, betrayal: a story in which "I" am the betrayer, conquering a fear by becoming the fear. Becoming not only a traitor but a cruel and finally cowardly one—all in the face of, because of, mystery (in this case, Michael's response to the mysterious actions of adult parental love).

Asked at the time (I wasn't), I'd no doubt have said that I wrote the story—or that the story had lingered all those years, demanding treatment—in order to tame my own waiting cruelty and to warn the unwarned or oblivious. And I'd have been right, partly. Roughly half-right. Yet could I—can I—expect any reader to come up with such answers, should he ever ask the questions? (Won't they, at least as often —anyone trained in American schools and colleges—come up with questions like these from a letter recently sent me by a highschool English class:

Is the bathroom Michael retreats to parallel to the Garden of Gethsemane?
Are we to assume that because Michael did not come out of the bathroom at the end of the story, you believe that Christ did not come out of the tomb?

—The apples of Milanion again; lead apples.)

I could expect answers like my own, yes—and do. The story seems to me still, whatever its size, what a friend of mine said it was—"an arrow to a target," that trim and swift. No reader would need any of the autobiography above to hear the story say, as it does, "Change your life" and to hint at some ways. He only needs the story, and that's on sale or loan.

What I couldn't have foreseen has been one of the real rewards—that readers (my students, age eighteen, the age at which I wrote it) would years later show me other questions whose answers helped me see another half of my intent, a harder and more original half, which may explain what life the story has had, its seductive threat. They asked why the narrator makes so few gestures, emotional or physical, to reach Michael in his silent ordeal, even to offer help? Why does he—"I"—after Michael's awful report of the mother's words lie awake in the bunk beneath Michael: "Once I sat up and started to reach out and touch him but I didn't. I was very tired"? And why, at the end when he has broken away from the other boys and returned to the cabin where he hears Michael behind a bathroom door, does he say, "I started to open the door but I didn't"? What decision does he make between "started" and "didn't"? What statement fills that silence?

Isn't it a chain of questions, not a statement; and aren't they these (in my voice, age twenty-one, nine months after presiding at the death of my father)?—I cannot enter the pain of another human being any more than the pain of a dog, a starling. Maybe I shouldn't try. Maybe weak tries—"started" and "didn't"—only strengthen, prolong the other's pain. Maybe he asks to be abandoned in his pain, accorded the dignity of solitude and silence?—not all human beings, but this one Michael and, since he is human, the others like him. Mustn't I learn to recognize and honor them?

What if all that is lies after all, however innocent or well-intended? Maybe it will be possible within a few years to show that I wrote "Michael Egerton" not for any of the reasons I've mentioned, public or private, conscious or concealed. Maybe I wrote it because, in November 1951 at the time I was required to produce a freshman theme, a chain of electrochemical events forced out this product—events related maybe not so much to kinetic designs on the world's behavior as to my genetic predispositions, my psychic and physical metabolism, the climate in my dorm, my dread of the Korean draft. Maybe we'll soon be strapping the electrodes onto would-be poets—or literate dockhands—and by accurate stimulation of precise loci within the brain, producing real poems, novels, plays. (Maybe the Crab Nebula is fanned in all directions by a central ring of doves in infinite flight.) What if, what if?

I've plunged too far; no one could answer—though in a culture where what we agree to call good poems could be produced cheaply and rapidly by any literate man who could reach the stimulating equipment, surely few of us would be reading and questioning one another. Why bother? —every man his own Tolstoy; the ultimate pornography. (Every literate man already possesses the apparent raw materials of any good poem— words and life—and most men have probably had more eventful lives than Shakespeare, certainly than Emily Brontë.) In any case, all questions of How? would be answered—by this silver needle, inserted *here*, charged with x volts for y milli-seconds. Wouldn't Why? survive though, a mystery still, the only one? And if there were a poet or electronic novelist whose answer to Why?—"Why do you seek this solitary stimulation?" and "Why has your brain been made to issue *this?*"—would be other than "Fun and profit," mightn't he say above crackling synapses what Prince Genji said in eleventh-century Japan to reassure a lady whom he'd caught reading fiction?—

> I have a theory of my own about what this art of the novel is, and how it came into being. To begin with, it does not simply consist in the author's telling a story about the adventures of some other person. On the contrary, it happens because the storyteller's own experience of men and things, whether for good or ill—not only what he has passed through himself, but even events which he has only witnessed or been told of—has moved him to an emotion so passionate that he can no longer keep it shut up in his heart. Again and again something in his own life or in that around him will seem to the writer so important that he cannot bear to let it pass into oblivion. There must never come a time, he feels, when men do not know about it. *

Till the age of electric inspiration then, my old claims hold—for me, at least, and for all I've written—and "Michael Egerton," early and lean as it is, answers the central question for me, in full and with the clarity of first-work and in much Prince Genji's way: so that man (no, a few) should not forget but remember and reply.

1963, 1972

---

* Lady Murasaki, *The Tale of Genji*, translated by Arthur Waley (Random House, 1960), p. 501.

THE LONELY HUNT FOR POWER

A NOTE ON "WAITING AT DACHAU"

In the summer of 1956, I drove out from Munich in my new Volkswagen with two friends to visit the remains of the concentration camp at Dachau. It was a visit which we had planned for some months. The three of us, two men and a woman, were contemporaries of Dachau (opened in 1933); and I at least bore childhood memories of the assault of the first photographs from the liberated camps, memories which eleven years had worked into questions. So I was surprised when one of the two quietly said, as we walked toward the gate, that he would wait for us outside—surprised and annoyed (at a change of plan) and baffled (why had he pulled back?—a perfectly hardy gentile English soccer-player whose father had died in the war, to be sure, but in England in a truck-wreck, not starved or gassed) and maybe wounded (was some refusal of trust involved, after six weeks of pleasant travel together?).

But under that, I was powerfully excited. I was twenty-three years old, with a year of graduate study in England behind me and two more years ahead; but I was also more than a year past the fervent and happy realization that the thing in the world which I stood a chance of making was prose fiction. Beginner though I was, I had known already the cold thrill of having the bones of a story stand up in life and seize me. Here clearly was a story—the balking at the gate—and I'll swear that I registered it as such at the moment (*swear* because writers are notorious for the manufacture of interesting origins for long-finished work). These, I knew, were the bones of a story; but since they bore no signs as to what their story was, I also knew that I must consign them to the charnel of my unconscious mind in the hope that the bones would one day rise, connected and walking, displaying their life and knowledge.

A decade passed, as it generally does for me with such consignments; and though that recalcitrant friend and I remained close as we still do and though I continued to read widely in the literature of the camps, the relics of that day at Dachau showed none of the twitchings of life. And nothing in my present life summoned them, required their galvanization. Then in 1966 I began to write a series of independent stories about an American at Oxford, stories published as "Fool's Education" in *Permanent*

Errors. Without going to tedious or indiscreet lengths, I can say that yes, the stories were summoned by strong needs of the present; yes, they feed heavily off my own past life; no, I cannot now sort precisely the truth from the fiction; and that it would be a good deal more accurate to describe them as mosaics, composed variously of fragments of experience, witness, and invention—all to the apparent end of examining the obscurities and dilemmas of those apprentice years which had persisted in my unconscious curiosity long enough to assume narrative shape in the hope of attention and answer. After I had written three of the stories and had clarified for myself their obsession with the poles of love and freedom, I began to want a story to conclude the group, to resolve the suspended and comically rapt relation of my two central figures; and the bones of my curious afternoon at Dachau began to seem ready to offer a sufficient and credible story—offer and refusal, contingency and flight. That they offered themselves in the summer of 1968—an especially bad time, outdoors and in —was not the least of their kindnesses.

It was only in writing the story, however (between August '68 and April '69), that I began to suspect not only a satisfactory end for my sequence but something more and luckier—an extension, an opening at the end for stories which had planned to end at a wall, a small blank point (an opening in fact for a whole volume of stories, all of *Permanent Errors*; and even for my previous and perilously resolved novel, *Love and Work*). In short, a reprieve—in work and life. I came to sense an older shape implicit in the slender form of my August afternoon as that form rose twelve years later encased in the tissue of invention (most of the action and the entire nature of Sara are invented) and subsequent knowledge (my reading in the sources)—my friend and I had sketched, safely and in lowercase through twenty seconds of gesture, not only the central act which made Dachau possible (for that had been my question after all, not *why* the camps?—any child knew that—but *how*?) but also the curse of most lives, the famished hunt for singleness and triumph, lonely power.

The story is now nearly five years behind me; its bones nearly twenty (or thirty or forty—they are my bones, it seems); but "Waiting at Dachau"—while I won't indulge in questions of *best* or favorite—still seems to me to make that one shape visible, audible, diverting, and oddly consoling. I'm glad to have seen it and glad to have it read.

1974

A START*

Wʜʏ sʜᴏᴜʟᴅ ᴀɴ apparently healthy child retire to his room, of his own will, and spend solitary hours in the composition of plays, poems, and stories? With the mass landing of federally-funded poetry programs in American schools, imaginative writing is now a commonplace of child life and has yielded occasionally dazzling results; but in my own North Carolina public-school years (1939–1951), such writing was not a part of the curriculum. I dimly recall composing and illustrating in the second grade a poem about rain. When I was in about the fifth grade, a female cousin and I began and soon abandoned a novel about boy-and-girl twins who sail to Europe on a liner; and in my senior year of high school, I took a course in writing with Phyllis Peacock. It was listed as an "interest"—i.e. hobby—course; and while Mrs. Peacock conducted it seriously, the "interest" label encouraged a good deal of moonstruck laziness in the pupils.

My own serious writing seems to have begun then on my own time and fuel, in the winter of 1946.** I was thirteen and in the eighth grade in Warrenton, N.C. That was our native county, and we had moved back there two years before—to general unhappiness. My parents' hopes of a return to family warmth had been dashed by family contention, and my own initial pleasure in new friends had been suddenly canceled by an unheralded and violent rejection. At the time (the fall of 1944), the rejection seemed to an eleven-year-old one of the vicious mysteries of fate—and in memory is still appalling—though now I can trace clear lines of inevitability: the new boy in town, and a very small town, innocently threatens to rearrange long-standing relations and dependencies; expulsion ensues. The boy, for whom solitude has always been a necessity

---

* Preface to *A Start (Early Work)* by Reynolds Price (Palaemon Press, 1981).

** I have said elsewhere what I believed to be true—that my first substantial piece was a play entitled *The Jewels of Isabella*. The claim was based upon my discovery among my mother's papers of such a manuscript, unsigned but in my sixth- or seventh-grade script. I have recently established that my manuscript—unsigned, as I say—is a copy of a seventeenth-century Italian original, translated and adapted by A.P. Sanford. I must have copied it for some potential school use.

as real as calcium, spends more and more time alone (albeit in a household containing three beloved others, plus a daily maid). His company comes from books, two or three movies a week, and (during school months) from the bused-in farm children who accept him as freely as their own plain futures—early marriage, hard labor.

From the months preceding composition of my first sizable piece— a play, *The Wise Men*—I recall two other kinds of writing that were crank- up exercises. The first was literal writing—an absorption in my own cursive script, with much experimentation in flourish and bravado, flexible nibs, many-colored inks; a fascination with forgery (I can still produce a re- pectable forgery of the signatures of George Washington, Frederic Chopin, and Franklin Roosevelt). The second was autobiography—a five-year diary with lock-and-key (meticulously heated with the fantasies of a truly Wag- nerian puberty) and a book-length log, now lost, of all the movies I'd seen with capsule reviews.

The surviving manuscript of *The Wise Men* is indeed inscribed in red ink in an elaborate made-up script—the temporary result of my ex- periments in calligraphy. Its mythical-historical theme, however, would seem to have no relation to anything in my own life at age thirteen. And yet—without remembering its conscious motives—I can guess that it came partly from the early stages of a mystical enthusiasm which developed rapidly in my adolescence. Certainly my cast of Hollywood-primitive Orientals contains no one with whom a lonely boy in the 1940s would readily have identified; but insofar as the theme is The Quest, then I was extrapolating at the start a central concern of my adult work. Still on my own, I wrote other pieces in the years immediately following—a screenplay about Bernadette Soubirous and a lurid supernatural tale, "The Ring," survive. But the other pieces printed here were written in my last two years of high school and my first year of college. Romantic obsessions had by then broken through to me. The pressures of old loneliness and new hunger would probably have sufficed to arouse an awareness of iso- lation and unassuaged ego; but I had also added to my boy's lean diet of adventure fiction such inflammatory fare as *Anna Karenina*, *Madame Bovary*, the stories and novels of Hemingway, and the poems of Emily Dickinson and T. S. Eliot.

Looking back at the poems and the prose sketches now, I mostly hear one question. *If I had been this boy's teacher, would I have encouraged him to pursue a life of writing?* (On this evidence, Phyllis Peacock urged exactly that.) He was clearly no Chatterton. Once past the unconscious charm of *The Wise Men*, it would not be easy to say that his syntax, imagery, or rhythms are fresh, though he is generally lucid (hundreds of eventual branch-bank managers are writing better poems in Poetry-in-the-

Schools programs today). What I hope I would have sensed was the already dangerous head of emotional steam in his undersized tanks, his compulsion to release it through hot but harmless valves. The strain on the gauges, combined with an unusual degree of attentiveness and a rare (in a child) curiosity about the lives of others, were probably the main early signs that he meant to run a course and stood a chance of finishing. *How would I have trained him?* Recalling Ben Jonson's advice that one must never tell a young poet all his faults, I hope I would have pointed him toward those older writers whose questions were similar to his but whose control of language and form were sure (I'd also have urged him to laugh a little more). Privately, however, I might have guessed he'd end as a melancholic priest or—with worse luck—an alcoholic politician. I doubt I'd have saved his manuscripts. If I had, I doubt I'd be publishing them all these years later. He did and is.

1981

A LIST AND A DARE*

When I began writing in earnest at the age of eleven or twelve, I assumed that I was speaking to and for someone. My first substantial effort, after the assigned verse of primary school, was a play—the most public of forms (and a play about the birth of Jesus, not exactly a marooned preadolescent). The someone was a teacher I'd fallen in love with that year, as I did most years, and the few relatives and classmates who knew of my effort. At the time I thought they were sufficient audience. I hadn't imagined hordes of the famished buying my wisdom.

Just as well. For while I've been mostly lucky in the reception of my adult work, I've come to see that my childhood aim was accurate. I've even come to believe more than half the time that in western culture, in any known century, there has been a mystically determined number of serious readers—larger maybe than the fixed number of Just Men in rabbinical tradition but an absolute, not a relative quantity, for each society. I suspect for instance that Homer had, head for head, as many serious listeners in the eighth century B.C. as Bernard Malamud or Katherine Anne Porter in American today—fewer than five thousand certainly.

I'm not speaking of sales figures or the number of eyes that traverse a particular work. Manipulated by ads, reviews, and self-fulfilling bestseller charts, the number of sold copies of a serious book is meaningless to anyone but accountants. I'm speaking of readers who actually meet a book with resources equivalent to its own—time, sympathy, intelligence, indifference to fashion. All good books find them eventually, and their response is a writer's second-largest reward.

The largest is the work itself. Good writers, like other good artists, are finally working for themselves and maybe some numinous judge— and working from the necessity to exercise a faculty, an intangible organ but one as *given* and demanding as a liver or pancreas. The primacy of that exercise explains why many writers are careless of reputation or even of the occasional Just Reader. As rattled as writers can be, in the short

* Preface to *Reynolds Price: A Bibliography, 1949–1984* by Stuart Wright and James L. W. West III, (University Press of Virginia, 1986).

run, by reviews or the vicissitudes of publishing, they ultimately rest (or fall exhausted) upon a few artifacts—a row of stories or poems. That's the paradox of their lives, speaking to be heard but at last accepting the speech itself as its own suspended end.

Which is not to say that even the most philosophic of writers— Shakespeare, Dickinson, Kafka—are not susceptible to surprise and gratitude at various kinds of attention from baked goods to propositions. Only that the attentions come from a world quite different from the one addressed. For their passionate witness and report, they receive intermittent ministry in an almost undecipherable language.

It's likely in fact that there have always been more good ministers to writers than there have been good readers, though the two categories are not mutually exclusive. Bankrollers, printers, biographers (there your writer must be dead), textual detectives, the immensely rare good critic, the bibliographer—even a curmudgeon is secretly grateful to them all. But the single necessity is the bibliographer. Without his meticulous hunt, his public list, no really adequate response to a prolific writer can hope to begin.

Children honor lists. They instinctively know their value as guides at the forks of life and comforts when waiting for full life to begin. As a grade-school writer I poured out lists like oil on the breakers—"The People I Love," "People Who Might Love Me," "Movies I Have Seen," "Great People I Have Seen or Touched" (Franklin Roosevelt, General Eisenhower, Marian Anderson), "Books I Will Write." Nearly forty years later here's an external list—"What He's Managed till Now."

What it will mean to anyone but me, I can't easily guess. Only an abjectly Just Reader will track down more than a few of the strays spotted here, and I wince at owning up to my righteous editorials for the high-school newspaper or the early book reviews in which I thought I was licensed to do a little turn of my own on a prostrate author or the interviews in which I rattled away (and got the misquotation I deserved). But the boy who unknowingly began a life's work with *The Wise Men* in 1946 is still alarmingly at large in the man who writes this; and they both are mainly pleased—a long careful list, a proof at least of time spent, a dare to augment it.

1986

USES FOR FREEDOMS

Allow a distinction, however rough, between novelists and pornographers. Then—total freedom to embody sexual acts and thoughts in works of serious fiction now appears to be available to American novelists. As long as the novelist *portrays* sexual behavior, as opposed to advocating it, it is difficult to think of images or language which would not roll smoothly off presses or bookstore shelves and past police and juries. Poets, playwrights, painters, and sculptors now share the freedom, though songwriters and filmakers do not; but my concern is with novelists.

The degree of freedom is new in America (though, despite cries of *terra incognita!* from both the joyous and the aghast, it is richly precedented in the past of eastern and western civilization; the list is by now a boring liturgy—the Hebrew Bible, Greek poetry and drama, Catullus and Petronius, Chinese and Japanese fiction, the tales and manuals of Arabia and India, and on into the night). Both its newness and the violence of its welcome have obscured an important fact—the totality of the freedom is illusory, theoretical, no more extensive than the uses made of it. Despite the tumble of barriers in the past decade, a number remain—high and maybe permanent, related to law and custom on sexual behavior, social pressures, and to the personal restraints of individual novelists, the tolerances and imaginative capacities of audiences—and an examination of the remaining barriers may reveal something about the nature of the freedom, its gifts and poisons, and about the effects of that freedom upon novelists.

For novelists are what will be affected, then the novel; and they'll obviously each be affected differently. The effect to-date, though, seems to have been considerably less profound than the effects of other new freedoms—the freedom of quick movement about the world, across cultures and maybe soon into space, for anyone with sufficient funds. Hence the rapid weakening or disappearance of many conditions and institutions which have shaped, even controlled, maybe originated, the novel—the sense of rootedness in a specific loved or hated place, language, style of gesture (previously the second most vital possession of a novelist, after his gift), the concomitant dissolution of family (the previous hothouse of all arts and the virtual subject matter of a majority of classical novels). And hence the proliferation of "down-here-on-a-visit" novels or the present effloresence of the exhausted and insensate literature of puzzle—the story as Fabergé Easter egg, jeweled musicbox tooled by one tinker for another. Enormously less profound too than the disappearance of silent countryside into metropolitan din. (Maybe the increasingly silent cities are metamorphosing through horrific death into new strange country with new lessons, *Arabia Deserta Nova?*)

But even such sexual licenses as are now issued to novelists have hardly amounted to unmixed blessing. Everyone has winced in recent years at the sight of gifted writers who—at the scent of musk in their nostrils—were whirling like dervishes in the freedom to make their personal unseen *seen* or, more probably, to send up their tittering fantasies as trial balloons (for air-worthiness, passenger capacity, commercial allure). For whom and why? News to whom? And, more seriously, there have been a number of visible cases of potentially valuable novelists so intimidated by the fear of new freedoms—fear of public self-confrontation—that they've sought refuge in silence or loud lying. I'll avoid contemporary names (seeing no reason to cause mischief through what may well be my own misinformation or ignorance) and will instead point to a few in the past who seem valid, and personally invulnerable, examples.

Assuming what I take to be true of *Madame Bovary*—that Emma's first adultery, in the course of a horseback ride with Rodolphe, is intended to be the first major collision between her dream of sex and a sudden actuality—then isn't Flaubert severely crippled by censorship in being unable to show, in the precise detail of which he was master, the moment by moment events and responses of that afternoon? Don't we really require to know—if we're to follow his full design and yield him the desired response—the size and performance-record of Rodolphe's equipment, the amount of carefully programmed dalliance employed (as opposed to hungry lurching), the exact degree and form of resistance from Emma, the degree of nudity, the positions chosen? In short, doesn't the story require a merciless graph of the confirmation or frustration of Emma's illusions *about* sex? Shouldn't we also possess an equally full account, earlier, of her bridal night with the fumbling Charles? Did Rodolphe, among leaves and grazing horses, give her more than Charles in dozens of botched tries? If so, what? Wouldn't such knowledge force us to become what Flaubert said *he* was—Emma ("*Bovary, c'est moi*")—and so make the novel a different and dangerous thing, a living unchained monster, not the lizard-in-ice it now remains?

Or Hardy in *Tess of the D'Urbervilles*. Surely we need full physical details of Alec's seduction of Tess. Hardy was forced to leave us with the assumption that Tess is deflowered virtually in her sleep (though un-drugged and sober) and that her quick sensualization in the ensuing affair with Alec occurs in an unconscious cellar of her brain. We are given only one sentence to cover this irreversible development in Tess's life and tragedy—

> She dreaded him, winced before him, succumbed to adroit advan-tages he took of her helplessness; then temporarily blinded by his ardent manners, had been stirred to confused surrender awhile: had suddenly despised and disliked him, and had run away. That was all.

If Hardy had been free to describe that first act and the following weeks —to dramatize them—and if he could have made clearer the extent of Tess's pleasure (public censorship was clearly not the only restraint on Hardy; there were strong internal reins), then we might be able later to enter into Angel's revulsion from her confessional narrative of those events on their wedding night (again, we are not given the confession; only told that Tess made it—and made it in detail with "re-asserting and secondary explanations"). As the novel stands, Angel's revulsion seems—even for a Victorian parson's son—prudish and stupid; and instead of responding to at least some of the agonized nobility which Hardy seems to have intended for Angel, surely our strongest responses are to his silliness, selfishness, his girlishness, the superficiality of his vaunted eternal love. Freedom— and courage—to face and describe the range of Tess's sexuality and, later, Angel's would have braced the novel unshakably at its now trembling center. (Still it remains as firm as all but two or three novels, in anyone's literature.)

Or E. M. Forster in *Maurice*. In a novel first written in 1913 (three years after *Howards End*, eleven years before *A Passage to India*), revised in 1960 and published posthumously in 1971, Forster attempts a story in which he probably had more personal energy at stake than in any other: the evolution in Edwardian and Georgian England of a young man who discovers, accepts, and happily fulfills his own homosexuality. Despite an occasional conversational obscenity (genuinely startling from Forster; were they added in 1960?), there are no explicit descriptions of erotic encounter. Maurice's early consummations, at Cambridge and just after, are the occasions for such a pulling down of blinds as to allow considerable doubt on the question of whether *consummation* is the word. His first encounter with Alec, the young gamekeeper who is to become his lifelong companion, though it appears to be total, is again unspecific; and even the crucial second encounter which cements their decision to share lives, is only communicated thus—

> [Alec] pushed him away, then heaved, pulled him close, put forth violence, and embraced as if the world was ending. "You'll remember that anyway." He got out and looked down out of the grayness, his arms hanging empty. It was as if he wished to be remembered thus. "I could easily have killed you."

Curiosity in all these cases rises from more than a reader's natural prurience; it proceeds from what any attentive reader will come to see are deep needs of the novels themselves. The need in *Bovary* and *Tess* is self-evident, but in *Maurice*? However repugnant or, at least, exotic homosexual encounters will seem to a majority of readers, *Maurice* would be a truer novel, more nearly itself (as Forster describes his intentions in a "Terminal Note"), if it could show us what it is that Maurice required to do with the bodies of the other human beings he loves—or to have done to his own body. (The intent of the passage above, with its reference to "violence," would seem to be that Alec willed to perform what English law until very recently punished as "buggery"—anal intercourse—or "gross indecency"—some lesser offense such as intercrural intercourse—and that Maurice welcomed the act or endured it without complaint.) To guess even that much is to go some way toward an understanding of both men, the literal stances which they must take in such a crucial but secret act. But to have been given a clearer picture of that central act—and an entrance into the heads of both participants by Forster, the single keeper-of-the-keys—would have greatly helped patient readers not only toward an understanding of the human evolution of Maurice and Alec but also toward an at least intellectual guess at the mysteries of homosexual love (which it is one of Forster's announced intentions to legitimate).

It would have helped in the case of *Maurice* because his story—like those of Emma, Tess, and Angel—is to an overwhelming extent a story of sexual discovery and response; of self-confrontation, self-understanding and finally communication *through* sexual relation: this piece of flesh laid thus against this piece. Or of the failure of those efforts. They are all three novels *about* sex—or novels which employ sex as their chief optical instrument, an instrument which fogs up (for three different reasons)—and any such fogging of lenses or veiling of the object of scrutiny can only obscure a total meaning. We can suspect that Forster, for instance, weighed the risk of alienating heterosexual readers by a detailed picture of homosexual acts and so chose his course as the lesser of two dangers; but isn't there a residue of feeling that, firm and brave as the book is at the edges, his central compromise is timorous, a little obsequious, a hole in his purpose, a function maybe of his mysterious inability ever to dramatize credibly the central claim of his ethic and art—the primacy of human love?

But some other novelists, roughly contemporary with those, were not crippled by limitations on the expression of sexuality in narrative. Far from it—some of the greatest of them were even helped by limits, were steered by them into diversions which extracted their most characteristic and rewarding solutions or were licensed by the ban to develop, in the unconscious or semiconscious, luxuriantly truthful allegories of love and pleasure, visions which law and custom and self prohibited their stating directly.

Again three examples. When Tolstoy reaches the moment in which Anna Karenina surrenders to Vronsky (well into the novel—part two, chapter eleven), he begins—in perfect understanding of the needs of this scene and these people, of his own needs from the scene—with the post-coital moment.

> "Anna, Anna," he said in trembling voice, "Anna, for God's sake! . . ." But the louder he spoke the lower she drooped her once proud, bright, but now dishonoured head, and she writhed, slipping down from the sofa on which she sat to the floor at his feet. She would have fallen on the carpet if he had not held her.
>
> "My God! Forgive me!" she said, sobbing and pressing Vronsky's hand to her breast.

The strategy is lean but conquering. Anna is shown at the moment of plunge into the guilt which will dissolve the center of her life and invite the cruelty of her peers (is her "Forgive me!" addressed to God or to Vronsky?); Vronsky in his sudden experience of the emotions of a murderer, a vision usual enough in Dostoevsky but shocking in the clear air of Tolstoy.

> He felt what a murderer must feel when looking at the body he has deprived of life. . . . But in spite of the murderer's horror of the body of his victim, that body must be cut in pieces and hidden away, and he must make use of what he has obtained by the murder.
>
> Then, as the murderer desperately throws himself on the body, as though with passion, and drags it and hacks it, so Vronsky covered her face and shoulders with kisses.

—And we are in possession of all we need to know, all we can use, about their act—and about their dreadful future. We have previously been subjected, through a hundred pages, to their instant and growing physical magnetism for one another, their creator, and ourselves. (Tolstoy invents in those pages the strategy which will become indispensable for many later novelists—Lawrence, Hemingway. He provides all the conditions, the physical and spiritual evidence, under which a responsive reader will fall physically in love with both Anna and Vronsky, thereby repeating their folly and enduring their punishment). Only later do we notice that he could not have told us more if he'd wanted. But he wouldn't have wanted. He knew his subject and it wasn't human sexuality in any of its forms.

And Emily Brontë. We know from other evidences of behavior, amply provided, how Heathcliff behaves in bed; and given Cathy's vehemence in all other matters, we can construct the necessary erotic scaffolding (as any nineteenth-century reader could have). And we are given, early in the novel, one light but chilling touch—so light that most readers miss it. As the narrator, Nelly Dean, describes the arrival of the gypsy foundling into the Earnshaw household, she adds quickly—

> I found they had christened him "Heathcliff," it was the name of a
> son who died in childhood, and it has served him ever since, both
> for christian and surname.

Heathcliff, then, was the name of a dead brother of Cathy's—now applied to her future, and eternal, love. If we recall the little that is known about Emily Brontë's own strong attachment to her brother Branwell, we may sense new depths opening onto views far stranger than the strange ones visible. And we may suspect, from that hint, that a greater available freedom of expression in sexual matters might have silenced her completely, petrified her with the direct gaze of her old need.

It would surely have panicked and might have silenced Henry James, who spent the first forty years of his career producing stories—"The Pupil" and *The Turn of the Screw* are only a little more than typical—in which a core of irregular sexuality is either ignored by James or is unnoticed or is rendered so elliptically as to be indecipherable. Without exception, in fact, sexuality in James's fiction before 1904 seems like nothing so much as a maddening dance round a huge veiled totem—a dance in which no participant may glance at the totem, not to speak of touching it, despite the totem's role as center and cause of the whole long rite. *No Touch* was the law of James's dance, as it was apparently the condition of his continuance as artist, maybe as man—until, at least, his monstrous triumph in *The Golden Bowl*: a win-through, a steady gaze at all the mechanisms of human sexuality (except love), as intense and courageous as any before Proust's and no less vengeful.

Those examples then—from a nearly endless resource—may finally suggest only what anyone might say of any sudden freedom: that some serious men will invent good uses for the new chance to face and record the motions, internal and external, of human sexuality; that some of the uses will give readers pleasure and stimulation which may in turn cast light, compassion, toleration, and laughter on a broad band of human experience. Some novelists have already begun to find such uses, though miserably few. Those who eventually succeed will almost certainly be those who understand and honor the fact that, for a long time to come in western culture, sexual behavior can be usably made explicit only when sexuality is the subject of the story, when a character's sexual nature is the chief index to his needs and destiny (usable as something other than pornography, though it may be possible to find new uses for passages which attempt sexual stimulation on a reader—one more means of compelling a reader to reenact in his own life, his own clock-time, the emotions and gestures of a fictional character).

The successful will probably also have active respect for a principle enunciated by an old landlady of mine—"It's not what it's cracked up to be": as an instrument for observing and understanding others, it's certainly not. The failures will drown, as they're audibly drowning all round us in a dozen books a day; but bad novelists—simply myopics or willful liars —have never lacked elements in which to drown. And, more disturbing, a large number of passionate men and women (gifted, by their total and exotic experience of the world, with complex secret knowledge and vision; fabulators by nature and need, allegorists like Emily and Charlotte Brontë, James, Tolstoy, Jane Austen, Melville, Shakespeare) will either fall silent in the steamy roar or, poisoned within, tell us less than they know, blocked by the glare of fashion. A fashion for lying—stick-men on stick-women. Truth being tellable only in tales.

1973

YOU ARE NEEDED NOW
AND WILL ALWAYS BE

A CHILDHOOD WITH BOOKS

CHILDREN KNOW THEIR NEEDS—food, loving touch, stories. Food and touch surround them from conception; stories arrive in their prenatal dreams (or from Mother's dreams, currents combing their sleep in the uterine sea). So they're born with knowledge that stories are vital, literally vital—food for their lives, pledges of love—and they force stories from us in the general extortion of babyhood. From anyone at hand. Any human who can tell a child the proper stories is quickly enrolled in the child's short list of servants and masters, the same to a child. And any child not told or read or shown stories—the proper stories—will spontaneously manufacture incomplete, maybe dangerous ones from the visible events of daily life, the invisible events of night: terrors, rewards. Or will die some form of early death, often not accompanied by cessation of breath.

Why? They're savage—ourselves in the wild, compelled by birth to continue the process, begun in the egg, of staging the long awful history of man in their single bodies. All men in the wild, all primitive cultures, exhibit the craving. It is visible—in advanced form, at the moment of discovery—in the presence at the core of any culture (tribal religion) of a cache of stories as permanent food. Or one story only. It is always the same, the one correct story which nourishes and saves either savage or child, any one of us.

The story is this. *You were made by a god working through your parents to bring you to life because you were wanted—precisely you. You are necessary. You are kept in the care of that god, those parents, your whole large tribe. There are threats without (and, worse, within—your father, your mother, your brother: armed). You can conquer those, or escape at least, through courage and skill and the deep strong care which caused your life. You will never die. Things rest on you.*

The message is crucial but so is the manner. Two things only are essential to its style—we must hear the story in the second person (never first or third; they are symptoms of sickness and danger) and in *human* time (the sequence of life, birth to maturity—no tricks with clock-time).

It can take any form; but it must say those things, to *us* and *in order*. Then it sanctions life, makes life possible.

Children once more show their appalling wisdom. They live on stories for more than the first decade of their lives; then they turn toward people and are generally hungry, seldom offered their story, seldom understood. For to understand any person's story—all the forms the one story takes for him—is to know him for good. It is also to have the power to please, terrify, and control. A child who would tell you all his stories would be your man.

All my childhood stories, I see now, were mysteries. I heard them as mysteries, whatever they were. What they were at first was Bible stories. The first book I owned was from my father's mother, dated *Christmas '35*. I was almost three years old, she was over seventy, and the book was *Wonderful Stories of the Bible in Words of Easy Reading* by Josephine Pollard.

I have it still. The cover shows Jesus in several colors surrounded by a realistic crowd of the wretched, all white but wretched—an apparently unconscious woman, a blind man, a crippled boy, an unaccompanied small boy and girl with their worldly goods tied up in a kerchief round a stick, a forest of crutches. Jesus gestures toward them but he stares at *you*. Inside—once you've passed some crayon work by me—are the honestly told stories of Adam and Eve, Cain and Abel, Noah, Abraham, Jacob and Joseph, Moses and Joshua, Samson, Ruth, Samuel, David and Jonathan, Solomon, Elijah, Daniel, and Esther (no mention of Jesus after the cover). Sex is veiled but implicit—"There was a woman named Delilah whom he loved"—and the stories are illustrated with apt ferocity by uncolored woodcuts: hairy men, breasty woman; all redolently middle-eastern in dress, fervor, odor. There is even one of God as He leans from the sky to accept Abel's sacrifice—the standard old man.

But the one burned deep in my earliest memories is Expulsion from the Garden. Adam and Eve, naked but for loin rags, are huddled at the huge left hand of a sworded angel pointing definitely *out*. What stopped me then, at three, was the general news—the worst could happen—and a single detail, an emblem of the whole. In the right-hand corner, over Eve's cowed head, were dark winged shapes. Now I see they are birds—gorgeous macaws—but I thought they were demons then. I must have heard the story, from my father almost surely—

Then because they had disobeyed the heavenly Father who loved them, God punished them. He sent them out of Eden, and before the gate of the beautiful garden He set angels with flaming swords to keep watch over the Tree of Life. The two went away to make a new home and to work for their food, but not to be away from God. He would ever be with them, loving them and helping them learn to obey.

And I must have registered the final consolation, but I knew this very clearly—there was something *left over*: demons in the sky who could fly past your suffering and watch and chatter. The list of contents will have indicated that much was left out in most of the stories.

Abraham stretched forth his hand and took the knife to slay his son but the angel of the Lord called to him, "Abraham, Abraham!". . . . Pharaoh tried to stop this thing by making a law that if a boy child was born to the Jews it should be put to death at once, but a girl child might live. . . . The house fell and most of the Philistines were killed. Samson died with them, and by his death slew more of the foes of Israel than he had slain in all his life. . . . David came out of his hiding place and bowed to the ground three times. Then he threw his arms round Jonathan's neck and the two friends wept as if their hearts would break.

I thought a good deal of such facts, at four and five. I already knew they were facts, not stories. I had seen my mother have a late miscarriage; I had seen my dog killed; I had intimations of my father's struggle with alcoholism; I breathed the thin air of Depression moneywoes; and I'd had several brushes with death myself (a violent allergy to egg, unrecognized, that threw me into fevers and hard convulsions).

I offer those not to suggest a Dickensian childhood—on the contrary, it was fairly normal for the time, place, and station; most children, then and now, endure more—but to suggest that the normal life around me and my first encounters with storybooks worked strongly together to create both my further curiosities as a reader and my compulsion to manufacture stories as a life's occupation. I had signed on for life as a sort of detective by the time I was four (my second major book—Hurlbut's *Story of the Bible*, with hundreds more pictures, many colored and by Germans, lusty and bloody).*

The mystery was *Why are they doing this?*—Abraham to Isaac? Jesus to Mary? my father and mother to their lovely selves? Surely I extended

---

* I was, maybe not incidentally, also four when an acquaintance of my father—Melvin Purvis, the famous G-man captor of John Dillinger—gave me a souvenir of himself: a chrome corkscrew concealed in the statue of a top-hatted grouch; twist his head and the screw rises straight from his tail.

the question by a phrase—*Why are they doing this to me?*—but what I remember is the whole wider bafflement. The world was all puzzle, just the little world around me; and that was growing daily. School loomed ahead (those hordes of *others*—I was still an only child), more Depression dislocations, the Second World War (which gave advance rumbles, passed to me through my father at the Philco each evening).

Since I had no playmates and we'd moved to the country, I held only three or four threads into the maze. Longest and strongest but much the most painful was observing my parents, still young themselves, struggling, and maybe too ready to ask for help in their own harsh puzzles from an unpropped child. Then I really had *nature*, my own Southern version of Wordsworth's rapture in the acres of woods behind our home. (Nearly twenty years before I knew Wordsworth, I shared his young conviction that nature was sentient—and sentient of me, concerned that I prosper; I talked at pines and creek rocks, dogs and birds; and felt I was answered). Then drawing and painting, which were other means of dealing with nature—a fixed concentration to see a thing's lines and copy them truly. Then stories and books.

I distinguish between them because life does. Books are written, stories told. I come from an endlessly storytelling family (only written down in letters); and I spent countless hours in rooms full of adults, listening to the litanies of family past, carefully storing them without conscious knowledge as if I were some apprentice curator, hereditary scribe. The stories though were dangerous. For the most part they flowed in hilarious streams; but sudden snags would rise (suicide, madness, abandonment, deceit—and all of them real, experienced by people sitting there or their kin or the servants out back), and seldom did anyone offer a child on the floor any chart past snags of his own. He was after all a child, not listening surely; and they knew of no charts, only various comforts for after-the-wrecks.

They were telling the truth; I was on my own. And I knew it by the time I could read with any ease, first and second grades, age seven or eight. The others in school confirmed that quickly; they were single like me.

So I fell on books. Before, as I've said, I mostly had pictures in the few books I owned (my parents were not big readers themselves—they had no more than a dozen books—and they rarely read to me; I'd ruminated on Bible pictures for four long years); but now there was this new skill in my hands. It even seemed a kind of power in my legs; and I tore off with it, down ways that I must have felt were escapes or at least safe but educational routes.

I was lucky several ways. Our town had a new bright public-library with a friendly keeper (I was well past cure as a book addict before I collided with the species of dragoness who guards so many school and city libraries). My parents, still seriously strapped for funds, bought me most of what I wanted from the local book-and-stationery; and my father's three sisters, who had all had disaster in their lives and walked round it —gave me good books at every holiday. Finally like most American middle-class children, I had free time—vast deserts of time—and I read to survive it.

I've tried to remember my favorite books of those years, from three to adolescence—the ones I owned and resorted to frequently as if they were self-renewing bottles, perpetual virgins. Here are seven which came after the two Bible versions (they retained their hold; Hurlbut's at least, which unveiled the sex). They are in the order I knew them in.

Wigwam and Warpath by Isabel Juergens—thirty-nine one-page lives of famous Indians with sober realistic drawings for each. I still have this, and it still reads well. The brisk prose never condescends or worships but clearly outlines a sizable tragedy—

> The Puritans, relieved to find their enemies exterminated, went back to their farming. All that remained of the once proud race were a few bond slaves and an exhibit in a Boston shop window—the scalp of Sassacus the Untamed. . . . Uncas, their ally, yielded to them and died ingloriously, a poor old man, stripped of his wide domains, a scandal-monger, sodden with the white man's rum. . . . Weta-moo's lovely head was cut off and set on a pole on Plymouth Common. Courage and beauty had not been enough. The Princess Wetamoo's short and unhappy reign was over.

Little People Who Became Great by L. A. Large—lost now and I can't find a copy; but I remember chapters about the childhoods (all rough) of famous figures like Mozart, Lincoln, Louisa Alcott, Andrew Carnegie, Helen Keller, with portraits of each as triumphant adults.

Richard Halliburton's Second Book of Marvels—the travels, to ancient and modern wonders, of a celebrated and eccentric young American, illustrated with photographs which are strong in my memory: reconstructions of the seven wonders of the world, Mount Everest, the wall of China (the only manmade object, he said, that would prove visible from the moon; was he right?). That he'd been to marvels and lived to write them down was an airshaft for me, onto possibility. I knew nothing then of his vanishing at sea.

The Disappearing Floor by Franklin W. Dixon—my favorite in the only series I read, the Hardy Boys: two early adolescents who refused to take mysteries with passive respect, not to mention fear. Their record was perfect.

Minute Biographies by Samuel Nisenson and Alfred Parker—one-page sketches of 150 great men and women, from pharaohs to presidents, with a drawing of each. I copied the drawings in a tablet of my own.

The Boy's King Arthur by Sidney Lanier—a dignified translation of Malory, with colored illustrations (not the well-known N. C. Wyeth set, though I can't find mine). The one I recall was a vision of the Grail, pouring light on its viewer—reward for courage and purity of heart.

Believe It or Not! by Robert L. Ripley (first and second series)—a collection of exotica from the popular newspaper series: men who survived steel bars through their skulls, prisoners who bombed their way to death with only the cellulose from a deck of cards and some bedspring-wire, the world's youngest parents (aged eight and nine).

Why those favorites out of so many hundreds?—for I read by the gross, as child-readers do, sensing virtue in mass (and rewarded for mass: a gold star on each year's promotion certificate for every ten books).

I've said that they all were mysteries; and they were, tales with a thick residue of *Why? Why could that happen? Why did it? Why tell me?* And my *why's*, as I've also said, must have turned inward well before I could read—*Why has the world done such things to me?*—but I was unconscious of the turn, for years. I was far on in adolescence before I began to want stories about myself, stories of lives recognizably like mine. One of the bitter mistakes of my childhood was reading *Toby Tyler or Ten Weeks With the Circus*. It seemed, very threateningly, about me. I'd had a long-held plan to flee to the circus as an elephant-keeper—fleeing both because I felt needed too much, and conversely, to preempt the abandonment I feared. After that (a shattered afternoon in my room), I learned to spare myself. Books were not meant to hurt.

I wanted allegories then and luckily I found them—my bafflements enacted and solved; but solved in concealment and in printed words, safe cold black ink. (I also loved movies but they'd scared me too often; and I learned to choose them more gingerly than books, as I now do television which is dangerously real—real people, really hurting.)

My favorite books all shared this much—they were mysteries allegorically related to my own life, successfully resolved (except for the Indians, who showed me the worst again, with flashes of grandeur) and resolved in human lives. They were all in fact biographies, the stories of others—possible, true, and finished—since I made no distinction in reality between young Andrew Carnegie and Galahad. Even Ripley's garish freaks were alive, burning will and courage as their fuel, however smoky.

All the lives, from Arthur's to the three-headed baby's, had plowed through mysteries, enemies, and failure to say a large simple thing—*You can live a life*. And to say it to me. I had known their stories without the burden of knowing them. Their stories were one, the only right story—*You are needed now and will always be*. They had lived for me then, to show me that. Lives of educational sacrifice, of which I was the object.

I never doubt that. With all my painful awareness of others, in the shapes of the lives of my parents and kin, I never much doubted before age eleven that I was the axle of their world at least and perhaps several more. They were giving me books; the books were for me. It never occurred to me to think books were meant for wide audiences. I knew of course that other children read, but I had no close friends to whom books were urgent. What was urgent for them was company and games, mysteries and skills I mostly avoided, from fear and incapacity. They didn't read because they didn't need to, I guessed (I guessed wrong—they got their stories elsewhere); so I can't recall, as a child, having given a book to a friend as any sort of present. And I wouldn't lend my books. They were tailor-made. I put in a good deal of time on their care—my father had a large case of shelves built for me when I was eight; and I'd find new systems for arranging the volumes every three or four months: much moving and dusting, no turning-down pages or cracking spines. In the seven years between learning to read and age fourteen, when I took to adult fare, I must have acquired some four hundred books. They were all hardbacked (paperbacks being scarce and as badly made as now); many were lovely physical objects; and I know that a real part of my first interest was in their *worth*. They were my big piece of the treasure every child needs to hoard for himself against ruin and desertion, bulwarks and weapons. I had other treasure, the usual kind—arrowheads, my brother's adenoids in a vial—but the books weighed more in every way. They were animate and spoke.

Did I ever want to thank them?—the consoling handsized amulets they were and the spirits they contained? Not for years, no (the care I took of them wasn't gratitude but homage, the fear that they'd vanish to mildew and worms); I was busy using them.

And I've never stopped that. But once I began to inch out of adolescence, lured by books, I met the only adult question—*What will you do?* Since I'd brooded sixteen years on childhood's question—*Can you do anything?*—I had hardly thought of futures. When I had, I'd assumed I'd be an artist, meaning *painter* (I had written a play, but painting was the hope). By sixteen though I'd looked at enough good paintings to see that mine were not. The discovery coincided with my having a high-school teacher, Phyllis Peacock, who urged me to write, praised and questioned my efforts. At first they were poems, like most poems—self-amazed, self-intoxicated: and therefore of no lasting value to me, who always craved others at however great a distance. But my teacher urged on; and at seventeen, I wrote a quick sketch of a poor dirty girl I'd seen peddling greeting cards; a stranger I felt compelled to know—and felt that I knew once I'd written her down.

I didn't, to be sure; but in one page of work, I learned that I might some year, after struggles, have a way to pierce objects and people alike and see to the centers they guarded in fear and say what I'd seen so they'd know themselves and me and welcome me into the dangerous room where they waited alone, as helpless as I. Hadn't I known, since *The Boy's King Arthur*, of sinful Launcelot's sight of the Grail?—

And anon a voice said to him, 'Flee, Launcelot, and enter not, for thou oughtest not to do it: and if thou enter thou shalt forthink it.' Then he withdrew him aback right heavy. Then looked he up in the midst of the chamber, and saw a table of silver, and the holy vessel covered with red samite. . . .

Now I sensed a grail of my own and headed toward it.

I never looked back, not for sixteen years. When I did, after writing a number of stories, I could see how not only *King Arthur* but all my childhood books had told me that, all along, though in secret, covered with samite. And I'd *known* it all along—where my own goal lay, which was everyone's goal, everyone's correct story—and been guided by the knowledge; guided in secret, the way to guide a child, toward a possible life. The knowledge of others, for my help and theirs; for our happy union, trusting and bare.

1976

FAMILY STORIES

THE CARTERS IN PLAINS

DESPITE THE WAVES of tourists and newsmen who, a week before Christmas, are washing over Plains (population 600) and providing brisk business for the Peanut Museum, the sandwich shop, and the new stores selling what Miss Lillian calls "Jimmy-things," the main pastime still seems to be memory—as it is in all villages, Southern or otherwise, where people lead lives of work and family. Stop most anyone you see—they're generally stoppable—and he or she will soon be spinning you a web of recollection to entertain you both. They tend to start with Carters, since that's why you're here; but soon they'll show you a crowd of human reasons for stopping at this wide spot in the road and listening well, even if Jimmy had been born in Savannah and was not their pride. He clearly is and they all call him Jimmy, to your face and his—no reverence yet —as they sketch in his family backward from him. For if you are quiet and let them tell what they need to tell, not what you think you want, then the story is family, unendingly.

There is one memory left to start the story *forward* and work down to Jimmy, who seems a tad still in that ongoing stream. Mr. Alton Carter, age eighty-eight, is Jimmy's dead father's elder brother. A short gentle-voiced man, he haunts his son Hugh's antique store on Main Street, meeting all with old-fashioned manners and a memory that runs back, clear and voluminous, to the early nineties—well before his mother Nina moved here to Plains with him, his three sisters, and his brother James Earl. For with all his tendrils of memory and hearsay that reach from the main stem back toward the Revolution, England, and Ireland, Mr. Alton starts his own tale where he knows it to start—with calamity his own eyes saw up close. His father William, Jimmy's grandfather, was killed in 1903, fifty miles south of Plains in a fight with a man named Taliaferro (pronounced *Tolliver*): "My daddy went over to his place to argue with him about a little desk that he took off. They fought in his store with bottles. They had barrels of beer bottles. They stood there busting bottles over one another's head. My daddy got out and started home, going this a-way; and he got out and started his way, his home was out that a-way. And Taliaferro run off out there about thirty yards and stopped and started shooting. He shot three times but he didn't hit him but once, in the back of the head. He never did have time to get out his pistol. I was as close to him as that truck" [fifteen feet away]. After four trials, Taliaferro was freed; and Nina Carter brought her children to Plains to be near her husband's brother (the family home had remained eight miles away). Alton was fifteen, went to work in the store where he still works daily (then a general store), helped support his family on twenty-five dollars a month, acquired the store in time, and saw Jimmy's father grow and pass him in success: "Everything Earl laid his hand down on, when he picked it up, there was three or four dollars. When he died he left about four thousand acres of land and a heap of money in the bank."

Mr. Alton smiles all through his story; but—today at least, and I haven't led him—it touches his nephew Jimmy only at the end, again in a family way, no thought of world fame: "We still got the family land in Webster County. Earl's wife and children, they got part of it." When asked if he'll go to see Jimmy sworn in, he says, "No sir, I'm too old to get that far from home" and turns to bagging peanuts as you hope some enterprising history-student is motoring toward him with deliberate speed and a carload of tape.

Earl's wife sits across the street at the depot, rocking most afternoons and greeting pilgrims with her tart high-spirits in spite of "muscle spasms from signing my name." Her name was Lillian Gordy; and since the early twenties when she came to nurse, she's been here—eighteen miles from her birthplace (except for two years in India, the Peace Corps). She married Earl Carter and bore him four children—Jimmy the first. Sitting with her there or nine miles away at Faye's mobile-home Bar-B-Q Villa in Americus, you may gather Miss Lillian has all but exhausted her desire to reminisce about Jimmy now. She's seventy-eight and has been hard at it for more than five years—his governorship and presidential campaigns.

She hasn't though. She adores him and, once her quick eyes have cleared you, she comes at her version of the big family story head-on, the way Southern women of her age and class come at everything—"I got my liberalism from my father. Papa was postmaster over in Richland. He'd bring meals from the hotel to the post office and let Negroes eat there; they couldn't eat at the hotel." Or when asked about her father's family—"I never cared much about my kin. I'll tell you why. We were the poor side of the family, and they didn't know me till Jimmy was governor." As straight as that. And whatever else of her version she offers, you're apt to lose in the sight of her strong rich face, lit with joy and the certainty of power around the great eyes. All her story is there. She has stamped all her children with the Gordy good-looks—a still grave radiance that slowly melts into broad delight at the life before them. The flat kindly

face of Mr. Earl's photographs has made no print on any of them except
the rufous Billy, a wily jester; yet Miss Lillian has claimed that they loved
their father better.

She may be right but you feel she knows that she won a victory in
them more important than the balances of household emotion, the victory
deep-cut in the face she gave them—her lockjawed passion for decency,
justice, and her life's conviction that the only honorable surrenders are
surrenders to laughter and mercy. If she's mostly given over now to laughter, pride, and sass, she has earned her fun; and within the fun, one can
still sense rock—a broad standing shaft of rock which one could reach
and stand on if one were in need, not a deferential tourist. She has told
of her struggle to nurse leprous children, a struggle she won. Like all
family women, she has lived for others' needs; and the story of her children
is spun on these poles—their need, her provision, now their various
repayments.

Her elder daughter Gloria, two years younger than Jimmy, is also
close by on the west edge of Plains with her husband Walter Spann. She
tries to place herself for you at once and tell a too-simple tale—"I'm a
farm wife and nothing else; listen, I'm *country.*" *Country* covers a good
many things—most of the life of mankind, for one—but what she seems
to be asking to mean is *naive, innocent.* Again the face talks when the
mouth reneges—her mother's face on Gloria, thirty years younger, broader,
lined differently but as deeply. Even if she hadn't, in self-defense, just
published an eloquent account (*Good Housekeeping*, January) of her own
large sadness—an imprisoned son William, thirty years old—you'd see
that her eyes and smiling mouth have long since given up attempting to
conceal a sizable and only partly-healed wound near the center of her
life. Yet she won't talk of that (and has written about it so she won't have
to talk).

She talks of happiness—"Up till now I've been the happiest member
of our family"—and the hard-won beauty of her face sets the claim. Then
she comes on a memory that has her beaming (they are all splendid
beamers since they knowingly beam against the grain of what they've
endured): "When Jimmy was a boy, we called him 'Hot'—he was always
fired up—but he never liked it; so when he got away to Annapolis, he
wrote me right away: 'Dear Gloria, Please do not call me "Hot" and please
do not write to me on lined notebook paper with pencil.' " That she and
her mother laugh long at the memory is one more piece of the story they
tell—a healthy piece. For anyone who sat out the parched family pieties
of the Kennedy, Johnson, and Nixon years, the sound of home-laughter
that laps round all sides of Jimmy Carter comes as welcome as water.

He is naturally more guarded—anybody who suggests the name "Hot" to his kin and turns up at fifty-two as president-elect was hardly slated to end as a joker—and even in Faye's cafe the next night with a handful of writers, his wife, and daughter, round a ten-foot table over perfect steaks, he is not prone to giggling fits. What he mainly does, or did in that company, is *listen* with a blowtorch intensity which makes most other brands of human attention seem dazed or bored. (And Rosalynn his wife shares the trait—an interest almost animal in strength and necessity, though her brand seems to come from her mother, Miss Allie Smith: a quiet impressive lady with the broad handsome watchful face she's given her daughter.) Some watchers that night—all but me non-Southern—found the gaze a little ominous: *Are we being sized up for future consumption?*

The opposite, I felt. In his own way, he was telling a private piece of the long family story. The son of strong lovable amusing parents (rooted in a place and confident there) and the sibling of vivid and irreverent juniors, he is trained to expect equal fare from the world. He can't often get it, but he's trained to go on trying—as courteous son, tried but patient older brother, as Christian fellow-creature; and as life-long veteran of small-town culture, which requires a sophistication of manners at least the equivalent of manners at Versailles.

The same night, for instance, as we sat at table, an elderly man in clean workclothes approached the president-elect from the rear and touched him on the shoulder. Carter quickly turned, smiled, stood, and called the man's name. The man apologized for interrupting but said that he wanted to say thanks again, that he'd never forget the help Jimmy gave. Then he greeted Rosalynn with the same unabashed dignity and left. Carter sat and, since we were silently curious, offered that the man had phoned him years before when the man's daughter shot the husband who was beating her, that the man had not forgot whom he turned to for help.

As my writer's pattern-making brain was seeing a neat circle close in the air of the past two days—tales of two lethal fights (Carter's grandfather, now this friend's daughter)—Carter quietly inscribed a larger arc: "You may not know what a warehouseman means to a working farmer." Born in a tobacco town half the size of Plains, I felt rightly chastened and remembered that I knew. I also guessed I'd heard one version anyhow of the story I came to hear—the oldest story, of blood-kin, desperate dependency, and mercy: the story we hope to hear in all human discourse. *Our kin, or our townsmen at least, love and guard us against ourselves and the perilous world. They use us kindly when we've turned and left.*

With all the cold fears our last four presidents have drenched us in, all the seedy disbeliefs they've sowed, I left Faye's that night feeling better for my own kin's chances now and lighter on my feet, which slid in

Georgia mud—purple Sumter County clay, the ground of many Carters over 125 years; apparently a national family at last to feed us with stories and the actions they cause: varied fare and nutritious, the stories of care and honest consolation that we've needed for very much longer than was good.

1977

PICTURES OF PRIDE

THE RISE OF Jimmy Carter—lifelong citizen of Sumter County, Georgia, son of Carters who have worked that clay since 1851—has stirred a moil of interest in all things Southern. But the things are only two—the land and the people.

The land constitutes a bull-shaped mass larger than Spain, France, Germany, Austria, Poland, and Czechoslovakia combined. Little more than a hundred years ago—within the memory of a few living people—that mass tried to stand as a separate nation, in defense of the will to possess human chattel, the only means it saw of continuing its life. The people, white and black, are those whose kin fought in or endured that ghastly war (180,000 Southern soldiers died, almost all on home ground); those who lived on in the same stricken place through a century of hostile occupation, the oppression of defeat, the taunts of victors; then a long contemptuous neglect in which to pick at wounds, compound old errors, and digest hard lessons. They are also—and not at all incidently—the people whose kin fought the last and bloodiest battles of the American Revolution, again on their ground.

Now the curious lovely land and people, though still despised by much of the nation as benighted or country-simple at best (in spite of their producing by far the better part of the first-rate original American fiction, verse, and music of the past fifty years and with no sign of flagging)—that land and people find themselves courted by numerous suitors, eager but fish-eyed.

Diplomats and managers with world-sized ambitions fly for job interviews to a south-Georgia village with no hotel or restaurant but a way of life as rich in complexity of manners, language, depth of realism and human comprehension as any Greek city built on rock, any Middle-Eastern village built on man's oldest middens—not to mention America's gorgon-faced cities. Flocks of reporters from world magazines flat-foot through the crossroads and countryside—and are so disarmed by the welcome they receive (the food and robust speech, the courtly self-confidence, the self-aimed wit) that they snap up the locals' own fabulated version of what it all means and head north to write one more total-miss

about Good Old Boys, Chittlin' Suppers, Racial Chasms. Political car-
toonists and television simpletons indulge in a round of Southern jokes
as ignorant and offensive as Earl Butz's blue minstrel-prank on blacks—
and a good deal older (anti-Southern humor predates the Revolution; and
some of the dumbest of the recent wave comes from decamped Southerners
who've fouled their antennae and lost the homing signal). Critical organs
which have long since blown taps over "exhausted" Southern writers are
imploring those same writers now for guidence through the ticking un-
derbrush of dark Dixie—as though we were nimble scouts, not the sad
sclerotics we so recently seemed.

I can say *We*, being among the new scouts—born in the village
South, formed in its culture, and resident in the town South for all but
four of my forty-four years. In fifteen generally gratifying years of publishing the fiction made from my life—therefore "Southern fiction"—
I've heard a few stanzas of taps myself, pumped out by various Northeastern
journalists who've understandably stultified themselves on a diet of Faulkner and Flannery O'Connor (writers whom some thoughtful Southerners
see as sports to the region—homeless rhapsodists, fantasts, mesmerized
haters); and I've felt the occasional chill breath of urban condescension
or bafflement which still awaits all educated Southerners who choose to
live south of, say, Falls Church, Virginia. Yet within recent weeks I've
been asked by a national news-magazine to visit Plains; interview as many
Carters as would hear me out; and write a brief essay on their family (I
did so with pleasure and was met with real kindness by people like the
people I've known since birth—tough, witty, broadly gifted, and mellow
with the wisdom of bend-and-yield and the open-eyed abandon gained
from centuries with blacks). And now the Washington *Post*, this paper
with old Southern ties in a city still largely Southern in tone, sets me this
tidy theme for variation on Inauguration Day—*The South Comes into
Her Inheritance*.

I happen to think that it is such a day of accession-to-rights, that
today a vast region and many million people sense their hard-won return
to a seat of trust at the height of power; and I'm proud to be asked to
perform on its morning. But I also think it's a far more complicated day
than that, so complicated in meaning and promise as to require the
upending of my theme.

First, though, to linger on the sweetness of the day.

Admitted that the South has a crucial share—through Washington,
Jefferson, Madison, Monroe, and a list of worthies—in the making of the
nation; that it held the White House for ten of the first seventeen presi-
dencies, till it forewent the right. Admitted, Jimmy Carter is the first
Southern-born, trained, and sponsored president since Andrew Johnson,

1865–69 (Wilson was trained in the North and elected from there; Lyndon Johnson was Texan, not quite the same thing, and rose to the office on a Washington record). Admitted that, while Carter carried all the Confederate states but Virginia, he won the white vote in only Georgia, Tennessee, and Arkansas. Admitted that a number of Southerners who did not support Carter are taking to the idea of a Southern president— and a Southern First Family—like the perishing to water; and that those of us who did so—who had stayed here and seen it through—exult this morning in an air of vindication and fragile hope. Admitted, that exultation has been earned—by a stream of great art, a work of racial union in advance of the country, by a care for wilderness and wildlife, by a hundred other quiet unadvertised victories.

In the face of all that, still I upend my theme and state it thus— *Today the Nation Enters on Her Southern Inheritance.* The variations follow.

The rural South—which is most of it still and its grandest gift— specializes in sunsets: not the addled-egg, operatic desert kind but a winey dying radiance in sky and trees that makes you all but pray to join the light in its rush toward rest. Or makes you expect to see an angel step toward you from the near pine-woods with the one word you've wanted from God, in gentle hands—*Pardon* or *Welcome* or *Reconciled.* For Southern country landscape still trembles in the grip of spiritual immanence— a land pressed on not only by the living stragglers who cross it but by spirits of Indians; early settlers; Revolutionary soldiers; all the soldiers and civilians who died in rebellion; the slaves and freedmen who tilled and tended; by the God of whom the region is convinced; and by Satan, Prince of This World, Prince of Lies.

I'm rural Southern, as I said, by birth and rearing but an avid indoorsman and no Civil-War student. I've never read *Lee's Lieutenants,* for instance (once a rite of Southern manhood) and cannot replay one battle for you, though my Grandmother Price (whom I clearly recall) was kissed by Lee and though I've known Confederate veterans and former slaves. Yet I've found myself lately, on no conscious search, in the midst of slow sunsets at two large places in the life of that war, empty of living souls but me. Those solitary evenings form an emblem, in my head at least, of some of the urgent gifts and warnings the South now brings the nation. Invisible as they are, I can only hope to hint them—a legacy the nation has requested at last, having finally earned it.

*

Appomattox Court House rides a long low ridge above a small stream in southern Virginia. It is kept now as a park to nail down the memory of Lee's surrender, the end of our fiercest struggle. In American fashion, what had been torn down of the village is now restored to the pristine state of Platonic Forms—no human buildings ever as fresh as these. The surrender house itself, honest family-dwelling of a man named McLean, was dismantled by speculators who planned to erect it as a commercial museum in Washington, then failed; it is now rebuilt—every thirteenth brick is from the original house. Yet you're shown the small parlor, where Lee and Grant never met, with reverence appropriate to the real boards and nails. Well, the *air* is the same; you're on the same old spot on the earth's old skin.

And the skin is the thing—the beautiful place, far from towns and noise, straddling this broad crest of land above the valley in a cold fall sunset. You can turn right from the house and walk a quarter-mile to a viewpoint on the valley. There's a little low contraption with a button to push. More in fear than hope, you push and stand looking over scarlet trees toward night. A clear male voice says that you are on the point where, at dawn on April 12, 1865, the final surrender parade occurred —27,000 Confederate survivors passed and stacked their arms. Then the voice reads a passage from Joshua L. Chamberlain, the Union general in charge of the scene—

> Instructions had been given; and when the head of each division column comes opposite our group, our bugle sounds the signal and instantly our whole line from right to left, regiment by regiment in succession, gives the soldier's salutation,—from the "order arms" to the old "carry"—the marching salute. Gordon at the head of the [Confederate] column, riding with heavy spirit and downcast face, catches the sound of shifting arms, looks up, and, taking the meaning, wheels superbly, making with himself and his horse one uplifted figure, with profound salutation as he drops the point of his sword to the boot toe; then facing to his own command, gives word for his successive brigades to pass us with the same position of the manual,—honor answering honor. On our part not a sound of trumpet more, nor roll of drum; not a cheer, nor word nor whisper of vain glorying, nor motion of man standing again at the order, but an awed stillness rather and breath-holding, as if it were the passing of the dead!

Something human has ascended to the beauty of the place and inhabited it—*one uplifted figure, with profound salutation.* You feel at last. Ninety miles from my house, alone in the place, the great-grandson of men who might have marched here, I feel some atavistic love of kin redeemed and rewarded. Southern kin, I mean—pitiful survivors of their own selfish folly, resourceful to the last in drawing figures on the air, the glorious and hair-raising pictures of pride.

These days there are two main places to visit from Americus, Georgia. Nine miles west is the town of Plains, a pretty (not prettified) standard farm town of the seaboard South—watertank, warehouse, row of old stores, a former railway depot selling souvenirs, skirts of good frame houses (mostly needing paint). Then the houses play out; and west a short way past a pecan grove is a road to the left which will take you through the cemetery another short way past rickety houses played round by black children, to a low yellow house almost in the road with the railway tracks maybe fifty feet in front.

You're at Archery. Miss Lillian has directed you—"You want to get there or see something once you do?" It's a settlement consisting of this sensible house, the disused chocolate-brown store in its yard, and the Negro houses sprinkled in view around it. Another *mental* place, no big ganglion of life, typical of a thousand more Southern place-names which only mark a general locus of feeling, no visible cluster of movement or sound. Any alien motorist tooling through here would see nothing much but the cheek-by-jowl closeness in which two races live and, in the Negro houses, a textbook demonstration of the startling durability of unpainted wood. The house painted yellow, though, was Jimmy Carter's home— the small accelerator, built of kin and work, in which his boyhood was raised to critical speed (his family called him "Hot") and from which he was spun toward the Navy, the statehouse, us.

You can turn just beyond the Carter house and retrace your path through Plains, past Miss Julia Coleman's (the crippled teacher who started Jimmy reading) and Jimmy's own street, now blocked by Secret Service. Then back through Americus and on from there on Highway 49 through the newer well-shaded suburban homes, to the other place.

Six miles northwest of Americus, the flat land begins to roll; and the color of the earth—almost purple round Plains—lightens to doeskin, topped by broomstraw like coarse Viking hair. No houses in sight. You cross Viney Creek, then Sweetwater Creek; then—still vacant country, nine miles from town—you come on some black iron gates to your right. You're at old Camp Sumter, called Andersonville.

Here in a stockaded twenty-six acres between February 1864 and April '65 more than 45,000 Union soldiers were imprisoned—unroofed, scarcely fed, watered only by Sweetwater Creek (soon a sewer) and a spring which appeared in the worst month, August (named Providence Spring by the prisoners). Thirteen thousand died.

A week before Christmas, it's quarter to five. I'm here all alone, only a park attendant waiting at the gate house to close up behind me when I've had my little tour. The sun is performing the grandeur I mentioned. I drive very slowly through the cemetery first; all the dead are there under close white headstones the size of shoeboxes—*William Pike, S. C. Paley, Conrad Drumond*. Then along a sand track through a stand of scrub pine to the campsite itself—the twenty-six acres open to the sky as they were a century back. The near-end offers another button to push—unvarnished facts of horror with laconic reminders that Union prisons were hardly more humane; that a Union prison in Elmira, New York had a death rate comparable with Andersonville's (the best guidebook to New York State will not tell you that; and even the tape at Andersonville ignores the Union's Camp Douglas in Chicago, which had the highest death rate of all the war prisons). Then a few mourning monuments and twenty-five deep holes, dug by prisoners—some for water, some for freedom. Down the gentle slope is Providence Spring and Sweetwater Creek still crossing the site. Nineteen feet inside the vanished stockade is a row of white posts—the Deadline, to cross which was certain death. Little markers for the Dead House, the fort, the hospital. I stop near the creek, walk over dry grass, and stand on the Deadline. No one to see me, not even a crow.

I've been more than one place that has borne great suffering over stretches of time—Dachau the worst, before it was doctored-up to museum status. Such places have about them, however many tourists, their own clear calm—a calm in proportion to the pain they witnessed, as though they had earned perpetual reprieve from mere perturbation. Here is no exception. I surprise myself. I tear a slip of paper from a memo pad and bend and, with the largest coin from my pocket, scratch up a teaspoonful of the dirt. It is sandy, the texture of clean woodashes. I fold it in the paper and mean to keep it always. Four hundred miles from my comfortable house—far from there as Manhattan—I still feel at home. Here at this dense core of human suffering caused—however haplessly—by countrymen of mine, I mainly feel pride and hope in a man I met the night before in a mobile-home restaurant over simple splendid food: James Carter Jr., whose blood-kin were working this country thirteen years before Virginia bureaucrats chose its peaceful hills to bear the thick nightmare of Andersonville. Men herded and starved and dying, no mercy.

Pride and *hope* for one large reason—he is from this place. Not only Sumter County with its special cause for knowledge but the South, the old Cause. What he knows—what my little spoonful of dirt knows—is the South's knowledge (white and black), shared on this continent by only one other people: Indians. *Pride of the self, its passion for power—to own other men and make their choices—will end in helpless cruelty, total defeat, punishment, long decades of shame at the hands of hypocrites.*

In a time when the whole United States has lost its first war, though on foreign ground (a war based on folly much like Confederate folly— the will to use others as tools for our gain), and when three out of our last four presidents are known to have deceived us in directing our lives, the nation has turned to a man who makes no effort to conceal his origins in and indebtedness to that tragic land, people, and knowledge called *South*. Still burdened with the blood-guilt of Vietnam, still fetid at the center of government, we have chosen to hope that such a man might help us cleanse ourselves, might guide us with the ancient human skills his home has shown him—guide us honestly out of the dreamy savage innocence we've wreaked on other peoples and on ourselves into knowl- edge of the wrongs incurred by us all and the will and wit to amend them humbly; then on into fresh lives as men and women on the ruins of our pride, sane neighbors again to a frightened world.

Maybe no man can do that. Maybe this one can begin.

May a countryman offer him profound salutation—this figure in words—as he bends to the yoke.

1977

HOMELESS. HOME.

THE WORD *home* is an obsession of the American language, not of the English. In four years of living in England, I never heard an Englishman use the word *hometown*, for instance. They have the parent-word of course and most of its offspring—there is even a Home Office in their government (concerned, significantly, with internal affairs of the entire country)—but if *home* ever bore the meaning it has for Americans, the meaning has faded. In fact, the dense ganglion of emotion which Americans keep round it only began to settle on the English word in the fifteenth century.

The Oxford English Dictionary has citations from about A.D. 900; but they all define a tangible place, a particular village or house "which one regards as one's proper abode." The *Dictionary* cannot find the word used in our sense as "The place of one's dwelling or nurturing, with the conditions, circumstances, and feelings which naturally and properly attach to it" before about 1460. The first citation is suggestive. In the Towneley mystery plays a character says, "In euery place he shall haue hame"; and *home* sprang finally to life—for a people who had wandered restlessly—as the symbol of safe warm rest, however brief. The root of the word had similar force for our Indo-European and Saxon linguistic ancestors, but many other European languages have no precisely equivalent current word. Modern French, Italian, and Spanish are content with their word for *house*. They have approximations, all connoting *hearth*—*foyer, focolare, hogar*—but like the British, they show little need for a word most Americans need many times a day—*home, hometown, homemaker, homebreaker, beautiful-brand-new-homes-for-sale, homesick, homemade, homewardbound*. Why do we?

We're a nation of vagabonds. Exact figures are hard to come by, but it's commonly claimed that one in three American families moves every year. It's fashionable to speak of such alarming mobility as a recent phenomenon—the product of economic, technological, and moral changes in the wake of the Second World War. Again, reliable figures for the movements of earlier generations are not available; but one fact may be stated and leaned on—*Every American, including the Indian, is here because he left somewhere else. Only black Americans came unwillingly. All except Indians came very recently on the scale of human change, genetic history.* And though the vast majority of Americans—nearly ninety percent—left the "somewhere else" for a tangle of spiritual, economic, and physical reasons, it's important to remember that a heavy reason in many cases was *family.* The "somewhere else" put so irretrievably behind was mostly the home of their family—the endless primeval slough of blood and duty, the puppeteer-hands of older generations.

It was only with the first generation *born here* that what had seemed a clean impulse to freedom began to seem a doom instead, a curse in the seed. The children grew on the labor involved in clearing land or spinning thread to feed family mouths; then once grown, they tore loose and lost themselves in the unimaginable distances provided by America—the Cumberland Gaps, the plains and forests so patiently eager to swallow and hide. Think of all the sons and daughters—labored over, nurtured for years in the natural hope of eventual return (a tended old age)—who one day said plain farewells and rode off westward, out of sight and voice forever: no phones, no regular mail, *disappearance.* Any country's history may be seen with some justice as a series of dramatic genres—tragedy, farce, melodrama, vaudeville turn. A large part of eighteenth- and nineteenth-century American history was a vanishing act; a large part still is.

Four hundred years after Raleigh's lost colony in North Carolina, the spaces still oblige an odd solitary or fugitive or aging hippie; but the monstrous cities now are the perfect maw of anonymity, stripped raw liberty. The girl in the subway—straw-blond and pale, accepting your look with a lucid smile—may be a long-sought Weatherwoman or the Kansas axe-slayer of a family of eight. (By contrast, it seems a fair guess that seventy percent of the present world population lives within fifty miles of its grandparents' birthplace and that eighty-five percent of all *Homo sapiens* in history have never moved more than one day's journey-on-foot from the site of their cradles.)

It's our ingrained American restlessness then, unique in the world for geographical scope and endurance, which demands that we nurse— in our various temporary camps—the idea of home as icon and amulet, gross sentimentality and bedrock truth simultaneously, a truth which has borne these centuries of violation but is murderously roused against us at last, implacably perhaps. The ignored centers of sane human life—literally homes, houses, and towns—are killing us over what we thought were safe distances we'd put between us in our need and fear.

The fear has been multiple; but if it's reducible to a word, then the word is *time.* If we stay at home, we acknowledge a past which, as one of its functions, has given birth to us (contingency then, not spontaneous generation); and worse, we see that past die before us—our parents age, sicken, dissolve in pain; we tend them as they go and learn our own mortality. But flight—ah flight! To leave all that is to cancel its claims. In a strange far place we are free to be ourselves, not subordinate units of a large sponge or hive; and the chance of evading decay and death is real, worth the wandering. But being alive, we require companions—the touch of other bodies. That touch is the friction which begins to wear us; and time finds us anywhere, the ultimate police.

So a sizable part of the premise of America was fallacious, that part we've always called *room-to-grow, a place-to-be-free-in*—when what we meant was a dream of escape, a selfish exile. And the fruits of that deluded planting fall round us now, threatening to smother—Medusa cities which no one can contemplate for long without yielding vital human qualities to stone, a once apparently limitless countryside now helpless at the mercy of a huge population in fevered pursuit of change and "rest," in pursuit of a happiness guaranteed in writing in the charter itself but alas not defined or regulated in any form more public than Jefferson's tabletalk and letters.

Despite sporadic eloquent attempts at rousing by passionate realists, from Thoreau to the Southern Agrarians, the dream careened on its way into nightmare; and only in the last ten years has there been any large-scale sustained effort to wake a giant as huge as the world's largest thoroughly mechanized society. Results to-date of the lengthy tocsin are hard to measure for depth and durability—a healthy new concern for the nonhuman world in all its organic and inorganic forms (which is subject on one hand to missionary excesses, on the other to the disbelief or disregard of the greedy); an apparent movement of population out of urban centers into small towns and the country; the apparent demise among bright young Americans of the notion, strong for the last century, that an invigorating life is only available in cities. I have for instance in recent years taught only one good university student who moved to New York, whereas in my own graduating class of 1955 there were mass dashes for the upper East Side. Graduates seem now to be seeking green places where the only clutter is a franchise-belt on the outskirts of town. What they don't often contemplate is going back home. Why?

—All the above reasons plus a crucial addition: they haven't *had* homes. There are, to be sure, a lot of exceptions; but a high proportion of students at any upper-middle-class American university in the past twenty years will have lived in many places by the end of adolescence. Even now, maybe too deeply rooted myself, I forget and often ask a student "Where did you grow up?" Their first reaction is generally surprise that someone cares enough to ask (odd and antique of me); then they recite me a litany of places—"Well, Cleveland; then White Plains, then Guam for two years, the Philippines for three; then back to Ohio—Shaker Heights, but I don't plan to live there." What they've had is a series of more or less prolonged tourist stops in a series of houses (called "homes" by realtors) in which they never paused long enough for emotional adhesion and which they'll never visit again—often *couldn't* revisit, given our propensity for razing whole neighborhoods every few years. So I was wrong to call their itinerary a litany. A litany is a prayer; in Greek *litanos* meant *suppliant*. A litany of places would be of sacred places. What makes a visible tangible place become sacred for us?

In the founding text of our civilization—the Hebrew-Christian Bible—a spot is sacred forever-after if God or an angel has deigned to touch it.

> It happened when Joshua was beside Jericho—he raised his eyes, looked and, look, a man stood opposite him with his drawn sword in his hand. Joshua went to him and said to him "Are you for us or our enemies?"
> He said "No. I'm come as captain of the host of Yahweh."
> Joshua fell on his face to the earth, bowed and said to him "What does my lord say to his slave?"
> The captain of Yahweh's host said to Joshua "Take your shoe off your foot. The place you stand on is holy."
> Joshua did.

But only the Indians and Mormons contend that America received such visits. For most of us, the chance of hallowing a place is through human means; the site of intense and/or prolonged human feeling becomes special for us. *Nostalgic* is not *sacred* however, and the apparently bottomless nostalgia of Americans for a past that often never was (recall the recent mob-fantasies of the Bicentennial) only half conceals our national puzzlement at lacking both central and local shrines—temples and homes.

Ancient Roman law contained an observation which is relevant here—"Every person makes the place that belongs to him a religious place by the carrying of his dead into it." Since it was forbidden to bury a body within the walls of Rome, cemeteries were just outside; the "religious place" then cannot refer to a citizen's house but must refer to the region of his city—his *patria*, fatherland (which surely does not mean "land that fathered me" but "land of my father"). The dwelling places of the makers of our culture—Jews and Romans—were made into *homes* by the presence, over sizable reaches of time, of spirits: transcendent gods or the souls of dead parents, who were either loved in life and memory or feared in death.

Does such a conviction suggest that hometowns—real *homes*; not the sites, however smiling, of our commerce, pleasure, and reproduction—are possible only for a people convinced of man's immortality? It very well may; the proposition *Are secular homes a contradiction in terms?* would be worth examining. But is there an essence in the old idea which survives theology and can offer us some grounding in a rootless time?

I believe that there is, but it's neither an easy nor comforting essence—individual homes and, around them, the sense of hometown and homeland require long stretches of human time and relative stasis in a circumscribed place. The classic, and continuing, American dream that home is where we hang our hats, that generation after generation of strong and satisfactory children can be raised in a series of widely separated camps—that dream is false and has maimed us near the absolute center of our complex lives: lives as single human beings, as candidates for marriage and parenthood, as citizens of towns and the larger nation, and as souls who crave immortality (if only genetic and geographic). A home is made by the homeless, or veterans of previous homes, when two or more generations of a blood-related family have occupied a dwelling in a single place or several dwellings in a narrowly circumscribed region. Why the requirements on time and mobility?

—Because a safe and rewarding home can only be built round a nucleus of sane and realistic people who have a keen sense of their own possibilities, as those possibilities are foretold and restricted by the visible successes and failure of genetic ancestors. The luxury of such prolonged human observation and deduction is only available when the nucleus stays together, and that is most practical within a single place. Long association with one homeplace has the further great advantage of permitting a person to gauge his own transitory life against the permanent cycles of nonhuman nature or the manmade monuments of towns and cities (though the physical shapes of American cities in this century have proved disastrously shorter-lived than their occupants).

Surely I'm wrong—or if not, then I'm baying at a moon so distant as to be beyond any hope of recall. There are strong objections to all I've said. To state only four of the strongest—

1. You talk as though family and homeplace were archetypal human institutions, natural and indeed indispensible to the species. But in fact both the much lamented extended family and the settled homeplace are

relatively new inventions, like romantic love. Settled homes—either houses or towns—were by no means the rule in most of the world before the middle ages; they're still rare in many countries. The family—as extolled, execrated, longed for—is a late bourgeois development, the inevitable product of a settled rural-urban life and the increases in human lifespan achieved by eighteenth- and nineteenth-century medicine. Before the late eighteenth century, families functioned chiefly as means for the protection of a husband and wife, who could hardly live past forty, and as a brief nursery for whatever children survived the perils of infancy before those children were launched in early adolescence on their own separate lives.

2. Far from being a curse, the American dream of freedom from blood and provincial ties has proved our greatest discovery—or rediscovery; for the American Revolution, in the broadest sense, was a refusal to accept the new bourgeois pieties of an *arriviste* Europe—the "bucket of ashes" of nationalism and paternalistic rule. And what the permanent revolution of modern American society continues to affirm is the ancient truth that happiness is best pursued by units of two human beings, briefly burdened with young, who move in response to their changing needs.

3. How can you as a writer inveigh against a way of life which has fostered a large proportion of the best American fiction and poetry of the past century?—James, Eliot, Pound, Stein, Hemingway, Fitzgerald, plus the subsequent legion of provincials who have worked and won fame in our own brands of exile (New York, San Francisco, or the circuit of universities).

4. Why should you—a bachelor—think that your opinions on home and family carry any more authority than those of the clutch of Italian and Irish bachelors who try to run the sex lives of numerous millions?

I hope my riposte to such objections is already implicit. If extended families and homes are new (but our oldest texts are based on them—the Old Testament, Homer, the Greek tragedians: all obsessed with blood and place), then they are among man's few improvements on nature and should not have been radically revised so soon. Most things described as *freedom* prove to have been only *short escapes*; and however much I admire the work of most of the famous exiles, I can't help believing that they all severely crippled themselves—in breadth of vision, depth of feeling— by abandoning the only places and people they stood some chance of comprehending.

The fourth question, though condescending, is especially strong. I could try to dismiss it by retorting, with my friend George Williams (the happily married father of three), "No one but bachelors knows how to rear children, and they forget once they're married." But I could start at least on a serious answer to this, and all other relevant questions, by speaking in some detail of the homeplace I've known. Like most of the world's living population, I definitely had one, and have it still.

In fact, I have two. I was born in 1933 in the rambling, one-story, wide-porched, oak-shaded house built by John Rodwell, my mother's father, just after his marriage in 1884. The same house had sheltered the births and rearing of his seven children (one died in infancy). He and my grandmother both died in it well before my birth; and his second daughter then reared my mother, who was orphaned at fourteen. The house was in Macon, North Carolina—a collection of some two hundred farmers and merchants, white and black, five miles from Warrenton, the seat of Warren County.

Warrenton was my father's home. His parents—Edward Price and Lula McCraw—lived with their five other children in a two-story house, the core of which was eighteenth-century, on the north edge of that architecturally distinguished town of a thousand, once an important political and social center of the state but becalmed after the Civil War into the immemorial doze of small commerce, tobacco and cotton marketing, and intense reconnaisance of one's neighbors: the life of a thousand other such towns.

Both families were solidly middle-class—Grandfather Rodwell was Macon station-agent for the Seaboard Railroad, Grandfather Price a courthouse clerk. Both had been in the country since at least my great-grandparents' generation and, before, had lived in adjacent counties—all within a hundred miles of their port of entry into southern Virginia.

My parents spent their childhood and youth in Warren County, never going farther than Norfolk or Savannah—short visits to kin. Their long courtship was all conducted on the county's backroads, by its creeks and ponds, in the homes of kin and lifelong friends. Though they were married from my mother's brother's home in Portsmouth, Virginia in 1927 (and honeymooned in Florida, exotic as Tibet), they first lived together in a rented house in Macon, a few yards from my mother's birthplace (my mother's best friend's brother had killed himself on the porch of the house a little while before). And they lived on there, changing houses several times through the difficult first years of marriage. In response to Depression anxieties, with his demanding mother five miles away, and pressed by my own mother's orphaned fear of abandonment, my father drank a good deal and earned almost nothing—unforeseeable misery, though neither family had lacked the occasional premonitory drinker. Still they held on—helped by family loans of money, homegrown food, and sometimes rooms—through five rough years. In 1932, as the slow curve of the crash was nearing bottom, my father got a job selling insurance in the nearest larger town—Henderson, fifteen miles away—where they lived with a distant cousin. Maybe on the strength of that small injection of hope and change, they started a baby. On January 31st, 1933—the absolute bottom—the baby announced its imminence; they drove to Macon to Mother's home and called Father's childhood friend, Dr. Frank Hunter. After an agonized dangerous night in which my father made a silent vow to reform, the baby appeared—me, battered but heavy ($9\frac{1}{2}$ pounds)—in the room where my mother had survived her own childhood, a few steps from where she herself had seen day and her own parents had died: home, a magnet grounded in a single place for fifty years, powered by a relay of actual lives; lives known and honored, repellent and adhesive, loved and resisted.

We stayed nearby—rooms in Henderson, Macon, Warrenton—for another two years as my father struggled to fulfill his vow while selling insurance to the handful of locals who had money left. Then he got a better chance, selling electrical appliances; and we moved even farther away to Roxboro, a little larger than Warrenton and with textile mills but with a similar atmosphere, minus visible kin.

Over such a short space, the kin continued to exert their attraction. Three letters to my father from his mother survive from these first years away. Her locally famous wit and beauty are burned off them by the heat of her age and sickness, the disappearance from her house of all her men (her husband was dead, her other sons had moved to Tennessee); and what remains is the unmitigated demand for solace, the confidence of a right to unaltered love. All are headed simply *Home* and the day of the week:

> I was never so hurt in my life as I was when the whole week passed and not a word a line nor a sight of you. . . . I can't tell you how glad I was to see you Sunday I just couldn't express myself. . . . I am still without [toe pads] and want you to see to my getting some at once.

No wonder he moved us farther west, a hundred miles—to Asheboro, a lively two-class textile town. A "promotion" to be sure, which he couldn't refuse after ten years of want, especially now that his drinking was over and he and my mother were settling happily into the eighteen unclouded years they would get before his death.

Still, neither of them questioned that *home* was *hometown*—the two hometowns, two houses, two people: his mother and the sister who'd reared my mother (plus the gang of other kin, all as hungry for laughter as my young parents, in a place and time where laughter mainly required live comedians—family jokers—on your own front porch). At our farthest remove, there was seldom a month when they'd didn't pack me, and in time my brother, into whatever Pontiac we could then afford and head for home: two days of talk, commiseration, and fun among those who had known us all our lives and would know us to the end, one of whom could be counted to answer when called (whatever the need), all of whom loved us because we *existed*, not for what we had done or promised to do. (It would be sentimental to conceal that *home* also meant, quite properly, continuous bounty—vegetables, hams, perfect preserves. We once sent my mother's sister a wire—"Planning to get there in time for supper." The notoriously erroneous station-agent in Macon received it as "in time for supplies"—"More truth than poetry," as Mother said.)

I trust it's clear that I shared their feeling. Home for me then was Macon—the house and specifically Mother's sister Ida in it. She served for me all the functions of an ideal grandmother—unquestioned love and generosity, without the rip-tides of parental love—and looking back now, I can guess that I served a similar need of hers. Her own sons were grown; she had suffered severe menopausal depression just before I was born. I was trusting and ready to take what she gave, give what I had. From the age of five, I would spend two weeks with her each summer. While her husband was overseeing farms and timber, she and I would sit in the green porch-swing (she scratching my head) and rehearse the past—always the family past, which already held me. And, with appropriate changes, that bond lasted all her life. She died when I was thirty-two; and years before, her love had settled on one of her young grandsons; but she I and maintained to the end the unbroken grace of flawless lovers. She never failed me—and may be the one person I never failed.

In Asheboro we shifted restlessly. In seven years there we lived in five places—four rented, one built by us to be ours but lost on a mortgage in 1941. I (a leaden soul) don't remember minding the moves at all, though it's hard now to explain them. With the exception of the house we tried to own, we lived in pleasant middle-class apartments and one nice house—no discernible social climb or fall. I can guess that my mother's bouts of the blues (this side of melancholia) required, and briefly responded to, change; but the fact that mattered was *We had a home. We could camp-out at will, May-dancers at the ends of pole-anchored strings. Someday our circling would gather us in.*

After ten years it did. Father was offered a still better job, traveling eastern Carolina. Warrenton would make an ideal base. He looked to the move with nearly fervent hope—his mother was dead but his sisters were there; so was my mother's larger family to whom he was devoted and his boyhood friends (mid-fortyish by then); so was the place itself, hardly changed to the eye. My mother was a little less enthusiastic—vividly gregarious, she had her own life of friends in Asheboro; plus some reluctance to be grounded that near the brainy keen wit of her inlaws. I was appalled. At age eleven I was only just emerging from a solitary childhood into friendships, games, Cub Scouting, school-success—the great American preadolescent barndance. Weighed against the prospect of my first conscious uprooting, the thought of being five miles from Aunt Ida seemed negligible to me; we had nothing to prove by proximity. My brother at three was too young to care. So I mounted a dog-in-manger campaign while my father decided. He decided to go.

It failed for us all. Not pure failure—there were happy days but the unchanged appearance of the town was illusory. Father's friends were long since sunk in their own lives—home, work, inlaws: very few lazy evenings at the eternal drugstore. Worse, both his family and Mother's naturally turned out to be more abrasive in steady contact than in weekend visits. And the town children rose almost as a body to reject the antigen of me. We stuck it out three years—in a hotel apartment and a rented house; then Father was promoted to department-head and transferred to Raleigh, sixty miles away.

We were happiest there, free again for visits home but free *of* home. In our own ample house on a friendly street, Father well-paid at last, Mother busy with a new set of neighbors, my brother and I content in our schools, we had a nice run of Indian summer—seven years, barely disturbed. In the midst of that, Father made a solemn gesture to confirm our happiness. He bought a grave-plot in a Raleigh cemetery, space for four exactly. For him, a great visitor of his parents' graves, to commit himself to lying all those miles from them was—I see now—the emblem of a deep change of heart in him, of his own mature intention and hope. *Home would be here now.* Then he died of lung cancer—1954, fifty-four years old.

I was twenty-one—a junior at Duke, half an hour away but gone for good, I knew, for a good American reason: the pursuit of freedom. Mother was forty-nine, my brother thirteen. They stayed in place through the pain of adjustment while I spent three far more amusing years of graduate study and writing in Europe. Yet however much I relished my distance throughout those years, however much filling-out (or stunting) I accomplished in a new unfiltered light, I never really thought of not returning—returning like my parents: *near* but not *there*. When I finished my graduate degree, my old university offered me a job; and I came back, to Durham where I'd spent four good undergraduate years—sixty miles from my hometown, twenty miles from my mother and brother in Raleigh in the one house we'd all been happy in.

I've been here ever since, nineteen years this fall, in a good country house in landscape very much like my home county—pine woods, gentle hills, wide hazy pastures, small brown bottomless ponds. The place I love most, in which I can work and rest from work; a place I call home, though I know it isn't.

Father was wrong, for me anyhow. His grave was in Raleigh for memorial visits and, much too soon, Mother's beside him; mine will probably be there. But the likable town has no deep resonance for me. When Mother died and we emptied and sold the good house, I was thirty-two. I experienced the vanishing of the older generation mostly as a dread of *homelessness*, an experience which many with their own children about them have shared. Much as I loved my house in Durham, it was *that*— a lovable house but hardly a "religious place" containing my dead. And Warren County was too tender with memory for comfortable visits. A scary time, recorded metaphorically in a novel of mine called *Love and Work*.

Work and friends got me past it. Through the writing—*Love and Work, Permanent Errors, The Surface of Earth*—I've transferred my dead here into my house, in the ways that matter for me. My brother has returned from the Navy and his own graduate study to Raleigh—not our old side of town—and his family there is happily my family. In his two daughters, whom our parents never saw, I see clear glimpses of their old sober joy in kin and home.

But *home* is Warren County still—for me, now that the tenderness has passed. Aunt Ida is dead, the Rodwell house is rented to a family friend, I haven't been in it for twelve years. My younger cousins have moved away. Integration has altered many old rhythms—some bad but some that were slow and attentive, productive of a broad deep compatibility. A small but ambitious franchise-belt has begun to close its ring; the overblown attempts at "old" houses sit gracelessly beside originals; the ladies clubs have taken to some brands of beautification which are hardly that (nothing new there though—in 1900 a cousin of mine said "Hogs, honeysuckle, and women have *taken* Macon"). Many of the landmarks remind me as much of adolescent woe as of happiness. Let me see it, however—as I do twice a year—and home it is, despite the fact that I know very little detail about its life in the last thirty years.

It knows me though, in the chief ways that seem by now to matter or help. It knows because for nearly two hundred years it has held in close quarters and watched closely most of the elements from which I was made—the runlets of physical life coming downward into wider streams, the literal blocks of heredity from which our lives are built like walls: good or bad but endless.

To state that more firmly—I can go there now (an hour's drive) and visit at either end of town two of the three survivors of my parents' blood-generation: Mother's nearest sister Alice, Father's nearest sister Lulie. Both are not far from eighty; both live alone, their children at a distance; both have had serious illnesses lately. Yet they welcome me with a cheerful vitality rarely seen now in children; and once we have got through a brief warmup ("How is so-and-so?"), they respond to my curiosity about their lives and the lives behind them in a generous rush of clear memory, wit, understanding, relief and urgency.

The relief lies in the fact that I care (though I'm not the only one); that all those great heads of human energy generated in their sight and hearing will not merely drift into space and oblivion, not yet. The urgency lies in their *knowing* it all matters—the shapes they can now see in what was once splendid and painful tangle, shapes which they know are both satisfying in themselves (symmetrical, diverting) and instructive.

What's to be learned of course is *Who I am.* Not simply that I'm a Price, a Rodwell, a McCraw, White, Egerton, Reynolds, Bondurant, Solomon, that a sixth-great-grandfather was the Huguenot emigrant Matthieu Agee (whom I share with James Agee)—though the litany of names itself is consoling, I could find it in the State Library. The vital addition is the stories that go with the names, the hundreds of stories which are (know them or not) the cards in my hand, to play or misplay or shuffle at will but never to discard. And from the stories, when they're dealt out before me in the voices of women who saw them and understand them now, comes a single smiling unanswerable voice, *You have your own story but you make it from ours. We are all you know, give or take the odd external fact, the odd external pressure to bend. You are all we know. We worked, in what seemed the urgent light of our earthly days, to have our own lives and know them clearly, when what we were really straining toward, blind as moles, was the chance that you and your generation would use us well, see us whole; that beyond you—endless stages past you—our story, stripped of even our names and yours, would state itself plainly: Life in the singular creature Man achieved its summit in stable centers of the Earth called* homes. *There, groups of blood-kin gathered for protection, love, and continuance. Also for punishment, cruelty, greed. But no other form of life was found possible by which significant numbers of the species avoided monstrosity or desolation.*

The voice says also, *Promise us to keep this story true, so our own laughing tragedies shall not have been vain.*

Any home-reared child, with whatever enormous reluctances, will make them the promise—hoping in his own turn to hear it, at home.

1977

A SINGLE MEANING

NOTES ON THE ORIGINS
AND LIFE OF NARRATIVE

A NEED to tell and hear stories is essential to the species *Homo sapiens*—second in necessity apparently after nourishment and before love and shelter. Millions survive without love or home, almost none in silence; the opposite of silence leads quickly to narrative, and the sound of story is the dominant sound of our lives, from the small accounts of our days' events to the vast incommunicable constructs of psychopaths.

It is odd then that nothing is known of the origins of narrative and that few serious attempts have been made to speculate on those origins —the conditions (supernatural, psychic, physiological, or social) which resulted in the development in man of a story-telling response to inner and outer events.

Of course, if we assume that narrative is specifically a human function, then we confess that nothing firm is known of the origin of the species itself. But the assumption that narrative is purely human is decidedly shaky—there is increasing evidence that apes, whales, and porpoises have elaborate narrative needs and powers and that almost all animals possess systems of communication, means for the transfer of information at least if not narrative—ants, bees, birds, snails? bacteria? That is a later question however—of the difference between narrative and information.

It is not immediately clear what questions should come first in any inquiry into sources, possible causes, of a need so universal and so ruthlessly pursued by seductive geniuses, paralyzing bores, deaf-mutes, madmen—almost all human creatures—but a question very near the beginning would be *When did man develop language?*

There is no answer yet. Paleoanthropologists change their minds annually after digesting each summer's African digs, but recent information available to laymen suggests that manlike creatures (*Homo erectus*) existed as early as three and three-quarter million years ago.* And some

New York Times, April 12, 1975, p. 29; March 9, 1976, p. 14.

recent disputed evidence would push linguistic ability in man, or at least the presence on the brain of the speech-essential Broca's area, back to between two and three million years ago.* Yet our oldest known samples of linguistic writing are only some five thousand-five hundred years old —considerable room for guessing. Linguists have obliged with centuries of speculation on the origin of language—divine gift (the theory of most ancient peoples and a few modern students), imitation of nonhuman sound (what Max Müller called the Bow-wow theory), response to pain or intense feeling (the Pooh-pooh theory), natural accompaniment to common acts of labor (the Yo-he-ho theory), mystic correspondence between sound and sense (the Ding-dong theory), inevitable result of brain structure, and on and on: the literature is immense. In the light of what follows, one guess deserves notice—Otto Jespersen's suggestion that

> the genesis of language is not to be sought in the prosaic, but in the poetic side of life; the source of speech is not gloomy seriousness, but merry play and youthful hilarity. And among the emotions which were most powerful in eliciting outbursts of music and of song, love must be placed in the front rank.†

A student of narrative who enters linguistic speculation is likely to feel soon, however, that while story and language are now solidly bound, they may not have been so for long on the scale of human time. He may even begin to wonder if the need to narrate was not in itself crucial to the origin of language—*to narrate* as distinct from *to inform.*

The informative and protective advantages of an ability for verbal narration are obvious, and it does not require the anecdotal etiology of "A Dissertation upon Roast Pig" to imagine other pressures to narrate upon mute creatures. Modern human beings tell themselves stories well before they possess speech or substantial experience of the world—all healthy babies dream. Given the proclivity of adults in most societies to value and fear and share their dreams, that pressure alone may have been powerful in the drive for speech, as it still seems to be. (Dogs dream but have not yet spoken in sizable numbers, though the fact that they are such new artifacts of man's genetic mischief absolves them of laziness— if not of the conscious frustration which dog-lovers suspect their pets to experience at the inability.) Few babies however can have launched their maiden speeches with "Falling!" or "Starving!" or "Dark!"—perhaps the common subjects of their dreams. To be sure, parents seldom prompt with such words; yet babies hear adults use and reuse thousands of words

* *New York Times,* April 21, 1976, p. 33.
† Otto Jespersen, *Language: Its Nature, Development, and Origin* (London, 1928) p. 433.

from large vocabularies. Why do they generally choose to begin with a family name?—Ma-ma, Pa-pa.

—Because there are needs which result in speech but are not needs *for* speech. Language is vehicle, almost never destination. So the first question in a search for the roots of story would not be *When did man speak?*, but it might be *Why?* The second would then be *What did he say?*

We have scant evidence, from any known cultures, to answer either. Oddly, few mythologies offer elaborate explanations of the origins and early nature of speech. The Egyptian god Thoth spoke the words which created the world; the Hindu goddess Vak created the world by saying "Bhu"; in Plato's *Cratylus* Socrates affirms that the gods gave all things their proper names and that Hermes conveyed those names to men; numerous peoples preserve explanations of the diversity of languages similar to the story of the Tower of Babel. But the fullest and most thoughtful account is that which begins the Hebrew Bible—Genesis 2, the story of the start of what is now western civilization.

Adam breaks silence first, like most children, to name his companions—

> God Yahweh molded from the ground each beast of the field and each bird of the skies and brought them to the man to see what he might call it and whatever the man called each living soul was its name. So the man gave names to all cattle, birds of the skies, and each beast of the field.

That initial speech fails. We are told at once "But for man he did not find a helper as his mate," and the creation of woman follows to remedy the lack. In Book VIII of *Paradise Lost*, Milton's Adam expands convincingly upon the lightly sketched but richly implicit dilemma of Genesis—

> *Thou [God] hast provided all things: but with mee*
> *I see not who partakes. In solitude*
> *What happiness, who can enjoy alone,*
> *Or all enjoying, what contentment find?*

And to God's subsequent argument that He is single also, Adam replies keenly,

> *But Man by number is to manifest*
> *His single imperfection, and beget*
> *Like of his like, his image multipli'd,*
> *In unity defective. . . .*
>
> (VIII, 363–366, 422–425)

Adam spoke, in Genesis and *Paradise Lost*, not to assert ability or do-
minion but to search for "a helper as his mate." Our central myth of the
origin of language says that man invented speech to define his solitude,
to confess his tragic incompleteness. (From Genesis we gather that Adam
also invented narrative; when God hunts out the human pair after their
fall, Adam says, "I heard Your voice in the garden and feared, since I'm
naked, and hid myself"—a chronologically consecutive account of more
than one past event, with attention to cause and self-defense: thus a
narrative.)

So while myths of the origin of speech are provocative, they will not
bear the weight of a search for bedrock. What is needed is a record of
early human speech; obviously there is none, though there are intriguing
modern fragments which look like survivors but promise more than they
tell—incantations in what appear to be, but almost certainly are not,
abstract sounds:

> *Da a da da*
> *Da a da da*
> *Da a da da*
> *Da kata kai.*
>
> *Ded o ded o*
> *Ded o ded o*
> *Ded o ded o*
> *Da kata kai.* *

Recent studies of primate communication also offer numerous openings
for luxuriant analogy; continuing investigation of the physiology of brain
and mind (and such humbler matters as the evolution of teeth, tongue,
and jaw) may yield leads; so may further studies of primitive languages,
further archeological and evolutionary findings. But anything resembling
an answer evades us and may always do so.

Whenever man first spoke, whatever he said, he seems to have waited
millions of years to make records. The earliest known "written" records
seem to be the engraved bones and stones which Alexander Marshack has
studied so freshly and convincingly—upper paleolithic remains from Africa and Europe, some perhaps thirty-five thousand years old. † Marshack
believes and argues strongly that they demonstrate sophisticated and partially decipherable methods for calculating and recording lunar phases
and perhaps menstrual and pregnancy cycles and for symbolizing the

---

* Aboriginal rain song, Australia. Caillois and Lambert, *Trésor de la Poésie Universelle*
(Paris, 1958) p. 25.
   † Alexander Marshack, *The Roots of Civilization* (New York, 1972).

elements of hunt and vegetation stories and rites. Hundreds of such examples are already known, and they push the history of both writing and narrative back ten thousand years beyond the famous cave paintings of France and Spain (the nature of whose narrative content, if any, is hotly debated).

Yet, to repeat, man as a recognizably distinct animal is perhaps four million years old. His use of a fairly complex range of tools is nearly as old; his control and use of fire is perhaps eight hundred thousand years old—and each of these skills tempts us to infer some form of oral communication, if only for the teaching of skills to others. Our oldest samples of writing in pictographic and alphabetical characters are only some five thousand years old; and our oldest narratives (*Gilgamesh* and a few other Near-Eastern stories) were recorded as recently as 2500 B.C., though there is reason to think they existed orally well before. Thus the known history of narrative begins roughly five-sixths of the way through what may be the *life* of narrative. The early stories which we call primitive come after millions of years of practice; they are intensely sophisticated products, though the conditions from which they proceeded may have resembled early man's so closely as to make the later stories much like his, in aim at least. Still, we know nothing of the causes and early career of a force so powerful in most daily lives. Can there be fruitful guesses? Why try?

I'll speak personally. Eight years ago I arrived, age thirty-five, at the traditional midroad of fatigue, choice, and question. The less private questions concerned my work. I'd published five books, all of them narrative; and while they'd been received with the rewarding if not smothering warmth that awaits complicated but communicative fiction in a prosperous country of two hundred-twenty million (only some few thousand of whom are committed readers of more than simple tales), I found myself questioning an impulse which had moved me since early childhood and which for almost twenty years had seemed a nearly central, surely permanent one. Could I go on for decades maybe, laboring to tell complex narratives to shrinking audiences? (the critically fashionable fiction of the late sixties was either urban-hectic or academic-experimental; it had not then become as clear as it since has to publishers, critics, or English professors that paying customers for those brands of chic would not stay amused for long). Whatever the difficulties of some of my work, I'd always felt that my own impulse—starting as it did among beloved kin who were not readers—had been toward simplicity, clarity, availability. At thirty-five I was not only doubting that such power was any longer possible to a complex narrator (as it had been to the writers on whom my adolescent ambition was formed: Dickens, Tolstoy, Twain, Hemingway)—I was also asking why I'd started at all in such an odd trade. Or landed in it; I'd started as a painter. In the midst of such questions, and while writing perhaps my least available stories, I found myself turning with increasing frequency to something new and strange—literal translations of short, almost blindingly lucid Bible stories.

They had not been the first stories I knew—both my parental families were ceaseless hives of oral narrative, and my earliest narrative memory is purely visual: my bedridden paternal grandmother slapping my own mother as she bent to kiss her—but they were the earliest I remember encountering in print. That same grandmother gave me *Wonderful Stories of the Bible* by Josephine Pollard when I was three—stories of Adam and Eve, Noah, Abraham and Isaac, Jacob and his sons, Moses, Samson, Saul, David and Jonathan, Solomon, Elijah, Daniel, and Esther. When I was four my parents, who were religious but not churchly, gave me Hurlbut's *Story of the Bible*—an essentially complete, surprisingly unlaundered version of Old and New Testaments, lavish with illustrations from nineteenth-century German art: none of your fumigated Sunday-school confections but credible ancient orientals, hairy and aromatic. Years before I could read, and I was seldom read to, I studied the pictures and built my own stories on the rapid summaries extorted from my parents. The two pictures I recall as favorites had tragic or violent implications—young Isaac bearing his own funeral pyre up a hill behind his father and young David hacking off the vanquished giant's head. I don't recall any fascination with gentler scenes—Jesus and children, the Good Shepherd and his sheep—though I do recall numerous pensive visits to the picture of Jesus raising the dead little girl (the magnet there was not the great feat but the unvarnished news that children were serious people and could die). Once I could read, I adjusted my versions to the textual norm and turned to other stories, though the Bible stories stayed in my head; and in a pious adolescence, the stories of Jesus surfaced again as straws in the dense hormonal maelstrom. The second sizable narrative I wrote was a play about the Magi (age thirteen—the first was a play about Queen Isabella); and a freshman course in Bible was one of the lights of my undergraduate years. But aside from a permanent interest in the hidden life of Jesus, I'd made no continuing resort to the central narratives of my culture.

Here I was however at age thirty-five like a well-fed, air-conditioned anchorite, studying the actual words of the stories, struggling to haul them into true modern English—first, Abraham and Isaac; then Jacob and the angel; then the risen Jesus and the fishing disciples. I didn't know Hebrew and, at first, very little Greek but worked from literal scholarly versions toward my own bare likenesses. Why, conceivably?

First, after years of planning, I'd begun to feel ready at last to work on a long novel. At that point in the late sixties, I thought of the project as a kind of realistic allegory of my own peculiar relation to my father; and my first translation, the sacrifice of Isaac, was a conscious calisthenic for the novel. I even went further and wrote a series of meditations on the narrative implications of Rembrandt's four pictures of the scene. * (My father was seriously alcoholic in the six years of marriage before my birth; when both my mother and I were endangered in a difficult labor, he made a vow to quit his drinking if both of us lived; we did and he quit. I was told of the vow by the time I was five and from then on saw myself in stronger light as a pledge, a hostage with more than normal duties and perils.) So while I was still a ways from starting the novel, the early translations did whet my interest and force me to dwell on the tight range of actions and characters which has proved of any enduring interest or use to the species—family dependencies and internal revolts, tribal war against unrelated enemies, personal revenge, single combat or union with a god.

The second reason is one that doesn't discuss well. In a hard time I was turning to the inscribed bases of beliefs which had supported me and my family. The stories I was choosing were the stories I needed; and the effort to bring those inscriptions over three or four millennia, faithfully and cleanly, seemed as potent a talisman as any. As I survived the time, began to write the novel, and continued the translations, I began to see that they were not only protective but instructive. I suspected I was learning, or relearning none too soon, essential facts about my trade—facts which made the long job move more easily than any previous; facts which slowly came to seem laws, visible there near what seemed both the roots of the hunger for story and of story itself. The root of story sprang from need—need for companionship and consolation by a creature as vulnerable, four million years ago and now, as any protozoan in a warm brown swamp. The need is not for the total consolation of narcotic fantasy— our own will performed in airless triumph—but for credible news that our lives proceed in order toward a pattern which, if tragic here and now, is ultimately pleasing in the mind of a god who sees a totality and *at last* enacts His will. We crave nothing less than perfect story; and while we chatter or listen all our lives in a din of craving—jokes, anecdotes, novels, dreams, films, plays, songs, half the words of our days—we are satisfied only by the one short tale we feel to be true: *History is the will of a just god who knows us.*

All these motives and no doubt others remained in force for eight or nine years—still do in fact since, while a piece of that novel is finished, other pieces are in sight; life is never scarce on quandaries, and all ques-

* See p. 125 above.

tions continue. Meanwhile, they've produced this collection of stories—
perhaps not quite the oldest surviving but the oldest which bear directly
on our lives, the line of our culture. They are offered with a prefatory set
of questions and considered guesses on the origin, behavior, and destination of story—the chief means by which we became, and stay, human.

The English words *story* and *narrative* come toward us through Greek,
Latin, and French from two Proto-Indo-European roots—*weid* and *gno,*
seeing and *knowing*. Thus other words related to *story* are *wisdom, vision,*
wit; related to *narrative* are *kith, recognition,* and *prognosis*. The etym-
ological messages might be expanded thus—a story is an account of something seen, made visible in the telling. A narrative is an account of
something known, especially by the narrator but partially by his audience
(their response to total *news* could only be bafflement). Such expansions
would seem initially unexceptionable; yet they are not entirely implicit
in the definitions given by the dictionary which provides the etymologies
(*The American Heritage*)—both words are defined from the point of view
of the teller; the audience is considered only as an object to be "interested
or amused." Even Webster's Third thinks of the audience only as a passive
thing to be cheered, despite the fact that *The Oxford English Dictionary*
cites as the earliest use of *story* in English a sentence which is chiefly
concerned with audience—"Me schal, leoue sustren, tellen ou theos storie
uor hit were to long to writen ham here."* (In the following, I use the
words *story, narrative,* and *tale* interchangeably because English does,
though clear distinctions would be useful.)
    Numerous European and American stories of the past fifty or sixty
years—say from *Ulysses* onward through Nabokov, Borges, and Beckett
to their many disciples in the present American academic tradition—have
shared the view of contemporary dictionaries. So far as we can measure
the pressures which produced them, they seem to have been more than
half reflexive—the story told for the teller's sake (amusement, relief, revenge, reward). Your local bookseller can, while unloading the day's gross
of cookbooks and whore's memoirs, tell you the average reader's response
to such sealed and guarded stories; and it's my experience that a majority
of readers when asked to define *story* will include themselves as audience
in their answer. For years I've asked the question of students as they enter
my narrative-writing class, before their views have been pressed on by

---

* From the *Ancren Riwle*, A.D. 1225.

mine. Here are three responses, thoughtful but typical, from American university students in the immediate past—

> A story is a re-creation of event played out by characters, real or imagined, which unites teller and audience in the recognition of some truth newly remembered or known in a new way.

> A story is a means of creating communion between two people, a teller and a listener, for the purpose of transmitting some knowledge from the teller to the listener.

> A story is a digression from the listener's life offered by the teller as a gift, serving its purpose through their mutual diversion.

A great weight of evidence suggests that an understanding of story as transaction has been basic to the life of narrative as far back as we can see. The very existence of such ancient acts of communication as *Gilgamesh* and the patriarchal cycles of Genesis; the opinions of Plato, Aristotle, Horace, Longinus, the Italian and English Renaissance critics, eighteenth and nineteenth-century European aestheticians—all begin from an assumption that verbal narrative actively seeks an audience. Sir Philip Sidney in 1583 summed the opinion of all theory before the twentieth century—

> [The poet] beginneth not with obscure definitions, which must blur the margent with interpretations, and load the memory with doubtfulness; but he cometh to you with words set in delightful proportion, either accompanied with, or prepared for, the well-enchanting skill of music; and with a tale forsooth he cometh unto you, with a tale which holdeth children from play, and old men from the chimney corner.*

The vehicle of early narrative (and of virtually all written narrative before Sterne) is simplified in language, rhythm, and structure not because it is "primitive" but because its communication, generally oral, was urgently desired by at least two parties: teller and told. Only as recently as the eighteenth century do we find that what Erich Kahler has called "the inward turn of narrative"† results in a trickle of stories which begin to be difficult of access—because they have no desire to be easy or because

---

* Sir Philip Sidney, "The Defense of Poesie" in Allan Gilbert ed., *Literary Criticism: Plato to Dryden* (New York, 1940) p. 427.

† Erich Kahler, *The Inward Turn of Narrative* (Princeton, 1973) p. 5. "The direction of the interacting development of consciousness and reality is shown . . . to be a progressive internalization of events, an increasing displacement of outer space by what Rilke has called inner space, a stretching of consciousness."

they lack the ability (among the revelations of Bible narrative is its vast demonstration that the most complex material imaginable may be contained and offered in lucid forms). The floodtide of real obscurity waited another two centuries, for the backwash of romanticism. There may have been difficult ancient narratives which do not survive, and from the beginning of the lyrical impulse there must have been difficult poems. Poets historically have made the more insistent claim to be god-inspired, therefore subject to tongues or babble; and the lyrical impulse is by nature more directly reflexive than the narrator's. No poet has stated that more fully than the Eskimo hunter Orpingalik—

> Songs are thoughts, sung out with the breath when people are moved by great forces and ordinary speech no longer suffices. Man is moved just like the ice-floe sailing here and there out in the current. His thoughts are driven by a flowing force when he feels joy, when he feels fear, when he feels sorrow. Thoughts can wash over him like a flood, making his breath come in gasps and his heart throb. Something like an abatement in the weather will keep him thawed up. And then it will happen that we, who always think we are small, will feel still smaller. And we will fear to use words. But it will happen that the words we need will come of themselves. When the words we want to use shoot up of themselves—we get a new song. *

That would seem a statement congenial to the one great poet who is also an actor in the following pages—David, dancing nude and ecstatically before God in 2 Samuel 6.

It is by no means sure that the chronicler of Saul's and David's reigns, who gives us that picture—the virtual inventor of modern history and biography, five and a half centuries before Herodotus—would have chimed to the sentiment. Nor Homer, who was more nearly a nineteenth-century novelist than a twentieth-century poet. Wouldn't they have spoken initially of preservation?—preservation of the deeds and thoughts of others for purposes of memory and instruction, the aim which moved Joshua to call for the cairn of stones, "these stones will be a memory to Israel's sons forever" (Joshua 4) or of John in writing his gospel, "These signs have been written so you may believe Jesus is the Messiah, God's son, and so—believing—you may have life in his name" (John 20).

Any such commitment to memory—to narrative simply—is a commitment to free-flowing transaction, to gift and receipt, to the detention however brief of easily bored, forgetful audiences. In fact, despite continuing uncertainty in some linguistic, textual, historical, and theological

---

* C. M. Bowra, *Primitive Song* (Cleveland, 1962) p. 36.

matters, there are no difficult stories in the Old or New Testaments, none which do not seem quickly visible in the arc of their action to a wide range of human beings and to virtually all veterans of Judeo-Christian culture. In the teeth of sectarian attempts to veil them, convert them into arcana, they remain firmly clear—the core of their meaning plain on their faces, when the faces are scrutinized slowly enough.

—Their meaning as stories, that is (their theological and historical freight, while lightly distributed on the narrative skeleton, can slip past a reader but the story cannot). It is a single meaning, however complex— a meaning evolved over the two thousand years of their composition and the further two thousand of our study; deeply suggestive as I've said, of both the origins of the narrative hunger so basic to man and of the possible future of complex written narrative in industrial societies.

Apparently the oldest words-in-order in the Bible are poems not stories—such fierce songs of triumph as those of Miriam in Exodus 15 and Deborah in Judges 5. The oldest prose stories were set in virtually their present verbal form in about 950 B.C. by one of the greatest of epic writers, anonymous, known to us only as the Yahwist.* There is considerable evidence of various sorts however—including the personal experience of anyone reared in a powerful oral-narrative tradition (contemporary American Southerners, for instance, or conservative Jews)—that the stories developed their present narrative armature and perhaps the greater part of their verbal form long before the Yahwist's editing. It seems increasingly likely that the historical figures who stand behind the first of these stories—the three generations of patriarchs: Abraham, Isaac, and Jacob—entered what is now Israel from Mesopotamia in about 1800 B.C. Unless we assume that the patriarchal and Mosaic cycles were invented from whole cloth by the Yahwist or an earlier figure (and no serious contemporary scholar assumes that; on the contrary, movement has been toward a confirmation of the historical reliability of these cycles), then we conclude that the stories are roughly as old as their heroes, surely not more than a generation younger. In that case—and I believe the conclusion to be true—the oldest tale translated here is the account in Genesis 15 of Yahweh's covenant with Abraham. Though it is only an episode in the long story of Abraham and the longer story of Israel, it contains the total germ of all those later stories (among the several aspects of narrative

---

* From his insistent use of the proper name of God, *Yahweh*. He is also called J from the German spelling *Jahweh*. The other chief redactor of the older stories here is called the Elohist or E from his use of *Elohim*—"God"—instead of *Yahweh* in pre-Mosaic stories.

perfection in Hebrew and Christian story is the ability to imply all other stories in one).*

A god—Yahweh, "I am,"† the strongest of a world teeming with gods—so needs one mortal creature that He summons that creature out of his native Mesopotamia; draws him to a new land (the god's home, Canaan); and there in a solemn and mysterious rite "cuts a covenant" with the creature, vowing to pour through his previously sterile loins a race of unique importance to the god, who will inhabit and tend the god's land and worship the god with appropriate rites, despite a period of exile. In a stunned trance the chosen man darkly guesses at the terror of the choice. (It is not however until the end of the exile, five centuries after Abraham, that Yahweh makes explicit to Moses on Sinai—in Exodus 34—"it is terrible what I am about to do with you," a promise whose story resounds through later history and continues.)

If that is a bare summary of the narrative which an audience would hear—ancient Hebrew or modern—what was the narrative heard by the creature himself, Abram or Abraham? So far as Abraham was the only human witness to the action, then the version in Genesis must represent his own understanding, however smoothed and shaped in transmission. Possible overtones heard by Abraham but not entirely explicit in Genesis might be phrased as first-person questions—"Why me? What now? What will any son born under this condition be?"

Isn't there possibly this question also?—"Is it because He loves me?" Ancient stories of divine passion for, even infatuation with, a mortal are not rare—Ishtar and Gilgamesh, Zeus and a multitude, Apollo and Hyacinth. It is strange however in the prevailing unerotic desert air of Genesis to encounter not a Hebrew parallel to the hijinks of other mythologies (which end at best in post-coital sadness, at worst in conflagration) but the startling chance of an origin-in-love, no less terrifying in the disproportionate capacities of the lovers but hushed here and ultimately consoling. The same possibility is implicit in a paired story two thousand

---

* A majority of modern students hold that the Pentateuch as we now have it, the first five books of the Hebrew Bible, is the product of four major sources or redactions— a Judean source (J) from about 950 B.C.; a North-Israelite source (E) from about 850; a source exemplified by the book of Deuteronomy (D) from about 650; and a priestly source (P) from the period of Babylonian exile, 550 B.C. and after. The later stories here, of Saul and David, are virtually contemporary with the events they portray, subject to Deuteronomic and Priestly redaction. A good introduction to such problems is Bernhard Anderson's *Understanding the Old Testament* (Englewood Cliffs, 1975).

† The etymology of *Yahweh* remains a subject of discussion, almost all of which assumes it a form of the Hebrew verb *to be*. The main modern theories are summarized in Anderson, *Understanding the Old Testament*, pp. 53–56.

years younger—the annunciation to the Virgin Mary (Luke 1)—the ancient covenant recut with a girl, an act also hushed and awful and consoling: *We are loved, even necessary, though we suffer for it to the point of cruel death.*

Twenty-six of the thirty stories translated here say at least that. They affirm the active presence of divine care and vindication in the lives of God's loyal servants. Four of the stories—one at the end of each group of three pairs—say appallingly less: *At times He is absent or stands, face averted. Creatures are left at the mercy of creatures; they die in agony, no hint of reward.* Yet even these clots of horror contain reassurance for a righteous witness. In three of the four stories—the rape of Dinah, Saul's last night, the killing of Jezebel—those who suffer are enemies of Yahweh, justly punished. Only in the sacrifice of Jephthah's daughter is the victim innocent—*Some wounds, though made by mere creatures, never heal: we are dreadfully free.*

Stories of violent justice are not rare in the Old Testament; but even in that harshly-lit world, the baffled face of a mangled innocent is glimpsed often enough to confirm the unfrightened breadth of vision throughout. For all the breadth, however, it is a proof of the Bible's rejection of *reportorial* wholeness and of its narrative wisdom that it seems to contain no innocent or virtuous creature dragged protesting toward painful death—Jephthah's daughter bows to her fate; Stephen, the first Christian martyr, dies in a vision of celestial recompense. I call that narrative wisdom since it acknowledges an absolute essential of the narrative transaction— it is impossible to tell an audience a story it does not wish to hear. Perhaps only Jesus—incarnate God—provides that final story which humans most dread; if so, it is given without comment and in only two of the four gospels. Mark, the earliest, records that Jesus' dying words from the cross were "My God, my God, why did You forsake me?" followed only by a great death cry. Matthew agrees. Luke and John provide later resigned, even triumphant speeches.

Any of the hundreds of separate tales in the Old and New Testaments may be classed under one of those four types—*We are loved and needed by our Creator, We suffer but accept our fate, Our enemies and God's are rightly punished,* and lastly *God is sometimes veiled from our sight.* Taken together as a continuing epic of the old landlocked Israel of Abraham and the new universal Israel of Jesus, they form one story which says nothing more. There is nothing more to say, no other story which a wide range of human creatures from all ages will sit still to hear; and those substantial stretches of the Bible which are not mainly story—genealogy, song, law, vision, and essay—only dimly suggest the one other claim a creature can

make: *I am here alone, there is no one beyond me, I will soon dissolve.*
The Preacher in Ecclesiastes sees that "the righteous man perishes in his
righteousness"; Psalm 115 that

> *The dead do not praise Yah[weh]*
> *Nor any of those who have gone down to silence.*

Such claims—insistent claims of much twentieth-century fiction,
drama, and verse—do not, from the point of view of Biblical narrators,
constitute a story at all; and in the Bible they are heard only in verse or
personal essay, traditionally brief forms. They combine to raise one more
or less lyric lament, tolerable to audiences only because of brevity, eloquence, and the desire of most men for occasional measured doses of
punishing fright. To become a story, such a soliloquy of lament would
not only have to acquire characters and an action—characters whom an
audience could be persuaded to watch, a major oversight of much modern
narrative—but, most importantly, it would need to leave at its end an
ultimately consoling effect.

Stories which tell us that the innocent suffer under God's mysterious
hand, that our enemies' joints are torn from their sockets, or even that
uncontrolled monsters patrol the world (most human beings assume themselves to be monsters, hence the child's fascination with wolves,
dinosaurs)—all these can console us in various ways, leave us firmed for
our public and private lives. Only the story which declares our total
incurable abandonment is repugnant and will not be heard for long. There
are no such stories which have won the abiding interest or loyalty of the
human species—neither in the Bible nor in the perhaps older surviving
tales from Mesopotamia nor in any subsequent literature. Why?

A reflex reply would be *Because such claims are literally intolerable
for long.* But the reply of the Yahwist, the Elohist, their oral predecessors,
the Christian evangelists, and of most human beings would certainly be
Because they are false. The all but unanimous testimony of human narrative has embodied, reflected, and sustained the opinion of the species
that the figure of man is a sizable piece in the total shape of seen and
unseen nature, that the shape itself is partially discernible and nowhere
more clearly than in man's own reports on his sightings and soundings
—tales, true stories.*

Granting that such stories are the oldest known, is there evidence
that these carefully formed and transmitted artifacts bear special resemblance to the narratives of early man hundreds of thousands or millions

---

* A recent Gallup poll indicates that 34% of all Americans say they have had a
decisive experience of conversion to Christianity. 40% of all Americans believe that the
Bible is to be interpreted literally, word for word. *Time*, October 4, 1976, p. 75.

of years previous? Perhaps not evidence but there are at least two kinds of likelihood, though it seems necessary to say that the very earliest narratives were probably secular, therefore eventually unsatisfactory.

First, there is the clear fact that narrative, like the other basic needs of the species, supports the literal survival of man by providing him with numerous forms of nurture—the simple companionship of the narrative transaction, the union of teller and told; the narrator's opportunity for exercise of personal skill in telling and its ensuing rewards; the audience's exercise of attention, imagination, powers of deduction; the spiritual support which both parties receive from stories affirming our importance and protection in a perilous world; the transmission to younger listeners of vital knowledge, worldly and unworldly; the narcotic effect of narrative on pain and boredom; and perhaps most importantly, the chance that in the very attempt at narrative transaction something new will surface or be revealed, some sudden floater from the dark unconscious, some message from a god which can only arrive or be told as a tale. Such needs might conceivably have been among the vaguely conscious longings of man before he spoke. It would seem irresistible that the pressure toward such advantages was among the pressures toward speech and therefore narrative. It is difficult, perhaps impossible, to imagine early man, prey as he was to a world of threat, producing stories which did less than arrange the evidence of daily life into sequential, even causal patterns implying order and a certain dependable continuity of life. I am not claiming metaphysical, theological sophistication for proto-narrative, only that certain permanent and orderly cycles of nature might soon have suggested the opposite of chaos (a regular feeding-time still suggests order and safety to mute animals) and thus have resulted in story—the seasons, moon and tide, menstruation, gestation, the rutting of herds, the annual waves of dearth and plenty: story which illuminated present and future by reference to a past both warning and consoling. The more clearly a creature comprehended time and cycle, the stronger his chances for moving with the massive flow of nature, therefore living longer. A skill at true story, as teller or told, made for survival then as now.

Second, once man acquired the complex ability to conceive sequential time, to guess at cause, and to narrate chronologically—*This happened because of that and may happen again*—there would soon have been pressure on teller and told to regress chronologically further and further toward origins, causes, the question *Why? Why did that happen?* It seems inevitable that some of the early answers to *Why?* are preserved in human mythologies. Almost all of those regress to a terminus—creation of world and man by gods. Some of man's remains, older than any known story, point to similar termini—evidences of ritual burial in Europe and the Near East, some sixty thousand years old, imply a hope of afterlife which implies a caring, and storied, god. And to glance again at paleolithic cave painting and the hundreds of exquisitely engraved stones and bones is to confront their radiant numinosity—something transcendent in beast, man, and nature is implored and entreated with delight and reverence.*

So while it seems probable that the early eons of narrative were secular—scraps of human hunt, flight, victory; domestic arrangements—the voracious hunger of historical man for origins and causes, operating upon the always ready mass of mystery and the even more basic hunger for solace, would soon arrive at sacred tale: the only perfect story, the story acceptable everywhere as true.

That sketch of an evolution omits the force which mythologies posit as crucial—the desire of gods to be known by man, the pressure of transcendent revelation upon creatures who must then narrate or strangle in awe. A contemporary sketch of an unexplored area like the origins of narrative must, in fact, initially omit such a force, if it hopes to reach a wide range of hands.

For the past fifty years, views of the origins of religion and religious story have moved toward polar positions which might crudely be called Freudian and Jungian—the first locating all roots of religious emotion in the structure of the human family, in the great Oedipal ganglion; the second, in the shafts and spelean pools of the collective unconscious. The second position has obviously been more attractive to students naturally inclined to religious emotion and to artists of various sorts, who find the mysterious nature of their own endowments more nearly acknowledged and explained therein. The first position, however—religion as Oedipal tactic—has held the castle of academic critical thought (and medical practice) and continues to do so, though with waning strength against younger generations strongly suspicious of the breadth, depth, and courage of the lines of defense.

I cannot discuss fully here the strengths and weaknesses of those views and of others less prevalent. What I want to do is suggest the beginnings at least of an alternate view, one both older and newer. It is a view which seems to me—and has always seemed, though never more strongly than after these eight years of work—to rise not from theology, dogma, sectarian rite, Oedipal tactic, or world soul but from a particular body of fixed and clearly legible story, unprecedented in the known history of earlier religions and never successfully imitated. Those stories are of course the

---

* Excellent illustrations are available in Marshack, *The Roots of Civilization* and Paolo Graziosi, *Palaeolithic Art* (London, 1960).

canonical sacred tales of Jews and Christians. Those tales, and above all the ones gathered here, are their own best witness to the ancient conviction of a sizable portion of the human race that a handful of men over two thousand years on a piece of land hardly larger than the state of North Carolina were brought into intermittent contact with an inhuman power quite beyond that available to comparable tales from other witnesses within our tradition—Assyria, Egypt, Greece.

To examine three tales, however briefly, may clarify some of that witness and suggest further study. I have chosen two reports of divine contact, one of absence and silence. *

Genesis 32, appendix below. Jacob—son of Isaac, grandson of Abraham, the wily thief of his twin-brother Esau's birthright and blessing— had fled to Mesopotamia from his brother's anger and had labored twenty years in bondage to his uncle Laban to earn his beloved Rachel, Laban's daughter. Now, having paid his debt, he is free to return to his homeland—the home of his father's god, "The Fear of Isaac," Yahweh. It is also however the homeland of Esau, whom he cheated twenty years before; and as Jacob reaches the steep-walled ford of Jabbok in the highlands of Gilead east of the Jordan, he receives word that Esau is advancing to meet him with four hundred men. After passing one fearful night in prayer that Yahweh deliver him from Esau, Jacob sends forward a guilt offering—a herd of some six hundred mixed domestic animals. The next night, with still no peaceful word from Esau, Jacob takes his household and belongings across the ford. Then back alone on the far side—to check for stragglers from the flock or in craven terror?—Jacob is assaulted by "some man" who wrestles with him silently and darkly in an uncertain struggle, won only at dawn when the man with a last move dislocates Jacob's hip and engages with him in a reluctant final dialogue. If the story—which must have come from Jacob, its only human witness—ever contained allusions to Jacob's inner questions as the fight proceeded, they are stripped off here in the Yahwist's account. Yet the tense expectation of the last episodes—the approach toward Esau, Jacob's terror—acts upon us as audience to oil the dry leather sinew of the tale with our own best guesses at Jacob's thoughts, the meaning: *Is this Esau, grown even more*

---

* Marshack's speculations on the origins of secular story are careful and interesting —Marshack, *The Roots of Civilization*, pp. 109–123. Evidence of the origin or confirmation of a sacred story is available in John Nance's account of the recent discovery and early study of an isolated stone-age people in the Philippine rain forest—*The Gentle Tasaday* (New York, 1975). Characteristic tales from the ancient Near East are available in J. B. Pritchard ed., *Ancient Near Eastern Texts Relating to the Old Testament* (Princeton, 1969) and Theodor Gaster, *The Oldest Stories in the World* (New York, 1952).

powerful with years? Or an agent of Esau, sent to murder me by night?
Surely in the early watches, Jacob cannot have known his assailant as
Yahweh—the previous night's prayer answered so soon and startlingly.
Yet by dawn he has struggled to a kind of recognition. What had seemed
"some man" now seems a power with grace to bestow. He has fought
with a god whom he still holds down and will not release till he gains a
blessing, as he'd gained Esau's from his dying father. And the blessing
comes but in strange bent form. The god demands to know his name; he
yields it at once, a reckless yielding—his intimate name, the lever to his
life, a means to harm him; and a scandal in the land, a swindler's name.
With that admission the god gives something more than a ritual
blessing—a changed name, a clean slate, forgiveness earned and strength
rewarded. The name is *Israel*, God's worthy contestant. Jacob asks the
god's name; the god will not say—it should be apparent. With a farewell
blessing He departs or disappears. At once Jacob-Israel in the rising light
performs the primal human act—the bestowal of name which is also
story. He calls the site of his struggle Peniel (or Penuel, both spellings
are given)—*God's Face*, "for I saw God face to face and my soul endured."
The story we read begins before our eyes in that two-word poem pressed
from Jacob in the dawn. The "man" was a god, the God of his father,
Yahweh the Fear of Isaac, who had guarded Jacob in his long exile and
has now annealed him for the meeting to come with the long-aggrieved
Esau. Jacob limps toward the meeting on his injured leg.*

The story is of a kind which Old Testament criticism calls
etiological—told to illuminate the origin of some fact or practice in tribal
history, often one attached to a place made sacred by the action described.
Such a view sees the story of Jacob's struggle as narrative validation of
Yahweh's cult center at Penuel on Jabbok and, less importantly, as explanation of the name Israel and of the Hebrew dietary ban on the sciatic
muscle; and beyond such a view, criticism barely goes. Beyond is
mystery—speculation, faith, subjective response. An eagle-eyed modern
student like Von Rad can point out the numerous possible strands of
ancient matter which the Yahwist has woven to his own later purpose†
but a modern reader, religious or not, faced with the final text, whatever
its vicissitudes and earlier forms, is likely to ask the central question
first—*What does this story ask me to believe?* Either kind of reader would
surely say *It asks me to believe precisely what it says.*

What it says, in the face of subtilizing comment, is *All-Powerful God*

---

* My reading of the story is indebted to, though in substantial disagreement with,
readings in the two distinguished recent commentaries on Genesis—Gerhard von Rad,
Genesis (Philadelphia, 1961 and E. A. Speiser, *Genesis* (Garden City, 1964).

†. Von Rad, *Genesis*, pp. 314–321.

descended in tangible form on a fearful man, fought him all night in hand-
to-hand combat, permitted him to win, then marked him with an injury,
acknowledged his strength in a new grand name, blessed him, and left him
strengthened for his future. The text available to us, fixed in about 950
B.C., does not permit allegorization or spiritualization of the action described. There is no chance of seeing the struggle as a metaphor of inward
event—nightmare, say. Hebrew sacred narrative roughly contemporary
with the Yahwist—the stories of Saul and David—does not confront us
with such undeniably physical intercourse between god and man (though
the tale of the boy Samuel sees the dim outlines of a visible Yahweh; and
later, Elijah can hear His whispering voice). With time and the gathering
decay of man, Yahweh had withdrawn such privileges. Whatever the
multiple theories of origin (personal memory, manufactured myth, transformed vegetation rite, developed etiology), and despite the nearly one
thousand years between the event and the Yahwist's final record, the tale
still says that plain thing, a wonder—*Who could have dreamt it? It happened; may again.*

Why should anyone believe it? (millions have, over nearly four millennia). As an object it curiously lacks those irregularities of texture which
we expect of true story—the unpredictable instants of visual precision
which signal veracity, a recollecting voice. Such instants are common in
other Old Testament stories, especially the accounts of Saul, David, and
the later monarchs—"They went to bury her and found nothing there
but skull and feet and the palms of her hands." And the gospels and Acts
swarm with them—Luke says that at the risen Jesus' first appearance to
the disciples, he asked for food and "They gave him *part* of a broiled fish"
(my italics). Here though, after the careful enumeration of Jacob's household, there is only a lean line tracing the progress of strange encounter.
If we try turning the Yahwist's third-person into first, we hear a doubly
convincing voice—"When I'd carried them all across, I sent my belongings. Then I was alone and some man wrestled with me there till
daybreak"—but in general we must choose among several explanations
for the smoothness of surface: the wear of centuries of oral retelling (a
process which often results in embroidery), some redactor's removal of
secular detail from a sacred story, or the filtering nature of supreme
confidence.

That last seems far the most likely to me. Jacob, the first narrator,
and centuries of subsequent transmitters told a story devoid of small narrative seductions because they were certain of offering one huge
seduction—*This story is true. I am the man. No one can doubt me. Why
would they, ever? I bring food for their lives.* The fact that Jacob's tale has
been believed by sizable portions of the human race for thousands of

years, and is still believed and acted on by millions, is the great reward
of his narrative success. No other narrator, except Abraham, has succeeded
longer or deeper in the first—and final—aim of narrative: compulsion of
belief in an ordered world.

John 21, appendix. A second tale of revelation, younger by nearly
two thousand years, provides an instructive set of likenesses and contrasts
toward a similar but different narrative end. The Gospel of John records
on a short page the third and final appearance of Jesus, physically raised
from the dead, to seven of his disciples. Contemporary students have not
agreed on a firm date for John or on an identification of its author; but
it would not oversimplify a complex and maybe insoluble problem to say
that in recent decades, a sizable number of respected students have moved
toward reaffirming the earliest witness (Irenaeus, Bishop of Lyons, in about
A.D. 180) who claimed that the gospel was written by John, Jesus' beloved
disciple, late in his long life when he was at Ephesus—presumably before
A.D. 100. Even those who argue against direct or indirect Johannine
authorship have steadily moved toward affirming an early date for the
gospel, one within living memory of Jesus.

Jesus was crucified in about A.D. 30. Whoever wrote the Gospel of
John—and my own study of the narrative and of its modern critics con-
vinces me that it is solidly based on the aged John's recollections and
homilies, recorded by a pupil and subject to later editing—it was written
within, say, sixty years of Jesus' death and the mysteries reflected in the
resurrection stories.* Sixty years is a short space in human memory,
especially short in a society accustomed to oral preservation—the chief
fact ignored by the dominant school of modern New Testament scholarship. (As I write this page I am forty-three years old but can summon
clear pictorial and auditory memories from forty-one years ago. The oldest
lucidly recollecting mind I have met was a woman ninety-nine in 1946
—she had been two years old at the deaths of Poe and Chopin.) In a tale
such as that in John 21 then there is an extraordinary opportunity to watch
the relatively fresh motions of what may be called sacred narrative
memory—but *memory* above all, personal recall that might have been
corroborated by other witnesses. Let me convert my close translation of
the episode into first-person narrative, changing only pronouns and the

---

* Students generally see Chapter 21 as an appendix to a book which intended to end
with 20. Many however see 21 as a genuinely Johannine story, appended later as too
valuable to lose. The account of the chapter in Raymond Brown, *The Gospel According
to John*, vol. II (Garden City, 1970) both summarizes recent study and sees in the chapter
a conflation of two or more differing tales. Despite Brown's meticulous intelligence, I go
on seeing only one tale in 21—an aged worn memory but seamless all the same.

few other words necessary to flush the beloved disciple from the near-hiding he has imposed on himself throughout his book.

Another time Jesus showed himself to us by the Sea of Tiberias—showed himself this way.

Simon Peter was there with Thomas whom we called "Twin," Nathanael from Cana in Galilee, my brother James and I, and two more of Jesus' disciples. Simon Peter said to us "I'm going out fishing."

We said "We're coming with you." So we went out and got in the boat. But all night we caught nothing.

Then when day broke Jesus stood on the shore though none of us knew it was Jesus.

He called to us "Boys, anything to eat?"

We said "No."

So he said to us "Cast the net to starboard—you'll find them."

We cast and the crowd of fish was so big we couldn't haul it.

Then I said to Peter "It's the Lord."

When Peter heard that, he cinched up his shirt—under it he was naked—and threw himself into the sea.

We others came on in the little boat towing the net of fish—we were only a hundred yards or so from land—and when we landed we saw a charcoal fire laid with fish laid on it and bread.

Jesus said to us "Bring some of the fish you caught."

So Peter got up and hauled in the net full of big fish—a hundred and fifty-three—and with all the number still the net held.

Jesus said "Come eat breakfast."

Not one of us dared ask "Who are you?" We knew it was the Lord.

Jesus came over, took the bread and gave it to us. Also the fish.

This was the third time Jesus showed himself to us after being raised from the dead.

To perform that neat transformation is not necessarily to demonstrate the existence of a nearly identical first-person original. Oral tales, since they seldom deal in internal emotion (thought, doubt, soliloquy), lend themselves more readily to interchangeable viewpoints than do dense, written tales. Any practiced novelist, however, knows that when an entire third-person narrative can be mechanically converted into natural first-person then there is likely to be a strong personal vision and voice beneath the strategies of distance and anonymity.

In the case of John 21, the voice resembles that of Genesis 32 so far as they both speak of intimate, even physical—but all the more mysterious—contact with what was taken at once and later as divine energy. John, near as he is to the contact, offers the convincing knotty texture which was largely missing in Jacob's struggle—Jesus' call to them as "boys" (plural of the Greek *paidion*, diminutive of *pais*, boy); the detail of Peter's dress (I've accepted Raymond Brown's view that Peter *cinches up* not *puts on* his shirt, revealing both his near-hysteria and his nudity); the professional fishermen's practicality in coming on slowly with the catch as contrasted to Peter's characteristic abandon; the odd note that "Peter got up and hauled in the net" (a further hint that the narrator is witnessing a pictorial memory but has neglected to communicate all his vision—where did Peter get up from: a bow at Jesus' feet or breathless prostration in the shallows?); the precise count of fish (in which centuries of commentators have strained for symbolism, without convincing result); and the unembroidered gravity of the plain but sacramental breakfast.

Comparison with a parallel incident in early uncanonical Christian literature would provide an interesting check on the quality of memorial vision in John. The promising fragmentary apocryphal *Gospel of Peter* (about A.D. 150) breaks off just as it begins to parallel John 21—

> Now it was the last day of unleavened bread and many went away and repaired to their homes, since the feast was at an end. But we, the twelve disciples of the Lord, wept and mourned, and each one, very grieved for what had come to pass, went to his own home. But I, Simon Peter, and my brother Andrew took our nets and went to the sea. And there was with us Levi, the son of Alphaeus, whom the Lord. . . . *

But the apocryphal *Acts of Pilate* (about fourth century) puts into the mouth of Joseph of Arimathea an extended first-person account of a resurrection appearance—

> On the day of preparation about the tenth hour you shut me in, and I remained the whole Sabbath. And at midnight as I stood and prayed, the house where you shut me in was raised up by the four corners, and I saw as it were a lightning flash in my eyes. Full of fear I fell to the ground. And someone took me by the hand and raised me up from the place where I had fallen, and something moist like water flowed from my head to my feet, and the smell of fragrant oil reached my nostrils. And he wiped my face and kissed me and said to me: Do not fear, Joseph. Open your eyes and see who it is who speaks with you. I looked up and saw Jesus. Trembling, I thought

---

* Edgar Hennecke, *New Testament Apocrypha*, Wilhelm Schneemelcher ed. and R. McL. Wilson trans. (Philadelphia, 1963) I, p. 187.

it was a phantom, and I said the commandments. And he said them with me. Now as you well know, a phantom immediately flees if it meets anyone and hears the commandments. And when I saw that he said them with me, I said to him: Rabbi Elijah! He said: I am not Elijah. And I said to him: Who are you, Lord? He replied: I am Jesus, whose body you asked for from Pilate, whom you clothed in clean linen, on whose face you placed a cloth, and whom you placed in your new cave, and you rolled a great stone to the door of the cave. And I asked him who spoke to me: Show me the place where I laid you. And he took me and showed me the place where I laid him. And the linen cloth lay there, and the cloth that was upon his face. Then I recognized that it was Jesus. And he took me by the hand and placed me in the middle of my house, with the doors shut, and led me to my bed and said to me: Peace be with you! Then he kissed me and said to me: Do not go out of your house for forty days. For see, I go to my brethren in Galilee.*

Despite the physical extravagance of the passage, it stands as perhaps the least fanciful of the numerous surviving uncanonical tales of the resurrection. There is of course the possibility that the author of John 21 was simply a narrator of greater restraint and skill than those responsible for uncanonical tales; but there are important questions which such a comparison raises, not only for New Testament scholarship and Christian faith but for the metaphysics of narrative—does *canonical* (approved, acceptable) in the matter of Hebrew and Christian sacred texts finally mean *credible*? Are Matthew, Mark, Luke, and John our only canonical stories of the life of Jesus because they are immediately perceptible as the best stories—the most credible in their consolations, the least manipulative in their fancies and designs upon us? Finally, the resurrection stories of the canonical gospels, especially those translated here, raise in ultimate form the question all narrative enterprise must face—how long will audiences accept, and to what uses can they put, any narration which is not, first, a reliable report? It is clear that large numbers will wait through fantastic, even terrifying, tales and return to them for years—provided they are labeled *false*. What if a narrator claims urgent truth, truth to bend our lives, but offers a lie?

Such a voice as that in John's resurrection tales or in Luke's is either reporting truly or lying brilliantly for political purpose, though we must consider the slim possibility that John and Luke were defrauded by events explicable in terms other than those provided them. I, like millions, am

* Hennecke, *New Testament Apocrypha* I, p. 466.

convinced and have always been by the stories themselves—their narrative perfection, the speed and economy with which they offer all the heart's last craving in shapes as credible as any friend's tale of a morning walk. And despite its greater age, its dimmer lines, I also yield to the tale of Jacob's struggle—helpless belief. If John and Luke tell me of acts more urgent for my own daily life, as a veteran of Christian parents and culture, that was their huge luck as witnesses and heirs of quiet events at the core of light. From the point of view of human need, the tale of Jacob at Penuel is as useful, in matter and manner. Both the Yahwist and John are treading the narrow white ridge of the summit of story in dazzling view of the perfect tale men dream and crave, yet not dazzled by it— watchful and capable in their certain joy to have seen the true tale and *lasted* as competent witnesses, actual angels to blinder men: *We are treasured; the wheel of the sky knows of us, turns to yield us light*. Fresh names, clean starts; a palpable god; bread, also fish.

    1 Samuel 28, appendix. The darker tales here, and in all sacred stories, are the gorges implicit in such bright peaks; and the extended account of Yahweh's abandonment of Saul, His first anointed king, is among the most carefully shaped and longest admired of all Biblical reports. The action described—eve of the battle at Gilboa in which Saul and his three sons died—occurred in about 1000 B.C. In the opinion of an important student, our tale of Saul and the witch at Endor derives from tradition local to Endor, perhaps even to the witch's own house, and is a basically untouched contemporary account.* Yet unless we assume that the witch herself transmitted the tale (not an impossibility, considering the sympathetic light in which she appears) or that it is invented, we are forced to conclude that the narrative bones of the present tale originated in the memory of at least one of the two slave witnesses —perhaps Philistines themselves; in any case, hardly worshippers of Yahweh. If that is the origin—a first-hand account of visible and audible events from a memorable night—then we also conclude that someone intervened later with an ear for Yahweh's dreadful silence and with a human voice for tragic comprehension and pity. Saul had once, eager for battle, usurped Samuel's priestly rites; later he had disobeyed Yahweh's specific command to exterminate the Amalekites; Yahweh had turned His face. The effects of the abandonment had gathered slowly—Saul's recurrent attacks of profound depression; Samuel's enmity; the rise (and Samuel's anointing) of David, Saul's protégé-turned-nemesis; and at last Yahweh's unrelenting silence as the Philistines wait for dawn by their campfires. Yet the silence does relent, in an awful way. Though Saul has

---

* Hans Wilhelm Hertzberg, *I & II Samuel* (Philadelphia, 1964) p. 217.

purged the country of unorthodox channels to divine or demonic energy—witches and wizards—a chance survives at Endor: one possessed woman. He and two slaves approach her disguised; and faced with the hope of consulting any spirit, Saul can only ask for Samuel, his prophet-anointer and the hectoring bane of his kingship. He had last seen Samuel alive at Gilgal when, before the ark of Yahweh, Samuel hacked to pieces Agag, king of the Amalekites, whom Saul had spared. The witch's power works and Samuel rises reluctantly from the dead to hear Saul's plea— "I have called you to tell me what I must do." The voice which, living, had poured a stream of advice to Saul can now only echo the silence of God—*You have disobeyed the Force that will not bear disobeying*; "*To-morrow you and your sons shall be with me.*" The speech is true; Saul is poleaxed by it. The spirit vanishes only the woman, the hunted frightened witch, and Saul's two slaves remain to console him with the last of helps—food: hastily butchered veal and flatcakes. He has been consigned to men—Yahweh's last worst punishment—and even men fail him. To-morrow in the battle the Philistines will miss him; and when he sees defeat and orders his armor-bearer to dispatch him on the field, the armor-bearer will refuse.* Saul must even kill himself. Swathed in a human tenderness as rare as water in the fierce hills, Saul's end says the thing all God's desertions say—*Stories of man, unassisted man, are the only tragedies: ignorance, waste, savagery of heart.*

The one scene comparable for situation and tenderness in western literature—that Plutarchan moment in *Antony and Cleopatra* (IV, iii) when Antony's god deserts him on the eve of his own last battle—does not approach the force and terror of the muffled night at Endor:

MUSIC OF THE HOBOYS IS UNDER THE STAGE

2ND SOLDIER   *Peace, what noise?*

1ST SOLDIER   *List, list!*

2ND SOLDIER   *Hark!*

1ST SOLDIER   *Music i' th' air.*

3RD SOLDIER   *Under the earth.*

4TH SOLDIER   *It signs well, does it not?*

3RD SOLDIER   *No.*

1ST SOLDIER   *Peace, I say.*
What should this mean?

2ND SOLDIER   *'Tis the god Hercules, whom Antony lov'd,*
Now leaves him.

1ST SOLDIER   *Walk; let's see if other watchmen*
Do hear what we do.

---

* Was the armor-bearer one of Saul's two companions at Endor?

*

To claim that those tales stand a strong chance of being true in a literal sense—that they offer us eyewitness reports of events theoretically visible to eyes other than the participants', events recordable on tape and film if such means had been available—is not only to risk a simplicity of comprehension bordering on the simpletonian but also to turn one's face on two centuries of investigation and speculation by hundreds of students of rite, myth, cultural evolution, comparative religions, the psychopathology of the sacred, and multiple schools of textual study of the Old and New Testaments.

The volume of such studies is now so great, and continuing, that a single reader can barely hope to encompass and synthesize. Weston La Barre has come as near as anyone.* It was in his classes at Duke twenty-three years ago that I began my own patrols through the field—first the labyrinths of Tylor and Frazer, then on without system but with undiminished appetite to the present: all, I think, in a long attempt to disprove to myself the preposterous claim of the earliest stories I had known and loved; an attempt to assault the bases of my life.

The attempt has failed till now at least, so I do make the claim or one form of it. A number of the theophanies in the Old and New Testaments give emphatic narrative evidence of claiming to be eyewitness reports of external events (another group make no such claim—such accounts as Exodus 3, 1 Samuel 3, and Luke 1 seem *as narratives* to permit our understanding them as metaphors of internal event; the choice between claims is one more gauntlet flung down to mother-wit). They bear their validation in the narrative bones, bones of the visible actions they describe, and in the reckless bravery on their cloudless faces. They well understand that they give us one choice—if we call them untrue, we must call them insane. They are plainly not deceitful; and I plainly call them true, in some awareness of the range of objections.

I would like to explore three things at greater length. First, the objections themselves and the pressure of motives behind them. Second, the narrative strategies of the tales as artifacts stunningly successful over time and place in their own first aims, and in aims accreted to them through millennia, and rich with lessons for recent generations of narrators oddly bent on repelling or petrifying a large waiting audience (especially interesting would be the question of how they carry for so many readers

* Weston La Barre, *The Ghost Dance: Origins of Religion* (New York, 1970). La Barre's text and notes provide an excellent guide to the literature; and the fact that I deeply disagree with his views on the sources of religion does not prevent gratitude for the bracing shock he administered to childhood predilections.

a reportorial conviction that sets them firmly apart from such seductive, partially satisfying but clearly fictional narratives as those of Stendhal, Flaubert, Tolstoy, Chekhov). Third, the psychic components of my long fascination with these few stories, my propensity to believe them.

I hope to do all three at another time—each is perhaps a separate book—but my purpose here was to preface a group of translated stories with the larger questions they have raised for me and to offer the lot in the hope of pointing new readers to an old and patient source of pleasure, instruction, and nourishment—a source of which their recent training has deprived them. I have also hoped to provide older readers with fresh and provoking but faithful tracings of deep-cut cornerstones worn smooth in their minds; and lastly, to share with colleagues in the craft of narrative a chance for contemplation of what has seemed, in our civilization, both the source and end of story itself.

Human narrative, through all its visible length, gives emphatic signs of arising from the profoundest need of one fragile species. Sacred story is the perfect answer given by the world to the hunger of that species for true consolation. The fact that we hunger has not precluded food.

APPENDIX*

GENESIS 32

IN THE NIGHT Jacob rose, took his two wives, his two slave girls and his eleven sons and crossed the ford of Jabbok. When he had carried them all across he sent his belongings.

Then Jacob was alone and some man wrestled with him there till daybreak.

When He saw that He could not win against him He struck him in the pit of his thigh so that Jacob's hip unsocketed as He wrestled with him. Then He said "Let me go. It is daybreak."

He said "I will not let go till you bless me."

He said to him "What is your name?"

* Translations by Reynolds Price.

He said "Jacob."

He said "Your name shall be Jacob no more but Israel. You have fought gods and men and won."

Jacob said "Tell me your name please."

He said "Why ask My name?" and blessed him there.

So Jacob called the place Peniel, *face of God*, "for I saw God face to face and my soul endured" and the sun struck him as he passed Penuel limping on his hip.

JOHN 21

Another time Jesus showed himself to the disciples by the sea of Tiberias—showed himself this way.

Simon Peter was there with Thomas called "Twin," Nathanael from Cana in Galilee, the sons of Zebedee and two more of his disciples. Simon Peter said "I'm going out fishing."

The others said "We're coming with you." So they went out and got in the boat. But all night they caught nothing.

Then when day broke Jesus stood on the shore though none of them knew it was Jesus.

He called to them "Boys, anything to eat?"

They said "No."

So he said to them "Cast the net to starboard—you'll find them."

They cast and the crowd of fish was so big they couldn't haul it.

Then the disciple whom Jesus loved said to Peter "It's the Lord."

When Simon Peter heard it was the Lord he cinched up his shirt—under it he was naked—and threw himself into the sea.

The others came on in the little boat towing the net of fish—they were only a hundred yards or so from land—and when they landed they saw a charcoal fire laid with fish on it and bread.

Jesus said to them "Bring some of the fish you caught."

So Peter got up and hauled in the net full of big fish—a hundred and fifty-three and with all the number still the net was not torn.

Jesus said "Come eat breakfast."

Not one of the disciples dared ask "Who are you?" knowing it was the Lord.

Jesus came over, took the bread and gave it to them. Also the fish.

This was the third time Jesus showed himself to the disciples after being raised from the dead.

1 SAMUEL 28

Now Samuel was dead and all Israel had mourned him and buried him in Ramah his own city. And Saul had put those that had demons and the wizards out of the country.

The Philistines gathered, came and camped at Shunem.

Saul gathered all Israel and they camped at Gilboa. When Saul saw the army of the Philistines he was afraid and his heart shook hard. Then Saul asked Yahweh but Yahweh did not answer either in dreams or by Urim or by prophets. So Saul said to his slaves "Find me a woman who has a demon so I may go to her and ask her."

His slaves said to him "Look, there is a woman who has a demon in Endor."

Saul disguised himself, put on other clothes and went—he and two men with him—and they came to the woman at night and said "Conjure for me by your demon and raise for me whomever I name to you."

The woman said to him "Look, you know what Saul has done— how he has cut from the land those with demons and the wizards—so why are you setting traps for my life to make me die?"

Saul swore to her by Yahweh saying "By the life of Yahweh no punishment will fall on you for this."

So the woman said "Whom shall I raise for you?"

He said "Bring up Samuel for me."

When the woman saw Samuel she cried out in a loud voice and the woman spoke to Saul saying "Why have you deceived me—you yourself being Saul?"

The king said to her "Don't be afraid. What do you see?"

The woman said to Saul "I see a god coming up from the earth."

He said to her "What is his shape?"

She said "An old man coming up covered in a robe."

Saul knew it was Samuel so he pressed his face to the ground and worshipped.

Samuel said to Saul "Why have you afflicted me bringing me up?"

Saul said "I am in bad trouble—the Philistines are fighting me and God has turned from me and answers me no more neither by prophets nor by dreams so I have called you to tell me what I must do."

Samuel said "Why should you ask me when Yahweh has turned from you and become your enemy? Yahweh has done to you what He spoke by my hand. Yahweh has torn the kingdom from your hand and given it to your neighbor. Since you did not listen to the voice of Yahweh or execute the fire of His wrath on Amalek so Yahweh has done this thing to you today that Yahweh may give Israel along with you into the hand of the Philistines. Tomorrow you and your sons shall be with me. Yahweh shall also give the army of Israel into the hand of the Philistines."

At once Saul fell prostrate his whole length on the ground and was terrified at Samuel's words. There was no strength in him for he had not eaten bread all day and all night.

The woman came to Saul and when she saw he was so frightened she said to him "Look, your servant heard your voice. I took my soul in my hand and listened to the words you said to me. Now please listen also to the voice of your servant and let me put a bit of bread before you and you eat so there's strength in you when you go on your way."

He refused and said "I will not eat."

But when his slaves and the woman also pressed him then he listened to their voice and rose from the ground and sat on the bed.

Now the woman had a calf fattening in the house. She ran and killed it. She took meal, kneaded and baked unleavened cakes from it and set them before Saul and his slaves and they ate.

Then they rose and left the same night.

1978

STORIES, MAYBE TRUE*

T̲HE NARRATIVES OF the Hebrew Bible have been watched with an unceasing gaze for more than two thousand years. They have meant more to more human lives than any other narratives, with the possible exceptions of certain Christian or East Indian texts. In the past two hundred years, they have been studied by a new army of heavily-armed scholars—studied linguistically, theologically, archeologically, and in dozens of other sane ways (not to mention the insane): indeed, in all the ways except the obvious, the one in which they above all invite study. They have barely been studied academically *as stories*, as works of narrative intent and accomplishment. (I stress the lack of academic study because, of course, it has always been as stories—seductive accounts of credible action—that the books of Genesis, Exodus, Joshua, Judges, Samuel, and Kings have reached the common believer.)

In the early pages of this eagle-eyed book, Robert Alter outlines the nature of that academic neglect and, while acknowledging his rare precursors in English and modern Hebrew criticism, proposes a pioneering effort of his own. He means to convey to contemporary secular readers the results of his delicate but deep penetration of the ancient texts in their original language (he is a professor of Hebrew as well as comparative literature). In the end, he summarizes his findings thus—"What I have tried to indicate throughout . . . is that in the Bible many of the clues offered to help us make these linkages and discriminations depend on a distinctive set of narrative procedures which for readers of a later era has to be learned. It has been my own experience . . . that such learning is pleasurable rather than arduous."

A stunningly obvious conclusion, you may think, for the amount of intense scrutiny applied. The stories of the Bible are intricately made toward a conscious purpose; and our discovery of those groundplans will enhance our reception both of the pleasurable tales of human action and of the divine agenda concealed in the fabric. In the face of the current cold gales that blow from French structuralism, Alter's conclusion is the

* *The Art of Biblical Narrative* by Robert Alter (Basic Books 1981).

principle that has powered the sovereign literary illuminations of our time—such works as Auerbach's *Mimesis* and Kitto's *Greek Tragedy*. It is the fact that the Hebrew Bible has largely escaped such illumination that lends freshness to Alter's enterprise—a blessedly old-fashioned freshness.

His procedure is straightforward and generally devoid of the narcissistic *son et lumiere* of most recent narratology. In successive chapters he discusses, with constant reference to the original language in his own close translation, what he sees as the strategies and vehicles of the stories— type-scenes, dialogue, verbal and gestural repetition, characterization, and silence. Though he ranges over the whole repertory of stories, he focuses most revealingly on the extended Joseph story of Genesis and the history of David from Samuel and Kings. And he steadily uncovers what seems to me virtually incontestable evidence for his contention that the stories —far from being the awkwardly conflated primitive documents that so much scholarship has led us to see—are as sophisticated in their verbal and formal devices as any other ancient narratives. The largest of his revelations may well prove to be that the narratives—some perhaps 3,700 years old—are as technically sophisticated as those twentieth-century novels which have preened themselves for dazzlement.

The most valuable consequence of that finding is, again, the best consequence of all the substantial literary criticism since Longinus—the realization that the most entertaining and enduringly useful kinds of literary complexity are those produced from within by a large and central complexity in the matter of the story itself. Since the mysteries of these brief narratives have provided fuel for most of the motions of Western culture—most frighteningly, in the present confrontation of Israel and Islam—any set of insights as devoted and intelligent as Alter's is all the more welcome.

Toward the end, he states the main questions he has found in his texts—"What is it like, the biblical writers seek to know through their art, to be a human being with a divided consciousness—intermittently loving your brother but hating him even more; resentful or perhaps contemptuous of your father but also capable of the deepest filial regard; stumbling between disastrous ignorance and imperfect knowledge; fiercely asserting your own independence but caught in a tissue of events divinely contrived; outwardly a definite character and inwardly an unstable vortex of greed, ambition, jealousy, lust, piety, courage, compassion, and much more?"

It is the richness of Alter's understanding that points up the three weaknesses of his otherwise superb effort. The first is a frequent lapse into distended and jargon-ridden prose. The second is brevity. The third is far more complex and damaging—a refusal to confront the effect upon the stories of the possibility that they are not merely artistic constructs but literally true records of events occuring visibly in time and space. The quality of his success elsewhere, however, can only make us feel that the present study is a sketch—a brilliant preface to the immense examination, line by line, of all canonical Hebrew narrative. May he start it soon.

1981

FOUR DISTINCT BUILDINGS*

THE GOSPELS OF Mark, Matthew, Luke and John are surely the most frequently translated literary texts. Through their nearly two-thousand-year life, they have undergone repeated honor, travesty, and assault at the hands of individuals and committees intent upon converting their extreme originality of content and form into virtually all human vernaculars. In English the supremely successful version has been that authorized by James I and published, with the remainder of the Hebrew and Greek Bible, in 1611. In its latest revision—the Revised Standard—it remains the most reliable of committee versions (its famous eloquence being largely a function of a dedication to literalness on the part of the men who produced and revised it). But the liveliest of twentieth-century translations into English have been the work of individuals. The versions of Moffatt and Goodspeed were controversial when new but retain large measures of intensity and usefulness. The more recent, and very free, versions of Phillips and Rieu have reached enormous audiences with their startling and often appropriate colloquialism.

What has been lacking, however, is a readable literal version that would do some justice to the peculiar paradox of the gospels—that they were written in the informal commercial Greek of the first century by men who, with the probable exception of Luke, do not seem to have used that language with native skill; and that, despite their occasional stylistic amateurishness and patches of jerry-building, they have nonetheless stood as the most persuasive of human narratives.

Richmond Lattimore, after many careful translations of Greek epic and drama (and an excellent earlier version of the Revelation of John, which is revised and reprinted with the gospels), has now attempted to fill the need. He says in his preface, "I have held throughout to the principle of keeping as close to the Greek as possible, not only for sense and individual words, but in the belief that fidelity to the original word

* *The Four Gospels and The Revelation*, Newly Translated from the Greek by Richmond Lattimore (Farrar, Straus & Giroux, 1979).

order and syntax may yield an English prose that to some extent reflects the style of the original." The principle, in its transparent intelligence, would seem unavoidable, though such highly praised recent versions as the New English and the Good News Bible have avoided it entirely, with disastrous results. What are the results of its use by Lattimore?

The sane and flexible adherence to original order and syntax does produce, almost automatically, clear ground-plans of the varying designs of the four evangelists—Mark's laconic attentiveness and urgency, Matthew's ponderous but nutritious Hebraism, Luke's suavity and occasional tedium, John's uncouth sublimity. Such a clarification of structure becomes also a delicate measurement of the unstated thought of the authors, a chart not found in any other easily accessible version since the King James (most modern translations pour the homogeneous personality of the translator like opaque cream-dressing over all four texts); and it makes Lattimore's effort very nearly unassailable in architecture—four utterly distinct buildings, made of similar stone, all opening onto a courtyard pounded by blinding sun.

Questions arise, nonetheless, at numerous details. The largest concern matters of vocabulary and consequent tone. Though the originals are not always couched in idiomatic or even lucid Greek, they are still linguistically *of* their time and make no sustained attempts at literary elevation through archaic diction. Lattimore has kept his vocabulary admirably small, though not as small as possible; but he adopts a generally stately diction which is often more reminiscent of glazed Victorian versions of Homer and the tragedians than of the uniquely precise and oddly grand hurly-burly of the originals.

To take a few small matters which finally acquire considerable weight—Lattimore follows the King James in too often translating the omnipresent connective *kai* as "and," thereby producing in modern English an unnecessarily simple sense of progression. He frequently writes "Jesus spoke forth" when the original verb is more naturally rendered "answered" or "replied." He renders several crucial recurrent words with English equivalents which, while accurate enough, smell of a later theology that is probably foreign to the authors. The word "gospel" itself is certainly more clearly rendered, from its Greek elements, as "good news." The words which he gives as "preaching" and "repentance" are as well rendered by "proclaiming" or "announcing" and "change"—and without the suggestion of millenia of institutional harangue. He gives the Greek *christos* ("anointed") as "Christ" when "Messiah" is closer and more illuminating. He follows the majority of English translators in obscuring the single most characteristic word of Jesus' own diction—the solemn

Hebrew *Amen* with which Jesus prefaced especially grave remarks (and which is preserved as *Amen* in the Greek) is inadequately rendered as "Truly." And throughout he has avoided the use of contractions, though they are justified by the structure of Greek verbs and would have lent ease to his steadily formal textures.

Lattimore's seriousness and scholarly competence are of course never in question, only the atmospheres ultimately generated by such apparently minor choices (since every word in the evangelists' limited battery is repeated so insistently, the choices become all the more difficult and dangerous). But when his conservative commitments and occasional departures from literalness invade the reported voice of Jesus—which is invariably more striking than the evangelists' surrounding narration, as any red-letter edition demonstrates—he falls short of reproducing in contemporary English the most persuasive element of his texts, the single human voice which has altered thought and action more decisively than any other.

In Matthew 22, for instance, Lattimore translates a parable in these rigid and distancing tones—"Then Jesus spoke forth again and talked to them in parables, saying: The Kingdom of Heaven is like a king who held a wedding for his son. And he sent out his slaves to summon the invited guests to the wedding, and they would not come. Again he sent forth more slaves, saying to them: Tell the invited guests: See, I have made the dinner ready, my oxen and calves are sacrificed, and all is ready; come to the wedding. But they paid no heed and went their ways, one to his own lands, one to his house of business, but the others seized the slaves and outraged them and killed them." And in John 8, the most impressive of all Jesus' speeches emerges thus—"Abraham your father was joyful over seeing my day, and he did see it, and was glad. Then the Jews said to him: You are not yet fifty years old; and you have seen Abraham? Jesus said to them: Truly truly I tell you, I am from before Abraham was born." A literal chart of the Greek in that last sentence would run, "Amen amen I tell you before Abraham came to be I am." More than three hundred years of memory confirm the inevitability of the King James version's "Before Abraham was, I am"; and Lattimore's variation clouds the eloquence and conceals the staggering claim of Jesus to share the name and nature of God, the sole *I Am*.

Objections aside—and a number of others might be made—the important news is that Lattimore has provided a generally self-consistent, personal, sanely literal version of the four texts most central to our tragic history. He has avoided the twin shoals of caprice and ego, and his dedication to the line of the originals has produced an air of solidity and reliability often missing from single efforts. It is an achievement which places us more deeply in his debt than any other in a long and dilgent career, and his publisher has recognized the fact in a volume whose design is worthy of its contents.

1979

A LAUGHING GOD*

THE CANONICAL GOSPELS OF Mark, Matthew, Luke, and John were almost certainly published before the end of the first century, within sixty-five years of Jesus' death. Mark, which is generally considered the earliest, was apparently written in the sixties—only some thirty years after the crucifixion and thus within the lifetimes of a number of first-hand witnesses. Why then (for all their immense power and formal originality) were the four gospels quickly surrounded by a maze of adjacent structures, the works we call New Testament apocrypha? This mass of poems, episodes from Jesus' birth and boyhood, occasionally startling (but more often boring) deeds and speeches from his later history was defined by the end of the second century as neither historically nor theologically reliable. The reasons for the proliferation of apocrypha are numerous:

—the inevitable, partly affectionate, partly stunned mythomania that follows the wake of any extraordinary life.
—the manufacture of historic and doctrinal support for rival Christian sects (what better defense for your position on chastity or money than a story in which Jesus pronounces in your favor?).
—most basically perhaps, in compensation for the grave deficiencies *as biography* of the canonical gospels.

It is fashionable now to argue that the canonical gospels were intended as proclamations of a faith, not as demonstrations or proofs. They mean to say that the one eternal God became man in a particular place, lived among other men, suffered the cruelest of deaths in atonement for the sins of all men, then affirmed his divinity and the success of his mission by rising bodily from the dead and appearing to his old colleagues. The argument explains the omission from the gospels of vast areas of Jesus' life and personality (and almost surely his teaching) by claiming that such details were unnecessary to the evangelists' purpose.

Yet an amateur may ask, why (if they were going to ignore so many normal narrative curiosities) did the gospels tell even the bones of a story,

* Preface to *Jesus Tales* by Romulus Linney (North Point, 1980).

a life? Why not confine themselves like Paul to assertion through letters and essays? The inevitable suggestion is that they were human enough to see how a proclamation is best and most truly made in a *story*, albeit sparse. Why is their story sparse? The possible answers are again numerous:

—perhaps Jesus was intentionally secretive.
—perhaps the evangelists therefore possessed no more facts than they used.
—perhaps (and this seems to me incredible) the evangelists themselves were secretive, concerned to convey a subliminal message to an elite while deceiving the unchosen.

The second answer seems much the most satisfactory. It is certainly the one which both explains the puzzling biographical omissions and preserves the integrity of the evangelists. Their accounts are not lives— not even in the limited sense of the great anonymous Old Testament life of King David (with its numerous unflattering, even criminal, revelations) and plainly not in the sense of Plutarch or the scandalous Suetonius— because they did not *know* the life in question. They were first- or second-hand reporters of an immense explosion; they did not know the formula of the bomb itself. Thus they tell us tantalizingly little or nothing about the family and youth of Jesus; the influences on his thought, his adult appearance, his marital status, his human proclivities.

The immediate successors to these first reporters were the authors of the apocrypha, and they were not so scrupulous. But standing at a safer distance from the blast, their responses were more normal. They proceeded, with instinctive narrative curiosity, to invent a personality for Jesus. Or personalities. Anyone who perseveres through the wastes of Hennecke's standard *New Testament Apocrypha* (or M.R. James's older but more charming *The Apocryphal New Testament*) will discover fragments of a multitude of men, all called Jesus—from the scary Superchild of the Protevangelium to the cryptic sex-mage of some of the Gnostic gospels only recently discovered in Egypt.

In the ensuing centuries the successors to the early apocryphal writers have been legion; and as narrative artists, they have often been much more satisfying. I need only mention the medieval mystery plays, such novels as George Moore's *The Brook Kerith*, Kazantzakis's *The Last Temptation of Christ*, and Rilke's poems on the life of the Virgin. And a majority of these later apocrypha have been orthodox in their theology, though D.H. Lawrence's story "The Man Who Died" is a bizarre modern sequel to the more absurd Gnostic documents. But with the recent decline of Christian inspiration in all the arts, the stream of apocrypha has shrunk. Devotional tale-telling (more nearly haggadah than apocrypha) has continued in church circles, but I can think of only two serious secular attempts in the near past—A.J. Langguth's peculiar but fascinating *Jesus Christs* and Anthony Burgess's *Man of Nazareth*.

Now Romulus Linney provides a third with his *Jesus Tales*. A good part of his early work, fiction and drama, imagines the personalities of baffling historical figures—men such as Frederick the Great and Byron. That personal human curiosity has brought him now to the central enigma of our culture—the private Jesus. He begins in the speculations (or embroidered memories?) of the oldest apocrypha—the marital dilemmas of old Joseph and young Mary—but soon he is very much on his own. With occasional nods toward traditional European folktales of Jesus and the disciples, he explores wonderfully the most lamentable omission of the four gospels—Jesus' capacity for fun, his comic sense.

The evangelists do hint dimly that Jesus was prone to jokes—Peter and the tax money, some of the exchanges with scribes and Pharisees, the comic potential of the resurrection appearances themselves—but their Lord is mostly grave. And in two millennia of institutional Christianity, that gravity has often been distorted into primness and murderous indignation. If Romulus Linney had done nothing else here—and clearly he has—he would deserve grateful readers for inventing a whole possible wing in the old house of Jesus' name and nature: a laughing god, approachable and tangible, mining our world with the sly cherry-bombs of his love and care.

1980

THE PROBLEM HALF*

In 1979 Richmond Lattimore published his admirably readable, if doggedly conservative, translation of the four gospels. In the same volume he reprinted, with slight revisions, his early translation of the Revelation or Apocalypse of John. Now with Acts and the apostolic epistles, he has completed a singlehanded undertaking that can not only take an honorable place near his own shelf of translations from classical Greek but equally alongside such other one-man versions of the New Testament as those by Goodspeed, Moffatt, and Phillips.

It was Lattimore's stated aim in a brief preface to the gospels to follow as closely as possible the word-order and syntax of the Greek in the hope of revealing what has generally been obscured in Biblical translation— the strong, even clashing, individuality of the four evangelists: roughhewn speedy Mark, ponderous Matthew, suave but tedious Luke, and John in his full battery of sublimity, tenderness, and violence. Whatever one's response to any particular choice of phrase, it was easy to concede that Lattimore had achieved that variety (if with an occasional archaic sedateness not often shared by his originals).

In the new version, his procedure remains much the same—and for similar reasons apparently. But in the epistles especially, he encounters an obstacle not presented by the gospels. (The gospels occupy only a little less than half the New Testament. What remains is a long narrative, traditionally ascribed to Luke the evangelist, of the vicissitudes and triumphs of the early heroes of Christianity in Palestine and the Mediterranean basin. After an initial focus on Peter, the most interesting of the twelve disciples, the narrative settles exclusively on the single fiery and stringy figure of Paul, a converted Pharisee who out-apostled the apostles. Acts is followed by the thirteen letters that tradition ascribes to Paul; they occupy about a fourth of the entire volume. The remaining epistles, including the only likely specimen of the writings of Peter, occupy less than a tenth.)

The problem for a translator of this second half of the Testament is

* Acts and Letters of the Apostles, Newly Translated from the Greek by Richmond Lattimore (Farrar, Straus & Giroux, 1982).

precisely the problem of variety, interest, monotony. Once the vivid but fragmentary narrative of Acts is ended, the translator must embark upon a vast flat sea of sermon, utterly devoid of narrative—amazingly so, if one considers the writer's proximity in time and personal memory to a story of such stunning power as that of Jesus. The authors of the epistles do unavoidably write in different voices—and Paul's own voice is a famous amalgam of styles, from dazzling eloquence to thudding brutality—and there are hundreds of fine distinctions of theological assertion. But even in the first decades after Jesus' death, a small department of verbal and structural stereotypes had entrenched itself in the fledgling Christian community. And so, for a modern reader with no special hunger for the wrangles and execrations of the first-century churches, the epistles can be a daunting and wearying (even repellent) experience—a long series of stops and starts, built in much the same way, enlivened chiefly by Paul's occasional bursts of feverish lyric and a few moments of sublimity in the very rabbinical argument of the Letter to the Hebrews.

Lattimore's unruffled solution to the problem makes no concession to the secular reader's dilemma. With his commitment to literalness, he is not free to break through into the refreshing (and arguably more literal) freedom of, say, the Phillips version. His reader then will be well advised to partake of the book slowly and in spaced segments.

A further problem for any translator of the whole New Testament who hopes to make a text readable by an audience other than ready-made Christians is the absence of Jesus as an active presence from the second half of the volume. He is of course steadily referred to and built upon, but only in Revelation's scary visions of an avenging Messiah does he have palpable presence and a momentary narrative compulsion. His absence is filled by the arrival of Paul (after quick appearances by Peter, John, and James in Acts). In Luke's narrative of the conversion and missionary travels of Paul, he possesses an intermittent picaresque charm, wit, and moxie. But if one reads his epistles in anything approaching the order of their composition, then one confronts a personality as repellent to secular modern taste as it apparently was to most of Paul's own Jewish, Greek, and Roman contemporaries. Continually, one hears Paul descend from magnificent affirmations of irresistible divine love into a slashing and almost certainly neurotic obsession with sex, the simple use of the human body.

Lattimore is unflinching in his communication of the ugly paradox. Indeed, in his very conservatism, he makes unusually clear a central fact about Paul (and the entire New Testament, considered both as literature and as revelation)—Paul had never known the man Jesus; and to a nearly overwhelming extent, Paul's theology is an attempt to make a virtue of that omission. The absence of the broad scent of Jesus' human variety, his flexibility and humor, his immense physical magnetism, acts as a blight throughout the letters of Paul (and, through the institutional triumph of a few partial strands of Paul's thought, on the entire development of Christianity and thus western civilization).

The two volumes of Lattimore's translation stand now as one of the trustworthy guides to the origins of a force as powerful as any in history. One should not expect the frequent perfection of phrase and rhythm of the King James version (nor, as I've suggested, the vigor of some other singlehanded efforts); often Lattimore echoes the King James only to crash—for the King James's "the wages of sin is death," Lattimore offers "the stipend of sin is death"—but he sometimes follows his originals up into a trim and breathy poetry, and that's a helpful lure. If what one's seeking is patient service to a mysterious and now partly unknowable original, without bright swags of personal conjecture, then Lattimore's stands in usefulness with another widely available conservative version, the Revised Standard. It remains only to hope that he will find some forum in which to publish a full essay, discussing his reasons for attempting the task and his findings in the process.

1982

A GOOD REPORT*

 $\mathbf{D}$ AVID RHOADS AND DONALD MICHIE have understandably denied themselves dubious assertions about the core of motive and purpose in Mark's little book, his gospel. For contrast, I'll sever the guywires and— instructed by their patient examination and by my own long study of the baffling text—I'll dare a few claims and hope the reader tests them.

The Good News According to Mark has proved the most enduringly powerful narrative in the history of Western civilization, perhaps in the history of the world. As the oldest of the four Christian gospels, basic to the composition of at least two of the other gospels, it has exerted an enormous and continuous influence over Western thought and action since its birth somewhere between A.D. 65–70. (And if it has affected the West so profoundly, then it has unavoidably and sometimes disastrously affected the East.) It has thus succeeded on a literally unimaginable scale in the first aim of all narrative—the compulsion and maintenance of belief. The simplest tale—a lost child, say, restored to its mother through terror and danger—labors to compel our temporary belief in both an action and the demand of that action, in the events described and the need for a changed human conduct which those events imply.

Mark labors (and it is part of his charm and power that he labors visibly; he is not a born writer) to compel our belief that a Galilean named Jesus discovered himself in early manhood to be the Son of God, that his discovery was confirmed by mighty acts over the powers of evil and the forces of nature but that he met with incomprehension from family and pupils, ultimately discovered a sacrificial destiny for himself, and advanced toward the spiritual nexus of his country to engage that destiny—killed in agony at the hands of uncomprehending strangers and apparently raised from death in invisible but eternal triumph.

Why does Mark wish us to attend and believe a story so initially incredible in detail and so repugnant in its picture of humankind?— Because, unlike most storytellers, he believes his tale to be *necessary for*

* Preface to *Mark As Story* by David Rhoads and Donald Michie (Fortress Press, 1982).

life, all human life in its significant eternal aspect. If we hear and believe the actual story—believe that the events so briskly described occurred in a particular time and place more or less as Mark describes them, then we can hardly avoid confronting the demand made by the events (the whole tale can be read aloud in little more than an hour). The demand is synonymous with the first words of Jesus reported by Mark—that we repent and put faith in the good news, the news that God has resumed control of history, the news that human life is no longer a dark bout of meaningless waste but is redeemed by boundless and permanent love. How a believer in Mark's tale is expected to behave in the remainder of his daily life is left, bracingly but frighteningly, to the believer's own deduction and invention.

In short, Mark passionately wants us to believe his tale because he knows it to be true. How did he acquire such conviction? Rhoads and Michie do not speculate, though in a note they mention the ancient tradition that a man named Mark was an associate of Jesus' chief pupil Simon Peter and that Mark committed to writing Peter's own memories of the words and actions of Jesus. That tradition is preserved in a brief passage from an otherwise lost work of Papias, Bishop of Hierapolis in about A.D. 140. A translation of the relevant phrases of the Greek original might go thus—

> Mark, becoming Peter's interpreter, wrote down correctly all he remembered of the things said and done by the Lord though not in order; for he had neither heard the Lord nor followed him. . . .

That straightforward claim was recorded by Papias some seventy years after Peter's probably violent death in Rome and some hundred years after Jesus' own murder. There are numerous difficulties in the way of a simple acceptance of so simple a claim; yet for reasons too complex to state here, I (and many other students) accept it. It is credible on its face, according as it does with our knowledge of the mechanics of human memory in history, and it explains both the uncomplicated surface and the internally convoluted originality of the work itself. No earlier literary document bears the slightest resemblance to Mark's. One man, overwhelmed by a second man's memories of a colossal third man, preserves these memories as an urgent legacy to our race.

Hordes of other men and women have preserved first- and secondhand memories in letters, diaries, poems, plays, novels, biographies. Why were Mark's memories—first- or secondhand—so successful in their purpose? His own answer might well have been "Because the memories were so astounding in beauty and importance." We can be sure, however, that a vast majority of us would have been incapable of committing similar memories to such powerful form. The success of the gospel then lies in two huge resources—its subject matter (the secret truth it knows and struggles to reveal) and its strategies for revelation.

Rhoads and Michie have clarified more thoroughly than previous critics the strategies of architecture and language that are Mark's designs upon our hearts. I will not dilute their findings by summary. But I would like to point in conclusion to one over-arching strategy of Mark upon which they do not elaborate and which seems to me to confirm the origin of the tale in a particular personal historical memory.

Notice the degree to which Mark's gospel, in striking contrast with the other three, lays its narrative bet upon described *action* at the expense of conversation or monologue. Remember the often paralyzingly long halts for dialogue or sermon in Matthew, Luke, and John—those waits which make the boorishness of Jesus' pupils seem all the more credible. Then look at Mark's committment to unflagging and clearly limned action. Jesus went here and did this; then he went there and did that; then the world did its will on him; then he did his last deed—he triumphed over death.

Human memory, especially memory more than a few hours old, is almost always the memory of action, gesture, scene. Speech is certainly not omitted or even slighted in Mark—though we may long to know what Jesus said about many things and though Mark seldom preserves short sayings of Jesus to match the plentiful staggering utterances of the gospel of John—but speech in Mark is almost always rendered as the direct result of prior action. Jesus is brought to an apparently dead girl; he says, "Little girl, I'm telling you, rise!" He is shown a child from the crowd; the child's body in his arms then evokes a long and interestingly connected meditation on human offense. Such a strategy could conceivably have resulted from conscious or even unconscious art. But for me, and for many of Mark's two milennia of readers, it is the surest validation of and signal toward the origin of his blazing immediacy—he reports, not invents, the good news: a thing that has happened and in sight of human eyes. The thing can recur each time the tale is read. Read and see.

1982

AVAILABLE HEROES

O UR NEED FOR HEROES is at least as old as our need for enemies. The earliest literary texts of Western civilization were propped in powerful compulsion round the names of actual men—large, honorable, and honored in proportion: Gilgamesh, Abraham, Moses, Achilles. The compulsion and its famous results continued, with few interruptions, till a hundred years ago. Tennyson's "Ode on the Death of the Duke of Wellington" and Whitman's poems on the death of Lincoln remain, oddly, the most recent in a line of heroic monuments nearly four millenia long. Where are their successors?

Maybe the pause is not odd and is in fact a break. Where after all are our epics and tragedies?—fragmented into novels and movies, ghosts of their old life-giving forms. Tennyson himself, in contemplating the Iron Duke's corpse, predicted the end—"Mourn, for to us he seems the last." Of later poets writing in English, only Auden in his elegies for Yeats and Freud succeeded in erecting sizable and apparently durable memorials. Where are the poems on, the distinguished portraits of, the hymns to Marie Curie, Albert Einstein, Douglas MacArthur, Pablo Picasso, Franklin and Eleanor Roosevelt, Claus von Stauffenberg? Where are the odes to the three popular heroes of the recent American past?—John and Robert Kennedy and Martin Luther King Jr. They are plainly honored in the national imagination—millions of chromos in millions of homes attest to that, and a grotesque hunger for news of their survivors (no gobbet too small or rank) continues to gorge itself. They are of course the subject of numerous memoirs, biographies, films. But is their absence from serious imaginative art only another sign of the disastrous separation of cultured life from common life; or have good writers, painters, sculptors, and composers been sensitive and responsive for years to a rising sound that is only now being widely heard?—*There are no present heroes. Most dead ones were frauds.*

An answer to the first question would lead far afield (though whatever claims are made for a national "arts explosion" can be quickly refuted by any good artist). My answer to the second is a quick Yes—artists in droves have turned their backs on their ancient love and preservation of heroes.

Why? Because artists of all sorts, as society's most attentive observers, began early in this century to abandon the traditional definitions of heroism and have found no equally fertilizing substitutes. The explanations, again, would be complex; but important among them are the growth of compassion for the poor and powerless (traditional heroes being mostly high-born and powerful), the backwash of revulsion after the Great War at the patent stupidity and savagery of politicians and generals, and—crucial—the steady spread by press, radio, and now television of intimate and accurate information.

It's the merciless flood of *information* that has made living heroes apparently so rare, if not invisible, and so perilous on their heights. The classical world decided wisely that any human being accorded the honors and monuments of a hero must be, above all, dead. Even with their primitive apparatus for the dissemination of news, Greeks, Romans, Jews, and early Christians saw that today's still-breathing "hero" may easily be tomorrow's criminal or fool. (The first hero of whom we possess anything approaching a full picture is King David; and if—with his womanizing, his murders, and family scandals—he seems more human and interesting than Moses or Elijah, he is also proportionately less inspiring of reverence and emulation.)

By contrast, Americans in the nineteenth and twentieth centuries have often rushed to elevate the living only to discover dark patches of fungus on the idol's face and hands—Henry Ward Beecher, Warren Harding, Richard Nixon: to name only three from a long roll of the fallen. All subsequent would-be heroes have suffered from the ensuing disillusion. (It's obvious but accurate to say that President Carter and his family are unavoidably attacked by the lingering spores of the Johnson-Nixon blight.) And in the past decade the dead themselves have proved alarmingly vulnerable. Posthumous allegations of sexual adventuring by Franklin Roosevelt, John and Robert Kennedy and Martin Luther King, Jr.—men who capitalized on the public desire for immaculate family loyalty—have shaken if not toppled their shrines. In short, another human need—for unashamed praise this side idolatry—has been balked; and any parent now searching the walls of his child's room for icons of heroes is likely to find no face older than a rock star's or an athlete's, no person likely to do what he presently does throughout a lifetime.

Alas, but ho-hum. It was always thus, you may well respond—and I'll partly concur. The cult of living heroes has always been dangerously close to adolescent crush at best and, at worst, to psychopathic craving. At the very word *hero*, a number of our heads automatically run vivid home-movies of Hitler, Mussolini, Stalin on balconies—genuine beasts borne grinning toward us on seas of faces damp with adoration. And far closer by, most of us endured the daily televised arrival in our homes of the villainous faces of the Vietnam war—as we continue to endure the efforts of newly skilled electronic artisans to stoke our old hungers to fever pitch for some man or woman with no greater claim than an out-of-hand ego yearning for worship. In such a dizzying tide, surely we could relish a period of calm, admiring the admirable souls we meet in daily life but sworn off the hunt for national saviors or personal outsized templates for glamor and bravery?

I doubt we can. The need is too old, too ingrained in the kind of creature we are (slow to leave childhood and capable of love). At its purest, the need has always been our strongest lure to education; lives of great men and women *have* always reminded us we can make our lives quite literally sublime—lifted up, raised above the customary trails our nature has cut for itself through eons. And while many of us have had the early good luck to encounter and recognize heroic figures in our own homes, schools, or towns, such encounters have not often permanently satisfied the full need. The need is for figures both grand *and* distant. Why?

Partly because grandeur is best comprehended from a distance—an eye pressed to the floor of the Grand Canyon is seeing only grit. Partly because grandeur seen close often reveals beer-cans, chicken bones, immortal plastic. Mainly though because distance itself implies a journey —time and effort, endurance and strengthening. Home-town models have a disconcerting tendency to seem too possible and to shrink as we grow. What we want are models visible on their heights and all-but-inimitable in gifts and achievements. Tennyson at Wellington's bier defined the hope—"On God and Godlike men we build our trust." Provided that our God is merciful and just, we have always profited from real demigods who lure us up.

And *up* is the catch. Illusory heroes have frequently lured us *on* if not *down*. Hence the current healthy suspicion and aversion, the falling off in attendance at all shrines, the consequent awarding of fame and awe to pathetic instant-celebrities. (In Warhol's dream world where everyone is famous for fifteen minutes, no one will have time to *see* anyone else; we'll all be at mirrors, awaiting our moment.)

But a lull is a good time to look back and forward, to brace for the next wave—bound to come. What, in an age of nearly total information, can heroes be? Can they exist at all, in any form worth noting? Must we choose them blind as romantic lovers choose—and accept them at our doors like foundlings, bane or blessing? Or may we exercise study and judgment and select what is likely to serve and last? Since I'm proposing a true fool's errand—laying down law for regions where whim has always prevailed—I'll push to a rash end and answer the questions.

Heroes must be figures whom we feel to be unnaturally charged with some force we want but seem to lack—courage, craft, intelligence, stamina, beauty—and by imaginary contact with whom we experience a transfer of the force desired. Since we require that they stand at a distance and since they no longer come to us veiled in impenetrable art, we learn of their triumphs from a press which is equally prone to discover their faults. We're lucky therefore when our heroes are chosen for qualities that function more or less independently of our personal sense of morality. If we admire a priest for his charity and self-sacrifice, our admiration will be shattered by news of his intricate involvement with a ring of superior call-girls. If the same revelation includes the name of an idolized professional athlete, the new light may only enhance the athlete's glamor and power (Tennyson was plainly undeterred by Wellington's parallel fame as the sexual hero of a thousand boudoirs).

Hence there's profound unconscious wisdom at work in the present mass-cults for athletes, actors, musicians. Since we honor them for what we perceive as *physical* skills, the honor is not so fragile as that we bestow on peacetime rulers, clergy, doctors, lawyers, all kinds of teachers (in wartime obviously soldiers are honored for defensive ferocity). Brilliant performing artists are the safest heroes. In the current state of moral tolerance, their heroism is seriously threatened only by their health (even a failure of health will not affect our memory of them)—and maybe by discovery of their involvement in the cruel exploitation of children. Ingrid Bergman in 1950 was the last great performer to be thrown down in America for offensive morals, and she was restored in less than ten years.

Ideally then, in prevailing conditions of scrutiny, our heroes should either be dead (and judged safe) or alive but revered for strengths that are relatively amoral, though never vicious. Such a caution isn't meant to preclude the finding of large rewarding figures almost anywhere one needs to look—commerce, science, literature, fine arts, law, the military, cookery, labor, even government. It is however meant to define again the original core of true heroism, its first and most nearly irresistible base—the human *body* (at its strongest, boldest, most beautiful) and the deeds that flow direct from that body, broad memorable gestures on the waiting air. Few of us are agile, graceful, picturesque, or eloquent enough to be immune to the use of models who stand today in that ancient line. And luckily there's a long line of candidates—from Leontyne Price, John Travolta, and Natalia Makarova to Johnny Weismuller, Bruce Jenner, Martha Graham and on: their recorded perfection preserved from age and failure.

Yet however heroic in their different ways such names seem to me, I cannot hope to convey them intact into your pantheon. For if the recent hawking of celebrities (solid or weightless) has demonstrated their fragility as models, it has simultaneously proved the impossibility of arousing the degree of permanent excitement and admiration which is indispensable for the choice of heroes, by masses or individuals. Lasting and useful heroes *are* objects of love—love of all sorts: altruistic, erotic, passive, potentially destructive—and are chosen by levels of the mind beyond the reach of external persuasion. They may thus be either helpful or damaging but not premeditated, interviewed, selected by cool personnel procedures. Their suddenness and mystery is precisely their power, their promise and threat. The best we can do, as we scan their dazzling faces and feel their strong pull, is to scan ourselves—to probe our own weaknesses, vacancies, and know which of them need filling and why. Then at least we can wait, informed and prepared, for the unconscious acts of choice and ardor.

It may in fact seem a bad time for heroes—their old gleam, the old force they promised to lend us, seem genuinely and justly tarnished, worthy of suspicion. Maybe it's always seemed so; maybe old Greeks, Romans, Jews, and Christians were no more pushovers than we for the lone dazzler with the yen for worship. (There's a good deal of evidence to confirm the guess—Socrates, Kind David, Caesar, Martin Luther hardly climbed unopposed to their eminence or rested there.) It also seems a bad time for love. There can be no question that it's always seemed so (world literature says very little else). Still the world has proved lovable year after year—though in shrinking enclaves of beauty, honesty, excellence, persistence. The chief surviving enclaves, now as always, are single human beings. The list of those whom we—at our best—can love, serve, honor, and use as anchors in the riptides round us is surely no shorter than it's ever been. To say we lack heroes is to come dangerously close to saying we lack the capacity to love. It is certainly to say that we lack self-knowledge of our own predicament as incomplete creatures, capable of height.

1978

THREE GOOD NOVELS
OF THE 1970s

1. *The Honorary Consul* by Graham Greene (Simon and Schuster, 1973).

Graham Greene is nearly seventy. He was born in 1904 and is, as he says in these books, at the end of "what should be the last decade of my life." I call attention to the fact not only because he has done so—in that statement and in the majestic collected edition of his works now appearing in England—but because the fact is shocking in a revealing way.

The shock proceeds from realization that a writer whose passion for movement, whose quickness of presence in the ganglia of our psychic life (bombed London, colonial Africa, occupied Vienna, Saigon, brutalized Haiti, now a terrorized Latin America), and whose persistent and attractive air of disrepute have affirmed a hungry perpetual youthfulness, has at last begun to wrap the drapery of his couch about him. Or is it more shocking, since happily neither his energy nor his gift seems endangered, to be forced to consider that he may now be the largest of living English novelists?—Greene, the ambidextrous producer of "novels" and "entertainments," the saturnine and elusive figure most visible to Americans in Americophobic letters-to-editors, Catholic chronicler of the sour hearts of adulterous and drunken slaves of God?

For me, at least, he is the largest English novelist alive. E. M. Forster was consistently deeper, though never as broad; but Forster is recently dead. L. P. Hartley, Christoper Isherwood (long an American citizen), Anthony Powell, and Henry Green have sustained perfections denied to Greene; but again in each case, the grasp and the quarry have been smaller. Of older living English novelists, only Graham Greene seems now to have created (over forty-six years in nineteen novels) the sort of world-in-language which has been the deducible ambition of a majority of novelists in Asia, Europe, and America—a world which differs from the particular novelist's observable and appallingly rich world of time and place (which is more than an image of that world) in one respect only: that it yields *stories* to the patient witness.

Anyone to whom that appears either platitude or bathos is unaware of the degree to which original fiction during the past twenty years—especially in the United States and France—has ceased to be story. The disappearance of story (as plot, narrative) is in fact far advanced, ceded to other forms—film, television, journalism. Since the appetite for narrative would appear to be as constant in all peoples as appetites for food or love, and only a little less urgent, it is one of the triumphs of contemporary journalists to have seized what so many novels have surrendered, as the camera seized image from painting or as the novel itself won story from the dying epic and tragedy. And since plot and character have been the two, and the only two, indispensable components of narrative for at least four thousand years, a serious reader may well wonder if the surrender by novelists of narrative in its traditional forms (accounts of broadly recognizable human beings as they move through time and are altered by it) will not prove fatal to the novel or doom it to a dwindling coterie audience.

Vital possessions are not surrendered without struggle unless the possession has come to seem untenable. There have been numerous explanations for the atrophy of narrative—the most frequently heard is that novelists have tired of story, that its usefulness as an instrument of scrutiny and discovery has been exhausted by three centuries of novels—but toward the end of Greene's new novel *The Honorary Consul*, a Catholic priest turned Marxist guerilla explains to a hostage why he is reading an ordinary detective story at a time of danger:

> 'Oh, there is a sort of comfort in reading a story where one knows what the end will be. The story of a dream-world where justice is always done. There were no detective stories in the age of faith—an interesting point when you think of it. God used to be the only detective when people believed in Him. He was Law. He was order. He was good. Like your Sherlock Holmes. It was He who pursued the wicked man for punishment and discovered all. But now people like the General make law and order.'

The thesis is profound and largely convincing; it confirms the secret contained in the Indo-European root of the word *narrative* (*gno*, to know). A narrative is something discovered by one man in the welter of life and told by that man to other men. The pleasure of the listener in the transaction will consist both in the comfort of a prior partial knowledge (no good story can be entirely new) and the delight of discovery, illumination—fresh knowledge, which may age into wisdom. Stories must be known before they can be told; and stories can most easily be discerned, traced, and communicated by men who approach the surface chaos of the world with the suspicion that chaos conceals order, conceals a plot —plot in the sense of story told with emphasis upon causation and in the sense of conspiracy.

Since 1938—*Brighton Rock*—all Greene's fiction has been a search for the existence of that conspiracy at the center, a conspiracy on the part of a Creator God and His ministers (human and otherwise) to lure a renegade reprobate creation back to Himself, toward rest. The instrument of Greene's search has invariably been *story*, the actions of men in specific time and place. And the fact that we experience the stories as natural and true or manipulated and false is the gauge not so much of the success of his search for knowledge and answers as of his strengths as a novelist— his power to fascinate and finally to console (all enduring novels have offered consolation, however indirectly).

There are novels in which a divine plot is discovered by the characters and is confirmed in their actions (*Brighton Rock, The Power and the Glory*), those in which a plot is suspected but not confirmed (*The Heart of the Matter, A Burnt-Out Case*), and those in which the fierce benevolence of God is not suspected but is startlingly confirmed in credible action (*The Comedians, Travels with My Aunt, The Honorary Consul*). Since that analysis proceeds chronologically, it suggests not only a movement in time but a development in the skills of the searcher—in the honesty of his methods, the reliability of his findings.

Since the action of *The Honorary Consul*—as in all Greene's novels—rests upon a net of suspenses, unexpected combinations, unpredictable outcomes, any full discussion at this point would destroy the greater part of a reader's legitimate expectation from the novel. It is a story of the interdependence of four people—a half-English, half-Paraguayan, unmarried doctor living in a small city in northern Argentina; the aging and alcoholic Honorary British Consul of that city; the consul's young wife (a former local whore), and a Catholic priest who is now second-in-command of a group of Paraguayan guerillas. The guerillas, in an effort to force release of political prisoners, attempt to kidnap an American ambassador. By mistake they seize the Honorary British Consul, who happens to be in the same touring party and whom they are then compelled to hold hostage. The doctor is seized to tend the consul (the doctor is a boyhood friend of the priest and believes his own father to be among the prisoners whose release is sought). The doctor has been conducting a secret affair with the consul's wife, who is carrying his child. They begin to move on one another.

And the story which they generate—while it resembles Greene's past three novels in being "comic," producing a sense of justice done, virtue rewarded—reaches its calm end only after violence and unfathomable brutality. Most interestingly, it produces—in the voice of the priest just before the catastrophe—a statement which so far as I know is unprecedented in Greene's fiction but which now illuminates both his bleak early novels and these later gentler ones:

> 'The God I believe in must be responsible for all the evil as well as for all the saints. He has to be a God made in our image with a night-side as well as a day-side. When you speak of the horror . . . you are speaking of the night-side of God. I believe the time will come when the night-side will wither away . . . and we shall only see the simple daylight of the good God. . . . It is a long struggle and a long suffering evolution, and I believe God is suffering the same evolution that we are, but perhaps with more pain.'

Without imputing the thesis to Greene (though heretical for a Christian, it is an adequate account of the theology of Aeschylus), veteran readers may guess as I do that in it he has found at last the ultimate story for which his work has been a search. Confronted with the bones of the plot, we can now look back on the previous fleshings and judge them again. They all seem alive and joined in a progress, however broken and bizarre, toward a huge destination; and the latest in line—*The Honorary Consul*—is one of the lithest, surely not the last. A story both known and told.

1973

2. *Winter in the Blood* by James Welch (Harper & Row, 1974).

James Welch is a thirty-four-year-old American Indian (Blackfeet and Grosventre). Last year he published a collection of poems, *Riding the Earthboy 40*, and now this first novel, the third volume in Harper & Row's Native American Publishing Program. Welch says, in a jacket note, "I have seen works written about Indians by whites . . . but only an Indian knows who he is." And three of the six jacket-encomiasts insist upon the book's special value as inside news of Indian life. A small part of its value may well be that, but to stress the Indian-ness of Welch or his novel is to indulge in the same obfuscatory inverse snobbery with which some black writers and journalists have recently burdened their work. (The oppressed can hardly be blamed for reluctance to admit that their oppressors have indeed understood them—and continued to oppress.)

Winter in the Blood is by no means an "Indian novel." There is nothing in it—character, incident, language, or emotion—which will not be familiar or quickly comprehensible to any middle- or working-class white or black Southerner, Jew, Hispanic American, homosexual, or other minority member, literate country-club social chairmen included. What it is is a nearly flawless novel about human life. To say less is to patronize its complex knowledge, the amplitude of its means, and its clear lean voice.

Not that Welch doesn't draw a substantial part of his emotional power and the echoes of his story from an intensely observed past, from a meticulous particularity of human and geographic reference—reservation Montana. His book is nothing if not firmly local, rural (implicitly anti-urban), in the main tradition of the European and American novel. Its locus and cast are in fact tightly constricted—an aging young man, his mother, stepfather, his dying grandmother, an important blind neighbor; the family ranch, nearby towns with bars and lonely women. But the story it tells, the knowledge it contains, has as much to say of the bone-deep disaffection and bafflement, the famous and apparently incurable psychic paralysis of several million Americans of varied origins now in their twenties, early thirties, as of any smaller group. Permafrost in the blood and mind—why and how and what to do?

The components of the story are these—the narrator, a nameless thirty-two-year-old Indian, lives on a 360-acre ranch on a reservation in north-central Montana. The spread belongs to his widowed mother; she and her ancient mother are (so far as he knows) his surviving family. His dreamy cheerful father and an older brother, remembered as a paragon of competence, have died years before—the father frozen while drunk, the brother run down by a truck in an accident for which the narrator still feels responsibility. In the same catastrophe, the narrator suffered a knee injury which was later the cause of his only extended stay off-reservation—an operation in Tacoma and the chance of a job there in rehabilitation, terminated by his revulsion from a nurse's anti-Indian remarks. His mother remarries early in the novel; her husband proudly assumes management of the land. The narrator continues his cycle of ranch work, fifty-mile trips to town for the glum sprees of drink and women which serve as both narcotic and harsh electrotherapy, returning him to the tangled and paralyzing peace of family—pride in his tough and capable mother but disdain for her cool independence from him; amused animal affection for his senile grandmother (a genuine survivor of the great Blackfeet past and, not incidentally, a victim of her own tribe's internal cruelties); perhaps most damaging, an obsessive and by now sentimental regret for his father and brother.

In short, a black sack tied firmly shut. But no more firmly tied than most human sacks—as Welch and his narrator both see calmly (and detail in richly humorous low-life encounters with mysteriously luckless whites)—and tied shut partly by the man's past refusal to do more than double his own binding knots. Not much of a story if it ended there, surely not a fresh one.

But just as it threatens to die in its crowded sack, it opens onto light—and through natural, carefully prepared, but beautifully surprising narrative means: a recovery of the past; a venerable, maybe lovable, maybe usable past. To describe that opening here would deprive readers of the pleasure of its sudden radiance within the whole book. Enough to say that it involves the narrator's late discovery of long-suppressed facts about his own heritage—the names and history of his grandparents, in fact— and that Welch's new version of the central scene in all narrative literature (the finding of lost kin) can stand proudly with its most moving predecessors in epic, drama, and fiction.

The future *use* for the narrator of even so joyful a recognition is not pressed or prognosticated. Near the end he speaks of "planning my new life"; but neither he nor Welch expands on what the practicalities of such a life might be; and since it seems to include a renewed pursuit of his wretched Cree mistress, the omens are sad. The amount of clear knowledge may only have been that—a moment in a long night, a quick flush of heat in frigid blood. But even a quick light can cut a deep image; and what Welch has shown, not only for his lonely Blackfeet hero but for armies of the rapidly aging young, is a truth engraved in iron—a society which has taken no care that its children love their past (and a past which has taken no care to be lovable or venerable—a ground for standing on, at least) will reap generations of frozen children, hateful and hated. Black, white, brown, yellow, red.

Few books in any year speak so unanswerably, make their own local terms so thoroughly ours. *Winter in the Blood*—in its young crusty dignity, its grand bare lines, its comedy and mystery, its clean path-finding to the center of hearts—deserves more notice than good novels get. Mere true stories.

1974

3. *Song of Solomon* by Toni Morrison (Alfred A. Knopf, 1977).

Stories exist in four varieties—long and short, good and bad. The great majority of human stories are communicated orally, and skillful brevity is the first requirement of oral tales—in modern western cultures at least. The only long *audible* tales we endure offer side attractions such as music or pictures—*The Ring of the Nibelung, Gone with the Wind,* baseball. It's a famous fact too, and puzzling, that audiences for *written* story generally abhor brevity and crave length. Any publisher will grant that sheer bulk, in today's fiction bazaar, constitutes attraction; and a glance at any American bestseller list will show the presence of several heavy-megaton bombs.

There are explanations for both phenomena. Faced by a breathing speaking narrator, we fear captivity and boredom. But alone in our rooms, we submerge gladly in the self-controllable indulgence of a story hundreds of pages long—*our money's worth,* in more than one sense.

But long stories—novels—are generally undistinguished. Partly because most artifacts are undistinguished but, in particular, because few writers possess enough complex, mature, interesting, and communicable knowledge of the world. The question of maturity is especially crucial—there have been juvenile geniuses of the lyric poem, but it's difficult to make even a short list of first-rate novels produced by writers much under thirty. The subject of the novel is the operation of time upon human nature; and most men and women, especially in a middle-class America dedicated to infinite adolescence, only begin to recognize the existence of that subject as they enter actual middle-age—mid-thirties, early forties. A good young writer's long fictions are generally lyrical—the intense impressions of childhood, necessarily a little marooned in the self (is Emily Brontë the one novelist to spring up full-grown and vanish at once?—*Wuthering Heights* must have been written in her mid-twenties; she was dead at thirty-one).

Toni Morrison's strong first novels sustain the theory—*The Bluest Eye* in the purity of its terrors; *Sula* in its dense poetry, the depth of its probing into a small circle of lives. Firm as they both are in achievement and promise, they didn't fully forecast her third novel, *Song of Solomon.* Here the depths of the younger work are still deep; but they thrust outward now into wider fields, for longer intervals, into many more lives. The result is a long prose tale which surveys nearly a century of American history as that history impinges upon a single family. In short, a novel—rich, slow enough to impress itself upon us like a love affair or a sickness—not the two-hour pennydreadful which is again in vogue or one of the airless cat's cradles custom-woven for the delight and job-assistance of graduate students of all ages.

Song of Solomon isn't, however, cast in the basically realistic mode of most family novels. In fact, its negotiations with fantasy, fable, song, and allegory are so organic, continuous, and unpredictable as to make any summary of its plot absurd; and absurdity is neither Morrison's strategy nor purpose.

The purpose seems to be communication of painfully discovered and powerfully held convictions about the possibility of transcendence *within* human life, on the time-scale of a single life. The strategies are multiple and depend upon the actions of a large cast of black Americans, most of them related by blood. But after the loving, comical, and demanding polyphony of the early chapters (set in Michigan in the early 1930s), the theme begins to settle on one character and to develop around and out of him.

His name is Macon Dead, called "Milkman" since his mother nursed him well past infancy. He is the son of an upper-middle-class northern black mother and a father with obscure working-class Southern origins. However obscure (and the father is intent on concealing them), those origins fuel Macon's father in a merciless drive toward money and safety—over and past the happiness of wife, daughters, and son. So the son grows up into chaos and genuine danger—the homicidal intentions of a woman (whom he spurns after years of love) and accidental involvement in a secret ring of his lifelong acquaintances who are sworn to avenge white violence, eye-for-eye.

Near midpoint in the book—when a reader may begin to wonder if the spectacle of Milkman's circular life is sufficient to hold him much longer—the man is flung out of his private maelstrom and forced to discover, explore, comprehend, and accept a world more dangerous than the Blood Bank (his boyhood ghetto of idle eccentrics, whores, bullies, and lunatics) but also more rewarding—the larger, freer world of time and human contingency; knowledge of the origins of self and the potential waiting in the lives, failures, and victories of dead kin.

Macon's search is finally a search for family history, though it begins as a hungry hunt for money; and when he has traveled through Pennsylvania and Virginia, acquiring the jagged pieces of a story which he slowly assembles into a long pattern of courage and literal transcendence of tragedy, he is strengthened to face the mortal threat which rises from his own careless past to meet him at the end.

The end is unresolved. Does Macon survive to use his new knowledge or does he die at the hands of a hateful friend? The hint is that he lives

—in which case Morrison has her next novel ready and waiting: Macon's real manhood, the means he invents for transmitting or squandering the legacy he knows of.

But that very uncertainty is one more sign of the book's larger truthfulness (no big good novel has ever really ended; and none can, until it authoritatively describes the extinction from the universe of all human life); and while it has its problems (occasional abortive pursuits of a character who vanishes, occasional luxuriant pauses on detail, and the understandable but weakening omission of active white characters), *Song of Solomon* lifts above them easily on the wide slow wings of human sympathy, well-informed wit, and the rare plain power to speak human knowledge to other human beings. A long story then and better than good. Toni Morrison has earned attention and praise. Few Americans know, and can say more than she has in this wise and spacious novel—splendid with knowledge of a family's history and with power to search for its shape and essence, to make them ours.

1977

STRONG OLD RHYTHMS

I FIRST CAME DOWN HERE from Macon County more than thirty years ago to nurse my cousin who was having a baby," says the fiftyish waitress who serves me my first cup of coffee on Main Street. "Now I can't even *find* the house I came to. Plains has changed that much—and all just lately. I think it's grand."

On my own first visit to Plains two years ago, the town was mostly elated at its sudden fame. The nine old brick stores on Main Street, some disused for years, had opened hastily with a limited stock of Carter souvenirs, all relentlessly featuring peanuts and grinning teeth. The railroad depot, which had been campaign headquarters, was a welcoming center that offered the admirably unpredictable Miss Lillian for several hours each day of autographs and bracingly candid talk with the few bellwether tourists.

Up the way, Jimmy (as everyone called him) was in his own low rambling house, making Cabinet choices to the accompaniment of comic gallops by the baffled world press up and down the narrow streets to interview job hopefuls, then on to the nearest motels in Americus (ten miles away) for sparse rest and food. The food came, famously, from the now legendary Faye's Bar-B-Q Villa—a good steak served in the Formica rooms of a "double-wide mobile home" parked in a mud lot behind a filling station near some rotting tourist cabins.

Yet for all the excitement, the media cynicism, the physical groanings-at-the-seams, one could strike off alone and explore the town and countryside, finding the various unadorned sites of Jimmy's life and early work. A polite visitor with an anxiety-dispelling Southern accent could even find and talk at relaxed length with members of the presidential family. In a three-day visit—during Christmas rush at that—I had cordial and substantial meetings with Alton Carter (Jimmy's uncle and keeper of the family tales, possessed of an excellent narrative tongue and the sweet will to use it); Miss Lillian, Jimmy's mother (as self-assured as the mistress of an English country manor in Fielding's England); Gloria Carter Spann (Jimmy's nearest sister, wife to a Plains farmer and the most retiring and impressive of the circle); Miss Allie Smith (Rosalynn's serene but clearly strong mother); and Jimmy and Rosalynn themselves (attentive as radar stations on the DEW line and pleasanter).

Now two years later, midway through the first Carter term, I'm back to see how the place is changed. From the mobbed television scenes of presidential trips back, I anticipate the worst. And the last few miles of the drive are ominous (you fly to Albany, drive forty miles north). My favorite American road sign is gone now—the darkly mysterious "Dot's Topless Oyster Bar"—but a mange of new signs has broken out, for gift shops, campgrounds, ice-cold Billy beer (all the remains of that sunken venture have drifted hither). Just beyond the agricultural experiment station, a new information center sits by a freshly dug pond with the regulation absurd Old Faithful-type fountain. Just inside the town limits, two new buildings vie in raw gracelessness, both souvenir shops. The rival tour wagons jostle Winnebagos, in flight from the snow of Nebraska, Montana, Minnesota, Illinois and hovering here at the dozen chances to buy a now amplified selection of interchangeable junk mementos—the grinning peanut in still more awful avatars, Billy T-shirts, yardsticks, local cookbooks (revealing how deeply the taste-destroying shortcut has driven in its charge south from General Mills). Carter family members who have stayed on move more carefully now, cautious of the speed with which packs of strangers can gather at a glimpse.

The newest structure in town is Maranatha Baptist Church, result of a schism precipitated in the Plains Baptist Church by a racial dilemma in the wake of Jimmy's election. The newest organic matter seems to be a small garden given by the citizens of Kaohsiung, Taiwan. In a chill evening wind, the shrubs seem afflicted and huddled in gloom along streets as empty as Sagebrush at midnight. And, I discover as hunger mounts, Faye has closed her restaurant and moved the mobile home. The old Plains may be buried past finding.

Well, no. A night's sleep, a warm bright morning, and a big grits breakfast begin to focus facts. The breakfast (paper plate, plastic knife and fork) is at the Kountry Korner Restaurant. I've been advised that a trace of old Plains may be found here. And here indeed is more than a trace: eight middle-aged farmers at one long table talking land, bean planting, the future of Taiwan ("You think the Taiwans got a word to say about it? Think one billion can't take seventeen million any day they want to?" One man just says "Viet Nam," ending that), and crime in the county (a man has been shot in a break-in attempt—"Funny thing, he's a *married* nigger"). None of them pays the least notice to me or the other two strangers eating within earshot. It's their place; we're invisible. While I sense that the N.A.A.C.P. may not wish to pass out brotherhood plaques here, I also smell the first spoor of real life; and the fact that two black policemen and one black councilman work across the street in the town headquarters makes for further fine tuning. (I recall, for instance, that "nigger" in many Anglo-Southern mouths is not a racial insult, but a dialect noun, one used for at least four centuries).

What begins to seem clear on a second look then is how *little* is changed, since the Inauguration at least. In a remarkable exercise of control under pressure, the town council has severely limited commercial building. In addition to the two shops mentioned and the church, I could count only one other shop (more souvenirs) and a small grocery store; no neon in sight. The nearest motels are still ten miles away in Americus; and while there are one or two opportunities for respectable snacks in Plains itself (try the Main Street Cafe), the nearest full menu is also toward Americus (including a startlingly good French country restaurant as recompense for Faye's).

The few short streets still show the mildly abraded middle-class homes of the past ninety years. The one long block of South Hudson Street still shows black hovels in what seems permanently frozen collapse. No sign of pork-barrel public works or decor (beyond merciful provision for human excretion), no Carter statues yet, no rumors of veiled Saudi peanut takeovers. Any conversation with a longtime resident is likely to reveal that, under some genuine annoyance with the present, the spiritual structures of the past are standing, for better or worse, and straining to survive till Jimmy is a private citizen (six years at most) and Plains can be a farming town again, with a few dollars now and then from hell-bent consumers of presidential history.

A visitor, however sympathetic, is prone to feel that the hope is deluded. The stripped-down Protestant faith of the townsmen should have readied them for that. Where two or three are gathered together, there first of all is Satan: pride of self, envy, greed. While it seems a near certainty that Plain's magnetism for tourists will diminish (when I was there, I saw a mere three hundred a day—lots of parking, no crush), it also seems certain that the green crossroads and its six hundred souls can never lapse into pre-Carter life. The cause is not Jimmy or his mother or wife or his sad younger brother or Cousin Hugh, whose recent ragbag memoirs spill prematurely a lot of what seem to be real family beans. The beans, after all, are everyone's family beans, only easier to see: mothers-in-law, problem children, alcohol, a taste for money (as someone told me, "The Carters are not a bit worse than the Kennedys; the Kennedys just have more cashmere sweaters").

No, the deep shifts sensed and regretted by natives are attributable not to one local boy but to history. The outspoken Carters may have speeded ventilation; but the bleeding holes in the oldest foundations are the same holes rammed everywhere in America by swelling population, the spread of wealth, racial change, and an active central government. Through every hole, the citizens of Plains see what we all see—the quick dissolution of ancient ties of blood, faith, and money: the primal mortar of society.

Yet an older mortar is visible, the oldest hope anywhere and still a strong refreshment. Two minutes by car in any direction from the center of town will put you in the fields and woods of Sumter County. So I prowled for hours on the nearly empty roads—bare flats of resting purple earth; gentle folded hills on which naked hardwoods are swallowed in tall pines black in winter green; slow wheeling buzzards, hawks stalled above like statues of hawks, long crepe ribbons of starlings drifting south. The fact that crucial landmarks from the formative years of a man of present immense world-power are spaced round at intervals with no signposts may come to seem trivial in the uninsistent grandeur of the place itself, the inhuman place.

But the place is human now for a while at least, clearly Jimmy Carter's home. Anyone with the time to wander the county, to wait for the strong old rhythms of its life to sound their bass beneath the cashbox jingle, will see how the place has added to the man large measures of its own calm, its silent demonstration (at field's edge, in shacks, on more fortunate porches) of the few but urgent needs of human continuance, of—more urgent still—the needs of the earth. You may even come away with something like my own sense that what is regrettable in Jimmy's life now is your and my presence in his native place; the fact that he cannot return here in peace and roam as I've done in absolute stillness past his boyhood house, the neighboring hovels, the empty woods, the acres of graves just up the road at the site of the prison at Andersonville, where almost 13,000 men died in fourteen months to feed brands of ignorance and malice still ravenous now as then—or spend a long evening in a house on the edge of town with friends and kin joining other local boys (Mac Lee and "Amos" Austin) in songs new and old to first-class guitar: mainly A *Satisfied Mind.*

1979

WHAT STAYED IN PLAINS

WHEN I FIRST visited Plains, Georgia in December 1976, a month after Jimmy Carter's election, the town was buoyed on various brands of delight—the native son's handmade personal triumph, the daily spectacle of famous TV newsfaces bolting along the quarter-mile street between Jimmy's house and the heart of downtown (where long-shut stores had opened to peddle a line of peanut souvenirs which then seemed more comic than dismal to a new stream of tourists), and the onset of Christmas. The victor's formidable mother, Miss Lillian, was freely available at the old depot, dispensing her startling wit and candor and the sight of an old-fashioned wife and mother who'd kept her head high, her mind clear, her eyes bright. His brother Billy was cheerfully posing for snapshots at the gas pump, permanent beer can ominously poised. His affable mother-in-law and warm hilarious guarded sister were closer to the ground but still in sight, going on with their earnest working lives in a place they'd known forever, thick and thin. Even the president-elect and his wife were not invisible, making occasional forays into shops and to greet childhood friends or to eat at the nearest restaurants—every forkful watched for significance by a post-Watergate press corps as merciless as Pasteur at his microscope. And a sizable slice of the citizenry were guiding the influx of strangers round the sites—Jimmy's birthplace, his country home, his father's simple grave (the ambitious monuments in the cemetery are not marked CARTER but WISE and FAUST).

In those few pre-inaugural weeks, the town and its people seemed —from present hindsight—to be fairly precisely the kind of America promised not so much by Jimmy Carter as by Ronald Reagan now. Its virtues and vices were *personal*. All contact was hand to hand, hand to mouth, or at least face to face, and the limits on life were human or meteorological limits—*How much do you need? How much can you get? Where do you come from? What color are you? How much will you bear? Can I help any way? Do I want to try?* Lest the picture cloy, note that the turning of a swift buck, mountains of them if possible, is not precluded by the limits of a simple life—nor is the all but total absence of bucks.

On a second visit two years later, halfway through Jimmy's term, I found relatively modest changes. A few new tourist enterprises had sprouted, stocked to the ceilings with more gimcrack-souvenir assaults on the two archetypes of the Carter presidency—peanuts and teeth (neither of which lends itself to much variety of treatment). The state had built a welcome center, with vast parking lot and artificial pond, on the outskirts of town; and public restrooms had appeared near the depot. There were two shops dedicated to selling good local crafts, and—miraculously and surreal-istically—there was a new genuine French restaurant in an old chicken-house outside town, serving one-star meals at half the New York (not to mention Paris) price. Larry Flynt was publishing a weekly newspaper, the *Monitor*, with a crusading editor imported from Kentucky; and a few other out-of-staters—widely viewed locally as carpetbaggers—had set up various tourist scams. But the post-election tourists had dwindled fast, roughly as fast as two facts dawned on the populace—that Plains wasn't going to be the Little White House (presidential visits were scarce as summer rain) and that Plains and Jimmy Carter might not be as intimately connected as they'd first seemed to be.

Under the onslaught of its fame, the town had behaved with mostly unruffled dignity and hospitality (it was after all anchored to the ground —miles of peanuts, soybeans, wheat). But after a few patently successful attempts at informal mass communication—the telephone call-ins, the fireside chat in cardigan sweater—Jimmy had retreated decisively into his "nuc'ear" engineer's privacy, screened by a Georgia Mafia who lacked even the abrasive charm of basic Good Old Boys or of the Kennedys' strident Boyos. My notes from that second visit preserve local theories for Jimmy's scarcity in Plains—possible embarrassment at Billy's spiraling hijinks, displeasure at the crude commercialism, or maybe advice from his pollsters to downplay small-town Southern roots in favor of a ho-mogenized national image. Certainly a home visit was a summons to pushing crowds, at least half newsmen; and resident family members had found it increasingly impossible to appear downtown. (Miss Lillian says, "They all wanted to *touch* me, and if there's anything I hate, it's being hugged and kissed by a woman." Rosalynn's mother could no longer sit on her porch, and his sister had to build a stout fence to keep out a public that included frequent borderline cases intent upon rushing paranoid dispatches to the White House.) But the peculiar economical and decorous motions of a farming community, miles from any city, were still in grand career; and the splendid flat landscape of fields, thickets, and wildlife was intact on all sides—briefly tolerant of the occasional trailer or other frail platform of human hope.

And now a third visit, little more than a month after Jimmy's defeat—so clearly stunning to him and his children in their early ordeal of televised concession (the absence of tears was a gauge of their shock). He had flown here election dawn to cast his own ballot, already informed of imminent failure; and in a greeting to his hometown supporters at the depot, the break in his voice had seemed an understandable response to their continued loyalty in the face of so much bafflement, so many craven defections—"I've tried to honor my commitment . . . to you."

What had that local commitment been? Was it different from his repeated blanket commitment never to lie to the country and to do his own best? (a paraphrase simply of the presidential oath, so recently traduced by other men). If you had lived a great part of your life in so intimate a place, one where sustained deceit is impossible, wouldn't you have promised to make them proud of their share in you, their contribution to the shaping of your faculties? That was surely implicit. Do they now feel the pride of four years ago, the fervent expectancy announced in his always fragile Irish tenor at his swearing in?—"that when my time as your president has ended, people might say this about our nation—that we remembered the words of Micah and renewed our search for humility, mercy, and justice . . . and that we had enabled our people to be proud of their own government once again."

The most direct and eloquent answer I heard came before I reached Plains, when I talked with a fellow traveler—a black native of south Georgia who has lived in the northeast for thirty years and was bound home for a funeral: "It wasn't so much that the people didn't like Jimmy. They didn't like the *country*, and they didn't want him to have to run it."

But then as I drove out from the Albany airport in my rented car, forty miles north toward Plains, the first clear fact was that the country hadn't changed—not the physical country, not hereabouts. The meticulously tended pecan groves stand on in the clean light; the well-grazed cows are still marching barnward in neatly spaced lines as if in rehearsal for their next State Fair. The two crossroad towns, Leesburg and Smithville, show a little new paint on the old stores; but otherwise the stretch looks much as it must have all Jimmy Carter's life—no billboards alluding to his existence, no huckstering.

That begins on the road from Americus to Plains, though with nothing like the quantity or hideousness that is standard issue now for the edges of almost any town. I note the chaste welcome center on my left with only three cars in the lot (I never saw more than five in four days of passing), then the silos and watertank, and then the nice row of brick stores that have easily endured their freight of souvenirs and the acid marinade of countless photographs to stand on as anyone's icon of small-town America. They are not exactly an architecturally distinguished row; but their variety and fantasy of ornament and color make pictures of Reagan's home street in Tampico, Illinois look dour.

A stop for coffee in one of the buildings, the Main Street Cafe, indicates that fantasy was not exhausted on the rooflines. The snack menu offers for instance such sandwiches as "Amy's All American" (peanut butter with optional jelly), "Billy's Road to Recovery" (cold turkey), and a green salad called "Rosalynn's Remedy." And except for the silent caricatures on souvenirs and the now touching postcard photographs of a younger happier Jimmy and an unharried Billy, that might well be all I'd have seen or heard of the Carters this time, unless I'd asked.

That's the first surprise, how the subject of Jimmy has vanished like the dew. It is literally true to say that in four days of engaging random citizens and family relations in casual conversation, I never heard the president mentioned till I brought him up. The silence didn't seem a result of gloom, and certainly not of shame or humiliation. Billy's breakfast hangout, the Best Western Motel in Americus, did list *crow* on the menu of November 5th; but that's only consistent with the air of amused and stoic relief which greeted all my inquiries.

Any close observer has seen from the start that Jimmy Carter was *from* Plains but not *of* it. His qualities, especially his pride and hunger, propelled him away; and no doubt he realized long ago that no over-achiever is ever thanked at home. Not while he's achieving. 161 of the votes in Plains were cast against him this second time, more than a fourth of the town's population.

But ask about him and, since they instantly know that you're not one of the inhabitants, the answer will almost always take the circuitous form of speculation about his future relation to Plains. Will he or won't he live here? Will the Carter Library be here or in Atlanta? Rosalynn, they tell me, has said in a recent interview that they'll keep a place in Atlanta but will mostly be here where Jimmy will be writing; and that Amy will go to public school in the county. It's frequently mentioned that the abandoned Plains high school would make a good site for the presidential library (one look at the tired old building indicates its inadequacy, however nice the thought). And the speculations resolve into two camps. The most enthusiastic are from businessmen who hope for Jimmy's return as a new charge on the tourist magnet (even in the Reagan rout, more than thirty-five million potential visitors did vote for Jimmy, especially the oldtimers who can drop off on their way to winter in Florida). Others, among them old friends and family, are more ambivalent. They're ready for a long dose of Plains's former peace, where the only prying eyes belonged to one's neighbors; and they rather dread the attractions of a former chief executive, whatever their feelings for the man they've always known. Steady throughout is the question of Rosalynn. "Rosalynn really loved that job; don't count on her staying home cooking dinner." "Rosalynn's liable to *run* for something—maybe vice president to Fritz Mondale."

So they wait to see how much they'll get from their famous son— or how much they'll have to bear. Some of the burdens are already lifting. The carpetbaggers are leaving, Larry Flynt has closed his paper, the junk shops are starving. With luck, Jimmy Carter will be the youngest man since Calvin Coolidge to return from the White House; and surely neither he nor his equally impelled wife can predict their own movements or calculate their effects. They have not really lived in Plains for ten years. But though their townsmen are curious, they're not postponing normal life—even his kin who, though still cautious, seem fifty pounds lighter in the duty department and more candid than ever (though not for reporting).

The whole last day of my visit coincided with the annual Peanut Jamboree, all outdoors on Main Street with maybe three hundred souls in attendance, very few of them tourists—a flea market, cake walks (for homemade cakes, each cook's name revealed so you know your source), bingo, food stands (one white, one black—with integrated patrons), puppets, a pleasantly inept bluegrass trio, somber teenage gospel singers ("Praising the Lord the best way we can"), an integrated high-school song-and-dance team (good enough for the Osmond Show), and the best clog-dancing I've ever seen from the Muckalee Mudstompers, a local troupe with a world-class clogger in Jeff Moss, a sixteen-year-old native of Plains. When I talked with him, he only talked of dancing—how he loves it, how he practices every minute he can but means to study agriculture in college. Jimmy?—"Well, everybody's guessing what he'll do. I guess he won't *rest*." With that Jeff was called off for a second fling on the cold asphalt.

The skies that had lowered all afternoon were threatening to pour. One young farmer near me pointed toward the cloggers and said, "They may not get to finish this." His partner looked heavenward—grinning in the drizzle—and said, "I need a good rain a lot more'n I need to watch a *dance*."

Whatever he's forgot about his native heath in all the years away, all the wins and losses, Jimmy Carter—a watchful and canny man— won't have misplaced the point of that. Most things come and go, however good to watch; a few things stay and matter to the end. Rain for instance, a few hundred people having harmless fun on a fall afternoon to honor their harvest and to brace against winter. Let him come back and watch this a long time before he writes a line.

1980

LOVE ACROSS THE LINES

FOR NEARLY two centuries now a love, almost Wagnerian in intensity, has grown between two kinds of English and American literature. Vast and enduring and often unrequited as it's proved to be, it is little noticed and hardly discussed. The lovers are novelists and poets. The epic and dramatic poets of the ancient world appear, from our perspective at least, to have been content in their roomy narrative-lyric forms. There were no long prose fictions by Homer, Aeschylus, Sophocles, Euripides, Vergil—or by Dante, Shakespeare, or Milton. And there are none by Dryden, Pope, Wordsworth, Coleridge, Byron, Shelley, Keats, Tennyson, and Browning.

If we consider writers in English who are mainly regarded in the recent and relatively unGreek sense of writers of verse, then the first important poet to produce a long prose fiction would seem to be Sir Philip Sidney. But he has no immediate heirs (unless we choose to argue over the amphibious but chiefly prosey Samuel Johnson and Oliver Goldsmith).

On the continent, to be sure, Goethe won his fame and profoundly affected the life-expectancy of nineteenth-century German adolescents with *The Sorrows of Young Werther* and in *Wilhelm Meister* achieved a rich combination of prose and verse which has too seldom been emulated. Victor Hugo succeeded enormously with *The Hunchback of Notre Dame* and *Les Misérables*. To the east rises the long range of Pushkin and, still beyond, Pasternak.

In English however the poet after Sidney to excel in prose is Sir Walter Scott, who is now read for his prose fiction—as is, in America at least, Edgar Allan Poe. With curiosities and grotesqueries along the way—such as Walt Whitman's temperance novel *Franklin Evans*; George Eliot's long poem *The Spanish Gypsy*; and such honorable versatilities as the poems of Emily Brontë, Robert Louis Stevenson, Rudyard Kipling, Stephen Crane, Gertrude Stein, James Joyce, and D. H. Lawrence—we arrive in Thomas Hardy at the first writer in English to achieve substantial and equal distinction in long fiction and verse. And rather quickly we come to our second and, so far as I know, only other truly ambidextrous

poet-novelist/novelist-poet of large productivity and equal distinction—
Robert Penn Warren. (The fact that they both earned first notice as
novelists is of interest, for I cannot think of an example of the reverse—
a writer first widely admired as a poet who then proceeded to extensive
excellence in fiction—and I cannot think why.)

Some lesser achievements are famous—the poems of Hemingway
and Faulkner, of interest to cultists, have recently been reprinted. Buried
forever perhaps are whole volumes of poems by William Dean Howells,
Willa Cather, and Theodore Dreiser (though some of Howells's poems
bear comparison with his best fiction and though Dreiser's volume—
Moods, Cadenced and Declaimed, which followed his successful *An Amer-
ican Tragedy* by a single year but sold only 922 copies—should probably
be retained in print *pro bono publico* by the National Endowment for the
Arts as a species of warning to heedless poachers across the genre lines).
Among American and British contemporaries, such poets as Stephen
Spender, Dylan Thomas, Randall Jarrell, Howard Nemerov, James Dickey,
James Merrill, Sylvia Plath, Maxine Kumin, Galway Kinnell, D.M.
Thomas, and Dave Smith have published good fiction; and novelists of
the quality of John Updike, Joyce Carol Oates, and Larry Woiwode have
published quantities of serious verse.

The lists could continue well into the night and might provide occasional amazements—what for instance of the great plastic artists like
Michelangelo who've managed brilliant poems in an idle moment?—but
the lists only postpone an obvious and necessary question: why, for the
past hundred years, say, has there been this ever-increasing trespass across
the boundaries of form; this oceanic if unrewarded yearning of poets for
prose, novelists for verse?

A first answer would note that the boundary between verse and prose
in English and other Western languages did not become rigidly fixed until
well after the development of the novel as the popular receptacle and
purveyor of narrative—extended imitations of interesting human action
(conflict and resolution) presented in the order in which sane human
witnesses perceive the world outside themselves: that is, chronological
order; the order of ruthless clock-time.

In most Western countries, the gradual triumph of the novel began
in the mid-eighteenth century but was not complete until the late nineteenth, when the maturing of the form itself coincided with (and no doubt
encouraged) the rise of mass literacy. Thus Tennyson and Browning are
the last major English poets to write long verse narratives. In America
the impulse survived a little longer in Edwin Arlington Robinson and
Robert Frost; but by the 1930s the wall between extended narrative and
verse had been raised and pretty thoroughly secured (a rewarding com-

parison could be made with the famous effect of the invention of photography upon painting—a similar abandonment of mimetic narrative content and a consequent inversion of attention and vision).

In short, those writers who by gift and training were inclined to the production of verse, abandoned as indefensible vast provinces over which they had long and fruitfully roamed. Those invaders or benign colonists who inherited by vigor and default the ancient treasures of epic, drama, romance, and tale were required to surrender the ancient containers and vehicles of those treasures—metrical line, paragraph, and stanza with all their still-uncomprehended and uninvestigated subliminal powers to enchant, seduce, and conquer; perhaps even to *control* for brief periods. Once those drastic mutual surrenders were made, however; once the border walls were in place (and the border guards—more of them later), the yearning could begin, the fraternization and the often furtive mergings.

A second answer would ignore the effect of the novel on poetry (and of the powerful influence of movies over both) and would remark simply that verbal craftsmen share with all other humans and beasts an impatience with forms, restrictions, shortages of material imposed upon their lives. But surely no one who has not chosen a particular *literary* form as the container of his curiosity and knowledge can know the degree to which the form itself—the sonnet, the free-verse paragraph, the epic, the realistic novel, the prose tale—will not merely receive an artist's questions and convey him to the Ultima Thule of an answer but will simultaneously shape, alter, distort, disfigure, clarify, even beautify both question and answer.

It is so obvious as perhaps to bear mentioning that *King Lear* could not be a novel nor even a long narrative poem; that Shakespeare's discoveries in the interior of human folly, cruelty, and devotion are to an extent beyond calculation forced upon him by his initial commission—a stage drama of manageable length written generally in lines of five-stress rising rhythm, interspersed with passages of a prose which (though it appears to obey looser laws) is also marching under iron discipline: the discipline of the form of the play, the form of the *idea* as it is conceived, born, and matured by the physical form of act, scene, verse, prose *and* by the presumed pressure on Shakespeare to write both quickly and lucratively for a commercial enterprise.

It is equally obvious, and made even more so by several screen adaptations, that *Anna Karenina* could not be a play or a poem. The immense prowl of Tolstoy's immense and glacial attention over an entire civilization at a particular moment of poise-before-collapse could only have been contained by the elastic and pawky realistic novel, the shaggy monster which Henry James so innaccurately deplored when he spoke of

Tolstoy and Dostoevsky as "fluid puddings," devoid of composition, economy, and architecture—a form, not at all incidentally, which required more than four years of Tolstoy's time.

That discovery then of the constricting and liberating power of particular forms is among the most enduring impulses which send novelists and poets outside their accustomed forms into new and strange country —promising, forbidding, and often treacherous.

A third important distinction between contemporary novelists and poets, and a force in their mutual attraction, is memorably stated in Howard Moss's illuminating introduction to an anthology of short stories by poets. The collection is called *The Poet's Story*; and among other acute observations, Moss says,

> The mirror is the totem of the poet, who looks *at* and *into* himself, who creates himself, as it were. And I would say the window belongs to the fiction writer, who looks *out* and *around*, and is a product of the world.

The generalization can stand a little adjustment of course; but at heart it's unassailable. Robert Penn Warren's *Brother to Dragons*, despite the incorporation of the character RPW into the poem, is surely a long poem whose totem is the window. So are the many related poems of Robert Lowell's *History*. But with the decline of verse narrative, verse drama, and with the virtual disappearance of the religious lyric (the song to and about God), contemporary poets are fairly strictly committed to self-contemplation—even in the multitudinous neo-surrealists, whose relatively brief poems are inescapably charts of their own preoccupations. And the general abandonment of strict poetic forms, in America at least, has perhaps deepened the poet's solipsistic entrapment—the old complexities of meter and rhyme being, arguably, skills which lured the craftsman out of his cave of mirrors into a world of similarly employed workers, a large guild of journeymen fabricating gold watches set to tell the same time.

Any novel of course is also a function of its author's preoccupations, and one of the obsessive aims of the experimental writers of the 1960s and 70s was the prose domestication of the verse surrealist's luxuriant access to memorable image and to revealing disjunctions in time and human nature. If their often gaudy and always academic efforts found few readers—and indeed assisted the serious novel in its drift toward the reader-desertion so lamented by poets—it's worth remembering how silently and steadily great novelists from Defoe to Malamud have smuggled the tools of verse into their prose: metaphor, heightened speech, interior monologue, and (far more often than is noticed) meter itself. So the

novelist at his window, scarily aimed at the world of others, and the poet
at his seldom flattering or consoling mirror have naturally yearned to swap
views.

Before moving on to what I think is the strongest of the attractions
between the genres, let me glance at a weaker though very real one. The
contemporary poet, with his sales in the hundreds or low thousands, envies
the novelist his book clubs and paperbacks, his *Today* show interviews,
his presumed larger audience (an audience which, when scrutinized, often
proves small and which may soon vanish altogether, given the present
lemming-rush by publishers to drown in an artificially heated marsh of
ephemera). The novelist envies the poet his ancient and still assiduously
maintained priestly robes and wand, his evident but inexplicable access
to the gods of language, his tiny but fervent band of disciples, summonable
at any American crossroads at the mere announcement of a poetry reading.
The novelist also envies, I think, the strong odor of smoke and blood that
hovers above American poets—a continuous effluvium from the ceaseless
poetry wars: the Redskins vs. the Palefaces, in whatever getups they fight
this season. If there was in American fiction a similar aesthetic division
in the 60s and early 70s between the realistic novel and the commercially-
doomed experimental, it produced few memorable skirmishes—perhaps
only Gore Vidal's massive napalming of the experimentalists. But any
novelist craving a touch of real aesthetic frostbite has only to write a
handful of poems, then dare to read them to a room containing a minimum of one licensed American poet. Any craven need for an alley fight
can be quickly satisfied by the novelist's daring to *publish* the poems.

I'm open to correction, but it seems to me that poet's novels are met
with actual tolerance from novelists. My own four years' service on the
literature grants-panel of the National Endowment for the Arts gave me
constant occasion to wonder why, when compared with the brawling and
backbiting of poets, most novelists seemed positively somnolent if not
beatific. Perhaps poets envy that tranquility—professional at least, if not
personal. And is the tranquility a simple result of the novelist's access to
larger audiences and more money? (We're speaking of course of relative,
and pitiably small, figures—a few hundred vs. a few thousand generally.
In any culture at any time there is apparently a mystically fixed number
of earnest readers for serious verse or fiction, not quite as small a number
as the thirty-six Just Men of rabbinical tradition but stunningly low; and
any trade-paper's news that a novel of Saul Bellow's or a volume of Frost's
poems has sold a hundred thousand copies is not to be interpreted as an
indication that the gross number of serious readers is increasing. An
informal canvass of ten of those buyers will silence your hopes).

If that last-mentioned attraction between poets and novelists—an

attraction of commerce and psychic violence—seems less than noble, let
me attempt to suggest how it produces and even disguises the most potent
attraction of all: the essence of this long rivalry between genres (I'm omitting entirely those dramatists who write novels or verse, those painters
who have so often written well, those journalists who serenade every
window in the House of Art). Look first at a sonnet by W. H. Auden.
It's called "The Novelist" and I'll quote it in its earliest published form,
not in Auden's late and damaging revision.

> *Encased in talent like a uniform,*
> *The rank of every poet is well known;*
> *They can amaze us like a thunderstorm,*
> *Or die so young, or live for years alone.*
>
> *They can dash forward like hussars: but he*
> *Must struggle out of his boyish gift and learn*
> *How to be plain and awkward, how to be*
> *One after whom none think it worth to turn.*
>
> *For, to achieve his lightest wish, he must*
> *Become the whole of boredom, subject to*
> *Vulgar complaints like love, among the Just*
>
> *Be just, among the Filthy filthy too,*
> *And in his own weak person, if he can,*
> *Must suffer dully all the wrongs of Man.*

Sweet words—to a novelist, even one who like me recalls that the
older Auden appeared to read no fiction more ambitious than detective
thrillers. Sweet and no doubt too simple, however interestingly it agrees
with Scott Fitzgerald's observation that in every good novelist there is
something of the peasant. (Is the corollary to that that in every good poet
there is something of the baron?—the lord of the manor, subject to
outbursts of largess and rage?) To stick with Auden's simplification for a
moment though, if we think of modern poets as hussars (cutlasses drawn,
hurtling on fevered steeds through hails of grapeshot toward larger ord-
nance and certain death), then we may think of the more prevalent kind
of novelist (that is, the clock-time realist) as footsoldiers or maybe even
mess sergeants, cooks, and bottlewashers.

However coarse such distinctions, they do finally chart the lines of
the strongest magnetic force that draws poets proseward and novelists to
verse. My own simplification is this. The novelist envies the poet's intensity
of emotion, language, consequent rhythm, and kinetic effect; the poet

envies the novelist his stamina, his endless enlistment, his helpless commitment to the long haul—the slowly drawn but finally enormous net of
fish, the ripe fields of standing grain in late summer light. What each in
fact envies in the other is his particular command of time—the literal
chronological realities of his form: the lyric poem's command of the
moment, the novel's command of human generations.

Howard Moss makes another interesting division which is relevant
at this point—" . . . Time is different for the novelist and the poet. The
fiction writer is dominated by the clock and the poet by the metronome.
They are just dissimilar enough—metronomes can be sped up, slowed
down, or stopped—to provide a fertile field of transaction." My own
suggestion is two-fold and so obvious as to be generally ignored. With
uncharacteristic exceptions like Joyce's *Ulysses*, novels concern themselves
with stretches of time which, by human clocks, are relatively long—
weeks, months, years. Most novels literally portray the passage of a good
deal of time: time is their subject but also their predicate and object. The
traditional novel (and the one still most popular with readers) is lengthy
—five hundred pages and upward, say. Lady Murasaki, Richardson, Stendhal, Dickens, Tolstoy, Dostoevsky, George Eliot, Proust, Roger Martin
du Gard—all actually depict, by various chronologically consecutive
methods, the flow of time through particular persons; and the length of
their depictions becomes in turn a slow stream of time running through
us, the readers. Only a postgraduate student of Speed Reading can consume the majority of classic novels quickly, and most of us suspect that
consumption is not synonymous with assimilation.

Like most readers, I've spent whole summers with *War and Peace*;
winters with *Bleak House*, a calendar year doing Proust like a job (tedious
but well-paid with grand office-parties). And many contemporary novelists
continue that traditional request for substantial stretches of the reader's
actual life, novelists from a broad spectrum of schools—from Anthony
Powell, Eudora Welty, and Saul Bellow through John Barth and Thomas
Pynchon.

But of the already-canonized great twentieth-century poems, how
many demand—for a single earnest reading—more than an hour of a
sane reader's life? (I discriminate here between reading and scholarship.
A perusal of the author's notes to *The Wasteland* and the academic barnacles upon its hull and that of the *Four Quartets* can take a long decade.
The same might almost be said of Pound's *Cantos*, William Carlos Williams's *Patterson*, Hart Crane's *The Bridge*, David Jones's *In Parenthesis*,
Wallace Stevens's *Notes Toward a Supreme Fiction*, Charles Olson's *Max-
imus* poems—though in those cases, the process of canonization is still
being argued.) Among living poets, an increasing number have attempted

relatively long poems or cycles—Anthony Hecht, James Merrill, John Ashbery, Galway Kinnell, Ed Dorn, Geoffrey Hill, and Ted Hughes— but a rollcall of widely admired twentieth-century poets from Yeats through Robert Lowell and, say, Philip Levine is its own illustration of my point: that modern poets, with curious diffidence, have requested or required relatively small portions of our clock-time. That the diffidence is new, odd, and sacrificial is indicated by an earlier muster—*The Iliad, The Odyssey, De Rerum Natura, The Aeneid, The Metamorphoses, The Divine Comedy, Paradise Lost, The Hind and the Panther, The Dunciad, The Prelude, Hyperion, Prometheus Unbound, Idylls of the King, The Ring and the Book.* And lest they be thought of as isolated continents amid rafts of small lyric islands, we could spend an all but endless night reciting the names of their failed long companions—a number of them by honorable poets.

However critical then, that difference in the clock-demand of contemporary verse and prose, it is still not the essence of the final attraction between the genres. (My generation may have been the last in America to memorize poems—I had an uncle who could recite perfectly Walter Scott's *Lady of the Lake*—but the memorability of traditional brief verse forms went a long way toward eliminating the difference. Over nearly thirty years now I have frequently recited to myself poems as short as Emily Dickinson's "Success is Counted Sweetest" or as long as Milton's "Lycidas," but I cannot recall one entire sentence from any great novel.)

The essence, again, lies in each genre's peculiar grasp on time. The novel, like the drama, is helplessly and gloriously dependent upon scene—present action, however portrayed (even the most radical experiments, even novels of irregular chronology and unreliable narration cannot stray for long from scenes-in-the-present: characters observed in motion and, whether observed with the actual eye or the eye of memory, observed *now* and conveyed thus to the reader). Even a philosophical novelist like Proust or Mann must stage frequent scenes; and the chief problem that their pages present to the common reader is impatience, the often protracted wait for *scenes*—impatience which easily becomes boredom and anger.

The contemporary poem however, with its liberation or expulsion from scenic narrative, has chosen or been compelled to ally itself with the traditional metaphysical monologue, the sacred or secular sermon. Not that numerous poets haven't continued to produce the occasional scenic poem—or the quickly sketched scene which becomes the text of the homily—but any broad reading will confirm the alliance. Poetry has indeed selected the mirror or the telescope (another kind of mirror) as its totem.

The novel remains on its knees at the window (though, since the window is glazed, it will inevitably interpose glimpses of the novelist between the reader and the world). Mirrors offer us a perpetual present —our faces aging instant by discrete instant, as long as we can bear to watch them. Windows also reveal a present, but their partial transparency is capable of producing at least the illusion of merger with external objects in slow or rapid flux. Mirrors are therefore, as Auden again says, "lonely"—and as most other poets might say "bored." Windows are— what?—well, if not lonely or often bored, then certainly fixed in place (in the novelist's eyes) and rather more humble than they can steadily enjoy being: humble in their servitude to chronology and appearance, peasants in harness from dawn till dark. By nature then they long for one another; who else have they? Any small-town decorator knows how the mirror in a room loves the window—accepts its constant messages of light and motion, both holds and returns them: a satisfying love. But they cannot really *become* one another, despite a clean window's dim reflectiveness.

Is it also the nature and fate of narrative prose and metaphysical lyric verse to love as mirrors and windows and human beings love?—as solitudes fixed to opposite walls? The history of literature before our own century says a long and thunderous No. The vast displays of Hardy and Warren reverberate the claim more recently. Are the present mutual solitudes and yearnings only another grim result of American obsession with expertise?—limited workmen at limited tasks in limited space? Or, to recall Virginia Woolf, did human nature really change early in our century? Did the human mind really begin a mass migration inward, into the perilous refuge of its own lone self? Contemporary verse says a clear if rueful Yes. So does a great deal of contemporary fiction. But so surely do the swollen and vaunting heroes of Homer, the baffled choruses of Aeschylus, the desolate lyrics of Sappho. Is the job of the literary craftsman in twentieth-century America really so complex as to require the set of stalls into which the craftsmen have sorted themselves?—with, as I've said at all this length, frequent trespass in the night. Is a perfect lyric narrative of Emily Dickinson's the perfect motto for the question?

> *I died for Beauty—but was scarce*
> *Adjusted in the Tomb*
> *When One who died for Truth, was lain*
> *In an adjoining Room—*
>
> *He questioned softly "Why I failed"?*
> *"For Beauty," I replied—*

"And I—for Truth—Themself are One—
We Brethren, are", He said—

And so, as Kinsmen, met a Night—
We talked between the Rooms—
Until the Moss had reached our lips—
And covered up—our names—

The questions posed by the voices of the poem, though whispered, are hardly idle. Neither are my own, which come down at last to a single question—can the narrative-lyric impulse, perhaps the oldest and unquestionably the strongest of literary impulses, recover in the hands of numerous willing but fractured craftsmen the sane and sanguine unity of earlier, even recent, times? I've glanced here at valiant and incessant tries by many. If few of them have achieved precise aim and brought down the whole breathing brilliant prey—well, surely few arrows achieve *their* mark; but driven archers still roam the woods.

1982

PANTHERINE, LEONINE, ORCHIDACEOUS

A LOVE OF THE female voice, especially as deployed in operatic solo, is not given to all. Is it too fierce a reminder of Mother, in all her contradictions of crushing strength and enveloping tenderness? Or of the wheedling siren, a magnet among rocks? Whatever, any lover of the infinite grades of sound will many times be forced by a friend's grimace to douse the volume as Schwarzkopf soars or Traubel dreadnoughts toward an altitude. "Whooping and hollering," one of my most civilized friends calls it. I call it one of life's best rewards, scarce and imperiled but permanent.

When did I first know that? In 1946, I think, when I was thirteen and traveled sixty miles with my mother to hear Marian Anderson baste Memorial Auditorium, Raleigh, with the ductile bronze of her Schubert. I was taking piano lessons at the time; I had boy-sopranoed my way through a dozen solos at the U.S.O. and in church; and Cornel Wilde's Chopin in *A Song to Remember* had just shown me a fact I needed in a truly epic adolescence—that music, performed in public, was a potentially triumphant means of displaying and expelling private pain. As a child who had spent many vulnerable hours in the gentle company of black men and women, I was maybe too ready to hear Anderson's vast endowment and discipline as the straightforward issue of a tragic heart.

In any case, I quickly acquired a rudimentary phonograph and set my traveling father on a hunt for records—Anderson's *Ave Maria* and *Aufenthalt*, her *Alto Rhapsody*. And though I soon heard recitals by the grandest male voices of the time—Melchior and Pinza—my internal receiver was already tuned to the sounds of women. Through the forties and fifties, I annexed the voices of Kirsten Flagstad and Ljuba Welitsch as further access-routes to private bliss (none of my family shared the interest, though no one scorned it); and I began a short stint as an in-person stagedoor fan and long-distance penpal of as many of my favorite singers as I could reach. Anderson and Flagstad were kind in short encounters, as was Melchior in a long interview for my high-school paper;

and Geraldine Farrar answered my numerous letters with startling prompt-
ness and unfailing warmth (I'd searched out her acoustic recordings after
hearing an inlaw's scandalous and maybe apocryphal anecdote of Farrar's
Carmen in Greensboro in the twenties).

Even among the inscribed photographs and letters, however, what
remained strongest was the draw of the voices themselves, on records and
radio and stage. Why? My own boyish piccolo had drowned in the hormonal tides of puberty; so there was no pedagogical attraction, no hunger
for technical instruction. And there was no fascination with the exoticism
of German, French, or Italian. My father would pass and say "I can't
understand a *word*." Exactly. Neither could I, that early, but I heard a
whole *meaning*, a genuine help; and it went far to save me.

The help became a craving which, though frequently satisfied, has
never ended. Since I was simultaneously studying music—scales, rhythm,
harmony—a part of the craving was and has remained for a severe perfection of intonation and pulse. I have never been able to listen to, much
less enjoy, voices that cannot deliver the composer's notes in time; the
present cult for expression at the expense of competence is incomprehen-
sibly absurd to me, a species of necrophilia. Other elements of the need
are more difficult to describe—the otherness of controlled female passion
and skill; some infant memory of Mother's lulling voice with the old
infant's longing for confirmation and completion; certainly the longing
of the mind for earthly glimpses of unearthly worlds of recompense and
rest.

Farrar, Anderson, Flagstad, Welitsch, Ferrier, Schwarzkopf—they've
been for me the senior line of messengers from bliss. But clear as they
were in their visions of perfection and their will and power to transmit
the knowledge, they've been heralds of a still more lucid, almost frighteningly steady gaze at the moving form of beauty. That gaze procedes
from the voice of a woman still at work.

In memory and in the quality of her present work, Leontyne Price
seems so young that it comes as a shock to note that she has now celebrated
the thirtieth anniversary of her professional debut—in 1952, Virgil Thom-
son's *Four Saints in Three Acts*. A further surprise is in store for the recent
complainers that she's the Garbo of opera, stingy with appearances, if
they will contemplate the achievements of those decades—the touring
Porgy of 1953; the great Mozart, Verdi, and Puccini roles (among them
her Donna Anna, Aida, Amelia, the two Leonoras, Butterfly, and Liu
are unequalled in our time or on recordings); a number of other serious
and revealing assumptions (her San Francisco Ariadne, for instance, out-

stripped all rivals); most of the standard masses (Bach, Mozart, Beethoven, Verdi, the Brahms *Requiem*); a rigorous annual recital tour of America and Europe which recalls happier days when artists felt some compulsion to share their work with more than a few large cities; and a still-accumulating legacy of recordings as astonishing in versatility and depth as in beauty and among the most popular since Caruso's.

Three decades of steady work, at the highest level of artistry, are virtually without precedent in American singing; we normally look to the bracing North for such longevity and rectitude—Melchior, Flagstad, Nilsson. And such stamina has earned Price most of the available medals and degrees, the reiterated praise of the judicious, and the barely containable adoration of a welter of fans (anyone present at her first appearance in the Met's revival of *Trovatore* last January was witness to a rare brand of ovation—long, fervent, and joyous but without the raucous tumult that is now usual at the Met for the efforts of any famous female).

The honor, praise, and love have been earned almost entirely by the voice itself and the concealed strength of the woman behind it; there's been a blessed absence of the television traipsing and variety acts which embarrass the memory of so many recent performers. Nor have chauvinistic or racial emotions been significant in the public response to a gift that quickly proved international in validity and appeal. (Such emotions were inescapable in the careers of black singers older than she. Even one so politically chaste as Marian Anderson was a lightning rod for forces that had little to do with her work and that certainly took heavy tolls from her energy and professional scope.) In general, Price has labored in private; stood up in public year after year, poured out her bounty, and garnered her rewards—enormous rewards, the latest saint in the American vocal communion.

Yet I have to add that I think she's the most underestimated soprano now singing. All the early praise and honor, the cries of *prima donna assoluta del mondo*, the gingerly statement by J. B. Steane that "of Leontyne Price it might well be proposed that records show her as the best singer of Verdi among the sopranos of this century"—all those and more, and the miraculous continuance of the voice itself, have never crystallized into the one statement that now seems ripe and ready for assertion, a defensible fact. I'll state it here—Leontyne Price is the supreme lyric-dramatic soprano who's lived in the reach of recording. So far as I can hear from ancient and modern discs (and from direct experience of other voices), she surpasses all others by a significant distance in beauty guided by sinewy intelligence and grace beyond reason. Thousands plainly agree with me and have for years. None of her predecessors is diminished by the claim; many of their strengths live again in her work—the granite

faith of Flagstad that the *notes-sung-in-time* (by a voice like a fountain
and a brain like an alp in sunlight) are sufficient service, the womanly
exuberance and wit of Lotte Lehmann, the serenity in Rosa Ponselle's
hirsute opulence, the girlish sheen of Welitsch, the dark draught of pain
and ecstatic wisdom that seeped from Callas like blood from a pierced
hand.

It's all her own creature, though—Price's and whoever set those
cords in her throat, those lungs in her chest, that mind inside the noble
head. Any writer worth his ink should want at least to hint on paper at
its complex life. And I've tried for years—*a platinum Frisbee hurled at
the sunset, a gorgeous and previously unknown bird suspended over snow-
banked mountains at dawn.* Or adjectives—*pantherine, leonine, orchidaceous.* All fail of course; the phenomenon is hopelessly multiplex and,
though audible, not convertible to words. Still, an orchid may be its
visible emblem (enormous, delicate, outrageous in its wealth, solitary in
grandeur, ethereal, and erotic); but an orchid would have to endure and
evolve, become an unbroken line of other things—violet, lily, the fleshy
hibiscus—and shed a constant fragrance that could heal daily wounds
and nourish the failing ember in us: the hunger for trustworthy promise
of permanent joyful rest.

1982

LETTER TO A YOUNG WRITER

Dear _____,

If you can stop, you probably should. Try cabinet-making, try building fine musical instruments (clavichords or Celtic harps), try forestry—
any trade in which you can work in brief solitude, at natural speeds, and
for which there is at least a steady demand, however small. If you persist
in writing novels, stories, poems, plays, you will almost certainly work in
long solitude with no materials but the fragile contents of your own
unconscious, many of which are irreplaceable; and you will be stunned
to find that the demand for your artifacts is extremely small.

As an American, you have grown up in a society with an apparently
inexhaustible taste for music and narrative. Forget music (your *verbal*
music requires a great deal more in the way of strenuous cooperation from
the audience than any song with instrumental accompaniment). Ah, but
narrative, you're thinking—surely I can fill a small portion of the vast
and ceaseless craving for *story* that continues to move the American public.

Wrong, probably. If you concentrate on fiction—and on relatively
traditional, realistic, chronologically consecutive accounts of the lives of
at least partially sympathetic characters—and if you're very good at the
craft, then you may well accumulate a loyal audience of five to twenty
thousand buyers (there will be other readers of borrowed copies and perhaps even of a paperback edition, but I'm talking here of what you can
hope to count on—a first trade-edition, in whose manufacture and proof-
reading you've had at least the role of adviser). If you're writing poems
—again, accessible to readers of a fairly normal taste and training—you
may realistically expect, say, three thousand buyers. Beyond those rough
certainties, you are casting your bread endlessly upon unfathomable waters;
and you must not await its return.

Why? Because you will be offering bread for which—however great
you may think the *need*—there is precious little demand. Without going
into the large question of why "serious" writing has been increasingly

estranged from popular audiences (or whether it has, whether there were ever sizable audiences for serious work), the explanation for the present small demand would seem to be simple—only a tiny group in any population will wish to turn, in its leisure time, to an activity as relentless in its own requirements as the reading of a truthful novel or poem. You will be asking, unavoidably, too much. To acknowledge the fact is to imply no automatic contempt for whole populations. Most people lead lives which they perceive as hard; in their moments of freedom, they are not likely to choose further degrees of hardness—a performance of, say, *King Lear* or *Endgame*, an evening alone with the poems of Robert Lowell, a novel by Robert Stone, or James Welch. The fact that a few hundred or thousand people do make such choices does not automatically attest to their personal virtue. Such a belief continues to poison considerable numbers of American writers, young and old.

There are other serious impediments. The dire fate of serious prose-fiction and verse in the hands of many trade-publishers is widely understood, and there is little point in reciting again the classic litany of horror—volumes that were pulped a few days before winning the Pulitzer, the universal cry of "No advertising," the by-now expected bolloxing of simple matters of distribution (that have long ago been solved by most other brands of American business), the abandonment of a young or old writer whose widely praised work has not met commercial standards appropriate only in a Book Utopia, the increasing indifference of both trade and paperback houses to serious work. My own twenty-year experience of trade publishing has been fairly lucky, but I have my own all-but daunting tales and have heard hundreds more from sane and sober victims.

What are not so famous are the pitfalls of any small degree of success. Here I don't speak of the genuine rewards of sympathetic response—the sustaining letters from friends and strangers, the rare near-total comprehension. I mean the temptations offered by the sizable academic industry that has risen in the past thirty years round university study of contemporary letters—reading circuits, college residencies, community arts programs. God bless them, of course—large numbers of writers, especially poets, support themselves on such troubadour rounds. But at an invariably high cost to their own central task, the prose or verse. Anyone can name the famous figures, whirling the map like Dante's Lost, revenants of their former selves—exhausted but spieling for tidy sums. Omit names of the living; think only, for warning, of Auden in his last tragic decade. Not that his muffled isolation, his air of slow dissolution, was caused by the annual months on the road; but surely the road—indispensable to his financial survival—contributed hugely to the misery. His late poem, "On the Circuit," is a ruefully hilarious capture of the dilemma—

I shift so frequently, so fast,
I cannot now say where I was
The evening before last. . . .

Seldom discussed also are the internecine wars of rivalry and reputation—the jockeying for grants, prizes, and jobs (though these particular wars seem more endemic among poets than novelists, a result probably of the comparatively direr state of poetry as a popular form but also of the characteristic psychic composition of poets as distinct from novelists).

How much of that is autobiographical bellyaching, applicable to me but to few others? Virtually none—I'd wager that there aren't ten serious writers in America who wouldn't subscribe to a similar bill of grievances. Are the grievances special to the class then, to writers as opposed to academics or stereo salesmen or network vice-presidents? My guess is, yes. The business of writing is unavoidably a cottage industry, a one-man band; it can be well or poorly performed according to the competence and will of the writer. The business of publishing is not remarkably unlike many other medium-sized American industries. It could be well-organized and humanely and attentively conducted, to the mutual profit of producer (the writer), middle-man (the publisher), and consumer (the reader). It almost invariably is not so organized or conducted. Indeed, the last really fruitful innovation in American publishing was the revival, in the 1940s, of a nineteenth-century staple—the inexpensive paperbound book. Maybe we should farm the whole business out to Japanese sub-contractors. A touchingly small amount of clever attention would issue in startling results, I'm sure. If you still doubt me, ask to see the liquor (or comparable drug) bills of any five *successful* writers.

So stop, as I urged some pages back.

You almost certainly won't. Then I must tell you what I've withheld till now—the reasons for continuing. The first is persistent compulsion, though not necessarily obsession (the majority of bad writers are gravely obsessed). You are compelled—by the pressure of your entire life to this moment, by the pressure of a need to reward your loved ones, to reward yourself, and to thank the Powers—to sit in your room alone and form comely orderly tangible objects in ink on paper. If you sense further that the source of your compulsion is transcendent—God or a god—both your strength and your difficulties will be greater. A compulsion derived from the love of other human beings, in the hope of serving them and securing their devotion, will be constantly endangered by the very quality which you love in them—their beautiful solubility in time. Whatever your sense of the source, you cannot know from one day to the next that it will endure; there are no visible gauges to measure the fuel. You will need great lashings of reckless faith. You have some now; you must ration it sanely and replenish as you can. You should also nurse a notion of how to proceed should faith or compulsion itself expire. My own notion leans on the comforting prospect of manual work—drafting or some job of joinery that requires whole days of patient mindless sanding (no one who hasn't done a long stint of writing knows the degree to which it's *manual* labor, but do carpenters dream all night of their joints?).

The other reasons for continuing are surprisingly subsumed under the name *pleasure*. The tradition for thinking of writing as one of the grander agonies of the race is so ancient and so assiduously maintained by contemporary writers and critics that the idea of writing as pleasure is likely to seem coarse, to smack of the atmosphere of summer workshops in the Finger Lakes (much cuddling in the conifers)—poetry as Fulfill- ment, as Revenge, as Spiritual Calisthenic.

Unfortunately, the more enduring pleasures do not submit to dis- cussion. They are experienced in the deep interior, in still isolation, and are no more communicable or desirous of communication than other mystic recompense. By a comparison with saints, I do not mean to imply that writers in their moments of rare satisfaction have exceeded other mortals. Again I suspect that craftsmen of the readily palpable—tables, houses, gardens—experience similar reward. Maybe the nearest hit would be this—the writer, successful in his own terms, knows the satisfaction of the parent of a perfect child: and a child who remains perfect long after the parent has ceased to care or to exist.

It is worth warning that the rewards seem to have no relation to external achievement or success. Many of the most "rewarded" of writers are famously miserable; the virtual hermits (Dickinson, Kafka, G. B. Edwards) appear to have known numerous exaltations. Without, again, barging farther into autobiography than would be useful here, I can add my own testimony—as a man who was reared in two large families whose only "creators" were fertile women, I think I can say that I've experienced more, and more continuous, reward from my writing than the big majority of workers I've known—whatever the work. I would hate to lose the impulse, though I trust it wouldn't kill me.

More ephemeral but real pleasures are concomitant—invitations to travel, chances to meet other writers who (whatever their normal neuroses) often make excellent short-term company, possible brief freshets of money, and an odd priestly status which the trade itself awards one. Interesting people who are not themselves writers (and alas, leaden bores as well) will yield you their total secrets at the flash of your writer's badge. You will be a sort of renegade confessor from here on and must view the office, with large grains of salt, as sacramental and of grave responsibility. You must also quickly develop techniques for stemming the flood of talk, with its vampire demands on sympathy and concentrated energy; you will need a battery of ways to say No, Oriental in delicacy and German in firmness.

With that, I've told you two-thirds of what I know after twenty-six years of steady writing—fiction, verse, drama, criticism, journalism. Since I plainly haven't deterred you in your own intention, though my initial Stop-sign wasn't displayed flippantly, I can close by speaking of the final and most important third, the way to proceed. Or ways—there are millions but all share certain inevitable traits.

The foundation of all else is the recognition that serious work commences in the unconscious mind, or is first received there, and is transmitted in quantities and at rates always in control of the unconscious faculties. The prime skill and discipline, therefore, is learning how to serve and thus partly master that source and governor. The discipline, as usual, divides into spiritual and physical departments.

The unconscious mind apparently resides in a physical organ, the brain. The brain has needs as urgent and as comprehensible as those of, say, the liver. You must learn the peculiar needs of your brain—how much sleep, how much sobriety; how much company, sex, drugs, fresh air. You must learn the rate of its movement—its *optimum* rate, the speed at which it will generate your work when you have dealt with it in intelligent respect. Such understanding is available only after a series of experiments upon oneself—how much of this or that can I take? Do I work most fruitfully in the morning or at night? How much must I produce in a day? (if I'm a novelist anyhow—one of the built-in blessings of fiction writing is its ready submission to diurnality; with the abandonment of long narrative, the contemporary poet is faced with a spasmodic and considerably more unnerving situation). But the understanding is as urgent and indispensable as the compulsion, the gift itself. Without it, you may give off a few smoky flares of reckless brevity; but a useful long-paced incandescence will elude you. If you answer that you positively desire brief flaring, then treat yourself to a careful study of the final letters of Rimbaud—not the brilliant nasty-boy letters but the achingly lonely groans from Africa.

The spiritual department must be your own look-out—yours and whatever masters you can find; even I won't venture to accompany you thence. I do know, however, that constant attention to physical and chronological discipline is among the strong tonics for all other healths.

To end then—it's a hard life. At least as hard as being a good parent and likely to last longer than parenting, harder than all the jobs which permit themselves to be switched off at the end of eight hours; maybe a little easier than being a good doctor or nurse, an earnest religious. But such gauging is absurd, in your case. You are not out for ease. You're out, I trust, for goodness—the perfection of your own peculiar compulsion, as a means of serving, maybe even augmenting the huge and permanent beauty of the visible world? the unseen piers on which the world rides.

Be good,
R. P.

1982

SENSUOUS LURES*

BY THE TIME he delivered these lectures at Harvard in 1952, Vladimir Nabokov had been teaching American undergraduates for ten years. After his debut in 1940 on a traveling circuit for the Institute of International Education—a harrowing round, even for one who in his Berlin exile had offered private instruction in languages, boxing, tennis, and prosody—he proceeded to a succession of institutions: a summer course at Stanford, then seven years at Wellesley, nine at Cornell, and a semester at Harvard. The holder of a first-class degree from Cambridge and the lifelong companion of his own mind, did he comprehend his American luck to have landed on such stable grounds, among such students? He taught in the golden age of American academies. (I speak as a veteran of the time myself—an undergraduate at Duke from 1951–55, one who might have been taught by Nabokov but wasn't. I first heard of him when I encountered the Olympia Press *Lolita* in a street bookstall in Rome in 1956 and identified it, by its green cover and the company it kept, as pornographic. Only an exorbitant price prevented my buying it.)

---

* A proposed preface to *Lectures on* Don Quixote by Vladimir Nabokov (Harcourt, Brace, Jovanovich, 1982).

The story of this preface might well have amused the ironic Nabokov. I was approached by the editor and commissioned to write a suitable preface to the forthcoming volume. He did not tell me that at least one other writer's introduction had been rejected. No conditions, as to content, were stated; and I spent several weeks preparing myself— reading *Don Quixote*, Nabokov's previously published academic lectures, and a biography. When I submitted my manuscript, on time, the editor responded with prompt and generous enthusiasm. But in a few days he reported that my text was unacceptable to Mrs. Nabokov in Switzerland; I was insufficiently respectful. Could I make certain excisions (and certain expansions) to render my text acceptable to her? I remarked that no possibility of family censorship had been mentioned at the time of my commission. Foolishly, however, I tried to comply. I knew that I was working in the face of lectures which were basically undistinguished, even dull; the work of a lecturer unenthusiastic about his subject. The first draft had already ventured more praise than I honestly felt. My revisions were quickly submitted—and, after a pause, again rejected. Again the only reason stated was that my manuscript was unacceptable to Mrs. Nabokov. At that point, angered, I retired from the field. After a long pause, I was paid my promised fee; and Guy Davenport provided a substitute that proved acceptable. The text printed here is my unrevised original.

Anyone who was a student in those post-Second War-Korean War years will remember their peculiar intensity. Anyone, like me, who returned from graduate school in the late fifties and began to teach in a respectable college will testify to a steep decline in the performance of students from the early sixties till today. As I write this page, the radio reports that 1982 Scholastic Aptitude Test scores for high-school seniors have reversed a downward rush for the first time in nineteen years; but even now the average verbal score is fifty-three points lower than in 1955 and fifty points lower than in the year of Nabokov's Harvard lectures (good universities can of course demand scores well above average).

If the 1970s and 80s have been a trough for American education—and in ways that Nabokov had scented out and foretold in the character of Lolita—in what respects were the fifties an upland (I don't claim that they were Himalayan)? Can any reliable sketch be drawn of the generation of students to whom Nabokov read his lectures and who, despite his old-fashioned European avoidance of any procedure smacking of the Socratic, must have shaped his choices of material and method? Any instructor who writes out his jokes—even his tongue-slips, as Nabokov did—is touchingly solicitous of his students' attention and approval; and that solicitude implies a quantity of curiosity about the students' capacities. What were they?

If I try unsentimentally to remember the atmosphere of those years and any prevailing traits of my contemporaries, I'd have to say that students were distinguished precisely by *capacity*. With all our differences of background and training, all our innocence (and admitting that, as now, a large portion of us were in college for no discernibly serious reason and with no valid credentials—one fraternity friend of mine called his brothers "mumbling masses of mediocrity"), we were vulnerable to a degree that would have present-day teachers weeping in unaccustomed gratitude. As another contemporary said the other day, "We took things *into ourselves*." By *we* she meant a substantial portion of undergraduate students of the liberal arts in an excellent private university in the 1950s.

To expand upon her largely accurate description, I'd assert that it holds true for a wide range, geographical and economic, of the students in Nabokov's various audiences. Impotent witnesses though we'd been of the exhausted last years of the Depression and homefront participants in World War II (there were even a few G.I. Bill-vets still among us, earnest and bemused by our youth), we were from an instructor's point of view almost ideally vacant of preconceptions and defenses. We thought we knew nothing and were ready for filling. How so?

First, being mostly white and middle-class, we had actually survived classic childhoods—dazed dreamy years with vacant wastes of time to be filled by our own wits, by silent witness of the adult lives near us and of the distant great world as revealed by the solemn evening radio and by hilarious and/or devastating movies. The great American youth-activity jamboree had not begun. Middle-class children were idle by parental intent, little forced Oblomovs. And as long-term children, we had with varying degrees of good will accepted the ascendancy of adults. We were prepared to believe that they knew more and better than we, and we were inclined to listen. But if we weren't truculent refusers, neither were we docile sheep (only the cantankerous, phenomenally self-absorbed, and often exciting students of the late sixties were more questioning than we). That natural acceptance of authority—which bore our bitterest fruit when we came to manage whole wings of the war in Vietnam—also bred numerous discipleships and friendships with our teachers, relations of an increasingly rare sort now that many students derive from fragmented families and thus bear a conditioned resistance to their elders, plus a frenetic squirrel-cage social life with their peers.

Second, all but the most slothful of us and the odd alcoholic (we drank like temperance-pledgers compared to current students) were impelled by a near-immigrant fervor of hope. The yeasty Depression camaraderie that had linked our parents and their friends, the breast-forward enlistment and unity of the war years, had left us with not unwary but generally cheerful ambitions to be working adults and family keepers. We trusted, as did the often uneducated parents who labored to send us to college, that teachers and books would expedite our climb toward a less threatened existence than that of our immediate forebears. Look at any college yearbook of the time—the faces are strangely contradictory, both too old and poignantly young; smiles are epidemic and a certain fixed gleam, both admirable and scary: *Just tell us how; we can steer the world.*

If that sketch is a likeness (and I trust I've implied the larger warts; the others were normal to the species), then it follows that by 1952 Nabokov had cased his audience and understood it. He had gauged their hunger and willingness; he had guessed, no doubt from his affectionate experience of family, that small amounts of warm and witty condescension (in the good heirarchical sense) would ease his task immeasurably. He had also, despite the accuracy of his academic charades in *Pnin* and *Lolita*, concluded on his students' receptive intelligence.

—Receptive, eagerly deferential but not unwatchful, as I've said. Among the four hundred students whom Harvard unaccountably herded into one room to hear this series, there would have been a substantial number who had not previously read *Don Quixote* and who wouldn't complete the long task in the brief span of the lectures (if at all; many an A has been won from *Master Plots*). A majority perhaps would have slogged along, trying to keep pace with the instructor's annoyingly unconsecutive approach. An elite would have completed the book before the course began and would have nosed about in related criticism and biography; two or three might even have read one of Nabokov's few novels then available in English and felt some muffled thrill in his presence. Those latter groups would have developed a list of questions and doubts, most of which—given Nabokov's method—would have been unaskable. If we could know the questions now, we would possess an interesting gauge of the success of Nabokov as the expositor and *vade mecum* of one enormous Sacred Cow of the western humane tradition.

Maybe it's possible for a veteran of those years to guess at some of the responses. I was a second-semester freshman at the time, six hundred miles south. Two years later I spent ten weeks at Harvard, attending the superb mass-lectures of Howard Mumford Jones and Hans Kohn and talking with a number of undergraduates. Surely they'd have thought the following at least.

—*He doesn't like the book!* (Despite the obvious care with which Nabokov has prepared, and though he never quite says so, his general lack of enthusiasm for a beast so shaggy as *Don Quixote* is apparent everywhere—both in frequent references to Cervantes' carelessness and in the dutiful but occasionally listless tone of his approach: a groping at times for handles on the endless text, less of the nimble and focused brilliance omnipresent in his lectures on writers whom he loved. All students, especially in a course of Sacred Cows, take an initial delight in a subversive instructor; but delight can sour if the iconoclasm is continuous.)

—*Why is he going on at such length about a book he thinks is poorly made?* (Can the students have known that it was a set book in a course set well before Nabokov's invitation to Harvard? Can they have known that, once rumors of Nabokov's sly but candid denigrations leaked out of the lecture room, Harry Levin informed him that "Harvard thinks otherwise"? Or so says Andrew Field, Nabokov's biographer. Can they have known of their instructor's long and sadly unrequited love affair with the idea of a permanent job at Harvard? And can they have comprehended that the kind of mass venture in which they were enrolled and Nabokov's particular mode of instruction depended heavily upon their hungry and trusting natures?)

—*He's got two seriously contradictory obsessions.* (If as he insists, there is no "real life" in novels, then why is Cervantes' "cruelty"—or the imaginary world's cruelty to the Don and Sancho—such a hindrance to the instructor's enjoyment? Either the Don is a "real" man, capable of pain and therefore of our sympathy, or he's transparent and farcical and no more subject to pain or deserving of pity than Abbot and Costello. In any case, since Nabokov will not discuss Cervantes' life or possible motives or the ethos of sixteenth-century Spain, he is prevented from attempting to clarify the purpose and function of violence in the novel.)

—*Why is this sophisticated gentleman resorting to the oldest chestnut of academic crowd-pleasers: the excruciatingly extended comparison of unpalatable material to an athletic event?* (One of the famous groan-producers of my own undergraduate career was a historian who described all battles in terms of football—"Here comes old Patton, far down the sideline before the Nazi forward-wall so much as spots his break.")

—Finally and centrally, *Why are we asked to read a book which the instructor assures us is slapdash, confusing, and generally not funny?* (Even in the non-utilitarian fifties, we were wary of unjustified raids on our time. We had grown up after all in the highest tides of the ninety-minute Hollywood movie and were far more accustomed to quality-in-brevity than today's victims of the sixty-minute television slot. We recognized boredom when we met it, and we'd have wanted to know why a certified literary expert was telling us that our demanding text was *A* boring but *B* good for us. Nabokov never really tells them, not in the case of *Don Quixote*; his brief conclusion is an interesting and honest mirror of his own estimate of the book but hardly a defense of the time consumed in its study.)

With all the questions, however—and I've only skimmed them—there'd have been numerous pleasures and gratitudes. I've mentioned his obvious care. Even at a college that specialized in crack lecturers, lavish evidence of homework by an instructor would not have gone unnoticed. Respectful and intelligent attention from adults was not rare in those last days of the extended family, but it was always flattering and welcome. The keener students would have heard, behind meticulousness, the intermittently fascinating clash of a large and fastidious imagination with an even larger but "scarecrow" imagination (and how odd that Nabokov, whose metaphysical concerns were so coincident with Cervantes'—fact, appearance, illusion, the dangers of art—could not have farmed the coincidence to a richer yield).

And they would have wished for portable recorders to preserve moments their hands would have flagged before capturing—"Odysseus in a blaze of bronze leaping from the threshold upon the wooers; Dante shuddering at Virgil's side as sinner and snake grade into one. . . . The nameless thrill of art is certainly closer to the manly shudder of sacred awe, or to the moist smile of feminine comparison, than it is to the casual chuckle; and of course in that line there is something still better than the roar of pain or the roar of laughter—and that is the supreme purr of pleasure produced by the impact of sensuous thought—*sensuous thought*—which is another term for authentic art."

Such sensuous lures, and the rare American spectacle of a virile sane adult plainly devoted to the pleasures of verbal art and undauntedly defensive of them, would have led a good portion of the Harvard four hundred to wait for his prime—the weeks to come with Dickens, Gogol, Flaubert, and Tolstoy: matched partners for his game.

1982

A CEASELESS CON-GAME*

W.H. AUDEN is reported to have begun a lecture on *Don Quixote* by saying "Like all of you, I have never read all of it." And when Vladimir Nabokov's Harvard lectures on the same novel appeared recently, it was clear that the Russian fabulist labored breathily to lash his class through a novel that has long stood high on the short list of Great Novels. I managed two university degrees without knowing more of the Don than I learned in a boyhood dash through *Classic Comics*. And today—while there are few educated citizens who couldn't give an outline of the windmill episode, even a physical description of the unquenchably elegant Don—the text of the novel is seldom traversed by English-speaking readers not forced to study it.

Has *Don Quixote* slipped into the crowded limbo of Stone-Dead But Revered Relics, with Cicero and the *Aeneid*? It may be too early to say; it was published less than four hundred years ago. Who after all but compelled students now reads Milton or *Moby-Dick*, and are we ready to pronounce them dead? Only a few dozen monks were required to keep Homer breathing through the Dark Ages for his present wide fame. Will a few hundred thousand students, in the western world, keep the Don and Rozinante and Sancho Panza alive for whatever millenia are left to the human race? (Abraham, King David, and Oedipus have had a fairly steady run for upwards of three millenia).

First, Cervantes' long text will have to be readily and attractively available; contemporary readers are not noted for the pursuit of hard-to-find books. There are several decent translations in print; and Farrar, Strauss, & Giroux has just narrowed the rank by publishing a handsome new edition of the long-unavailable translation made in 1755 by Tobias Smollett, the Scottish surgeon-novelist whose *Humphrey Clinker* and *Roderick Random* may still be read with pleasure. Though Smollett worked well over a century after Cervantes' death, his own florid and vigorous prose and his abundant and sensitive love of the original are patent in

---

* *Don Quixote* by Miguel de Cervantes, translated by Tobias Smollett (Farrar, Straus & Giroux, 1986).

each of the 800 pages (accompanied by charming eighteenth-century engravings that show a younger, less withered Don than usual).

Can the revived Smollett accomplish what so many translators have failed—kindling in numbers of modern readers the translator's own love of a tale that is not only immense but frequently repetitious, predictable in wit, and far from fresh in its study of the perils of narcissistic romanticism?

It's too soon to speak for more than me, but I'm won at last. Unable to read the original Spanish, I've attempted to haul myself through other versions—all tedious. But I've found in Smollett my final access to the delicious lure that has drawn centuries of Hispanics into helpless entrapment by a slight tale distended to near-infinity. Whether or not the scent of orotund yet lively eighteenth-century English resembles that of the original, I've been granted an understanding of the story's enduring fame.

In his complex introduction to the new Smollett, the Mexican novelist Carlos Fuentes examines an elaborate metaphysics of reality and illusion that he finds central to the novel's power—its many-handed and ceaseless con game with the reader. But it's Dr. Smollett, with his writer's headlong love of and imaginative sympathy with another writer's revealing parable of the universe who stands a good chance of bringing Miguel de Cervantes and his laughing tragedy forward to us: a permanent need, permanently fed.

1986

A PLACE TO STAND*

A "YOUNG NOVELIST" is a contradiction in terms. The subject and essence of a novel is inevitably time, its motions and effects on the shapes and actions of human creatures and the scenes they inhabit. Any hope of comprehending, ordering, and exhibiting such clandestine and gradual effects is dependent upon intense and deeply registered personal witness. Premature skills in music, graphic art, oral expression, mathematics, even lyric poetry are not rare. But a child prodigy of the novel is almost unthinkable, even now when prose-narrative techniques are commonplace items in grade-school curricula. Raymond Radiguet's *The Devil in the Flesh*, produced at the age of seventeen, stands almost alone (and isn't it significant that Radiguet was dead at twenty?). A glance through the lists of serious novelists is likely to show first novels emerging late in the third decade of life, toward age thirty. Even the most uncanny of fictional debuts waits till age twenty-nine—Emily Brontë's in *Wuthering Heights*, a first and only novel, cyclonic in intensity.

Intensity is never the problem. Most five-year-olds are already the managers of bank vaults of memory, indelibly etched. The generally overwhelming dilemma for a young aspirant to the novel is perspective, distance, literal length-of-deposit in the vault. Those images of crucial stasis and gesture that any child hoards as his debit and capital seem to demand long submersion in the lower reaches of the mind—the zones in which transformation can occur; the alchemies beyond any conscious control that may in five, ten, or forty years accomplish an altered deliverable object, larger and more useful than the initial private matter. Anyone younger than, say, twenty-five is unlikely therefore to have had sufficient time for the unconscious marinade of the first experiences of adult life, the passions and desolations of adolescence. Hence the classic subject matter of the apprentice short story—childhood and youth. And external pressure is generally required to extract even those, the pressure of class assignment or other undeniable request.

In the spring of 1955, I was twenty-two years old, a senior at Duke

* Preface to *Mustian* by Reynolds Price (Atheneum, 1983).

University, enrolled in William Blackburn's English 104 (Narrative Writing). For nine years I had been writing sporadically but with some persistence—first, plays and film scripts (in the never-realized hope of directing my friends in productions), a few short stories and sketches, numerous high-minded school-newspaper editorials, a steady issue of poems in direct proportion to the hormonal drench and ensuing bafflement of the decade. Only the poems, and a partially autobiographical story called "Michael Egerton," bore any obvious relation to my visible experience; and that relation had made them the most difficult experiments I'd tackled—most of the plays and prose narratives had been in the nature of fantasy and therefore as easy as warmwater floating. In my first three years of college, I'd continued to think of myself as a writer; but though "Michael Egerton" and a few poems of love and solitude surfaced, I'd gladly accepted the pressure of course-work as an excuse for not writing. Only the idle summers at my parents' quiet and congenial house—a room of my own, no insistence that I take a moneymaking job—forced me to confront the fact that I had no presently accessible subject for narrative prose. I recall a good many vacant hours, prone in my locked room, gasping at the ceiling like a ravenous carp. Time, I'd suspected—and all my reading assured me—would furnish the food at its own wise rate. Till the day of delivery then, I had worked at my courses with a fervor that was two parts natural bent and two parts dread of the hot wind blowing our way in those days—the Korean War draft and its aftermath, Khrushchev and Berlin. Most of my male contemporaries were enrolled in the various officers-training corps to insure four uninterrupted years of college. On the advice of the state director of Selective Service, I had tight-roped on a shaky line of grades, gambling on an armistice.

Three weeks after my twenty-first birthday, my father had died of lung cancer. Less than a month before, he had seemed his normal strong self—a fifty-four-year-old traveling salesman in improving financial condition after twenty-odd years of serious straits, a desperate lover of family, a cured alcoholic, a ceaseless hypochondriac, a brilliant natural mime and verbal wit. From the day of the confirmed diagnosis, he requested, quietly but firmly, as much of my presence as I could give. We had not been a casual father-and-son. With all his laughter, his compulsion to win love through performance, he was late-Victorian in his sense of self and dignity. Neither my younger brother nor I romped on his large immaculate body. He played few child's games with us; we were treated from birth like confirmed, if fragile, adults. But from the age of five, I'd been conscious that my own birth—a first child and a dangerous labor—had been the occasion of his soon-successful undertaking to abandon alcohol.

And our always unstated awareness of that mutually sacrificial bond proved stronger than either of us had suspected.

In the final two weeks of his life, I was with him more or less steadily; and in the ghastly aftermath of the removal of his lung, I spent all the nights on a chair in his hospital room, his main companion through the rush of mutilations and reductions that killed him. On the night before his death, however, I accepted my mother's persuasion and went home to bathe and sleep. When Father discovered my absence, he raged and lashed in his oxygen tent till they phoned me at dawn and urged my return in the hope of calming him. Once I was back and he'd seen me, he sank without a word into deep sleep. The day was Sunday and numerous witnesses passed in and out—his sisters, various relations of my mother, doctors, nurses, short visits from my mother (who continued to respect his implicit demand to have mainly me now, telling herself he was sparing her the gasping sight). Whenever I'd leave his side for a moment, I'd find a small clutch of kin at the door, quietly searching me for omens. And always beyond them, across the hall, the open door of another patient's room.

I no longer recall who the patient was—male or female, young or old—but in traditional rural fashion, other members of the family had set up a rudimentary yet thriving brand of housekeeping in the rented room. Their patient left them sufficient relaxed time in which to stare nakedly at my father's door, presumably on the chance of catching a view unusual enough to redeem their wait. I remember three young men who looked like brothers, all with long necks and thick country-skin. There seemed to be no women in attendance, not in my recollection. I was partly repelled by their eavesdropping but secretly helped by their obvious sense that I was the main visible actor in a veiled but plainly serious drama.

Just after dark I was back in Father's room with my friend Patricia Cowden. The nurse had gone to get his next sedative. I sat by the bed and held his left wrist; he'd never stirred since morning. A thin thready pulse was the sign of life. Suddenly, beneath my fingers, it stopped. The body enacted a long convulsion. A half-hour later as we left the room for the final time, our country watchers were undauntedly in place, upright in their open door, unblinking as we passed.

Three weeks into official adulthood then, I had seen, at the closest possible range, a death I'd feared since infancy. His mortality had been both a frightening and a comic mutual concern. One of my earliest clear memories is of the night when he powdered his hair, came into my room, and sang "When I Grow Too Old To Dream" (I'd recently deduced that gray hair meant age; I was three and he was thirty-six, just at the end of his drinking and well before he developed its substitute, hypochondria— the dread and hope of death). In the dazed months that followed—a return to college work, a summer of study at Harvard, new expectations at home—I did not suspect that a gear had engaged and was waiting to turn.

But almost exactly a year after the death, two things conspired. First, as I've mentioned, was the necessity to produce a final short story for William Blackburn's class (in the fall semester I had only revised "Michael Egerton," a story conceived three years before). Second was the sort of apparent accident that eventually seems a peculiar gift of writers. I had gone to Duke Hospital to visit an ailing friend; and as I walked through the usual stunned population of hospital corridors, I encountered the nameless trio of men who'd stared so fixedly at my father's door. They were coming toward me, no visible purpose; and as I passed, they showed no recognition. Were they there a year later, in another town, with the same sick kinsman? Did they have any real home or merely haunt hospitals, doomed to watch pain? Were they actual men? Were they messengers to me? Unconsciously I chose the last question and answered Yes. I would let them signal my move into sustained work; they would be both fuel and steering column. In a matter of days, I was planning their story.

Yet it never was theirs. By a process I can no longer reconstruct, I began to generate a fictional center—a girl who had not been part of their family. The name of a fellow student, Rosa Coke Boyle (whom I think I never met, though I knew her sister), was additional fuel. But the moment of ignition was another chance meeting. A friend, Fernando Almeida, and I had gone to Howard Johnson's for a late Sunday lunch. A young couple entered and sat at the counter. He left no impression; she is still intact in every line—a tall girl, maybe nineteen or twenty, with the strong bones and skull that would carry her beauty undimmed to the grave; long ash-blond hair, a straw church-hat, a white good-dress, and pale blue eyes that alternated looks of grave self-sufficiency and half-smiling bottomless imagined need: all aimed at the boy.

She would be Rosacoke, I knew at once—Rosacoke a few years younger in life. The fact that I chose instinctively to show her first in adolescence was, I understood later, the central clue to her origin and meaning (for me at least, at that time in my life). She was the fictional equivalent of any one of a dozen girls who had treated me kindly eleven years before when we moved to my parents' home, a small county-seat in eastern North Carolina. My counterparts in the town itself quickly rejected me—childish violence, real as any. But my rural schoolmates, bused in from distant tobacco farms, accepted me warmly; and for a long three years, age eleven to fourteen, I resorted gladly for validation to the daughters and sons of subsistence farmers. They were ebullient and trusting, if prematurely long-sighted; and they were calmly primed for early adulthood—marriage, children—and lives of hard work at the sufferance of nature, the cruelest employer.

My choice of them—a female delegate from them, imagined though credible—as a lens for examining a parent's death was an act of gratitude for old friendship. More important for the resulting fiction, it was an unconscious annexation of a sufficiently distant perspective yet one still capable of radiant energy—the heat of admiration for a generous heart. Narrative has always refused to function for me unless I prime it with at least one partly admirable protagonist.

The first draft of a story grew quickly through the conflicting chores of winter and spring—I was also writing a senior history thesis on John Milton's politics—and when it was submitted in May to the composition class as "A Chain of Love," I sensed for the first time from my colleagues' responses the eerie pleasure of having been the medium through which an independent life has chosen to emerge. Though her story was not published for nearly three years, and though I continued to tinker at minor details, Rosacoke had stood up, live from her first paragraph—in my mind at least and those of a few friends who dealt with her at once like a palpable creature, warm to the touch.

Four months after I'd released her in the final sentence of the story, I left home for three years of graduate study in England. That was another turn pressed on me by the accident of winning a particular scholarship. Since I'd long planned to live by teaching English literature, I'd have gone to graduate school in any case; but the luck of a long stretch of work abroad was a further, and crucially timed, gift of perspective. I was awarded not only money but four thousand miles of distance from recent experience, the leisurely pace of advanced study in England (virtually all one's time dangerously at one's own disposal), a larger circle of literarily-inclined contemporaries than any young American of the time could have found in the States, and (I soon knew) a low-grade but durable case of homesickness.

Despite the startling, if eccentric, warmth of my welcome in an Oxford that more nearly resembled Max Beerbohm's and Evelyn Waugh's than the crowded welfare-outpost of today, I found myself thinking and feeling steadily about—and maybe longing for—not my home in Raleigh with my mother and brother (however much I missed them) but a largely imaginary childhood home built from my present needs and raised on a foundation of the credible people and landscape of Warren County, North Carolina. The facts that the actual place and its inhabitants were greatly,

if subtly, different from any I'd read of (their nearest relations appeared
to exist in Tolstoy, Turgenev, and Chekhov) and that no one had yet
memorialized them in fiction were further strong components of both the
longing and the pressure to capture, fix, and transmit.

In my first two unbroken years abroad, I therefore stole perilous
amounts of time from my studies and wrote stories called "The Warrior
Princess Ozimba" and "The Anniversary," both redolent of the distant
air of eastern Carolina. I also continued to tinker with "A Chain of Love."
The sustained exploration and creation of that real and fantastic world of
memory became so large a concern of my life that, by January 1957, I
found myself seated in freezing digs in the home of a working-class couple,
unknowingly on the edge of another accident of the sort that had so far
proved propitious. One of my father's sisters had given me a subscription
to our county newspaper, *The Warren Record*; and I was reading through
a stack of issues delayed in midAtlantic by the Christmas rush—the usual
murmur of village politics, love-brawls and knifings, social notes of monumental placidity, and (a seasonal feature) children's letters to Santa Claus.
When I'd scanned a few of the want-lists—burp-guns, dolls, sweets—my
mind suddenly produced a picture. I developed it backward in a matter
of seconds. A young woman dressed in a makeshift costume was seated
with a live baby in her arms; she was Mary in a small-church Christmas
pageant, the kind I'd acted in as a boy; she was Rosacoke Mustian; she
was pregnant though unwed; the father was Wesley Beavers, a boy evoked
but never shown in "A Chain of Love."

I went to my worktable and wrote down the impulse in skeletal notes.
Propped against the wall before me was a color postcard I'd acquired after
seeing the original in Holland the previous summer—Vermeer's pregnant
girl in blue at a window, absorbed in a one-page letter in her hands, a
large map suspended on the plaster behind her. Surely it had silently
inserted itself into whatever crowd of motives had brought me my own
instant picture, so slowly evolved.

In the next few days other images flew to the central figure and my
notes continued. But by then, caution had knocked. I was midway through
the second year of a two-year scholarship. Fiction writing, travel, and my
first tempestuous acquaintance with requited romantic love had left me
little time to work on the substantial thesis required for my degree. My
director, Helen Gardner, was rumbling ominously. A pair of certainties
faced me—in the new Rosacoke idea, I had the components of at least
a novella; but unless I meant to return home in disgrace, I could not
begin to write it now. The thesis took precedence. A smaller but real
impediment was my sense that, given an inveterately chameleonic nature,

I should wait till my immersion in British voices and rhythms had ended in a homecoming.

For twenty-one months then I turned to, first, a study of Milton and Greek tragedy (steady days in the Bodleian); and then an extension of my scholarship when it became apparent that I wasn't going to finish in two years and that, in any case, I wanted to stay a little longer in a place so conducive to fermentation; and finally to an instructor's job at my undergraduate alma mater and a return there to life in a trailer in the woods by a pond. Through the diversions and travel, I added almost daily to my notes for another Rosacoke story—long and short meditations on plot, character, psychology, language, theme, narrative strategy, the lessons of my concurrent reading (Tolstoy and Hardy were especially instructive), my own doubts and insufficiencies, and the relations of it all to my own luxuriant toils of early love and work.

By October 1958 I'd settled into my trailer, my first autumn back at home was in gorgeous cry at the windows, my mother and brother were in stronger shape twenty-five miles away, my first scouting trips to Warren County were just behind me; and I sat at a new worktable to write what I was already calling A *Long and Happy Life* (the title, though a common phrase, had volunteered some months before when I first saw the film *Bridge on the River Kwai* and heard William Holden wish it for a young soldier doomed to swift destruction). Still propped before me was Vermeer's girl in blue; and beside her stood the forthright mysterious Botticelli portrait of a young man from the National Gallery, London—he had served as the image of Wesley in my plans.

I was teaching a full schedule at Duke, two courses of freshman composition and one in major British writers. I managed to arrange my university duties on a three-day cycle, thereby freeing three days for writing (I took Sundays off). And slowly, with many balks and falls, I entered the long peculiar tunnel of novel-writing. Strangely, through the entire process, I continued to believe I was writing a longish short story or at most a novella; in fact, even when I'd finished, I submitted it to publishers as the final piece in a volume of short stories and was only with difficulty persuaded to publish it alone as the novel it plainly was. But my life quickly took on the tone and shape of a novelist's life—long days of silent solitary work (relieved importantly, in my case, by easy access to a pond; woods with deer, foxes, swarms of birds; and fields under broomstraw), work that soon exerts an imperious sway over one's other activities: job, friendships, loves, family duties. One lives so steadily, waking and sleeping, in an imagined world that the tangible world of houses, meetings, comrades begins both to fade and to swell in urgency. Throughout the writing, I found that an almost actual door stood ready to burst open between life and work. For long unnerving stretches, daily actions seemed manipulated to the point of puppetry by the needs and discoveries of fictional people. Other times, the intensest strands of private emotion would pour into the work with the vibrance and rhythmic inevitability of strong music. And always through the door came the pure inventions that gave the real joy.

It lasted a little more than two years. In December 1960 I completed the final revision of the scene that embodied my initial image—Rosacoke, pregnant, as the Virgin in a pageant in Delight Church at Christmas. It had taken four years, mostly happy, of my life to bring me and her back to the starting point; and the happiness was largely a product of the time spent in her and her family's growing presence, the malleable shapes of their gestures and choices. (I notice only now that I transformed the three anonymous watchers of my father into the three young men of the stories—Wesley, Milo, Rato.) As I released them into the typescript that was ultimately to become the book that delivered them to readers in thirteen languages, I remember a newly clear glimpse of adulthood. I, and my ROTC friends, had escaped armed combat. The Korean War had ended before we were tapped; Berlin, though ticking, had never exploded. We'd been left alive and unappalled to pursue past and future. There had been no public socially-certified rite of passage for our middle-class generation. When I'd finished, I suspected I'd been through a private rite and had someway described it—death and survival, freedom and love—by setting it loose to roam as it would, far from my own dreads and bafflements. If not an old soldier, then a parent of sorts and marked with the normal parental badges.

It was published fifteen months later. By then I was back in Oxford for a year. I'd abandoned the thought of a doctoral degree but had saved enough money in the three years of teaching to allow myself a stretch of time in the hope of new work. A few weeks after completing *A Long and Happy Life*, I'd conceived the idea of a story that would complete a volume of stories (now that the novel had been corralled out of my five earlier stories). It would be, I noted in March 1961,

. . . 'about' my father and me: I could write about a man who six years after his marriage was childless and an alcoholic, whose wife became pregnant. Her labor was long and painful, and the man promised God that if the child were born alive and unharmed, he would not drink again. The child was born, unharmed; but the mother died—he had forgot to ask for *her* life. My story would be about the relation of father and son.

That summer, in my old freshman rooms in Merton College, I tried to begin it—total recalcitrance. It wouldn't come. With considerable anxiety (I'd touted my trip to friends and employers as one of guaranteed productivity), I set the notes aside, not knowing that they'd season at their own rate and produce *The Surface of Earth* more than ten years later. I turned to translations of Hölderlin and Rimbaud, to one more polishing of "A Chain of Love," and then (on a commission from Stephen Spender for the hundredth number of *Encounter*) to a story called "Uncle Grant"—a Warren County story but this time a memoir. Those, and my friends, saw me through the frigid months till March when *A Long and Happy Life* appeared complete in a single issue of *Harper's* and simultaneously from Atheneum in America and Chatto and Windus in Britain. Its generally handsome reception consumed the remaining months abroad, and only when I returned to America in the summer was I able to begin a story called "The Names and Faces of Heroes" to flesh the older stories to a volume. The story dealt again—fictionally, at a distance—with my father's death. And for years to come, it closed that account.

Another was opening. I had come home again to the trailer to find my mother in Raleigh, fifty-seven years old, going rapidly blind for no reason doctors could at first discover. The next year saw her finally diagnosed with twin aneurysms deep in her skull—drastic surgery followed by a partial slow recovery of vision, all under the sentence of imminent stroke. As I returned to teaching, the external world served up the Cuban missile crisis; then the murder in Dallas of John Kennedy. Running beneath, a constant thirst, was a private relation in which I released more havoc than I'd thought could flow from what had first seemed the wish to protect. Through the months I had gone on with notes for a father-son novel, but by August 1963 even those had stopped.

So it was in a state resembling crucial need of peaceful employment that, in bed one night in January 1964, I thought of a story that promised to be comic. A few days later with no pause for plans or notes, I began to write it under the working title *A Mad Dog and a Boa Constrictor*. By the time it was finished in October 1965, my mother had died of the hemorrhage that had hung fire above her. The apparently comic story had become a muted near-tragic romance—a long fiction but not a realistic novel—and its final title was *A Generous Man*. It had explored in a thoroughly different, almost hallucinatory way the lives of Rosacoke's brother Milo and Rosacoke herself some years earlier than "A Chain of Love." That it had also explored my own simultaneous concerns, private and public, was inevitable (I've discussed its development elsewhere*).

With its publication in March 1966, I had come to the end of eleven

* See p. 40 above.

years' involvement in the imagined life of a single family. There were to be at least two more engagements with them—a commissioned but still-unproduced screenplay of *A Long and Happy Life* and a stage play called *Early Dark* that examines the relations of Rosacoke and Wesley from a distinctly altered perspective—and of course they'd never kept exclusive hold on my attention, even in their long run. But when I'd revealed Milo's final choice at the end of *A Generous Man*, I had (it now appears) no further need of reliance on his family's history. Strangers occasionally inquire the whereabouts and present fortune of a particular Mustian; and in 1970 I thought briefly of taking them up again, almost in middle age. But no story came; they were silent by then as disused oracles. Other actions and lives stood to fill other needs.

Yet from here, twenty-seven years after the invention of the family, maybe I can be allowed to look back with some degree of puzzled gratitude at the odd arrangements of fate, luck, and will that led a young writer—long on ardor but short on distance—to adopt a fictional family and their satellites (in most ways different from my own kin and friends) as the means of watching, subduing, and transmitting large tracts of his own experience. When they receded as available tools for further work, it was probably because of the peculiarly complete set of jobs they'd so patiently and variously done for me. That "A Chain of Love" and the two novels have been continuously in print since their first appearances—and that they are now read by generations of students young enough to be the grandchildren of Wesley and Rosacoke—suggests, in this present Dark Age of American reading, that their ability to do serious duty was not an offer to me alone. If they say nothing else, they attempt to say now, as they always did, the fixed unalterable injunction of narrative, to me and all readers—*The world exists. It is not yourself. Plunge in it for healing, blessed exhaustion, and the risk of warmth.*

1983

PENNY SHOW

THOUGH I'VE LIVED in the country continuously for twenty-four of my adult years, I'm thought of by my friends as the Great Indoorsman —one who loves nature from behind glass most of the time, the ideas and images of nature more than its touch and smell. As a child however I was different and better. We only lived in close contact with a relatively wild environment for some two years, when I was age six to eight; but in that time, wandering without brothers or sisters or regular playmates, I was lured quickly into an intense harmony with our suburban woods, creeks, and small animals. It was a harmony amounting to mystical union with the vital intelligence I suspected in nature; and while I knew nothing of Wordsworth then, I later found in his poems numerous close parallels to my own early raptures and faiths—a conviction that the inhuman world took benevolent cognizance of me in what seemed to be silence but was surely a secret code, decipherable with patience (one of my methods was to plunge my hunting knife into live wood, then to bite the thrilling blade and feel the tree's message).

The great majority of these moments were solitary; and perhaps of necessity, they did not long survive puberty. The flood of physical maturation tears a child's attention from its old objects—and deposits it forever on other human beings, freshly magnetized poles of inexplicable love. Seldom thereafter can many adults, barring saints or lunatics, plumb the deep blissful well of singularity. All the stranger then that one of my own clearest, most resonant, and most refreshing memories of such a moment involves two other people—my mother and my cousin (near-sister) Marcia Drake.

Marcia and I were seven or eight, which means that my mother was in her mid-thirties. Someone in her family had died. Maybe it was Uncle Brother, one of her father's two bachelor brothers who'd survived into his eighties (stone-deaf, asthmatic, but neat as a bridegroom) in the back bedroom of the Rodwell home in Macon, North Carolina. In any case, Rodwells, Drakes, Rowans, and Prices were gathered for a funeral in comfortable weather. The memory of flowers is strong—banks of cut flowers in the big dining-room, traditional pausing place for family coffins—and contagious tears from my mother's old sisters and my mother herself (my own continuing lachrymosity is almost certainly the result of a Rodwell gene). Marcia and I caught the prevalent tone of lament and were soon disconsolate, demanding some sign that the day's heavy air would break and not last the rest of our lives.

My mother took the challenge and, not changing her funeral dress, led us outside. The house in those days stood on two-foot brick posts, no underpinning; and the visible dirt expanse beneath was a warehouse of disused implements patiently awaiting new purpose. By one post were jagged panes of glass, removed from windows but never quite discarded. Mother crouched and found a piece the size of a platter. Then she found an old garden-trowel and led us far forward in the shady front yard. One of the big oaks near the road had a bowl-shaped arrangement of roots above ground. Mother crouched again there, laid her glass down gently, and (with us watching speechless) began to dig a small basin in the earth in the oakroot harbor. When she had its boundaries clearly sketched, she stood, brushed her hands, and passed me the trowel—"You and Marcia dig it deeper. I'll be back soon."

The funeral air still kept us silent—no complaints or questions. We dug on in peaceful turns, unsure of the depth prescribed for this mystery, and were working when Mother returned with her hands full of flowers. At the time, we didn't ask where she'd got them; now I see they must have been discreetly removed from memorial sprays. Yet my memory of their color is mostly purple (purple flowers at a funeral? what could they have been?). She approved our dig, then bent and slowly arranged her flowers in a nest on its floor. Then she told us to turn our backs for a minute.

When she called us to look, she had risen and was standing by the site of our dig—vanished now. Still neither of us questioned her. "Ask me what happened," she finally said.

So Marcia asked her (maybe I was prevented; isn't "What happened?" the primal unaskable child-parent question?).

Silent, Mother bent and with a clean hand swept at what had seemed firm-packed dirt. It slid back easily and showed her secret; she beckoned us toward it. The pane of glass, only lightly dusted, was a window again. What it showed was flowers under the ground, a garden buried under the earth. Mother covered it again. "It's a penny show," she said. "When people pay a penny, brush back the dirt and show it."

We had a few cents, and were happier, by the end of the day.

*

Only now, more than forty years later, have I asked any questions of the memory. In a recent random search, I could find no other friend or acquaintance who'd heard of a show like my mother's. For all her surging vitality, she was not unusually inventive or handy. Was the idea of small subterranean gardens a family invention, passed down to her? (She'd been born in the house where she showed me the first one; I'd been born there too, the only American my age that I know who was born at home.) Or had her own pronounced periodic melancholia responded so strongly to an old man's death, and her own son's distress, as to give her this tangible poetic invention?—a brief consolation, to be shared with others for a nominal fee: the reward of your inventiveness.

Whatever, she'd quietly given me one of her largest gifts. An adult I trusted had confirmed my suspicion—from that day, a conviction—that the ground itself, the earth and its products, was inhabited in hidden ways. That many of the ways were hurtful, I'd known from the start; any infant knows danger. What she'd shown me, at the edge of a family death, was the fact of veiled beauty, discoverable by hand and of some small profit. It's by no means the least of the thanks I owe her.

1983

A FAIRLY CRUCIAL CHOICE

F OR MORE THAN two decades, I've taught English literature and the writing of prose fiction. Before that I spent the usual twelve years in public school and seven years in universities. Through those nineteen years, I was guided by a blessedly large number of gifted and dedicated teachers —in fact, there was really only one bad teacher in the lot—but as I left those institutions and began my own independent work, I discovered with considerable pain that there was a single indispensable principle that none of my good teachers had pointed out to me. The principle is the virtual foundation of effective individual human thought; and it seems to me so necessary not only to orderly thinking but to the pursuit of life in most of its other departments that, at the risk of unveiling an open secret, I'll speak of it here.

First, the principle itself: *Serious and fruitful thought is possible only when pursued on a regular and unflagging basis.*

In late twentieth-century America, we are still oppressed by the Romantic notion of "inspiration" and prefer to believe that creative thought will find us—will strike us as lightning strikes solitary oaks on the plain —when we least expect. The cartoon cliché of an incandescent bulb switching on overhead *is* a crudely accurate metaphor for certain valuable but limited kinds of thought. Any successful creator—artist, scholar, engineer, economist, whatever—has known rare happy moments when, while immersed in some chore as dull as mowing the lawn, he becomes the sudden host of an idea of which he has long felt the need but which has evaded the conscious hunt of deductive reasoning. Such moments, welcome as they are, are only beginnings however—the fragmentary "givens" upon which dogged days, maybe years, of labor must be expended if any usable result is to be achieved.

In the case of my own work as a writer—fiction, poetry, plays, and essays—the labor must be daily if possible; if not, then predictably regular. When I am at work on a substantial project, my ideal schedule runs like this.* I rise after a maximum of six or seven hours of sleep. I eat a small but sensible breakfast and am at my desk by eight or nine o'clock. With whatever agonizing amounts of will are required, I overcome the torpors of the night and the fears of the morning and begin the writing of that day's quota of words. Some thirty years of work have taught me that my personal metabolism is geared for the production of three-to-five hundred words of finished prose in a day (poetry comes at a less predictable rate but still benefits from consistency of approach). If I force upon my unconscious faculties a steady demand for that much daily progress, then it obliges me with relatively little complaint some ninety percent of the time. I award myself one day of rest each week—Sunday since that's when most of my friends pause. At first glance, my rate may seem intolerably slow. But consider that it's calculated for a long haul. A six-day week worked at through a calendar year, with a month off for vacation and a few days for illness and the accidental, will give me some 250–300 pages of finished prose, prose that's ready for publication without further extensive revision. It is also a rate which gives the unconscious faculties time in which to breathe; in which to invent and reshape character, plot, and action before my consciousness can rush ahead with its characteristic errors of haste and judgment.

I stress the concept of "unconscious faculties." After nearly a hundred years of psychiatric theory and a prior three millenia of poetic speculation, we still understand little of the nature of those functions of the mind that occur beyond our waking control—that, in fact, flower so notoriously in our sleep. Yet every creative thinker I've known affirms strongly that large portions of his or her work are conceived by those mental faculties over which the waking creature exerts slim *mental* influence.

Are writers, painters, sculptors, choreographers, composers, physicists, and astronomers—in fact, all workers at any but the most manual tasks—at the whimsical mercy of a mysterious function of the human brain? To a discouraging degree, yes. And the biographies of many of them testify tragically to the inability of many creative workers to live in bodies controlled, as it were, remotely. Any one of us, from the first grade on, has had numerous opportunities to despair of his power to realize the aims of conscious will and to feel justifiable terror of his own daily proclivity to illustrate the law of absolute entropy—vacuum and stasis.

However mysterious the mind, though, it does seem possible to affirm that it resides in specific human bodies, primarily in an organ called the

---

* Since the winter of 1984, when paraplegia awarded me the bounty of increased writing-time, my schedule and its result have altered substantially. In the eight months when I am not teaching, I now write from six to ten hours per day, six days a week. The manuscripts then mount at a proportionately faster rate.

brain. If so, then even the unconscious functions of the mind would seem to require those conditions of nutrition, rest, and discipline by which the remaining organs of the body are known to profit. A novelist friend of mine has said very precisely that "The unconscious mind is like children and dogs; it loves routine and hates surprises." And without plunging further than is comfortable into the realms of Uplift and Self-Help, I'd add a claim of my own—*All human beings work and conduct their personal relations best when subjecting the total organism to a sanely strict and regular discipline.* I'd grant that the claim sounds suspiciously like a quote from some early edition of the *Boy Scout Handbook*; but I continue to claim that it embodies a truth ignored by an astounding number of those, young and old, who wish to work and love competently and consistently. The unconscious mind appears to perform an enormous amount of our work. Our best hope of negotiating its mysteries (unless we're prepared to plunge into the steamier aspects of the occult, drugs, food fads, and private ritual) is through an attempt to coax it to work in the ways we consciously desire. And a consensus of active intellects, east and west, seems to agree that a routine of regular requirement is our one chance at steady access to the enormous submerged and dangerous portion of our lives.

To proceed beyond a statement of principles—and a sketch of my own work-habits—would really be counselling at the TV-talk-show level. But I will venture, at the end, that any reader who has accompanied me this far and who has persistent problems in thinking his or her way through substantial pieces of mental work (from term paper to book to plans for a bridge) would do well to begin a serious effort to organize and maintain a realistic individual schedule for daily work and diversion, one which can be followed with as few guilt-producing betrayals as possible. Don't attempt more than is feasible for a day; work in the same place and at the same time whenever possible.

I wouldn't presume to commend my own schedule to anyone else; I've described it only by way of illustration and suggestion. But if a personal schedule cannot be arrived at and followed, not only for days but years, then the odds are excellent that the sporadic distractible mind will prove unable to think or communicate in any way that will prove of permanent interest or use to its body's colleagues. Again, my tone may sound ludicrously like that of the parent who urges an anorexic child to buck up and *eat*. But I know of no other way to state a frighteningly simple fact. The question is one, finally, of human worth—whether or not one chooses to *signify* beyond the limits of the personal epidermis (or the mind of God).

The choice of course is hard, maintenance of the choice is harder, but a failure to choose is hardest of all. One can spend a dismal lifetime watching the stain of one's daily failure spread through all one's resting places, one's family and friends. Many millions do.

1983

A DIM WARM CAVE

THE TREASURES of childhood mostly vanish. A toy, a book, an irreplaceable hat is passed on to a younger child or is obliterated by love and use. Fifty years into my own life, I retain from childhood only three or four books, an arrowhead, and a Christmas crèche consisting of thirteen plaster figures. I know that I got it before the Japanese attack on Pearl Harbor in December 1941. At that time I was eight, and the figures of my dime-store crèche were plainly made in Japan (when the phrase was synonymous with "shoddy" not "elegant"); they're bound then to be pre-war. The faces of the holy family, wise men, and shepherds are unmistakably Japanese. The artist, in one selfless gesture toward late western tradition, gave both Virgin and Child blond hair. I at once took my poster paint and made her brunette, leaving the child blond for reasons I no longer remember.

What I haven't forgot, and what revives with ambush force each year as I lift them from their shoebox, is the intense meditations they occasioned in me, years before I knew of the existence of theology or the questions of ancient history. Till then as the only child of struggling young parents, living in relative isolation in the country, I thought with the laser-focus available only to an innocent of the miraculous potential of any human birth. My own birth had worked seismic changes in the lives of my parents, for good and bad. In their innocence, they'd told me again and again of the changes—my mother had nearly died in labor; my father had vowed to control a drinking problem; I'd been a sickly baby, and financial burdens had multiplied during the late years of the Depression. With such knowledge I was well-prepared to concentrate for long minutes on the way a specific child (this boy in his manger, the size of my thumb) could bring quick joy to the whole winter world. But then as now, my mind was incapable of more than a few seconds' abstract thought. I considered, without naming them, the mysteries of incarnation and redemption by concentrating on the story of this child's gift to these dolls I'd bought with my weekly allowance—some neighboring shepherds, a sheep and a camel, three Persian kings, in a slope-roofed Bethlehem stable in our living room.

My Japanese artist had respected the medieval notion that Jesus was

born in a manmade stable, a wooden building of the kind familiar throughout rural Europe and America. He may have known and felt literally
nothing about the story his dolls depicted; but on his assembly line, he'd
made me a durable holy place. What I see now in cooler hindsight is
that he'd made a receptacle for my own need to have such a place, a
socket for my own need to ground a powerful current of awe and fear in
a visible, tangible, portable place.

My response then was both prepared and surprising when I reached
the actual Judean town of Bethlehem some forty years later and confirmed
on the undeniable spot what books had warned me—that the birth of
Jesus occurred in a dim limestone cave the size of a modest suburban
kitchen. The cave is located in the east end of the plateau on which the
small town huddles; and like dozens of caves in the area today, it no doubt
sheltered both humans and animals from winter rain and the scalding
pure sun of summer and fall (Bethlehem, though a hill town, is only
twelve miles from the lowest point on the earth's surface, the Dead Sea).
We know from Justin Martyr, a reliable contemporary witness in about
A.D. 130, that the cave was venerated well before Jesus had been dead
a hundred years. And we know that in about A.D. 327, the emperor
Constantine began the construction of a basilica to protect the cave and
enshrine its meaning. The present Church of the Nativity, accessible to
any tourist, is the direct descendant of that first basilica and still guards
the cave. As direct a connection existed between my childhood dreaming
on the place's great moment and the years of adult curiosity that brought
me there on Christmas Eve, 1980.

I came, the last six miles at least, by foot. A few weeks earlier I'd
suggested to a friend that we spend Christmas in Rome (home-Christmas
is a prospect at which I always experience strong mixed-feelings). He
considered the proposal a moment, then said "Why not in Bethlehem?"
I'd never been to Israel nor any other region of the old Roman province
of Palestine, and like most Americans I shared the impression conveyed
by television that the area bristles with a constant threat of violence. But
in as little time as it took my friend to propose it, I accepted his suggestion.
A man as physically unadventurous as I had sprung to the idea of a visit
at a no-doubt-crowded season to one of the world's most volatile places.
In subsequent moments of doubt, I consoled myself with the assurance
that an early craving in my own mind had overriden fear and would see
me through the trip (as it had seen so many million pilgrims to the eternally
troubled place through two thousand years).

We arrived in Jerusalem on the night of December 23rd; and when we dragged our exhausted feet through the walls of the Old City for supper, we stopped at the warm but empty Citadel Bar and began to talk with its courtly proprietor, a man who'd come as a boy to Jerusalem before the Turks departed. When we asked him the best way for reaching Bethlehem next day in time for midnight mass, he told us that the road would be closed to auto traffic (we'd rented a car) but that we could take the Arab bus. Then he paused and said as easily as we'd resolved to come at all, "Why don't you walk?" We must have winced. He smiled—"It's only seven miles."

So once we'd finagled our way into tickets for the service, we tied on our hiking boots and set off from downtown Jerusalem in warm cloudless sun. Half an hour later, beyond the toy English-village railway station and a suburban fringe no more winning than most, we passed a single street-decoration strung overhead (an Arab Santa Claus in floor-length nineteenth-century robe). He marked the point at which private cars stopped; beyond him we were in the scenery of my early imagination—the backdrops of engravings in childhood Bible-stories. Small fields worked by donkeys, gray knots of olive trees, hills that after ceaseless clearing still breed stones more easily than food, sudden plunging views through air clear as glass across a dazzling wilderness toward the Jordan rift and the mountains of Moab; in the middle distance rose the artificial mountain of Herodion (Herod the Great's fortress-palace and tomb). And once we'd topped the rise on which the monastery of Elijah sits, we could see Bethlehem strung along its bony ridge above the drops and chasms of a country more like a living shifting body than the usual inert mineral corpse. Somewhere near the desert edge of the town, in a dense warren of belfries and roofs would be the actual defended cave—as clandestine now as the night it harbored a girl in labor, changing the world.

Another hour of walking through the dusty souvenir-store fringe of town, then the final climb toward Manger Square and a grimly earnest body-search by Israeli soldiers securing the place for its annual splurge. Then at once on our left the pile of the church itself, leaned on by a convent, another church, even a modest one-story hotel. I knew it by its pictures—a gray and tan jumble of hurled-together stones, the record of an often desperate life as the oldest continuously maintained sanctuary in Christendom. As little like the sensibly planned, safe churches of America as a dangerously radiant mystery is like a flourescent tube. It was much more sudden and available than I'd intended. There was no big crowd, but a few others who'd cleared security were streaming toward the famous five-foot-high door. For a moment I felt like a reluctant lemming caught in the first rush of tribal suicide or like one of the souls in Michelangelo's *Last Judgment*, hauled deadweight toward heaven by the hasty mercy of overworked angels. There was no choice but to enter.

The nave of the church is, first of all, empty—no benches or chairs, no confessionals or kneelers—and the emptiness belies its unexpected smallness. It's a short but tall box with two rows of noble rose-stone columns to each side; and except for the dim fragments of paintings and mosaics from successive rebuildings by the emperor Justinian and the Crusader kings, and the glum devotional barnacles of nineteenth- and twentieth-century Orthodox and Latin piety, it might easily be a basilica in the original Roman sense—a court of justice, sufficient space for the sane conduct of serious *business*. Again, there is nothing to slow our advance toward the business itself—descent to the cave. On either flank of the hidden altar there are semicircular stairs smooth as skin, no handrails for help. My eyes are poor for stepping *down*, but the stairs are mercifully deep and few. Five seconds and we're there.

Outside it's three o'clock, the sun still holding; in the cave all the light is red candlefire. The walls are covered with protective leather and asbestos hangings; the floor is paved with marble. The first impression is of a longish narrow room with a low niche at one end and a pantry-sized room down a few steps to the left. The rock roof is barrel-curved, barely out of reach; so the air is cave air, close and thick. The space is packed with other lookers, and a covey of German nuns has begun to sing carols in English. A dedicated claustrophobe, I suspect I'll need to surface soon and return another day. The security net outside has made me more conscious than ever of the ease of violent attack—anyone can kill anyone with astounding ease; a single grenade rolled down these Crusader steps would finish the fifty of us. And within the next minute, fulfillment to my prophecy, there comes a loud crash. Now the panic surely. But no one budges and then it's clear that we're all alive and safe—one of the ceiling lamps has shattered on the floor. A furious custodian appears and demands an explanation; the nun nearest me speaks out clearly, "Just keep singing." They do. We join them and the knot of fear loosens.

So, in another few minutes, does the crowd; and for an inexplicably long stretch on Christmas Eve, my friend and I are alone in one of the two germinal sites of Christian history (the second is Golgotha and the Holy Sepulcher, seven miles back up the road in Jerusalem)—the matrix and terminus of a small set of dolls that had shaped my childhood sense of human purpose and continued to signify throughout my life. I know that it's fashionable among historians and biblical scholars to doubt that Jesus was born in Bethlehem; but my own sense is that we possess at least as much evidence for the authenticity of the site as we do for, say, that

of the cremation of Julius Caesar, which no Roman historian doubts—
Matthew and Luke are unequivocal on the matter; John appears to allude
to it ironically; and here are these continuously tended remains, in a
country so small, so humanly intimate and contentious, as to make top-
ographical fraud or error unthinkable. After a few minutes of
preparation—pacing the length and breadth of the cave, exploring the
side room (traditional site of the manger, a wooden and clay trough which
Constantine's mother, the empress Helena, took to Rome, where it's now
visible beneath the altar of Santa Maria Maggiore)—I move to the niche
of the birth itself. If you wish to see it, you must kneel or crouch. I crouch
and slowly bend to touch the fourteen points of the silver star that bears
in silent Latin this lean assertion, "Here Jesus Christ was born of the
Virgin Mary." I'm moved as at no other juncture I remember. I think I
could spend the rest of my life here in this close air, grainy to the eyes
and warm as the lips of a healing wound.

Very ponderable men have felt similarly and acted on the thought
—St. Jerome, for one, spent the last thirty-odd years of his life a few yards
away in an adjacent cave, producing the Vulgate Bible and a warehouse
of other books. To bend and kiss the heart of the star seems the only
available gesture of return for the promise delivered on this spot two
millennia before—the tangible hope thrust annually toward us in the
normal bloody birth of one child: the appalling miraculous threat of
renewal, in my own slowing life and the leprous world.

Before I've heard the slightest sound, three others are behind me. I
stand and retreat. An Arab woman in a loose dress and shawl has brought
two children—a boy and girl, maybe five years old, in thin dark sweaters.
They fit themselves neatly down into the niche; and from a hidden pocket,
the woman produces a bottle of oil and a clean white rag. With the
unfailing hands of a weaver or harpist, she opens her oil and replenishes
the lamps that had all seemed full. As she works, she instructs the boy
and girl quietly, turning to check on their understanding. They never
look away but absorb each gesture—a strange new skill they may need
someday. When she's corked her bottle, she carefully wipes the marble
with her rag (no drop has spilled). Then with each hand, she draws a
child toward her. They understand with no further word. In a unison
bow, all three brush the star with open lips.

I didn't stay of course. In two weeks I was home and prowling my
accustomed underground shafts (some lighted, some dark). But the power
of that memory strengthened, especially the Decembers when I'd haul
out my chipped crêche; and three years later I returned to Bethlehem of

Judea. This time I consciously avoided Christmas and came during the Jewish high holy days of September 1983, partly for reasons of personal exigence and partly to test the air of the cave at a more neutral time. The thin incredibly clear light of winter was now a ferocious late-summer force, pouring down its last assault; and the town was more crowded than at Christmas, plagued by jittering cars and buses (why don't the citizens exclude auto traffic from their center at least?). The people now though were not the half-fervent, half-bibulous northern Europeans and Americans of Christmas Eve but the permanent Arab shopkeepers and the only recently anchored Bedouin of the gorgeous lethal wilderness that waits just yards from any Bethlehem street.

I drive down from Jerusalem in a rented car with another friend; and when we're baffled for a parking space in the packed Manger Square, a local boy maybe nineteen approaches in a baseball cap and leads us to a slot on the steep south side of the ridge. When we climb out, he grunts at us smiling and waves urgently toward the church behind us—what about us has told him instantly that, of all the town's offerings, we've come for the cave? We nod; he signals that he'll guard our car (unnecessary in a town safe as any, but the job he's defined for himself in his home); and we walk the hundred yards to the low door.

Inside a small television crew are packing their cameras—some footage for Christmas? Otherwise we're alone, not even an Orthodox monk in sight. I walk us quickly past the trapdoors in Justinian's floor onto Constantine's mosaics (two feet down), past the screened Greek altar, to the semicircle of steps to the cave. A Monday, September 12th, more than three months from any of the several dates on which the place celebrates its perpetual moment; and yet it's as likely a day as any to be the anniversary of Jesus' birth (the presently celebrated days in December and January are the results of guesswork in the eastern and western churches). Sobering to think that I may have stumbled here accidently on the day itself, a few days before the Muslim feast of Id al-Adha and the Jewish Yom Kippur, which is also this year the first anniversary of the massacre of Palestinians at the camps of Sabra and Shatila in Beirut.

The cave is empty of all but us and its uncanny air. I slowly pace it off again, touching what I can of the actual live rock. (One of the deep satisfactions of eastern holy places is the absence of museum guards to prevent human contact with the facts; a wonder at all that there's any stone left after two millennia of stroking hands. In the west, this would have long since been sealed in bulletproof chambers; and in America there'd be worthy ladies in first-century dress and gold-rimmed bifocals to recite the meaning.) Then I sit on the marble bench six feet from the star of the nativity and study it again. Still grogged from the twenty-four hours of travel—North Carolina to Judea—I nonetheless feel as strongly as before that this is the peaceful heart of the world. Or the heart of peace. I could stay here forever. I understand hermits, monastics, pilgrim-tramps. I'm readying myself to bend and touch the place. Then the unwelcome sound of more feet.

A middle-aged Arab guide in red polo shirt, with embroidered alligator, is leading a young man slowly down. The young man's shirt is white and takes the red blaze of candles like a screen. His face swims round and I see he is blind. He extends, like an unintentional chastening rod, an utterly unguarded trust. The guide leads him first away from us to the room of the manger. But the young man faces straight ahead at the wall. Then he firmly says, "I should see the star first." The guide turns him round and bumps him toward the low niche of the birth, freeing him there and stepping back. First the man leans forward till he finds the floor, the marble outer ledge of the spot; then he kneels on the stone, upright as a tree, no support fore or aft. Then he bends, slow and steady as a small beast to water, and kisses the disc at the star's green core. Then he seems to pray.

Ten minutes later when I stand to leave (feeling mildly disjointed to be blocked from the place), the young man is still planted straight on his knees, head aimed at the star. Even my boyhood dreamings on the child could never have mustered a purpose like this. Upstairs in the different air of the nave, we move through bare space, again the only humans. The first word said is from my friend as we crouch to step through the last door to daylight—"I guess he had a lot to say."

It's also the last word; I know that at least. I come back four more times in three weeks and have my own chance to say at last, in solitude at one of the earth's still centers, my own lifetime's weight of thanks and hope. Faster than my box of Japanese dolls, the thick air and smoked rock absorb the mute speech—as though they themselves (the whole honored place, now supremely threatened by manmade Armageddon) are famished and grateful for any peaceful visit.

1983

A RECURRENT FACT

I F YOURE NOT a farmer, the main advantage of a home in the country is not simply the absence of human crowds but the presence of non-human creatures. Apart from their hidden crucial service in the chain of being, their short fragile lives provide an assortment of mirrors in which we can study the shifting aspects of our own slightly longer expectancies. Possibilities range from Disney-anthropomorphic (comic or pathetic) on into the higher reaches of transcendence and exultance. I've had re-lations—probably one-sided—that have lasted from minutes to years with particular spiders, snakes, squirrels, foxes, and deer.

Through the past twenty-six years I've lived at the edge of a pond in Orange County, North Carolina—first on the east side in a pre-World War II trailer (more like a trim yacht than the sad boxcars that now strew the countryside), then in a larger house on the west bank. And all that time I've been at work on novels, stories, plays, or poems. The animals, though often unseen, are constant and have insisted on entrance into the work. Individual hawks, bats, cardinals, snakes, and deer have in their different but always uncanny ways materialized beside me and assumed roles—occasionally large—in whatever was in progress: novels, stories, poems.

But the most impressive and persistent encounter of those years has been with what I'm convinced is a single great blue heron, the most self-possessed and resplendent bird to visit this landlocked but rolling county of pines and small stock-ponds. I saw him first (I think of it as male, though I still don't know) in the late summer or fall of 1960 when I was nearing the end of my first novel, *A Long and Happy Life*. He was feeding with unhurried dignity in the shallows of the pond, and he soon entered my manuscript—as a visual relief unnoticed by my two burdened char-acters. In the novel I made his color white—maybe because the fictional time was winter, and white seemed more seasonal and startling. The following year I was in England and never thought of him. But on my first Christmas back—1962—he was suddenly there again. He fished for the best part of a day, then vanished.

A cycle had begun, or my part of a cycle. How long before me had he made these annual stops at a teeming three-acre pond on his migratory sweep? And how long could a single great blue survive in a world increasingly hostile to his complex, splendid, all-but-secret trajectory?

Whatever the answers, he continued the visits for another decade—having adjusted his arrival to within a few days of Christmas. He'd fish for a morning, sometimes be there the next day or two, then lift off laboriously for wherever he wintered. The South Carolina marshes, the Everglades? Once in the early 70s, the pond froze hard, which it's done only four times in my experience. But the heron arrived and lingered on the booming ice, unable to eat and lethally becalmed. After several days I feared for his life and, in a ludicrous-disastrous error, threw out a dressed fish for him. He scorned it but the smell lured dogs in the night, and next morning there were scattered lilac feathers where he'd stood. I thought I'd been the instrument of his death. But the next year, on schedule, he was back; and I began writing a long poem about him. It took me years to finish and was only published in 1981—"The Annual Heron."

The various omens I'd read from his beauty and timeliness, his endurance and solitude, led me to think that this bird (who by now was surely reaching the end of a normal heron's span) might at last be freed from his punishing cycle by the poem's completion. Mightn't the transmission to strange readers of whatever private relation he and I had constructed through two decades release him to die in the rushes of warmer water than mine?

Ludicrous again. I take a chastened joy in reporting that he appeared during Christmas '82. As I went down to deposit garbage by the road, I alarmed him from where he waited at the near edge of the pond; and he flew on his way. This year, as the coldest Christmas on record passed without him, I thought again that I'd laid his living ghost.

But on the morning of December 30th as I stood cooking eggs, I turned for a towel and caught him upright on the hard-frozen pond. I'd been given binoculars only five days before. I reached for them carefully—he shies at the slightest movement—and stood still as he, studying him at last. He's four feet tall and Egyptian in his sideways ravenous grandeur, inscrutable glare. He'd take three or four slow steps on the ice, then halt to gaze at his own perfect image in the impenetrable mirror. If he could see the torpid bass below his suspended feet, he never stooped for a futile strike. My phone rang; a neighbor had seen him. And the friend who was showering upstairs arrived in time to witness. He'd look up and wait through each of our moves; but he bore us twenty minutes. Then he left at his own will, unalarmed though hungry.

Can it be the same bird each year, that punctual? To my untrained eye, he's always appeared to be (for a few years he seemed to have a peculiar growth at the hinge of a leg, but that's gone now—maybe cured). Is he really a heron or something larger and even less imaginable? Am I the urgent target at which he flies one cold day each year with necessary news that I'm meant to convey? Or on which I'm meant to reform my life? My poem asks all those unanswerable questions, some crazy.

This year, though, I'm choosing to stop at what I begin to trust is the glad blank fact of another return, offered to my prying fingers but sealed. He at least was here—and for three sober witnesses—working in perfection at his private mystery, which may only be life.

1984

A GOURMET CHILDHOOD

IN THE 1930s and 40s my father moved us restlessly around North Carolina, in search of a living in those hard times. But *home*, for both my parents, was Warren County. More specifically, it was the village of Macon, my mother's birthplace and mine. Though her parents had died when she was a child, the low white house in thick oak shade survived and was occupied by one of her elder sisters—Aunt Ida and Ida's husband Marvin Drake. Their open-armed bounty and the quality of the table they set was not only a source of continued wonder and magnetism but also of family jokes. (Once my mother sent a telegram to Ida, saying "Will arrive in time for supper." The local telegrapher erred and decoded the message as "Will arrive in time for *supplies*." And his error was a closer approximation to the truth. We never departed Macon without full contented stomachs and a backseat stacked with produce, cakes, jars of preserves.)

With a whole acre of the back lot given over to a vegetable garden, with chickens in the yard, and pigs on their nearby farm, Ida and Marvin seldom sat down to a meal that was not splendid, and splendidly prepared. The cooks were Ida herself and her long-time black helper, Mary Lee Parker. So I began life as the recipient of great cooking; and like all my kin, I acquired in childhood an unconsciously sophisticated palate—no squeamish refusals of the complex masterpieces that poured from the small black woodstove. By the time I was six or seven, I began to pay month-long summer visits to the homeplace. The strongest magnet was Ida and her endless resources of love. But her table was an attraction only slightly less powerful.

All the more amazing then that the kitchen contained no cookbook (and in the other rooms, there were only a few books—the Bible, a few devotional scrapbooks, an atlas). The recipes were stamped in Ida and Mary Lee's brains; they could no more have written them down than you or I could write *Paradise Lost* blindfolded. Yet my memory doesn't contain a single failure from them. Day after day, they produced three large and elegantly balanced meals—all from scratch and with the raw goods at hand from the garden, the yard, and the farm.

My main recollection is of the astounding variety they could offer from a strictly limited supply of fresh materials. Pork and chicken were the steady meats. The only drinks were tea, coffee, and water. All desserts were based on delicate pastry and fresh or home-canned fruit. On an occasional Friday, Ida would buy fish from Henry Watson, a local black man who imported a weekly iced barrel from Norfolk. And once a month, she might risk a beef-roast from the white man who clanked into the yard with an ancient truck full of unrefrigerated beef—all red and dripping, hung on cruel hooks like a Rembrandt anatomy lesson, and attended by flies.

The scarcity of beef was my only complaint. My parents' budget was slender, but we did have steak or roast at least weekly. My cousin Marcia and I would commiserate in secret—"If we could just get one good taste of *steak*." And we'd grind our teeth like the lifelong carnivores we were fast becoming. But I never voiced the longing. Even then, I knew my luck and protected it. I well knew that I was the object of a vast skill, exerted thrice daily (seven days a week) by two master chefs; and I wasn't about to stem their flow.

I knew because I'd already acquired other experience. My mother's cooking, for instance, was tasty, reliable, and ample. But her natural bent was hardly toward the kitchen; despite an eternal war with fat, her hunger for movement and company allowed her little time or energy for the stove. (My father called her "an excellent short-order cook"; and my younger brother said only recently that he was grown and in the Navy before he knew rolls and biscuits weren't supposed to be black on the bottom.) And I'd "eaten out." As late as the end of World War II, it was considered mildly common to eat in cafes or restaurants. Any such visit revealed either a shiftless mother or an appetite for trash. My mother of course leapt at any chance to take a night off; and we'd go to, say, the Puritan Cafe and eat on white plates heavy as flat-irons—tasteless breaded veal-cutlets or gray corned-beef hash or steaks broiled to leather, forced down with presweetened tea and followed by soggy pies.

So at Ida's I counted my blessings and reveled. How good a judge was I; how much is my memory gilded by the passage of forty years? Sober reflection says "Not at all." I've since dined in the best restaurants of America, Europe, and the Middle East—and am grateful for the chances—but nowhere have I encountered food more carefully and cunningly prepared and served.

The genius of North Carolina country-cooking before the advent of frozen and packaged foods lay precisely in its loving respect for the raw materials. Though they couldn't have told you so, the aim of Ida and Mary Lee was the enhancement—not the disguise or tarting up—of superb fresh vegetables, chickens killed only two hours before cooking (and that delay was only to allow the "animal heat" to leave the flesh), pork aged and smoked by men with centuries of practice behind them, berries picked that day from the garden or the roadside and baked in a pastry as exquisite as any Parisian *pâttisiere*'s. The only spices were salt, pepper, cinnamon, sage, and ginger; the only condiments were vinegar and sugar (sugar was occasionally sprinkled on acid tomatoes).

But the secret ennobling ingredient was time—time and pride and family affection. If either of the women once regretted the stewing-hot hours spent daily at the stove, the lightning disappearance of their careful creations, the endless dishes washed in hand-drawn pails of well-water, they flew no visible signal. It was what they could *do*, their sole creation after their children. And their children were its aim—children in the wider sense of kin and friends. Indeed the cooking gave them far more reliable rewards than the children. Like the proud artists they were, they knew their worth; and they took their reward from the faces of the audience—an endless succession of gratified guests. I'm aware that I speak as a man and am therefore in danger of sentimentalizing an enforced drudgery. But children are never fooled; and the child I was for years still affirms the fact, still thanks their ghosts.

1985

A VAST COMMON ROOM

AMERICANS BORN before the Second World War may well share with me one of the disquieting memories of childhood—a hermaphrodite (or "morphodite" as the creature was often called). With the obese and the anorexic, the hairy and the bald, they were features of freak shows at carnivals and fairs. One might even come to your town, rent a vacant building, and set up its own little private exhibit. Your father might ask you one evening after supper if you'd like to take a walk. You'd accept his hand, stroll through a mild evening to the drugstore, eat a cone of cream; and then he might say "Want to see something strange?"

Strange is the last thing you hope a parent will show you, but you say Yes and know you're locked on a course you can't change. You enter the door of that once-vacant building. The only light seeps up from the back—some greenish glow from behind a screen. A rusty man steps out in your path. Your father produces two thin dimes; the man waves you on. You hold the hand tighter and know you're lost. Your father leads you on toward the glow. He never breaks step till you round the screen, stop in the outer edge of glare, and are eighteen inches from the morphodite.

It's real, no fake—you see at once. The shrunk face all but shudders with a frail smile launched your way. The head is more like a man's than not—lank tan hair, though you see no stubble on the crinkled cheeks. The skin is pale and soaked, parboiled; and the eyes are worse than you dreamed—sky-blue and not too steady but aimed your way.

Then it does the worst. It parts the flaps of the rayon kimono and points to what you hadn't known you dreaded most in the whole real world. Down there, in a space the size of your palm, waits a moist and intricate compromise of father, mother, person, or thing. You can't look up; you'd meet its eyes.

I've set that scene to evoke the ancient nexus of lure and terror that western culture advances in the face of blurred gender. However many prophets and frauds urge otherwise, we're generally unnerved if not routed by sexual ambiguity. The Elizabethan and Jacobean theater had its brilliant boy-actors (for whom Shakespeare wrote his Cleopatra, Lady Macbeth, and Gertrude—to name only the least easily imaginable). The Japanese classical theater still offers male actors in a female disguise so complete it amounts to metamorphosis. My father's generation had its farcical Womanless Weddings; and we have unisex clothing, hair, makeup, and drag shows. But during the last, say, thirty years, the public's revulsion from sex-change surgery and the accelerating openness of exotic sexual behavior are only the peaks of a growing fear of blended genders and a submerged plea against the significant if fragile advances toward freedom and understanding made in the 1960s and 70s—*Let men be men, women be women; let the world proceed.*

International horror at the concentration of AIDS on male homosexuals only confirms my sense that the wider fear is growing at an alarming rate. And the fear may go some way toward explaining the increasing rarity of an old and immensely useful species of fiction—the reversed gender novel. Feminist critics have recently investigated the phenomenon, and they've discovered interesting new shadows in the work of those classical male novelists who offer sustained portraits of women. But the new findings are not always offered without their own set of blinders, and the results have had little circulation.

What needs much wider notice are two facts—first, that one of the earliest triumphs of the English novel was the female first-person narrative written by a male. Defoe's *Moll Flanders*, Richardson's *Pamela* and *Clarissa*, and Cleland's *Fanny Hill* are only the most enduring of the pioneer efforts. (In older drama and lyric, male poets had steadily built their first-person female speeches into credible women.) The second fact is the reverse of the first—male first-person novels written by women— have always been rarer.

The earliest such continuously read and admired novel in English seems to be *Frankenstein* (1818) by Mary Shelley, the daughter of an important early feminist. If we pass over the numerous popular exceptions in English, the proven-durable specimens are distinguished but scarce— Emily Brontë's *Wuthering Heights* (which soon settles into the voice of a woman instructing the male narrator), Willa Cather's *My Antonia*; and several of Mary Renault's novels of ancient Greece, including a unique fence-sitter, *The Persian Boy* (narrated by a historical figure, the castrated lover of Alexander the Great). In French, Marguerite Yourcenar's *The Memoirs of Hadrian* has made its own majestic place—a profoundly convincing portrait of not only a man but a man of absolute power.

Throughout the eighteenth, nineteenth, and early twentieth centuries, however, male novelists not only frequently wrote in the female voice but, even in the third person, provided us with many successful entries into female consciousness (I call "successful" those portrayals that have won approval from generations of women as well as men). To name Tolstoy's Natasha and Anna, Flaubert's Emma, Hardy's Tess and Sue, Dreiser's Carrie, and Joyce's Molly only begins the roll.

The best female novelists have not only seldom attempted the metamorphosis but have also seldom focused on central male characters—men seen all-round. In English and American fiction, the salient example (ineradicable after a century and a half of memory) is still Emily Brontë's Heathcliff. Jane Austen's men, exemplary or foolish, are invariably pictured in the company of women. Of George Eliot's many substantial men, none is revealed in the core of his erotic nature (as are Bovary, Anna, and Tess to name three parallels). Despite the spectacular but scarcely probed gender reversal in *Orlando*, most of Virginia Woolf's men are translucent masks through which a cool soprano streams—though Mr. Ramsay in *To the Lighthouse* emits the convincing odor of male failure. And from living female novelists, the few central males who come readily to my under-read mind are in Anne Tyler's *Celestial Navigation*, Toni Morrison's *Song of Solomon* and *Tar Baby*, Laurel Goldman's *Sounding the Territory*, and Josephine Humphrey's *Dreams of Sleep* (all richly internal portrayals of men with sexual lives, the aspect most consistently neglected); then a few of Joyce Carol Oates's hag-ridden worser-halves, and Iris Murdoch's collection of brainy but touchingly underpowered saints. There are dozens of isolated exceptions but the point survives.

Granted, for every male novelist who has succeeded in creating women convincing to female readers, there are numerous examples of the opposite—female characters who are peculiarly unresonant and seen from a doggedly "masculine" perspective, as receptacles of phallic fantasy. Most conspicuous among the failures are Conrad, Faulkner, and Hemingway. But if there's an imbalance between the literary male and female impersonators, why is that so; and can or should it be altered?

The beginning of my guess at an answer paraphrases that of David Cecil. He suggested that the imbalance is owing to a fact of family organization. Male children are reared in the fairly exclusive company of women; so are female children. Boys, by genetic heritage, contain the vague but palpable psychic and physical components of masculinity; but in the first five years of their lives, they are surrounded by instructive concentric circles of women—mothers, sisters, their mothers' friends, aunts, grandmothers, and teachers. Girls, by inheritance, are female (not at all the same as describing femaleness in any of the traditional ways); but in the formative years of their youth, girls are given few opportunities to observe adult male character. And in our own constricted nuclear family, they are deprived of the resident grandfathers and uncles frequently present in earlier homes. Men are the creatures who leave after breakfast and return at dinnertime. Most women then are excluded from close psychic relations with men until the women are pubescent. (Is it meaningful to note that at least three of the exceptions—Mary Shelley, Emily Brontë, and George Eliot—lost their mothers in infancy?)

However partial, the explanation is grounded in prevailing gender structure as far back as we can see in western civilization—the rigid assignment of male and female roles and duties. The structure has unquestionably benefitted the male children, who become male writers, at the expense of the female. Further barriers have been raised in the path of the female who ultimately writes—she has, notoriously, been forbidden to work at anything less palpable than children and food; and even the courageous visionary outriders (so frequently unmarried or lesbian) have been shouted off the reservation of male sensibility; above all, the preserve of male *sexuality*—so huge a force. No wonder at all then that the imbalance exists.

Yet isn't it an old and tenacious belief that great artists are above all androgynous? I've alluded to the women of Aeschylus, Sophocles, Euripides, and Shakespeare. But remember too the women in Goethe, Wordsworth, Ibsen, Mozart, Verdi, Puccini, Vermeer, Degas, and Picasso. Maybe the question is unfair; still, can we assemble a comparable gallery of men from the art of women—Sappho, Emily Dickinson, Mary Cassatt, and Edith Wharton? There are imposing male presences in many of their poems and novels (think of Lady Murasaki's astounding Genji, convex and thrusting beneath his poetic robes, Katherine Anne Porter's broken but heroic Royal Thompson in *Noon Wine*, Carson McCullers's halt and lame, and Flannery O'Connor's poisonous starvelings); and I'd welcome further powerful examples. But aren't men, in women's art, more often than not portrayed in the act of bending, with protection or threat, toward a woman? Is the myth of creative androgyny another lie, at least when applied to female artists?

Surely not. Surely the rarity of their attempts owes less to childhood deprivation than to the warning so sternly heaped atop the deprivation— *Be women only; dare nothing more.* If creative androgyny is a lie, then the lie has resulted from our applying the myth to artists alone—actors, writers, composers, painters. It didn't take Freud to inform us of an innate bi- or polysexuality in all creatures (indeed, he deferred to writers as his teachers). Aren't all human beings, like other visible animals, possessed of a born or trained comprehension of all the needs and emotions of their species? And since our forebears thought it a crucial condition for the maintenance of a perilous balance of power in family-centered societies, hasn't our most devastating lie as parents and teachers been the stripping away, in infancy and childhood, of our offspring's infinitely complex set of entire human sympathies? Aren't we now faced with a population unnaturally deprived of its most benign instincts, its earliest skills?

The instincts are those that unite a majority of boy-babies in virtual symbiosis with their mothers and girl-babies in a psychic union with their fathers, a union so close that, in fear, we have blinded ourselves to the goodness of the intimacy and converted a tragic excess into a current obsession: father-daughter incest. (Mother-son incest is still too unthinkable a subject for discussion, though any acute male will have heard from his friends dozens of hints of that greater taboo.) What "men" presently don't know about "women," and vice versa, is largely a power-guarding delusion in whose maintenance we are enlisted early. You take your half of the family, and the world; I'll take mine—the men's room, the women's. And hasn't the accumulating pressure of the lie through crowded millenia, combined with the increasing threat of unconventional sexuality, now resulted in the near closing down of the gender gates in art?

In American fiction, the answer is a certain Yes. Henry James was the last spacious male American novelist who specialized in the intimate investigation of women recognizable as such by both men and women (and his only distinguished predecessor was Hawthorne). Then Tennessee Williams peopled a long dramatic gallery with credibly parched women, though he was ignorantly condemned for insinuating the homosexual's blighted worm's-eye view. (The contributions of male and female homosexuals to cross-gender art have not begun to be appropriately valued, despite their offer of some of androgyny's richest rewards.)

After Williams, who is there; what women likely to detain us for years to come?—Styron's Peyton, Updike's *Witches of Eastwick*? Ruth in his Rabbit trilogy? (though Ruth is seen almost entirely through Rabbit's own knothole), Romulus Linney's nameless diarist in *Slowly by Thy Hand Unfurled*, the baleful Lucy in Roth's *When She Was Good*, the transfigured Sister Justin in Robert Stone's *A Flag for Sunrise*? With scattered exceptions, most male novelists of this century have joined the majority of their female contemporaries and acceded to an overwhelming public will that artists abandon half the human race as knowable only in terms of vatic if not gorgonian mystery.

Can we change? And should we? My own answer is an obvious Yes. Men should excavate and explore, however painfully, their memories of early intimacy with women, and attempt again to produce novels as whole as those of their mammoth and healing predecessors. More women should step through a door that is now wide ajar—a backward step, also painful but short, into the room of their oldest knowledge: total human sympathy.

Failure, for either, would at worst be courageous. But the likelihood of new and usable modes of understanding is enormous—an understanding portable from the page into life.

To speak of my own experience, my first novel was called A *Long and Happy Life* and was published in 1962. It was narrated in the third person but with frequent plunges into the sensibility of a young intelligent woman. The oddness of my choice had not struck me till I read my reviews. Nowhere was I attacked for chauvinist audacity, though there were suggestions from male reviews that my knowledge was "uncanny." (As if I, like many of them, hadn't spent the first eighteen years of my life in the steady company of women.) As decades have passed, I've often been approached by women, asking "How did you know?" And often, mixed with gratitude, I've detected the suspicion that I was somehow weird—a pre-surgical sex-change. My own answer was a resort to Flaubert's famous, and true, canned-answer when asked how he understood Emma Bovary—"Bovary is me."

Yet I suspect that the strangeness of the response to my Rosacoke Mustian was a powerful force in directing my later fiction to its occasionally broken concentration on male figures. It was only three years ago, when I was fifty, that I began receiving demands from my unconscious—create another central woman. By then my curiosity had taken the form of a thirst for knowledge of my own mother's past, the twenty-eight years of her life before my birth. She had died in 1965, when I was thirty-two—too filial still to question her closely. Her parents had died when she was a child; she'd been reared in her birthplace by an elder sister and the sister's family (a husband and three boys). She'd been noted for youthful rebellion but then for impeccable loyalty to my father when, in the early years of their marriage, he was drowning in alcohol. Despite a nearly fatal labor at my birth, a nearly fatal miscarriage three years later, then a hard time with my brother, she had been a warm, attentive, strong, and tolerant but hungry mother. *How had she done it?* was the question I finally needed to answer.

There was no one I could ask. She'd died at sixty, all her early contemporaries were dead, there were no written records (she'd been too fervently committed to negotiating the rapids of her life to pause and commit herself to paper). I was on my own—precisely where she'd labored so hard to put me.

So I sat down and began with little forethought to write in a female voice, one whose atmosphere chimed in my ears with the timbre of my mother's lost voice, which I no longer remember. The story the voice told—of a woman born in North Carolina, residing there and in Virginia from her birth in 1927 till 1984—grew in ways that moved far from my mother's own constricted path. But however far my Kate ventured in rebellion and independence, she achieved in her voice and in all her acts a credible expression of my mother's own spiritual potential—a life whose courage and headlong drive I might have awarded my mother had I been able and were it not a life with even more pain than hers.

The job took more than two years—years which, for other reasons, were unusually complicated—but I never relished work more, never felt my daily life more enriched by daily work. It's traditional for writers to lament the wretched solitude of their calling. I've mostly loved those parts of my life spent on paper, arranging a destiny that (once I look up) I cannot alter. But this time there was an unexpected saving benefit. Not only was I mining the dark shafts of my mother's mind; but in the face of complications, I was entering my office each morning and becoming someone else—not only another human being, with another name and other troubles, but another gender: one with similar eyes for the gathering of light, though with subtly altered lenses.

I may, of course, have deluded myself. I may not have earned a place among those writers who entered the vast room of their androgyny and calmly generated a large portion of literature's enduring characters —characters who have taught us a large part of what we know about love and tolerance in the actual world of sight and touch. If my own attempt fails, still I assert the original claim. The most beautiful and fragile of our birth-gifts is an entire humanity, an accessibility to all other members of our species—all shades of gender and private need. The gift lies not primarily in our sexuality but in something simpler and more complex —an early comprehension of the *means* of human life, packed as they are so lovably, transparently, delicately, frighteningly in bodies and minds called male and female but deeply kin. It's in our power—writers and readers—to take the next step, back and forward, to a common gift: our mutual room.

1986

THE BURNING CENTER*

ONE OF THE real puzzles for a contemporary student of art and religion is *What did the old Greeks think gods were?* Did they believe in them, for instance, with the fervent physical literalism of American Christian fundamentalists? Were susceptible educated Greeks subject to visual and auditory manifestations of the gods comparable to those experienced by numerous apparently sane modern westerners?

Whatever the particulars, in individual cases, the Olympian gods were obviously transcendent, invisible, and aweful. They were also pesky, helpful, sexy, local, palpable, odorous. Any girl at the well (lovely or self-possessed enough), any boy in the pines or on the blinding strand, might be—permanently or as a momentary condensation—Artemis herself or the beneficent but lethal Apollo. Cursed or lucky enough, you might actually know them—enter their flesh; be interpenetrated by them, though you are woefully incapable of absorbing the bounty they need and yearn to give you.

Hence surely an unplumbed tenderness in the attitude of early Greek sculpture and painting toward the carefully imitated bodies of girls and boys at the breathless moment of their all-too-sudden turn from childhood to the brief procreative splendor of youth (those dry bud-breasts, those tight-cupped balls ready to bloom and pour forth gifts). A beautiful child *becoming* a beautiful grave self-propelling young adult is our nearest visible image of the endless but far more miraculous metamorphosis that we trust to be the steady condition of divinity.

Indeed a whole sentimental branch of Anglo-Saxon-American aesthetics—the Lilac-Hellenic division—has existed to hymn the continued production of such easily consumable copies of such an apparently endless supply of lordly youths. And much has been written about the dedication of Yannis Tsarouchis to a portrayal of that point of fusion in human-divine life—the sailors and street spivs beneath whose tacky gabardine getups lurk the bodies of Dionysos and Hermes, waiting to dazzle. But as these reproductions attest, no one can claim that Tsarouchis has

* For a collection of essays on the work of Yannis Tsarouchis, with reproductions, forthcoming from Sylvester & Orphanos.

begged more for his vision of the male form than the fully rendered painterly evidence will bear.

He gives us a strong face with, above all, relentless eyes and an ample body (though by no means American or old-Athenian gym-perfect—the nutritional deprivations of Hitler's war often glare sadly through Tsarouchis's subjects in their narrow chests and in bones that can never reach their goal). It is plain from first glimpse that the painter has been chosen by the subject's face, not the reverse; and an absolutely crucial component in our response to the numinosity of the experience is our willingness to grant the painter's abduction in the enterprise.

When he has composed his model and so apparently quickly peeled off his visible contemplable integument for the canvas, it is then our turn to accept the game and complete a rite that the painter's own grave persistence slowly but irresistibly demands.

For it is a rite much more than a game. If you cannot, by a suspension of will at least (if not an admission of your own erotic susceptibility), imagine a worship of the male principle, then you can no more appreciate the work of Tsarouchis or the founding faith of Greek religion than you can comprehend the ultimately monotonous, boring, and untrue female worship of French impressionism and contemporary American pop-culture.

The worship invited by Tsarouchis's icons—as by any splendid Apollo or by the Zeus at Olympia—is precisely a supreme awe of the *potential for grandeur* of a being whose visible body is composed thus, a body that (with luck) one might glimpse tomorrow in the ring, the market, or the subway. The being is portrayed nude because only in its true unshielded statement can its whole identity be guessed, its divine secret core.

His icons are not properly objects for erotic self-satisfaction simply because sexual union should ideally be the final (not first) stage of worship and attempted knowledge of a god. And how the Greeks warned against that brand of knowledge!—a whole burn-ward of hapless victims is strewn through their myths and plays. Lest we fall back on denunciations of the danger of anthropormorphic religious art and long for the cool blank offered us by the fantastic or calligraphic art of Judaism and Islam, it is well to see that the veiled gods of Tsarouchis are ultimately as sexual as a Chinese vase.

And like the vase, they are specifically receptacles. They await the insertion of at least three kinds of energy. The gods inserted into the painter's soul a motive and skill for the adequate imitation of their own inherent grandeur, the painter then literally bore that laden image forward from his own mind and body, then we the witnesses assent to two things. Or we refuse entirely. The two things are the technical and the spiritual skill of the painter—can he seduce us to watch this image long enough for our minds to discern its motor core?

In the case of Tsarouchis, if we refuse to look slowly, calmly, thoughtfully and come away devout—what's left? Well, perhaps a lifetime's production of wistful and lovingly executed images of human vitality, a haunted literal Fayoum-impressionism in which the flowers (and the girls) have become men—no mean achievement, especially when pursued so long and singlemindedly. And not altogether irrelevantly, there are endless rich remainders from contemporary Athenian streets of how all those snow-white marble Greek post-adolescents must have looked on the Acropolis in the warm flesh, despite all the millenial intervening infusions of other blood (Macedonian, Scythian, Roman, Germanic, Turkish). If we assent, ah then the current flows; the wires burn. Incandescence. Stand back. The god lives. *You must change your life!*

The command is of course spoken by Rilke's archaic Apollo as he strides into life at the end of one of the most famous of twentieth-century poems. The paintings of Yannis Tsarouchis, so justly portrayed here at last, announce a parallel law. *Look. The world is godly. That boy there, gazing off toward home (the sea, the hills, the vines, his girl) is the burning center and focus of the universe, deserving all knowledge, all kindness, all care. Ease his path. Declare him to the world. Change your life!*

1986

REAL CHRISTMAS

ALL MY CHILDHOOD Christmases were spent in North Carolina—
in the modest rented houses of my parents or the rambling oak-shaded
home of my mother's family, the home that had been my own birthplace.
So my present sense of the season is entirely conditioned by the memories
of my first experiences and the memorable accounts by my parents of
Christmas in their own childhoods.

So that the following doesn't seem ridiculously pious, let me acknowledge first that my early anticipations of the season were given their
highest excitement by the luminous but greedy expectation of exorbitant
and perfect gifts (the Noah's Ark, for instance, that my parents could never
find or the actual live elephant they couldn't afford). Beyond those annually renewed delusions however was the safe assumption that, in our
huge family of superb cooks, no curb would be set on the provision of
wondrous feasts (for a family in which even the children were not sniveling
consumers of bland macaroni-from-Grand-Rapids but demanding and
hearty *gourmands*): feasts of food and unstinting love. My own less noble
expectations then repeated those of my parents' early recollections.

Both my parents came from small towns close together in Warren
County, North Carolina—a once-prosperous, now impoverished, farming
area northeast of Raleigh adjacent to the Virginia state-line. Neither family
was wealthy but each was well-housed, comfortable, and able to splurge
a little in anticipation of the miracle that comes to revive both us and
time as the grim short days of the old year flicker.

My father's most frequently repeated memory was of his mother's
annual cakes. In his own childhood he had been one of six (three boys,
three girls); and early on, his mother established the principle that each
child might request the cake of his or her choice. With the help of skillful
black cooks (chief of whom was a man named Walter Parker), six cakes
would rapidly accumulate on the sideboard in the dining room. I've long
since forgot the names of the favorites (my father could recite them all);
but I do recall that my father's was a Lord Baltimore, a lavish confection
I've never seen. And I recall my early envy of the inconceivable opulence

of a household in which each child might have the proprietorship of an entire cake, labored over for him alone—to eat or barter.

My mother was one of seven (four girls, three boys); but by the time she was old enough to enjoy Christmas, there was only one other sister in residence with her. Her memories, though warm, were not of a pouring abundance but of something truer to normal human reality. There was a year for instance in which her want-list (which always included the horse she never got) was met with a Santa-Claus gift of ashes and switches, literally. She'd had a mischievous year, and the Judge of Children had rendered his merciless but just verdict. (Her parents simultaneously gave her oranges, raisins, and dried figs—all special favorites in a time when even dried fruit was a treat as welcome as toys.) Years later, hearing of such a blow from the sky, I was mightily impressed, though I doubt my deportment was much improved.

Yet my own early Christmases were not without their bitter edge. I've mentioned my annual dreams of perfect gifts. They were the seed of my grim Christmas secret—that by ten on the morning itself, my un-grateful perfectionist mind was ashy with disappointment. However hard my willing parents tried to assemble the reasonable items on my list, I was left with the inevitable realization that human desires—well, my young ones at least—were once more proved hopeless. The dreamed of carbine rifle, close up, was gimcrack. The Indian suit was embarrassingly cheap. The Dopey doll from *Snow White* had an ear quickly gnawed off by our puppy. So that I don't seem spoiled beyond tolerance, let me record that I'm far from the only ex-child who remembers the painful ambiva-lence that struck in the middle of Christmas morning. My parents sat there, awaiting every kilowatt of my delight and gratitude; and I was struggling mightily to conceal a powerful backwash—*Oh no. It's over now. Greed failed me again. I must wait another 365 days for the next shot at success.*

Luckily what remains far stronger with me however, a childhood memory that survives to fertilize the sterile commercialized present, is the core of history at the center of the dazzling festival. For of the two realities which undergird all that we mean by American Southern culture (the presence in society of a great many, sometimes a majority, of black men and women *and* a universal adherence to the Christian faith), the belief in the divine nature of a single real human figure called Jesus is still the most unifying fact. Fifty years ago it was even more so.

When I was two or three, I received as a gift from my parents a thick Bible-story book with numerous illustrations—pictures from which I could construct tales of my own long before I was able to read. In many of the paintings and drawings, a boy not much older than me was central to the action and meaning—young Isaac or David or the infant- and then boy-Jesus. I pored on those, imagining for my own lonely self (I was then an only child) some sudden capacity for significant deeds in the actual world of adults as pained and puzzled as my parents.

When I was four or five, I was taken to see my first Christmas pageant at a local Protestant church. We went because a grown friend of ours played the Virgin Mary. I no longer remember but I suspect the Christ Child was played by a doll, to avoid the wailing inconvenience of an actual infant. Whatever the case, the take-home message for me at the time was urgent. I wouldn't have been able to state my personal logic, but the substance was something very much like this—*A child is the center of Christmas. All these adults are gathered to watch him. A child is the center of an entire faith. I am a child. I matter in the world.*

Soon after, at about the age of six, my parents gave me my next heart's desire—a Christmas crèche composed of numerous plaster figures made in Japan (with unabashedly Japanese features) and a rudimentary wood-stable. Almost fifty years later I still have all the figures but the angel and the manger, early casualties. Annually through childhood (and since), I spent crucial hours each Christmas carefully deploying the figures for maximum narrative effect. And each year, unaware of the European custom, I independently invented it—I waited till the crucial hours of late Christmas Eve to place the figure of the Child in his manger. The hero of the story, for whom all else waits—his parents, the three rich kings, the poor shepherds with their livestock offerings, even the sheep and the camel—the heroic infant God appears in his own good time, not ours.

That's not to suggest that I was subject to dangerous delusions of grandeur or blasphemous identifications with a deity. It does suggest that the meaning of Christmas, for a child of my time and place (an almost entirely Christian region of America in the 1930s and 40s) could still easily be located in its precise, in fact its only, sane center. I've admitted that Santa Claus, his sleigh and deer, were likewise important to my pleasure and my hopes. But all the other decor of Christmas, even in those necessarily penurious years, was genuinely unwelcome to me.

I heard adults sermonizing each year about "putting the Christ back in Christmas." What most concerned me then, and now, was putting the *child* back in Christmas—or keeping him there, where he'd been from the start. The child who, whether as Messiah or ordinarily lovable and difficult boy or girl, begins at least to redeem (at the dark end of the sun's year and ours) the soul's oldest hope—the hope of Christmas, even now in a time of nuclear dread, that our swelling race of creatures spread so wickedly but gloriously over the entire face of this gorgeous blue planet is loved by the mind at the core of space and will somehow be spared a permanent death.

1986

A WORLD TO LOVE AT LEAST

I T HARDLY SEEMS an accident that I met Caroline Vaughan twenty years ago when she enrolled in the elementary class in Narrative Writing that I was teaching at Duke University. She was a freshman and Duke's home—Durham, North Carolina—was her birthplace. I was a young writer who had published two novels and a first volume of short stories. She responded to the class assignments with an immediate flair. I remember still the vividly imagined line of her early stories. It was some time though before I knew of her passion for photography. In fact, it was only two years after her graduation that she assembled the first show of her pictures (one image here, "Lindsay," was in that show).

I was at once excited by the prodigious authority of her visual work but I wasn't surprised. Just from her lucid imagistic prose, I should have guessed that beneath her photographs there would ride the insistent pulse of story—the compulsion to narrate which is only a little less urgent to *Homo sapiens* than the need for food. From the first, and even in her nearly-abstract images of landscape, she allied herself with the long and honorable gallery of narrative photography. Even Cartier-Bresson is not more pregnant with story.

Look though at the no-nonsense titles she attaches to images as story-laden as most of those reproduced here—"Self Portrait," "Virginia Farm"; "Oak in Snow, Carolina Farm"; "An LaBarre, Bonnie and Jody"; and "Waterlilies, North Florida." Only "Eskimo Spirit, Mammal Breath," and "Image from a Past Life" acknowledge a poetic content.

Aren't we led to conclude that her eye and mind are powered by calm but polar impulses? The first is an impulse to assemble, from the natural world, the minimum ingredients of a plot (let "plot" be defined as "a story with emphasis on causality"; what is fascinatingly omitted from most of Vaughan's stories are firm hints of cause). Those ingredients consist of one or two characters, including animals, and a place—sometimes benign, occasionally threatening. Among those components, the current of energy that the artist implies is so strong as to compel—in a patient viewer—his own story or poem, his variation on a theme by Caroline Vaughan. The final component that the viewer is invited to bring to the transaction is *cause*. Why has this image happened and why here? For instance, I might today respond like this to some of the elements offered:

—This woman has come out to stand beside a still pond at dawn, with a pregnant mare and a dog, because. . . . then a sudden voice from the near-shore (where I also stand; have I spoken?) calls their names. The horse and dog, but not the woman, look and see that. . . .

—These naked women lie near one another in a strange pure light, but what do they see? Does each know the other? If they speak, what imaginable words will they say?

—The photographer herself stands with a stick among derelict farm-buildings. It's winter and both she and the place are awaiting my approach since I bring them. . . .

—That circle on the water which seems ice is not ice but an object that rose from the depths, or settled from the sky, at dawn. It is sent for me. I step toward its unmarked whiteness and find. . . .

But because none of Vaughan's present images is part of a sequence (as in Duane Michael's haunting sequences, so imminent with story that the anxious photographer has scrawled his own word-accompaniments in the margin lest we miss the implicit content) and because we are given no encouragement by her anti-poetic titles, we are left alone with her meticulously arranged moments—her frozen instants of history, biography, or silent song. We can attempt to treat them purely as photographs, the arranged accidents of light. Indeed, some viewers feel strongly that Vaughan's nearly-theatrical arrangements are as innocent of narrative as an oxblood vase or a T'ang horse.

A nature mystic like Ansel Adams can photograph Yosemite Valley, seduce us to ignore the fact that hundreds of thousands of befouling human beings visit it annually, and set us meditating upon inhuman Creation and its Creator as quietly and profoundly as Poussin or Constable. "Moonrise, Hernandez, New Mexico"—for all its poignant huddle of graves in the foreground—can rivet our eyes to the moon and the sky, not the low crosses that briefly mark the eternal resting-sites of individual human beings.

But even in Vaughan's landscapes and nature studies that contain no hint of human presence or influence, the threat of story is never entirely banished. Those waterlillies conceal, or protect, *something*. That ice-glazed pond is not *empty*.

And certainly a picture like "Constructivist Double Portrait," as technically complex in its arrangement as a three-act play, invites any number of different readings. Those two long bodies at first seem as innocent of conscious thought or intention as any seashell, seem lit by a near-lunar shine. Yet slowy they radiate from within (with what mysterious fuel of their own?). Such questions and deductions will finally say far more about my own narrative needs than about either Vaughan's own compulsions or intentions. But it's hard to imagine a viewer who can see such images without at least the stirrings of narrative speculation. Where are these people (if not in extraplanetary space), why are they before me, what am I meant to do with their presence?

For me, from my first exposure to them, Caroline Vaughan's photographs have been as rich in narrative potential as Vermeer's dazzling records of the deeds of light while it prowls human faces and manmade objects. But then, for me, most enduring photographs are freighted with story. Even more than in the other visual arts—and perhaps it's because, however technically altered, they acknowledge a rock-bottom origin in tangible reality—the deeply memorable photographs, from the humblest photojournalism to the near-abstractions of a Weston, are those which survive in our minds as icons: objects for narrative extrapolation and contemplation, even for a kind of awe and worship. Far more things than we guess in the world are worthy of our *notice*—whether formed directly by God, Time and Weather, or by Man. They silently require our concentration, our slow comprehension, or at least our awe.

The grand camera images earn their place beside the best paintings and sculptures because they are equally striking and trustworthy representations of earthly and heavenly truth. In their general fidelity to unaltered surface, photographs are far more selfless than any painting. An apparently faceless painter like Vermeer is a flaunting egotist in comparison to the grandest of realist photographers. A great photographer—and Caroline Vaughan is one—is therefore as much an oracle of truth as any other devoted artist, however comic and gypsy their apparatus compels them to be with balky equipment, stuffed canvas-bags, and fistsful of tinfoil litter. And their greatness is measured, as with all other workers, both by the size of their attempt (how much of the world they attempt to annex) and its seriousness (how deeply they pierce).

Like her forebears from Brady to Wynn Bullock and Minor White, she stands at an opposite pole from the news photo, the stunning snapshot peeled bleeding off the face of history. The photojournalist gratefully acknowledges his huge debt to chance, his luck at being in the right spot at the right moment. Vaughan almost never gives us that sense of nervous luck. Her gifts are patience and the slow but audacious eye of an astronomer, a microbiologist. She is thus in fierce battle with the potential ease and triviality of her medium and her instrument. No young photographer knows better than Vaughan that, with the advent of the automatic single-lens reflex camera, any intelligent citizen with a keen visual sense can shoot three rolls of film and bring home one or two memorable-or-better images from the drugstore.

So no bearded monk on Mount Athos, painting his hundredth charged icon of the Risen Christ; no Michelangelo at age eighty-nine with a candle in his cap, relentlessly hacking a last *Pietà* from the already ruined block, has sought more seriously or successfully than she to force from the visible world its invisible messages—the perfectly beautiful Ideas and Forms that teach us to live, that prepare us to accept a world far grander than ourselves that nonetheless awaits our attention (or our ignorance, if we are so self-absorbed as to ignore it).

The world that Caroline Vaughan reveals is literally awesome. If we pause to see it, it may really be seen. Every item in her catalog is clearly shown; nothing is suppressed, vandalized, or glamorized. It is a world rare in the work of contemporary American photographers for its beauty. Yet it is a world not necessarily in love with us. There are no mothers with laughingly extended arms, no children beaming their gratitude, no tall men granting us warm safe harbor, no serpent-free gardens. But in the strenuous calm of the apparently endless beauty she discovers (a summoned natural beauty, not a staged human drama), her world demands our love and maybe more. What patient witness will not bow to its heart?

1987

MAN AND BOY

A LIFE ON CAMPUS

(an Address to the Annual Meeting of the
Friends of the Duke University Library)

A s a teacher at Duke, I'm not quite yet a thirty-year man. That anniversary will come in September 1988—if I, or any part of our world, is here to observe it. But as a human being with intimate attachments to the University, its surrounding village, and even to the surrounding town, I date back almost thirty-six years—to September 13, 1951.

It was on that day that my parents drove me the long twenty-two miles from our home in west Raleigh to West Campus, Kilgo Quad, House N, Room 111: an all-freshman and, thank God, all-male dormitory and a room which has now had one of its walls removed and the space incorporated into a larger faceless lounge in that dim old memory-freighted building. So much for the sanctity of my former Duke spaces. My sophomore single room has likewise vanished into the Few Federation lounge. Only my junior-senior single, also in FF, seems to survive.

The first room was tiny, built to be a single—twelve feet by ten— an early victim of the University's continuing and incorrigible temptation to overstuff our already inadequate space. But by the benign hand of fate that guided so much of my student career, I was paired with a thoroughly compatible roommate. His name was Jack Hail from Richmond, Virginia—quiet, witty, and studious. (He also smoked incessantly, a habit that would separate us now but that barely fazed me then—the son of chainsmoking parents.)

We shared few professional or intellectual interests, beyond a mutual love of music. I had spent seven years of my childhood at the piano; Jack was a passionate trombonist and quickly copped the honor of a chair in the Duke Ambassadors, that more than respectable local big-band. But we left our instruments at the doorsill and settled at once into as peaceful a living arrangement as I've since managed with any other member of the species. We studied, talked endlessly, laughed, and slept the bottomless trances of the American adolescent (on rickety bunk-beds) in that tight space—barely larger than a piano crate—for nine months without a cross word.

I spoke of laughter. If it was not our main activity, it was a prime component and might well be noticed first. Firecrackers were by then illegal in North Carolina, doubly so on campus. If you were caught with the smallest cherry bomb, you were expelled and thrown unceremoniously onto the next bus out of Durham. In a present less certain of its moral values, you can do far worse and walk away scatheless—free to cut all tomorrow's classes too.

The harsher rules of those brave days of course encouraged students to import tons of TNT and to employ them in hugely imaginative ways to punctuate the torpor of dormitory life. (Most of the West campus dorms, with their grim brick-and-terrazo mile-long corridors, breed thoughts of mass destruction. The more realistic English principle of staircase organization precludes such thoughts.) It was normal enough, thirty-six years ago, to hear a quasi-nuclear detonation on the fringes of sleep—say at four a.m. on a Sunday—then to enter the bathroom at nine and discover a ponderous porcelain commode in thousands of white shards round the floor. Much laughter.

Or lighter fluid. In those bad days of near-universal student smoking—when the major tobacco companies were permitted to distribute free packs of cigarettes during lunch hour on the quads (a close approximation to the current Crack dealer lurking by the schoolground)—there were frequent incidents fueled by lighter fluid. Jack Hail and I were shut in studying one night when he noticed a pool of liquid creeping beneath our door. We watched it spread with interest, only to see it flash into flame. Lighter fluid was being blown toward us by a pyromaniac friend in the hall, and soon our expensive oak-door had ignited. Much laughter.

Or feathers! Early in the first semester, before the hardcore stunts had taken root, Jack and I awoke one Sunday morning—Sundays were debris time—to find that an apparent blizzard had afflicted us in the night. Our floor, the furniture, our own bodies in the bunks were blanketed in a mantle of white. Close inspection revealed the mantle to consist of high-grade chicken down. Another inventive friend had come up the hall, confiscating pillows from sleeping heads, and opening their ticking. Since our room happened to be last in line, we had been the recipient of his gatherings—all broadcast in at us, over a period of considerable silent time, through an open transom. Much laughter.

Laughter at what?—surely at our own ebullient and self-loving youth, our fertile minds' prankster inventions, at our indifference to consequences. Lighter fluid and fireworks dangerous?—it never crossed our minds. Hadn't we lived through the leveling of west and east Europe and a good part of Asia in the Second World War, which was after all only six years behind us? Wasn't the Republic of Korea being noisily leveled just out of our hearing at those very moments, awaiting only our strong young bodies to help in the chaos once we'd finished or failed here? (We stayed out of service in those years by one of two courses—by safely joining an ROTC program and promising the government later years, or we winged it scarily on high grades.)

We were also forbidden to drink in the dorms; and in surprisingly fearful respect, we mostly obeyed. So unless we gambled our physical safety on the dangers of downtown Durham (white townies were notoriously hostile to us all-white Dukies) and took ourselves to the profoundly funky Chili House (now Anotherthyme) or the Donut Dinette (now a parking lot beside the dead Ivy Room) or to Rinaldi's Italian Cafe (a parking lot also, beside a funeral home) our body poisons were limited to tobacco and the cholesterol-larded diet of the time.

I never so much as heard rumors of any drug more illegal than caffeine on campus before 1966. And that at last was marijuana, a drug which—on my first campus whiff—I recognized as identical with the cigarettes smoked legally by my ancient great-Uncle Brother Rodwell in Macon, North Carolina throughout my childhood for his near-paralyzing asthma: so-called asthma cigarettes that he bought over the counter at the local pharmacy. When I told my mother's surviving sister that poor unfulfilled confirmed-bachelor Uncle Brother—age near-ninety—had been blissfully stoned out of his gourd every night of his adult life, she only laughed and said "Well, I knew every time I went in his room, I got real *woozy.*" So much for the Puritan consciousness in our Confederate family.

And actually achieved (as opposed to dreamed of or elaborately plotted) sexual interchange was so nearly non-existent on campus as to constitute little problem except for the two deans, East and West, whom we fondly called the Sex Deans. Abortions, venereal diseases—not to mention AIDS—and the sad-to-tragic array of other physical and psychic reproductive woes that afflict any university today were all but unheard of among us then. So—lighter-fluid fires? beerbottle bowling-matches in the halls? exploded urinals? whole rooms of furniture instantly dismantled while the owner ran to the nearby Dope Shop for a Coke and reassembled to exact scale outside in the Quad, complete with floorlamps alight, fungoid socks and jock straps on the ground by the bed, and all in plenty of time to greet the occupant's flummoxed return? Well, surely—much laughter.

A Tom Sawyer decade, you might say, the harmless white-washing of harmless white fences—though twenty years later we somehow discovered our old ballistic pyromaniac selves or our friends as the junior-managers and staffers of an extended overseas-amusement in a country whose name none of us had heard in 1951, though it lay not far south of the Korea in which we'd rightly dreaded fighting.

And I spoke of studying. Both Jack Hail and I—and with one or two epically slothful or prodigiously lecherous exceptions, all our hallmates —spent long hours studying: at a conservative estimate, some fifty to sixty hours a week. It was fashionable then as now to abandon the dorms as impossible study-halls and to repair to the crowded public-rooms of the Main Library.

That was not yet called Perkins, though most of its present non-electronic services were in place and functioning with the smoothness that has always made our library one of the almost unfailing local pleasures, second only in reliability to the supply of near-boiling water in any campus faucet. In those days the stacks were closed to undergraduates, however desperate for quiet desk-space—except those few who were mature-enough-looking to forge through the swinging doors by the old circulation desk and gamble on being taken for one of the aging, often World-War-II-vet, graduate students who still populated the place.

But Jack and I were united in a homebody nature. He could work through any decibel of outrage, any megatonnage of barrage. I couldn't; but like the teenager I was, I could sleep through it. Often I'd brush my teeth, slip into bed on weeknights at eight, and snore like a morphined baby through whatever stone-splitting degrees of hijinks exploded at my ear. Then I'd wake at three, make myself a bottomless mug of strong tea, and study at my own desk—five feet from my unconscious roommate and with the otherwise riotous dorm and campus stretching away in silence from the pool of warm light in which I memorized the elegant classifi-cations of Zoology 1–2, one of the genuinely exciting courses I ever took and by far the hardest.

I'd read on too till dawn broke coldly over the old post office in the basement of the Union. Then I'd pause long enough to eat a field-hand breakfast in what is now a good-deal-too-grandly called the Gothic Dining Hall—if we name one more thing *Gothic* around here, I for one am going to yell and not stop—or in the bleak overhead jailhouse-lighting of the University Room. To quit grumbling for an instant, my memory awards a smiling A-minus to the Duke kitchens of those years and of the present—that cafeteria bacon! those Oak Room club-sandwiches! the cin-namon-and-raisin cookies on the late-night outdoor Chow-Man carts, long abandoned for robot dispensers of Dupont snacks!

Or perhaps I was running behind and would skip breakfast, working on as the dorm woke around me; and I continued to conquer the multiple-document theories of the composition of the Old Testament for Religion

1–2 with Chick Sales (another pulse quickener for a traditionally-raised Tar-Heel Methodist), or memorizing French subjunctives for Tom Cordle, or marveling again at the lucidity of the verbatim notes I'd transcribed from the History 1 lectures of the quietly flabbergasting Harold Parker (still the supreme teacher in my book, and my book runneth over with fine teachers), or writing my next theme for English 2A—a special section in which I'd landed, thanks to one of the rare advance-placement tests of the time.

In one of the few others during freshman orientation-week—in mathematics—out of a possible perfect score of 99, I managed a resounding 14. And when I passed through the winningly personal pre-registration procedures of those days, the realistic freshman dean, William Archie, noticed how comically my math score contrasted with my English, delivered his famed peacock-hoot of delight, and wrote across my permanent record, "The uniform requirement in Mathematics is waived in the case of Mr. Price." That sentence, which I can still see in Dean Archie's imperious hand, is one of the two favorites of my life. The second was scrawled in a mean child's penciling by a scornful sergeant at the end of a line of nude males in Raleigh seven years later, "Price examined and found unfit for military service."

The writing of weekly themes for that advanced section of Freshman English and the response the themes received from my classmates and my instructor were probably crucial to my reaffirmed decision to continue hoping to "grow up to be a writer." I had harbored the ambition since at least the eighth grade when—just before Christmas—I wrote my first substantial thing that survives, a play about the Wise Men. In the second half of that school year, I had the luck to encounter a teacher—Crichton Davis—who was herself a writer, having published short stories, one of which had been honored in an O. Henry prize anthology.

But I was even more impressed by the fact that Mrs. Davis, a lifelong friend of my father's, was also a good painter. Then in my life—and since age four—I was fascinated by my growing ability to make visible copies of imposing objects in the world around me: landscapes, trees, human faces, elephants. She and I met occasionally outside school and painted still lives of fruit and flowers or decorated prune-juice and shaving-lotion bottles. And those hours gave me the instantly addicting whiff of the unique happiness available to a self-sufficient artist.

My love of the graphic arts had continued through my high-schooling in Raleigh; but it was not until my junior year there—at the age of sixteen, when I encountered the extraordinary teacher Phyllis Peacock—that I began to see two important things. My drawings and paintings were skillful but unimaginative. I was chained to realistic copying, the literal reproduction of a visible palpable object. And at a time when abstract expressionism—which I saw as self-absorbed calligraphy—reigned as the certified mode of American art, I knew that my own abilities doomed me to a career in commercial illustration. Phyllis Peacock, with her encouragement of my poems and narrative-prose sketches had simultaneously shown me a way to detour round my discouragement in painting. With my talent for recognizable copying, I could render the world in a different but parallel way—in words, the English language.

So by the time I'd landed in Philip Williams's English 2A in Carr Building, East Campus, in September 1951, I was eager to write. Fortunately for me, Williams permitted me to write narratives—autobiographical sketches to the standard freshman-theme length of five hundred words. I still possess most of them, with my instructor's thank-God salty remarks.

I say *thank God* because one of the most difficult things for a talented young American to get, in a public-school system always short on talent, is anything *but* delirous praise. As a highly praised student, I'd known for years that I needed discerning criticism. Scared of it as I was, I wanted it. And deep in my mind still, still worth noticing, are such comments of Williams's as "See how much better Hemingway is when doing the same thing."

Though I continued to study with him in the second semester of that year—Chaucer, Shakespeare, and Milton in English 55—and though he was my faculty advisor for another year or so, I never got to know him and certainly never thanked him with anything approaching adequacy for that important early help. By the time I was a senior, he was dead.

He had left Duke, returned to his origins in Charlottesville, and died by his own hand. If he can hear me at all now—Mr. Williams, though I'm twenty years older than you waited to be, I see you plainly still: your endless in-class cigarettes stubbed out on the hapless legs of the desk, your extraplanetary profile, your weak eyes goggling at me in half-respect, half-amusement as you say "Mr. Price, I think you'll find that Emily Dickinson retains a mystery or two that even you haven't plumbed. Back to the saltmines, my boy, and good luck to you." I've been in the mines, sir, more or less ever since; and I've had good luck, found a handful of what I trust is not fool's gold. Warm thanks forever.

By the end of that first full year then, the components of my Duke (and extra-Duke) life were all visible—laid out before me, my hand to play. Two components, as I trust you'll understand and be glad of, I don't want to discuss here among the ruins of a pleasant dinner.

The first was a huge reality that Americans of my unhurried generation often discovered early in their college careers—romance, a first intense all-stops-pulled love affair. I dived into my first Wagnerian commitment early in my first semester and pursued it through most of the following four years with an intensity almost equal to the voltage I expended in study and writing. In some ways the experience was damaging, even devastating; in perhaps more important ways though, it was a real part of my early education, and as such I can't regret an amp of the power.

The second undiscussable component was a rapid evolution in one of my oldest concerns, religious faith. Like many children of my time and place, I'd had a mystically fervid relation with the transcendent creator of all things whom I believed—and believe—to stand waiting only just a little beyond us behind a not-entirely-opaque curtain.

The fact that the building which stands at the head of West campus is, for architectural purposes at least, a cathedral proved important for me in a way that neither J. B. Duke nor orthodox churchmen can have foreseen. Back then the Chapel was available most hours of the day and night for meditation and, above all, for private worship. Very quickly in its resonant and spacious beauty—its adequately partial metaphor of the grandeur of God—it discovered in me a trait I share with my hero John Milton: an absence of need for membership in an organized religious sect.

That trait has remained with, and strengthened, me ever since. And when I was invited last year to write a preface to the new book of photographs of the Chapel, I was finally able to express some of my long gratitude to a structure in which I've thought about—and pled about—everything from a forthcoming boxing-exam in Phys. Ed. to my father's lung cancer.

By the spring of 1952, as I've said, I dimly saw that the shape of my whole life lay before me. The components were work, love, friendship, play, and worship. So in June I returned to Raleigh to spend an edgy idle summer. I was mainly waiting to resume life in the one place where I'd felt entirely alive and at home; the one place where all my strengths and abilities were not only wanted but accepted, treated with dignity and honest discrimination, and valued or rejected with the kind of precise intelligence that a sane human craves. It seemed to be a place that promised to go on shaping and using the remainder of my life—and rewarding me for that use.

It's an index to the importance of the University in my mind, after only nine months of furious participation, to realize that I possess no sustained memory of that post-freshman summer. I half-think I attempted to expand a short story I'd sketched in my English class; if so the results apparently don't survive. I existed, as I've implied, in a kind of not-quite-miserable torpor of waiting for September, campus again, love and work and real life.

And instantly in September, it did recommence even more rewardingly. Not only was I completing British Representative Writers—Pope to Yeats—with a for-me new and challenging teacher, herself a nationally-known poet, Helen Bevington. I also began to explore what was to prove a lifetime passion—my love for the poetry of John Milton, first encountered in Philip Williams's literature class in the spring of 1952. The exploration began in an undergraduate seminar conducted by an unsung but superb teacher, Dean Florence Brinkley. Plus more French with the dashing Jean-Jacques Demarest, more of the dreaded then-compulsory Physical Education, the Anthropology of the American Indian with Weston LaBarre (one of the real gadflies of Duke's history, as opposed to egomaniacs-posing-as-gadflies), and Elizabethan literature with William Blackburn.

Though Blackburn is one of the mythical figures in this young university's past, though a number of his students have gone on record with their affectionate memoirs; and though many of you remember him, I'd still like to expand here on his nature and methods. I didn't study fiction writing with him until my senior year, so I'll say at once that his initial deep effect on me, and on most of my contemporaries, resided in the valid force with which he convinced us that a thoroughly masculine and mostly sane man of our fathers' age (he was fifty-three when I met him; and he was never entirely Mr. Mental Health, a fact he knew and laughed about ruefully)—that such a man could love the poetry of passionate discourse as much as other sane men loved football or money.

He could read the whole of a long poem—say, Edmund Spenser's *Prothalamion*—to a crammed room of post-adolescents, read it with a voice and skill as impressive as John Gielgud's, bring himself and many of us to the reluctant point of tears, and convince us that the making of such objects—permanently beautiful works of verbal art—was among the highest honors available to individual members of the human race and, however immensely difficult, was an honor not closed to us: the students here around him.

Further, he was not ashamed to deploy in the classroom that riskiest of strategies—the overflow of personal emotion, an occasional glimpse permitted to the students of a teacher's own heart: the terrors, depressions, and elations of an adult private life. This is not to say that William Blackburn indulged in the sleazy brand of heart-on-sleeve theatrics so permanently popular with American students, not to mention a behavior of which he stood in great fear—the brand of risk involved in student-teacher erotic politics. It's only to say that he understood profoundly how poetry, the art of controlled articulate passion, cannot be conveyed to students without an unashamed admission by the teacher that the matter under consideration either alters him profoundly or leaves him coldly in place.

As I watched Blackburn with the unbroken scrutiny that only a knowledge-hungry adolescent can muster—well before he approached me with his elephantine courtesy and offered friendship—I learned that vital secret about the teaching of poetry. I learned further that the love and communication to others of the beauty, the use, and the art of literature were transactions at least as urgent for the continued life of mankind as nuclear disarmanent or the conquest of space.

What could I do then with my own dimly perceived skills and passions but attempt both tasks—the making of such complex sacred objects and their communication to that portion of the population likely to be most receptive, the captive and needy young?

That was his prime service to me, surpassing the welcome encouragement he gave my narrative prose two years later when I experienced his English 103–104—a course taken by a number of other eventually published writers, many of whom studied with me also when I returned here from graduate school in a whole new hat: William Styron, Guy Davenport, Fred Chappell, James Applewhite, Wallace Kaufman, Anne Tyler, David Guy, Josephine Humphries, Charlie Smith, and Michael Brondoli. Many of them have confirmed, in essays or interviews or conversation, my conviction that the best of Blackburn was most visible in his literature courses—especially his sixteenth- and seventeenth-century courses.

As a writing teacher, he could offer an intuitive and trustworthy ear for raw talent—especially in male students. He seldom persisted past graduation in the encouragement of a woman; and years later he told me the reason (sad but often valid in a co-ed college of those days)—"I've tried but they walk off, get married the week after graduation, have a houseful of children, and I never hear from them again."

But despite his spellbinding and hilarious skills as a raconteur and the attentive vitality of his letter writing, Bill Blackburn could not write fluently when he attempted critical or narrative prose. It was his chief personal disappointment, I suspect. So even with his male protégés, he was hampered by an inability to point to the word-by-word weaknesses of a given manuscript or to suggest the work habits and conditions of daily life that any beginning writer most needs.

Thus there came, to most of us who completed our own self-training and went on to publish in the big world, a painful episode of paternal rejection by him. Blackburn came to feel wrongly that most of us had outgrown him or, worse, grown to despise him. He repeatedly cast himself in the sad role of Mr. Chips, the once-loved but elementary and discarded old codger. Luckily, in almost all our cases, we were able to assure him of his continuing value to us and to make the necessary repairs before his death.

I, for instance, was able to be with him on each of the hard days of the end of his life when—blinded and baffled by brain cancer—he was nonetheless able to turn his frightening cyclopean gaze on me and say in his then-ruined bass "I don't see how you *stand* this." I think he meant "How can you stand being here, watching me die like the crazed tormented Lear I taught you long ago?" And that almost unimaginable degree of self*less*ness, at the very moment of final shattering assaults on his proud self, was perfectly emblematic of his greatness as man and teacher. He was standing in the mouth of a distorting and agonizing death, a death that was doing all it could to unman and humiliate him. But he was thinking of me, concerned for me—how much I could and should ask myself to watch and bear. What more useful message could any teacher offer?

At the time of that death, his monumental fears and humilities had simply fallen away. At the end he never once mentioned them to me, and I can affirm that William Blackburn died with a firm sense of his sizable accomplishment. He had drawn for some of his thousands of students—boldly and brilliantly—the large figure of a magnanimous creature on fire for that beauty which is the province solely of the lucky man or woman who is gifted enough, disciplined and hard-working enough to create and communicate new objects of lucid verbal beauty.

I have mentioned the names of other teachers and singled out the name of Harold Parker, historian of the French Revolution and the reign of Napoleon. He doubled Blackburn's example of the teacher incandescent with love of his subject. In his own thoroughly different way, Parker was as resourceful, academically sound, and enduringly impressive a performer—and a great teacher is, before all else, a great actor. Parker surpassed all my other early models in being himself the ongoing master of an eloquent and unchallangeable narrative prose.

If he has yet to publish the wise summary work all his students await, he had even then (more than thirty years ago) already given us the exemplary *Cult of Antiquity in the French Revolution*. And in his *Three Napoleonic Battles*, we could contemplate one of the masterpieces of military history. It was, not at all incidentally (since it was finished just before his own induction into the World War II army)—one of the eloquent denunciations of war as an instrument of human policy.

I have spoken also of the luck of guidance from Florence Brinkley in Milton and Helen Bevington in Representative British Writers and later in Twentieth-Century Poetry, a course that opened a vital new world for me. Scarce as women then were in the faculty, those two multiplied their rarity by distinctly individual but equally visible kinds of dedication. Dean Brinkley was the classical unmarried scholar-writer-teacher. She could bring her students both the extra time and energy available to the chaste, though the chaste far from always focus their gains as intensely as she. She was also unafraid to give the characteristically shy but all-the-more credible affection of the childless; and when she invited us on December 9th to her annual Milton's Birthday Party, we went in part-amusement at her naive charm but with firm admiration for her lifelong dedication and her odd ability to communicate a pure devotion.

And as my undergraduate years proceeded, I encountered an unbroken line of the richest gift Duke University offered—a troop of thoroughly skilled, often brilliant, always committed scholar-teachers. Time permits me to name only four more, all of them still nearby—Allan Gilbert, Louis Budd, Joel Colton, and Weston LaBarre. I hope I've hinted, in my discussions of Blackburn and Parker, at the help they all so variously gave.

The remainder of my undergraduate years brought little else that was genuinely new, though the years were crowded to near-exhaustion—with more of the same. Work again, and love (some of it happy and reciprocal), and even more play.

The later play was provided by membership, from my second year on, in a social fraternity—Phi Delta Theta. Then the Phis were an athletic fraternity with, like the Betas, a successful sideline in masculine good-looks. Their induction of Reynolds Price—whose freshman grades in P.E. were thudding Cs and whose athletic skills just about covered a gentle walk through the Gardens—can only have been a tribute to my grades (despite the Cs in Phys. Ed., I still finished first in my freshman class; so there!). I could singlehandedly raise the group's academic average and keep if off Social Probation. I could help the brothers write their English papers; and further I suspect that my undisguised love of learning amused and amazed them. They wanted me in their large raucous bawdy and friendly zoo.

Maybe I was a pleasant sort of marmoset to have in a corner of the chapter room that was otherwise populated by the larger benign anthropoids and to introduce to their dazed and/or terrified dates at cabin parties in the Duke Forest or at the Saddle Club on Hillsborough Road. Their nickname for me—*Mister Phopheles*—is a clue to the latter interpretation (I'd published in *The Archive* an essay on the character of Mephistopheles in Marlowe's *Doctor Faustus* and was never allowed to forget it). In any case, I enormously enjoyed their company, though I managed always to avoid rooming in the heavily ballistic fraternity-section.

And as I came down through the storm of my father's death in the winter of my junior year toward graduation, I was permitted by the University to meet two writers whom I—and the English-speaking world—admired and honored. The Anglo-Irish novelist Elizabeth Bowen came to campus for a lecture in my junior year, read the one short story I'd written in Williams's class two years earlier, encouraged it with a dead-accurate diagnosis of its structural problem; and when I drove her on to the next engagement in Winston-Salem, she displayed to me in the unmatched privacy of a car her joy in the craft of fiction and the artist's life.

And in the second semester of my senior year, the American Eudora Welty came also for a lecture, read a recently expanded and repaired version of the same story (entitled "Michael Egerton"), and called it professional. She asked if she might send it to Diarmuid Russell, her agent in New York (a man who was not only the son of A.E., the Irish mystic poet, but also a friend of William Butler Yeats and Lady Gregory); and he remained my invaluable agent and friend till his death in the mid-1970s.

Eudora Welty continued to encourage me through the remainder of my senior year by permitting me to give first publication in *The Archive*, which I then edited, to her now-famous essay "Place in Fiction" and above all—and most unimaginably, because I knew she was plainly one of the rare masters of the short story in American literature—by treating me quite simply as her peer through the remaining slow years of an unpublished apprenticeship.

In another place I'd have stood slim chance of meeting two such impeccably professional and spiritually generous models—two who, by placing their wordly benediction atop those of my Duke teachers, convinced me decisively that I must leave here and learn to become the two things I seemed fated—rigged—blessed to be: a writer who could teach, a teacher who could write.

In providing for me the various opulently rich environments in which I could learn those crucial things, after so much else, Duke University had in fact nearly matured me. It had already presided over one more agonizingly slow but unquestionably live birth from childhood into manhood—a manhood hardly completed but at least commenced, a labor induced by many local hands and by the place itself.

So a boy who had driven here from Raleigh on bloodcurdling old two-lane highway 70 in the fall of 1951—all adolescent pimples, bobbing Adam's apple, uncertain baritone voice, and gnawed fingernails—drove away in the spring of 1955 for three years of further burnishing and fitting in England. He was still far from sleek with self-love and confidence. If anything he was hungrier than ever; but he was at least reliably informed of what to order, savor slowly, and build into sinew at the banquet table of a Europe still groping to its knees ten years after the War and all the gladder to trade its wealth to a Yank with a few pounds to spend and a mind that—despite sixteen years of storage—still offered miles of warehouse space.

As I went, I partly knew what, here and now, I strongly affirm—this beautiful place (admittedly more beautiful then because more leisurely and with a far greater variety of excellent students from many more levels of the American society and economy, certainly a less crowded place and—with all the fireworks—a more peaceful one)—this place had put its broad deep stamp on the crown of my head.

The head, as some of you may recall, was black then and dense as monkey fur. It's patently now a thinner silver. But it's still embossed with that same mark—not quite the Great Seal of the University with cross, gleaming landscape, and its motto's forthright promise (*Eruditio et Religio*) to free me from roughness and bind up the scattered parts of my soul but still the stern and loving brand of a bountiful parent, a nourishing mother: *Alma Mater*.

1987

AT THE HEART

In my childhood I often heard a radio program called "This I Believe." Conducted by Edward R. Murrow, a native of my home state, it consisted of brief first-person credos by famous artists, politicians, and athletes. I don't remember any particular statement, only my own fascination with the general premise—that there were successful adults who knew what they believed, who were prepared to stand in public and describe the platforms on which they had built whole lives and earned applause. Since it never occurred to me to doubt that every adult would eventually know such things or that anyone might simply manufacture a set of lies or empty hopes for the occasion, I was an ideal audience for the program. And its premise became one more of the hundreds of chances I awaited—a time when I'd have firm true beliefs on which I was basing my life, that I'd know what they were, could state them clearly, and that anyone would care.

Here now—at fifty-four, a little past the age at which my father died—I find that I do in fact believe a great deal. Far from paring down, in the scraped-bone simplification that's promised for maturity, I believe more now than ever—passionate convictions on every subject from home cooking, prose style, and child rearing to the peaceful management of outer space.

The broad central beliefs though are the ones that may be worth stating, those I seem to have held forever and from which most of the others can be deduced, if anyone cares to. In my case, the indispensable weight-bearing structures are driven into what I think is bedrock along the seismic narrative line of the Apostles' Creed—a formulation of historical, theological, and ethnical beliefs that was not apparently made by Jesus's own disciples but that had solidified by the fourth century and which I can recite now as easily as in my fervent adolescence, with no reservation through all its enormous looping implications. Here it is, not in its most familiar form but in my own literal translation from the Latin—

I believe in God Almighty Father, maker of Heaven and Earth, and in Jesus Christ, his only son our lord who was conceived by the Holy Ghost, born of the Virgin Mary, suffered under Pontius Pilate, crucified dead and buried, descended into Hell, on the third day rose from the dead, ascended into Heaven, and sits on the right hand of God Almighty Father. Thence he shall come to judge the living and dead. I believe in the Holy Spirit, the holy catholic church, the communion of saints, the forgiveness of sins, the resurrection of the body, and everlasting life.

Since I subscribe to such a demanding statement—and subscribe without rationalization or allegory—and though I am not a member of any sect, I am thus an orthodox (though not fundamentalist) Christian. The visible reasons seem to be that I was reared in sane Christian families in a traditionally Christian region of the United States and, more crucially, that I was further shaped in childhood by experiences that I took to be direct and graceful contacts from God and his messengers (trees, rocks, animals, angels, angelic humans).

Then as a studious adult, I was confirmed in my training and vocation by the credible narratives of the four gospels and the specific and implied ethic of Jesus (though I reserve my assent to some other texts of the Christian Bible). The miraculous events of his life are reported in a straightforward manner that compel my belief—above all, in the fact of his healing power and his bodily resurrection from the tomb. And his own ethic, as reported in speeches and exchanges and implied in his deeds, is unparalleled for humane compassion in prior or subsequent history.

All my other beliefs derive from that core. I'm convinced for instance of the creator's gift of natural and manmade beauty to lighten our lives. I struggle to trust that what we creatures experience as evil—the dreadful steady presence of almost unbearable cruelty, from human or inhuman sources—is a temporarily mysterious function of a loving creator. I believe that I'm expected to return an interest on the creator's generous investment in me, through my capital ventures as writer and teacher, friend and lover. I cannot doubt that my own prosperity lays upon me the duty to share my luck with all creatures, even those who deny my premises.

I believe finally that the history of our universe is an infinite *story* told to himself and, in part, to us by the sole omnipotent creative power. In his own self-sufficient perfection, the creator cannot require our existence or our worship. Yet in his eternal singularity and in his desire to enact the boundless love which is his essence, he has chosen to create us and to endure our trying lives and willful choices—his witnesses, companions, lovers, and traitors through the long haul of time and eternity. (I refer to the creator in masculine pronouns because the founders of my faith, all of them observant Jews, were inspired to do so and because recent experiments with other, or with no, pronouns have not convinced me of their superiority.)

We are then unruly and improvising actors in the crowded unforeseeable and perhaps unscripted tale in which he has cast us for his own purpose—delight or education. The tale is likewise for us, for our pleasure too, for our training and growth; and the lethal agonies of cruelty and disaster that are such steady features of the plot are apparently didactic, literally educational—intended by God to enrich and strengthen us, to deepen both our humanity and our comprehension of his unfathomable power and diversity and our own inexplicable failures of mind and body. Despite his creation of Sunday mornings, mountain brooks, colts, and dolphins, he is unconcerned to charm us—to buy our love with easy bribes. On the contrary and for whatever reasons, our world is now so fouled that we must struggle to contemplate him through a scrim of drought, flood, starvation, cancer, monstrosity, and the torture of children.

The most difficult and constant of our struggles is with ourselves, with our predictable but always surprising tendency to choose the wasteful course, our busy devastation of other creatures and of the planet itself, a succession of error that blinds us to the rare glimpses God permits of his moving hand. When those choices have led us into harrowing dark nights of the soul, and he and our fellows seem absent or unwilling to help, then the next likely cry—parched and blameful—is "Abandonment! No just god could treat me thus."

But as the mystics of many creeds assert, God does not entirely abandon us. He does however take us seriously; even more terrifying, he loves us and craves our love. A great part of what we call evil is not the result of divine sadism or fickle disappearance but of the reverse.

We steadily flee a creator who can tend both the slow wheel of the galaxies and our own feverish escape while he awaits our return. For his own purpose as he waits, he may hide behind all but impenetrable screens—holocausts, individual agonized lifetimes—but the merciful intent of his hand is eventually discernible by an attentive patient witness.

And the tale he is choosing to tell himself and all creation will not finish but will amend and augment itself, blossoming ever more grandly like the radiant choruses of Mozart's *Magic Flute*, swelling to transform a world of farce, trial, and pain—unfolding with unimaginable and individually appropriate rewards for each worthy creature (perhaps for all human creatures if each—as seems increasingly possible—was bought by the voluntary sacrifice of his only son), a goal of unbroken justice and joy for all creatures known to God by name.

I acknowledge that such a creed can be stated but not defended with a satisfying dossier of empirical evidence. To base a life on the counter evidence however—death camps, torture, famine, and disease—is to ignore the enormous resources of natural and manmade beauty, of human compassion, and the unquenched faith in immortality that has fueled *Homo sapiens* since at least the caves ("the opinion of the human race is worth considering," my philosophy teacher used to say).

The final help I can offer the proof-hungry is a reminder that virtually identical beliefs powered perhaps a majority of the supreme creative minds of our civilization—Augustine, Dante, Chaucer, Michelangelo, Durer, Milton, Rembrandt, Pascal, Racine, Bach, Handel, Newton, Haydn, Mozart, Wordsworth, Beethoven, Kierkegaard, Dickens, Tolstoy, Hopkins, Bruckner, Tennyson, Stravinsky, Eliot, Barth, Poulenc, Auden, O'Connor (to begin a long roll that includes only the dead). Pressed by their unanimous testimony to a dazzling but benign light at the heart of space, what sane human will step up to say "Lovely, no doubt, but your eyes deceive you"? Not I, not now or any day soon.

1987

Reynolds Price was born in 1933 in Macon, N.C., a village edged by cotton and tobacco fields but split down the middle by the Seaboard Railway. His father, a salesman, led the family to various small towns in search of work toward the end of the Depression. He began school in Asheboro, N.C. but moved back to his native county in 1944. There he met the farm children who, a decade later, were the prototypes of his early fiction. He also encountered splendid teachers—in the seventh grade, a woman who taught him hundreds of lines of poetry and, in the eighth, a woman who had published a short story in an O. Henry Prize volume. He had long been fascinated by books; by adolescence he was addicted, a craving which his family cheerfully supported.

When the family moved to Raleigh in 1947—his thirteenth move in fourteen years—he met other fine teachers and began the serious writing of fiction and poetry. The luck continued through four years at Duke University and three at Merton College, Oxford where (as a Rhodes Scholar) he studied John Milton, Italian Renaissance criticism, and Greek drama with such teachers as W. H. Auden, David Cecil, Nevill Coghill, and Helen Gardner. Again he spent a perilous amount of time writing fiction and poetry but at last wrote his thesis and received a B.Litt. degree.

He returned to Duke in 1958 and began the teaching which has occupied a satisfying part of his year ever since. In the ensuing thirty years, he became James B. Duke Professor of English and has had the pleasure of witnessing the early work of such writers as Fred Chappell, Anne Tyler, Josephine Humphreys, Charlie Smith, and David Guy. All that time he has lived within a few yards of a pond in Orange County, N.C.—the habitat also of fish, mallards, blue herons, king-fishers, snapping turtles, muskrats, foxes, copperheads, black racers, chipmunks, raccoons, and a noble though voracious herd of deer.

In 1984 an astrocytoma in his spinal cord resulted in paraplegia. The new access of time and energy has enabled him to complete two novels (*Kate Vaiden* and the forthcoming *Good Hearts*), a collection of poems called *The Laws of Ice*, this collection of essays, and a trilogy of plays called *New Music*. He continues teaching at Duke, and a list of earlier books appears at the head of this one. His fiction has been translated into fifteen languages.